For Polly Watkins Opyr

mother, confidante, friend

SHAKEN
and
STIRRED

Joan Opyr

Ann Arbor
2011

Bywater Books

Copyright © 2011 by Joan Opyr

Bywater Books First Edition: June 2011

Printed in the United States of America
on acid-free paper.

Cover designer: Bonnie Liss (Phoenix Graphics)

Bywater Books
PO Box 3671
Ann Arbor Mi 48106-3671
www.bywaterbooks.com

ISBN: 978-1-932859-71-3

Mixed Sources

Product group from well-managed
forests and other controlled sources
www.fsc.org Cert no. SW-COC-002283
© 1996 Forest Stewardship Council

FSC

Acknowledgments

I have so many people to thank that I scarcely know where to begin. My partner, Melynda Huskey, has been my best reader, my best critic, and my strongest advisor. Without her, this book would not exist. Without her, I doubt that I would be writing. I'd be sitting around, talking about writing. She is my inspiration and my coach. I don't know what I'd do without her, but I'm sure it wouldn't be anything good.

Thanks to my mother, Polly Watkins Opyr; my grandmother, Mable Johnson Watkins; and my sisters, Micheal Opyr Pender and Nicole Opyr. All have been very supportive of this project in particular and of my work and life as a whole. I'd also like to thank Kelly Smith, Marianne K. Martin, Andi Marquette, and Bett Norris for reading the manuscript and offering advice and encouragement. Thanks to Lynne Pierce and the lesfic_unbound list for reading and commenting on a "Sneak Peak." Thanks, especially, to C.J. Werlinger and Mary Vermillion, who voluntarily completed painstaking edits! Thanks to Bywater Books for publishing *Shaken and Stirred,* and thanks to Val McDermid for a terrific title. I was stumped as to what to call this book. Val had the perfect answer.

Thanks to my children, Sofia Opyr-Huskey and Harry Opyr-Huskey, for their good sense, generosity, patience, and affection. Both are wildly creative, and I learn so much just by watching them. Kids, it's an honor to be your mother.

Finally, I'd like to thank my late grandfather, Charles Randolph Watkins. Shaken and Stirred is not about you, PaPa, but it is about family. You were always my support, my cheerleader, and, in wit and humor, my perpetual inspiration. I miss you terribly and think of you every day. I wish you were here.

2002

Chapter One

My surgeon lied to me. A hysterectomy is not like an appendectomy. No one misses a vestigial organ, particularly one that's trying to explode inside her guts and kill her. There is also no comparison between a hysterectomy and having your gallbladder removed, your tonsils out, or your bunions shaved, and as for the friend who told me it was no worse than having a root canal, well, that's just proof that friends lie, too.

Nothing prepares you for the feeling of loss. You have a hysterectomy because something has gone very wrong, because you're in pain, and because you want that pain to stop. I was only thirty-four. True, I didn't have any children and I didn't plan to. I'd come to think of my uterus in purely metaphorical terms. It was there, but it didn't work—kind of like a broken-down muscle car in a redneck's driveway.

But I liked children, and, from time to time, I'd had vague ideas about finding the right partner, settling down, and maybe having a few. I didn't find the right partner, and so there my uterus sat, up on blocks, leaking oil all over the driveway.

Still, it wasn't until I was popping Vicodin like Pez—until the fibrous cysts and a raging case of endometriosis made a hysterectomy inevitable—that I thought about what I was losing. Posterity. Parenthood. A legacy. Had I known that my window of fertility was only open a few inches above the sash, would I have done anything differently? Would I have married hapless Dave, the guy I'd dated in high school? Would I have gone to a sperm bank? What kind of mother would I have been?

I tried to imagine myself pregnant. It was surprisingly easy. I closed my eyes and saw me, Poppy Koslowski, only this time, everything would be right. No wastrel father, no alcoholic grandfather, no hand-wringing women making po-faced excuses. Best of all, no me in the middle, causing trouble but also keeping the peace. No acting the family clown. No feeling tied down. The small me I'd give birth to would rise above it all, borne aloft on the raft of my experience. She'd go to Smith, she'd be a poetic genius, and she'd talk like she had a horse's bit between her teeth.

Yes. Probably best that the Koslowski line came to a screeching halt with me.

In my post-surgery haze, I'd blamed Abby for the hysterectomy. She was the one who'd insisted I see a gynecological surgeon. You know what they say—never see a surgeon unless you want surgery. Abby was a nurse and, when it came to medical matters, she was a tinpot dictator. She was also my best friend. We'd known one another since we were thirteen and, though I never questioned her off-the-cuff diagnoses, I occasionally resented her medical infallibility.

"Would you like pelvic inflammatory disease?" she had asked. "If you think this is painful, try that. You'll wish you could pull your guts out through your vagina with a pair of salad tongs."

"Thanks for that image. Who says it'll come to that? You do exaggerate."

"Nonsense."

"Okay, you fib."

"I do not."

I went for the low blow. "Do you remember that I wrote your term paper for Kaye Grabbel's class?"

"That was in the eleventh grade, and you didn't write it, you edited it."

"Believe me," I said. "In your case, it's the same thing. You sprinkle commas on a text like pepper on your eggs."

"You're high," she replied blandly. "How many Vicodin have you taken?"

"Two," I said.

She frowned. "Let's try this again. I know you take two at a time. I mean how many have you taken today in total?"

I tried to think. Abby waited, her head tilted to one side.

"You've counted the bottle," I accused.

"Of course I did. Your prescription was filled two days ago. Forty-five pills with the proviso that they must last the whole month. You've got thirty pills left. Either make an appointment with a surgeon or check yourself into rehab. Your choice."

I went to see the surgeon. Three weeks later, I was minus a uterus and one ovary. Abby took time off from her job in the Trauma ICU and hovered around me in Med-Surg being bossy and efficient. It was amazing to watch her in action. With the surgeon, she was cool and intimidating; with the nurses, funny and irreverent. A few minutes after the anesthetist put the sedative into my IV, I told Abby that I wanted to be a nurse. She said I wasn't nearly sick enough. The other nurses laughed.

Beneath the surface irritation, I was insanely grateful to Abby. Some small, irrational part of me was convinced I was going to die on the operating table. The surgeon would open me up and find a big cancerous blob, or a blood clot would form in my toe and travel to my brain.

Whenever I'd done something stupid or dangerous as a kid, like jumping from the garage roof onto the trampoline, my mother would say, "For God's sake, do you want to wake up dead?" I didn't want to wake up dead. I wanted to wake up alive, and the first thing I wanted to see was Abby's familiar, cranky, reassuring face.

I didn't tell her any of this, of course. We'd been inseparable for nearly twenty years. I loved her, and I knew she loved me, but we didn't gush. We cracked jokes. I asked the surgeon if I could take my uterus home in a jar. Abby offered to take pictures of the nurse giving me my surgical shave.

She stayed with me all three days that I was in the hospital, sleeping on the recliner in my semi-private room, and, when I went home, she moved into my spare bedroom. She said she'd stay for a week, enough time for me to get back on my feet. It was a cozy arrangement, just as it had been when we were roommates in college. We fell into a comfortable routine. We talked, we watched movies, and we enjoyed one another's company. Apart from the fact that my stitches itched and I had one hell of stomachache, it was better than a week at the beach.

On the morning of the seventh day, Abby left for work, and I turned to my stack of paperbacks. I'd read only ten pages of Agatha Christie's *Postern of Fate* when the first wave of grief washed over me. Abby was leaving. This was her last night. I'd have no one to talk to, no nurse at my beck and call, no one to share the sublime and the mundane of everyday life. I tried to shake it off. I threw myself into the usual distractions. I played cards on the computer. I watched television. I listened to music. As the day wore on and the drugs wore off, I realized there was more to my melancholy than just feeling sorry for myself.

I was in my mid-thirties, I lived alone, and I was at a genetic dead end. Three million years of human evolution, from Lucy of the Australopithecines to the unlikely union of my parents, a Southern Baptist and a Polish Jew—all of that ended with me. The human race would go on, but I wouldn't. I was the last of my kind, no great loss, maybe, but when I was dead, I'd be well and truly gone, and I'd take all of my ancestors with me.

The fact that in Lucky Eddie's case I'd be doing the world a favor was no consolation. My worthless father had managed what I couldn't. He'd helped to make me. I'd helped to make no one. I wept for my lost uterus until I felt thoroughly stupid. I cried until Abby's dog, Belvedere, stopped trying to comfort me and took refuge in a far corner of the living room. I ran out of Kleenex and shuffled through the house, looking for something softer than the roll of paper towels in the kitchen. The toilet paper I ended up with was no improvement—I'd bought it in bulk from a cheap warehouse store and it might as well have been fine-grain sandpaper. I wiped my eyes and blew my nose until both were red. Then, even though I wasn't in any pain, I took two of my wicked, addictive painkillers and fell asleep. At three, I woke up and took two more. When Abby's key turned in the lock at a quarter to six, I felt numb, like a longtime resident in an opium den. I swam over the living room carpet and met her at the door.

She was wearing her green scrubs and a baggy purple cardigan, the pockets of which were stretched out from carrying pens, wrappers, and all the other assorted detritus of her work in the ICU.

"You're upright," she said, smiling. "Drop your drawers and let's have a look at your incision."

"This is so sudden. Can't I have a drink first? Or a kiss?"

"I wouldn't kiss you on a bet," she said, "and I think you're already drunk."

She closed the door behind her, leaned me against the wall, and bent over to examine my incision. The plastic beads on the ends of her braids made a clicking sound as she moved, like hundreds of tiny castanets. I liked her hair braided, though I'd kept my opinion to myself. For years she'd worn it straightened and brushed into what she called the modified mushroom. When I'd suggested that she grow it into an Angela Davis afro, she'd given me a sharp look and said that a black woman's hair was a sensitive subject and not open for discussion. I didn't ask why. I expected it had something to do with her mother, who had "opinions" about Abby's hair. Abby's mother had opinions about everything to do with Abby, and none of them were positive.

My own hair wasn't interesting enough to discuss. It was dark brown with little bits of gray, and I wore it short. Every five weeks, I had a standing appointment with a hairdresser named Clyde, who kept up a non-stop commentary about my cowlicks.

"The incision is a little inflamed on this end," Abby said. "You need to clean it with some hydrogen peroxide."

"I put Neosporin on it this morning."

"That's good, but you still need to clean it. Okay, exam over. Pants up."

"What a disappointment. As long as you were down there, I thought . . ."

"Yes, of course you did. And how sexy you are—a drugged-out woman with a five-inch wound. I had six babes just like you in the ICU today. There was a wreck on the interstate. A semi-truck hit a bus full of women on their way to some Christian hootenanny. Two DOAs."

Belvedere trotted up, and Abby scratched him behind the ears. "Do you need to go outside, you evil hound? Do you need to go?"

Belvedere wagged his tail furiously. He was an ancient border collie of noble bearing, who had more decency and common sense than all but the best of humankind. Abby should have named him Jimmy Carter or Mahatma Gandhi, but she couldn't resist the chance to spend a dozen years calling out, "Belvedere, come h'yar, boy."

She fixed me with a sharp brown stare. "Have you let him out today?"

I thought for a moment. "I don't know. If I did, I don't remember."

"It's a wonder you're not swimming in dog pee." She opened the sliding glass door in the dining room and Belvedere stepped out onto the patio. He sniffed the air, savoring it like the cork from a wine bottle, before trotting off in the direction of the single tree in my backyard, a Japanese maple in full autumnal glory.

"When did that happen?" I asked.

"What?"

"Those leaves. Look how red they are."

Abby shook her head. "Where have you been? That tree turned two weeks ago."

"I was preoccupied."

We stood at the window, watching the dog and admiring the tree. Belvedere chose to heist his leg on my last living rose bush, wobbling a bit as he tried to maintain his balance.

"His joints are getting so stiff," she said.

"That's not surprising. He's twelve. That's . . . what?"

"Eighty-four in dog years. Look how white he is around the muzzle."

"He's as lively as ever, Abs. What's he taking for the arthritis?"

"Glucosamine, chondroitin, and forty milligrams of enteric-coated aspirin twice a day. It's time for his second dose. What did you do when I left this morning? Did you start on that pile of murder mysteries or did you sleep all day?"

"I invented a new card game."

"Oh?"

"On the computer. Lesbian FreeCell. You play it just like regular FreeCell, only you can't lay a queen on a king. It makes for some tricky moves."

"I'll bet. So you felt good enough to log on. Did you check your email?"

"No."

"Do you want *me* to check it?"

"No. Can you help me over to the couch? I'm starting to feel dizzy."

"Okay," she said, her beads clicking as she shook her head in disapproval. "You're not off the hook, Koslowski. That woman is a psycho. She's stalking you."

I backed up to the sofa and slowly sat down, placing my left hand on the armrest and leaning on it heavily while Abby held my right hand in her firm, professional grasp.

"Thanks," I said. "It's hard to imagine I'll ever sit like a normal person again."

"It's hard for me to imagine that you think you can change the subject."

I didn't want to talk about Dolores Sanchez. She was the latest in a long line of romantic mistakes, all of which I preferred to forget. I closed my eyes and rested my head on the back of the sofa.

"I'm recovering from major surgery. I want to forget about my fuck-ups."

"You've had a hysterectomy, not a lobotomy." Abby sat down in the recliner opposite and put her feet up. "What are you going to do about Dolores?"

"What do you want me to do? Call a cop? That's how I got into this mess in the first place. Fucking burglars. It would have been cheaper just to buy a new stereo."

"Call her sergeant," Abby said. "Cops have rules about cops stalking crime victims."

"She's not exactly stalking me," I objected. "She's just persistent."

"Ten emails a day for ten days straight? She filled the tape on your answering machine. 'Call me, call me, please, call me.' She's probably on her way here right now to boil a rabbit in your crock pot."

9

"She's not that bad, Abs. She didn't bother me at all when I was in the hospital."

"You didn't tell her where you were going."

"She's a cop. She could have investigated." I opened one eye. Abby was frowning at me. I sighed heavily. "Look, she's angry now, but she'll get over it. I've told her so long, farewell, auf wiedersehen, goodbye. She'll meet someone new. Someone will rob someone better than me, and she'll forget that I ever existed. She's probably already forgotten. No calls today."

"You really are out of it," Abby said. "I unplugged your phone."

"Oh, for God's sake." Slowly and carefully, I slid down the sofa and flipped the switch on the telephone. "I'm not afraid of her, Abby. I just don't want to date her."

"You live on wishful thinking," she replied. "You hope she'll forget, but you of all people should know better."

"What do you mean me of all people?"

"You know exactly what I mean." She paused for a moment. We stared at one another, and Abby backed down. She was sensitive about her hair. I was sensitive about other things.

She said, "It's all fun and games until someone loses an eye. You pretend to be all casual and lah-dee-dah, but you never let anything go, Koslowski. You brood. If the shoe were on the other foot . . ."

"Belvedere wants in," I interrupted.

"Belvedere can wait."

"Poor dog. Are you really going to make him stand there on his stiff old joints?"

Abby had long since perfected the nurse's glare, the one that said, "You can have the problem, or you can have the solution." She gave me a healthy dose of this, but she got up to let Belvedere in. I feigned oblivion.

"Fine," she said. "We won't talk about Dolores. How about your other source of discomfort—any resolution yet?"

"I am not going to talk to you about that either. Stop asking."

"Don't get testy. I'm a medical professional. You can't shock me. I get paid to ask about these things. Besides, it's not like it's a personal failing. Constipation is routine after surgery."

I looked out at the Japanese maple. "Nice weather we're having."

"Water and walking, that's the cure—or an enema."

"If you don't mind," I said firmly, "I thought I'd order a pizza tonight. Pepperoni with extra cheese. I may need some help with *that*. I can't remember where I put my checkbook. I also seem to have trouble holding a pen. Do you think I'm losing my fine motor skills?"

"No," Abby said. "I think you should lay off the damned painkillers and, while you're at it, you might stop laying women in uniform. Your checkbook's in your left-hand desk drawer. No, stay where you are, all hopped up and comfortable. I'll let the dog in. I'll get your checkbook. I'll even call the goddamn pizza parlor. Just pepperoni?"

"And extra cheese. And maybe onions."

"No onions. They give you heartburn."

"Fine." I shifted in my seat and felt an unpleasant pulling sensation. "I might be hopped up, but I'm not comfortable. I can't sit up straight. I think that fucking doctor has sewn the top of my vagina to the bottom of my lungs."

"I wish she'd sewn it shut. Is Old Chicago okay with you? They do the best deep dish."

"I prefer thin crust."

"Too bad," she said. "I like deep."

"I'm paying."

"I'm ordering."

When Abby sat back down, Belvedere climbed onto her lap, his head and tail hanging over the arms of the chair. They both closed their eyes. Gingerly, I lifted first one leg and then the other up onto the sofa and settled a cushion behind my head and shoulders. I'd just eased onto my back when the phone rang.

"You want me to get that?" Abby asked, her eyes still shut.

"No."

"What if it's Crazy Cop?"

"I'll tell her you said hello." I picked up the phone.

"Poppy, is that you?" My grandmother's voice crackled across three thousand miles.

"It's me. Hi, Nana."

11

"It doesn't sound like you. You're all out of breath. Why are you up? You said you were going to have someone there to take care of you. I told your mama we should fly out there and make sure you don't—"

"I do have someone with me. Abby's here."

"Abby." My grandmother hesitated. "Abby. Do I know . . . ?"

"Abby Johnson," I said wearily. "We went to high school together, and college. She moved with me to Portland five years ago. It was a four-day trip by U-Haul, and her dog kept throwing up in my lap. Nana, you've known Abby for twenty years, since she and I were thirteen years old."

"Oh, your *black* friend," said Abby.

"Oh, your black friend," said my grandmother.

"Yes," I said simply. "How are you, Nana? And how's Mama?"

"We're just fine," she said. "I went to Asheville last weekend with my Sunday School class, and we went to the Biltmore House. Two-hundred-and-fifty rooms and sixty-five fireplaces, can you imagine? I like the gardens best of all. Someone famous designed them."

"Frederick Law Olmsted," I said.

"I can't remember who," my grandmother continued without a pause. "They charge an absolute fortune to get in. My ticket was thirty-six dollars. I tried to get your mama to come, but she said she'd rather stay home and watch some old movie she's seen a hundred times."

"Oh? What movie was that?"

"*Fiddler on a Hot Tin Roof.*"

I covered the receiver with my hand and repeated this to Abby.

"Of course," Abby said. "Elizabeth Taylor and Zero Mostel. It's a classic."

My grandmother said, "I told your mama she could buy the video, but she said no, so I had to share a room with Daisy Burt. She was up and down all night long with colitis. I didn't get a wink of sleep. Do you remember Daisy Burt? Her son is the one who killed himself. Went upstairs one day and blew his brains out with a shotgun. He was only seventeen. How are you doing? Are you still constipated? If you would just take two tablespoons of mineral oil . . ."

"How about this one?" said Abby. "*Father of the Bride of Young Frankenstein.* No, wait. *Blazing Cleopatra.*"

12

"Would you shut up? No, not you, Nana."

"Now, when your mama was just a little thing, I used to give her Fletcher's Castoria, but I don't suppose they still make that."

"I am fine," I said loudly. "My plumbing is working just fine. Is everyone well at home? Is Mama there?"

"She is," said my grandmother. "Do you want to talk to her?"

"Sure."

The sound of the phone clattering to the floor, and then being picked up and dropped again, was followed by the sound of Nana shouting to my mother as if they were separated by the Berlin Wall.

My mother said, "I don't know why she hollers like that. I'm standing not three feet away from her."

"I hear you skipped Daisy Burt's colitis tour of the Biltmore House."

"I did. I had a weekend all to myself. I watched movies, I read books, and I cooked exactly what I wanted for dinner."

"Meaning you ate a hamburger steak junior from the Char-grill every night?"

"Exactly."

"So, what else is happening?"

"I was getting to that," she said. "First, how are you feeling?"

"I'm up and about."

"Well, that's good. And everything's moving along now?"

"If you mean am I still constipated, the answer is yes, but don't tell Nana. I'm not taking mineral oil, I don't want an enema, and I have no idea what the hell Fletcher's Castoria is. I don't care if I never go again, I just want to stop talking about it."

"Fletcher's Castoria." My mother made a shuddering sound. "No, you don't want that." There was a pause, and then she said, "I don't mean to worry you while you're recovering, but your grandfather is in the hospital, Poppy. He has pneumonia."

"Good lord. Is it serious?"

"Probably. If you can manage it, I think you should come home."

My mother's tone was always deadpan. She felt things more keenly than she ever let on, but in order to know what she was feeling, you had to listen to what she said rather than how she said it. I'd left home

13

at eighteen, but no matter how far away from Raleigh I'd lived, my mother had never asked me to come home. Not that she wasn't glad to see me when I did—it was more that she liked to feel that the visits were my idea, something I did out of a genuine desire to see her rather than a sense of obligation. This, of course, had the opposite effect of making me feel guilty by scrupulously trying not to make me feel guilty.

"I think I could pull myself together in the next couple of days," I said carefully. "Why the hell did Nana waste time telling me about Daisy Burt and the Biltmore House? Has she gone off the deep end?"

"Denial," my mother said. "Or Alzheimer's. Hunter doesn't just have pneumonia, Poppy. There's something else going on. We're meeting tomorrow with a lung specialist. There are dark spots on his X-rays."

I put my hand over the receiver. "Black spots on his lungs?"

"Lung cancer," Abby said. "How long did he smoke?"

I did some quick math. "Sixty-nine years. From age eleven to age eighty."

"I heard that," my mother said. "It's what I thought."

"Is he in any pain?"

"I don't think so. He's breathing hard, but he's on morphine. He's out of it. He didn't even wake up when we went by this afternoon."

"Okay," I said, trying to shake off the effects of my own painkillers. "Call me tomorrow after you meet with the lung specialist. I'll hop a flight out of Portland as soon as I can, sometime in the next few days. Don't worry about picking me up at the airport. I'll rent a car. I think I'll get a hotel room, too."

"Uh-uh," said my mother. "I understand the impulse, but I wouldn't if I were you." She dropped her voice to a near whisper. "Nana has already cleaned out your old bedroom. She's moved the ironing pile and made up the bed. If it gets to be too much, you can always go over to Susan's."

"Susan?" I said blankly.

"Didn't I tell you? She got back about a week ago from wherever it was she's been these past three years."

"The former Yugoslavia," I said.

"That's it. The war is over and now she's home. Here to stay, too, or so she says. She was on call when they admitted Hunter, and I can tell you, we were glad to see her. She's so calm. Nothing seems to faze her."

I wished the same were true of me. Abby and Belvedere were both staring at me.

I took a deep breath. "She's staying with her father?"

"For the time being. She'll be right next door. You can pop over whenever you need a break, just like you used to."

"I don't think so."

My mother sighed. "That was all a long time ago, Poppy. None of it was your fault, any more than it was hers. Susan couldn't have been more professional with your grandfather or friendlier to us. She asked about you."

"Did she?"

"Of course. I told her where you were and what you were doing. She said she'd like to see you. It's a shame you two lost touch, but, well . . . we'll talk when you get home. I'll let you go now. You're probably tired."

"I am. Good night, Mama." I hung up the phone and settled back into position on the sofa. Abby and I looked at one another. The doorbell rang. Abby shoved Belvedere off her lap and got up to answer it.

She set the pizza box down on the coffee table. Without looking at me, she said, "Susan Sava returns and you're on the first plane back to Raleigh." There was a long pause. "You're not fit to travel."

"I know that, but my grandfather . . ."

"Which is why I'm going with you."

"What? Abby, you can't. You've just taken a week off."

"I can," she replied firmly. "I have a million hours of annual leave, and I intend to use them. The ICU is fully staffed. I won't have any trouble getting someone to cover for me. I'll stay with my mother."

I laughed. "Oh no, you won't. Your mother's favorite game is fingernails on a chalkboard. You wouldn't last five minutes. Listen, my grandmother be damned, I'm not sleeping in that hard little bed next to her ironing pile. You and me, we'll share a room at the Velvet Cloak Inn, my treat. It's the least I can do."

"I suppose it is," Abby agreed. She handed me a slice of pizza, took one for herself, and sat back down. "You've just compared my mother to Captain Quint in *Jaws*."

"I'm sorry," I said. "I should have given her top billing."

Abby sighed. "I'm not saying that it's not accurate, only that it's not nice. So, you can also spring for the plane tickets. I want the window seat. You can have that cramped one in the middle with no armrests."

Chapter Two

Sometimes I think my story is about slutty Avon ladies. And not just one—one I could chalk up to chance. Two slutty Avon ladies feel more like a curse than a coincidence.

Today, the Avon lady is an anachronism, like the vacuum cleaner salesman or the Fuller Brush man. The only thing people sell door-to-door these days is eternal salvation, but when I was a kid, "Avon calling" was a regular event. A woman stopped by at least once a month, and whatever my mother happened to be doing, she put it aside for half an hour to sit down and sample the hand lotion, lipstick, and perfume. Like most of the women in our blue-collar Michigan neighborhood, my mother didn't wear a lot of makeup. She was a low-maintenance woman. At our house, the Avon lady's profit margins were small. The only thing we bought on a regular basis was Skin So Soft body splash. We used it to take fleas off the cat.

Avon lady was a high turnover job. We seemed to have a new one every six months. I could never tell them apart—not, that is, until Karen Rostenkowski.

It was the first day of summer vacation, and I had big plans for the three months before I started eighth grade—softball, swimming, and building myself a mini-bike. I'd bought an old frame for five dollars at a yard sale, and my mother said I could have the engine from the broken lawnmower in the back of our garage. My father had forbidden me to use any of his tools, but I didn't care. My friend Jack Leinweber's father had died back in January, leaving him unrestricted access to a two-tiered mechanic's chest.

17

I was on my way to Jack's house when the phone rang.

We lived in a three-bedroom ranch just outside of Detroit. The houses in our subdivision were small brick bungalows, built so close together that when our next-door neighbor stood in his bedroom and blew his nose, we could hear it in our kitchen. Everyone on our street knew everyone else's business, and there was a well-established telephone tree for up-to-the-minute reportage.

The caller was Jane, Jack's mother. Grief had done little to dull Jane's interest in neighborhood events. Grief had done little to Jane, period. Like my mother, she was a transplanted Southerner. Jane was from rural Georgia, my mother from Raleigh, North Carolina. They'd both married Yankee men, moved north with them, and lived to regret it. My parents' marriage was far from happy. Lately, I'd gotten the distinct impression that my mother envied Jane. God knows I envied Jack.

"Listen, honey," Jane said. "Jack's waiting for you out in the garage. I don't know what all mess ya'll are fixing to make, but I don't want any more oil on that concrete floor. After Bob died, I spent a month of Sundays cleaning up the drips from his motorcycle, and I have just finished painting in there. I'd rather you did whatever it is outdoors, but Jack says you have to be inside. Bring some cardboard or newspapers to put down, would you? I told Jack, but he won't remember. Takes after his daddy."

"Sure," I said.

"Good girl. Now, is your mother handy? I want to speak at her."

My mother sat at the kitchen table reading a book. I held the phone out to her. "Are you handy? Jane wants to speak at you."

"And she means that literally," my mother replied. "What does she want?"

"She didn't say."

"Hell's bells."

My mother put the book down and pulled off her left earring. I handed her the receiver. Jane and my mother had a love-hate relationship. Jane loved to talk; my mother hated listening to her. Their friendship was based on close proximity, cultural affiliation, and my mother's thinly stretched politeness.

"Hello, Jane," she said, settling in for a long haul. "What's happening?"

I leaned against the back door. Jane often had an interesting tale to tell, and, thanks to the volume of her voice, it was easy to eavesdrop on her phone calls. Only the odd word or two escaped me.

"Well," Jane declared, "the new Avon lady just left here. I sent her across the street to Janice's house in case you needed time to straighten up. She caught me by surprise. I can't imagine what she must have thought—my kitchen looks like the junk room on the *Titanic*."

"I'm sure it was fine, Jane." My mother glanced around at the collection of disasters that comprised our own kitchen. It was 1979. My father had begun installing green patterned wallboard in 1976. He'd put up two pieces, one on either side of the window, and then stopped. The floor was dirty, the table was covered with newspapers and coffee cups, and the sink was full of dishes. Sensing what was about to happen, I opened the back door.

My mother held up her hand. "Stop," she said, and then, "No, not you, Jane."

"I just thought I'd give you a heads up," Jane went on. "Is Eddie at home?"

"Yes. Why do you ask?"

"Well, let's just say that this Avon lady is quite a change from Mrs. Orlicki."

"No mustache?"

Jane laughed. "No mustache, honey, and no babushka. She wouldn't want to cover up that Farrah Fawcett hair-do. A piece of work, let me tell you—about as trashy as they come. Her name is Karen, but she pronounces it Kar-ahn."

"Good lord. What's her story?"

"She wants to be a model. She doesn't have a prayer—she's strictly Barbizon and boat show—but she thinks she's big time. If I were you, I'd send Eddie to the store for a pack of cigarettes or some toilet paper. Men are fools for the peroxide bottle."

"Hmph," said my mother. "Thanks for the warning, Jane, but I don't think I'll bother. Eddie's asleep. It would take an earthquake to wake him up. You'd better let me go so I can vacuum."

"Of course, but call me back with a full report," Jane insisted.

"Okay." My mother turned to me as soon as she'd hung up the phone. "You know the drill," she said. "You pick up the random debris and vacuum the living room. I'll whip through the kitchen and bathroom. And here," she picked the cat up off the counter and handed him to me. "Shut Fonzie in your bedroom. He can't resist the smell of Avon lady. He'll be up on her lap as soon as she sits down."

"But Ma," I objected, "Jack and I are . . ."

"Jack can wait."

The cat didn't take kindly to being relocated. Sucking on a freshly bitten finger, I cleared off the coffee table, emptied the ashtray, and kicked my father's work shoes underneath the sofa. I could hear my mother in the kitchen shoving dirty dishes into the oven. I'd just taken the vacuum cleaner out of the coat closet when she came in carrying a can of pine-scented air freshener.

"What about Dad?" I asked. Lucky Eddie was asleep on the sofa, his feet propped up on the armrest.

"Never mind him," she said, spraying his feet with the air freshener.

My father sat up. "What the hell . . ."

"Avon lady," my mother explained. "Your feet smell like dead animals. Why don't you go sleep in the bed like a human being?"

"Jesus Christ," said my father, lying back down. "Take her into the kitchen."

"I was planning to." The doorbell rang. My mother gave the room at large a generous spray, tossed the can and the unused vacuum back into the closet, and opened the front door.

"Hello. You must be the new Avon lady."

Karen Rostenkowski looked like she couldn't decide if she wanted to be a prostitute or the head of General Motors. She wore a beige linen suit and a shiny red halter-top. Her high heels, which were also red, were a shade lighter than the halter-top but darker than the plastic headband that pushed back her blonde, wispy hair. As she stepped through the front door, she trailed a cloud of perfume so strong that it overwhelmed the pine spray. She introduced herself, smiling brightly.

My mother's answering smile was polite but cool. I'd seen her use it on Avon ladies before, as well as Mormons and Jehovah's Witnesses. It said that she was willing to look but that she wouldn't be doing much buying. "I'm Barbara Koslowski, and this my daughter, Frances." She gestured apologetically in the direction of my father. "Don't worry about that body on the sofa. We've called the undertaker."

Lucky Eddie opened one eye and prepared to roll over. Then he caught sight of Karen. He sat bolt upright.

"Sorry, I was just having a little nap there. I work nights." He stood up and extended his hand. "I'm Eddie," he oozed, "Eddie Koslowski."

Ordinarily, my father couldn't be blasted off the sofa with dynamite. It didn't matter who knocked on the door—the Girl Scouts, his mother, or a SWAT team—Eddie woke up for no one. He was skilled in the art of interpersonal avoidance.

By the time Karen Rostenkowski arrived on our doorstep, Eddie had long since moved out of my mother's bedroom and taken up permanent residence in the living room. He came home from work at six o'clock in the morning, kicked off his shoes, and slept on the sofa until five-thirty. Then he ate a TV dinner, took a shower, and went back to work. His routine never varied, and there was never any conversation. Eddie and my mother spoke to one another only when it was absolutely necessary, and, apart from yelling at Jack and me to get the hell out of the house and go play quietly somewhere else, he and I didn't talk. The man who was now grinning like a fool and enthusiastically pumping the Avon lady's hand was a stranger to me.

I looked at my mother, who looked pointedly at Karen's hair.

Lucky Eddie followed us into the kitchen. My mother offered Karen a seat at the table, and Eddie pulled out her chair for her. I abandoned my plans to meet Jack and sat down to watch the spectacle. I was not disappointed. For the next half-hour, Eddie was all over Karen Rostenkowski like a cheap suit. He made jokes, lit her cigarette, and offered her a mixed drink.

21

My mother, her face perfectly placid, said, "Don't you think it's a little early for cocktails?"

"Sun's over the garden," Eddie replied, opening the refrigerator.

"Yardarm," I said.

Eddie held up a jar of pickled onions. "We've got gin and vermouth. How about a dry martini? Shaken, not stirred, ha, ha."

My mother took a deep breath. "It's eleven o'clock in the morning, Eddie. Miss Rostenkowski is here to sell Avon. You use olives to make a martini, you use onions to make a Gibson. Why don't you go back to sleep?"

Eddie grinned broadly. "It's midnight in France, Barbara. I was just showing some of that Southern hospitality you're always on about, and I'm not tired. You want a beer, Karen? We've got Budweiser and Pabst. You could be a model, you know—has anyone ever told you that? You're a double ringer for that Cheryl Tiegs."

"Dead ringer," I corrected.

"I wish someone were dead," said my mother.

Karen smiled weakly. "Yes," she said. My father handed her a beer. "I mean, no. I don't want anything to drink. But I am a model. I've done some local work, department stores, that sort of thing. I'm just getting started."

"Really?" Eddie was all agog.

"Really," echoed my mother. "Now, if you'll just . . ."

"Do you have a portfolio?" Eddie continued, ignoring her. "If not, I'd be happy to do one for you. I'm a professional photographer. My studio's out back. I've got a full set up, lights, backdrops, you name it. Reasonable prices."

My mother rolled her eyes. My father worked as a press operator at the Ford stamping plant. Photography was merely the latest in a long line of expensive hobbies that had come and gone—rock climbing, skiing, scuba diving. His studio was a space in the garage behind a disassembled motorcycle and a rusty bass boat. He had a light table, a Pentax, and a box of business cards that said *Photography by Edward* in loopy italicized script.

He took one of these from his wallet and handed it to Karen.

"Thank you," she said, glancing at it quickly before dropping it into her handbag. "I'll certainly keep you in mind." Fixing her gaze firmly on my mother, she opened up her sample case. "Avon has several new products I think you'll be interested in, Mrs. Koslowski. Lipstick, perfume, moisturizer . . ."

My mother feigned interest in a bottle of foundation. She didn't really need makeup. She had perfect skin, and she didn't work outside the home. From time to time, my father would suggest that she "do something with herself," but this was only the prelude to a fight.

Eddie sat down at the table, beer in hand, and lit a cigarette. "Of course, I'm also 'Have camera, will travel.' We wouldn't have to do the portfolio in my studio. I could come to your place. Sometimes a subject feels more comfortable in her own home ambience."

"Environment?" I suggested.

He leaned across the table and pointed the cigarette at me. "No one likes a smart ass. Shut up or go to your room."

My mother pushed the sample case back across the table. "I don't believe I need any Avon today, Karen. Why don't you leave me a catalog, and I'll call you later?"

"Come on now," Eddie objected, sitting back and smiling again. "We can't let her leave empty-handed. Maybe you could use some of this." He picked up a white plastic compact. "What is it?"

"It's pancake," said my mother.

"Oh yeah? What do you do with it?"

"You eat it."

Karen closed her sample case and stood up. "My name and phone number are on the back of the catalog. If you want anything, Mrs. Koslowski . . ."

"Call me Barbara," my mother said. "I'd prefer not to be Mrs. Koslowski."

My father laughed. "And you can call me Eddie. Let's dispense with the formalizations."

"Formalities."

"I warned you," he said, taking aim once again with the cigarette. "Twelve years old and you think you're a goddamn genius. Go to your room. Now. The adults want to have some adult conversation."

"About Avon?" I asked incredulously.

I shoved my chair back from the table just in time. Eddie's hand missed me by inches and slammed against the wall, flattening the cigarette.

For a long moment, no one moved. Then my mother made a clicking sound with her teeth and tongue, a noise like the pin being pulled out of a grenade.

"You," she said to me. "Go wait in the car. I'll be out in a few minutes."

I stopped just long enough to take the keys off the hook by the back door. Once I was safely ensconced in the passenger seat of my mother's station wagon, I switched on the ignition and rolled the windows down. Five minutes ticked by. Jack came over and leaned in the window.

"What's going on?" he said. "I thought you were coming over to my house."

"My mom's inside murdering Lucky Eddie. She told me to wait out here."

"Oh." He opened the door and sat down. "Plenty of room in the way back for a dead body." He opened the glove box and pushed the trunk release button.

"Go shut that," I said. "You know I'm not allowed to play with it."

"That's because of that time you opened it going down I-94."

"Just shut up and close it before she comes out here."

"God, you're a crab," he said. "If you're not coming over, can I get the mini-bike frame out of your garage?"

"Go ahead." I turned on the radio. John Travolta and Olivia Newton-John were singing "You're the One that I Want" when Karen Rostenkowski came out, walking so quickly that her sample case beat time against her thigh. She walked right past me without even looking. Then she got into her car, a brown Mustang with rusty rocker panels, and drove away.

A few minutes after that, my mother stepped onto the front porch. She was carrying her purse, the cat, and a cup of coffee. My father stopped just behind her and stood in the doorway.

"Goddamn it, Barbara . . ." he began.

The coffee cup smashed against the doorframe above his head. He stood for a moment, brown liquid dripping from his hair onto the welcome mat. Without another word, he turned on his heel and went back in the house.

My mother dropped the cat onto my lap. "Ramada, Howard Johnson's, or the Velvet Cloak Inn?"

"We don't have a Velvet Cloak Inn."

"No," she replied, "but Raleigh does. Buckle up."

Chapter Three

My mother ran out of steam in Columbus, Ohio. We had long since run out of 8-track tapes. We spent the night at a hotel on the edge of town with the cat curled up between us on the bed. The next day, we slept in late and ordered room service. At noon, we drove back to Michigan.

There was a receipt on the kitchen table for $258 worth of Avon. My father had ordered a boatload of makeup, every shade of foundation, eye shadow, and lipstick available. My mother called him at work.

"Just what the devil is this?" she asked. "You know I don't wear makeup. Can't you send flowers like a normal man?"

"What are you talking about?" he said. "That stuff isn't for you. If I'm going to be doing model portfolios, I need a full makeup kit."

After explaining that models who really were models used their own makeup, my mother told Lucky Eddie that she and I were leaving. We were going to North Carolina to live with her parents. She also told him that she would be back for her things, that she would bill him for the U-Haul, and that, in case he'd ever wondered, he was indeed the prize prick of the universe.

We spent the next two days packing the back of the station wagon. I said goodbye to Jack and gave him the mini-bike frame and the lawnmower engine. I wished him luck. He cried. So did Jane. My father didn't come home, and he didn't call.

We drove the eight hundred miles to North Carolina in just under sixteen hours.

When she opened the front door, Nana said, "What in the world," and then, "Why didn't you call us? I had no idea you were ... where's Eddie?"

"Don't know and don't care," my mother replied. "I've left him."

Nana leaned against the doorframe, shaking her head in disbelief. My grandfather sat just behind her at the dining room table, shelling peanuts. He popped two into his mouth and crunched them loudly.

"It's about time," he said. "Eddie Koslowski is a no-good sorry Polack bastard."

My mother got a job as a clerk at the Olivia Raney Public Library, and we settled into my grandparents' house. She took possession of the bed and the bedroom she'd had as a teenager. I got the hide-a-bed sofa in my grandmother's sewing room. In a few weeks, we rented a U-Haul and drove back up to Michigan to collect our things. My grandfather and his younger brother, my great-uncle Fred, followed behind us in my mother's car.

We spent the night at Smiley's Motel in Charleston, West Virginia. My mother refused to share a double room with Hunter and Fred. Instead, we got our own room with a Queen-sized bed. In the morning, we had breakfast at Bob Evans and drove the rest of the way straight through, stopping only for gas and bathroom breaks. It was six-thirty when we pulled into the driveway. Jane ran out of her house to greet us, rivers of mascara-stained tears running down her face.

Lucky Eddie didn't have sense enough to stay away this time. He opened the door with a smile on his face and offered everyone a beer. No-one said anything except Fred, who said, "Don't mind if I do." The rest of us got to work.

When Eddie wasn't sitting at the kitchen table, drinking a beer and smoking a cigarette, he hovered around the edges, watching the proceedings with a disinterested eye. Eventually, he made a friendly offer to help us pack. My mother, also friendly, suggested that he pack his head up his ass and roll down to hell.

He left the house then. Jane, still crying, laughed so hard she choked.

It took me less than an hour to empty my room. Most of my clothes were already in North Carolina; I just needed to pack up my comic books, my Nancy Drews, and the old pieces of pipe, wire, and nuts and bolts that I kept stored in mayonnaise jars on the top of my dresser. These I put on the front seat of the U-Haul. Then I went to find Jack. He was in his garage, sitting on the mini-bike frame, rolling back and forth. He said he'd had no luck with the lawnmower engine.

"I can't figure out how to mount it," he said. "It needs to go on there sideways so the gears will be right, but then the engine mounts are in the wrong place. Maybe I need to weld something. My mom is pissed because it leaked oil on the floor."

I said, "Let's put some newspapers under it and see what we can do. My dad has a stack in his garage."

The newspapers were against the back wall, behind the light table. The studio had become a more formal space since we'd been gone. A new expanse of dry wall separated it from the boat and the motorcycle. Umbrella lights were arranged to shine down onto a black chaise lounge that sat in the middle of an oriental rug. As I gathered up an armload of newspapers, Jack flipped the switch on the light table.

"Hey," he said. "Come check this out."

Karen Rostenkowski reclined on the chaise lounge. She had clothes on in most of the pictures but not all of them. Jack and I examined each slide closely using my father's loupe. Without saying a word to one another, we each took one of the nudes and slipped it into our jeans' pockets.

When my mother finished packing the U-Haul, I told her about the rest of the slides. She looked at me for a moment, but she didn't say anything. She went into the kitchen and made bologna sandwiches, which we ate in silence at the kitchen table. After she'd cleared our plates, my mother opened the big garage door and dragged out the barbecue grill. One at a time, she dropped the slides into it. Jack and I watched, mesmerized, as she doused them with lighter fluid and set them ablaze.

Hunter and Fred sat on the back steps and drank up all of Lucky Eddie's beer.

For a while, I carried the slide around with me like a talisman. I looked at it only when I was sure to be left alone, and I remembered to take it out of my pocket every night and hide it in my underwear drawer.

I'd seen my mother naked hundreds of times, but Karen was a revelation. She was slender where my mother was round, tall and gently curved where my mother was compact and muscular. One of the walls in my grandparents' bathroom was covered with mirror tiles. Sometimes I held the slide up to the light fixture and compared the image with my own figure on the wall opposite. It was disappointing. I wasn't built like my mother, and I wasn't built like Karen. At five-foot eight, I was taller than either of them, but I was muscular all over, completely lacking in curves. My shoulders were broad, my waist was straight, and my hips were narrow. One day, I overheard Nana telling my mother that I looked like Lucky Eddie in a training bra.

"And feet like gunboats," she added.

I stopped looking at the slide after that. I grew careless with it. One day, Karen wound up in a pulpy mass at the bottom of the washing machine.

Living with my grandparents proved to be a challenge. As the only child of their only child, I found myself under intense scrutiny. My mother withdrew into her books and her work, and Nana took over much of my day-to-day maintenance. She declared my Michigan wardrobe—ragged jeans and flannel shirts—unfit for a Southern girl. It looked sloppy, and, even worse, it was unfashionable. I didn't argue with her. She knew more about it than I did, and I was nervous about starting school, anxious to make a good impression. I'd had the same friends since kindergarten. I wasn't sure I knew how to make new ones.

Also, I'd begun to notice something about Southern girls—they all seemed smaller, prettier, and somehow better assembled than I was. The youngest teenager applied makeup with an expert hand, and they all seemed to smile and laugh and be charming and confident. Michigan might have been crawling with beautiful women, but six months out of the year they were swallowed up in parkas and toboggans. In Raleigh, there was no escape from sun-kissed loveliness. The girls I'd seen out and about in my new neighborhood made me feel even more gawky and awkward than the slide of Karen. And, to top it all off, I was now under the thumb of the former head cheerleader of Broughton High School, Class of 1941. Nana wore a girdle even when she was mowing the grass.

It was with deep reservations that I agreed to spend the Saturday before school with her, clothes shopping. Nana's taste ran to the floral and frilly; mine ran to the boy's department. I'd already tried on and rejected several outfits when she appeared in the dressing room doorway carrying a blue cotton dress with a white Peter Pan collar.

I folded my arms across my chest. "No way."

"Why ever not?"

"I hate dresses."

"You need at least one."

"Why?"

"What if someone dies? You don't have a thing you could wear to a funeral."

"Okay. If someone dies, I'll wear that."

I was allowed a brief sulk. Then, attired in the blue dress and my red-striped sweat socks, I stomped dutifully up and down the Hudson Belk's Junior Miss aisle. Nana regarded me with dissatisfaction.

"It's not hanging right," she pronounced. "You need to stand up straight and practice your walking."

"What's the matter with the way I walk?"

"You're galumphing," she said. "You walk for all the world like John Wayne. Tuck your hips in and keep your knees together."

"Like this?" I asked.

My mother, who'd taken no interest in the proceedings thus far, now leaned against a dress rack and laughed helplessly. "Now you're walking like Jerry Lewis."

"You need a book on your head," Nana continued. "That'll sort out your posture. And we'll have to buy you a pair of heels."

"No way!"

"You'll need something to wear with that dress," she said.

"I will never wear that dress."

"You're nearly thirteen years old. It's high time you started acting like a lady."

I cast a pleading glance at my mother. She was the original tomboy—I had pictures of her at my age wearing a baseball cap and a dirt mustache. She considered for a moment and said, "I think pumps would be more suitable with that hemline." I cursed her for a traitor. She laughed again and then shrugged. "Well, it's not up to me—I'm not buying it, and I don't have to wear it. You two better work it out."

After much wrangling, Nana and I reached a compromise. She bought me a new pair of jeans and two plaid shirts, and I agreed to let the dress hang in my closet until somebody died. Preferably me.

"I hate Southern women."

"You do not," Abby said. "You can't leave them alone. Isn't Crazy Cop from Alabama?"

I made a vain effort to stretch my left leg, jostling the laptop on the tray table of the man next to me. He grunted unhappily and went back to typing.

"I've got the shakes," I said. "My legs are driving me crazy. It feels like spiders are crawling up and down my veins."

"Hmm," said Abby. "Spider veins. It's probably withdrawal. You're jonesing for a Percocet."

"I wish I'd brought them with me."

"I brought them with *me*, but you don't need one. You're not in any pain."

"How do you know?"

"We're not in North Carolina yet. When we get there, we'll each take two."

"I'm starving. I wish they still fed you on airplanes."

Abby laughed. "How can you possibly miss airplane food? A stale bread roll. A miniature chicken breast on a bed of cold dry rice. Trying to slice things with no elbow room using those tiny knives and forks."

"That's what I miss—the tiny knives. I could use a couple to saw my legs off."

"You should've sprung for first class. You're too tall for coach."

"Tell me about it," I said. "I'm sorry."

Abby was jammed against the window. We'd raised the pointless armrest between us, but my left leg was sharing the edge of her seat. If the plane were to catch fire while sitting on the runway, they'd need a can opener to get us out. She said, "Did you at least rent a decent-sized car? Tell me you didn't get a compact."

"I got a Ford Explorer. It cost the earth."

"You can afford it. I'll drive."

"That hardly seems fair . . ."

"You have stitches. You shouldn't be driving for at least another month."

"Then for God's sake give me a Percocet. That was the only reason I was trying to remain sober." I reached over the head of Mr. Laptop and rang for the stewardess.

"What are you doing?"

"No food, but there is a beverage service. I'm going to have a beer."

Mr. Laptop put his computer away and got up to stretch his legs. He yawned for a moment or two and then ambled down the aisle towards the bathroom. I unfastened my seat belt and, through a laborious process designed to keep from pulling out my stitches or knocking Abby's tomato juice into her lap, I reached under the seat and retrieved my jacket. I fished my wallet out of the inside pocket, picked out a credit card, and used it to release the telephone from the back of the headrest on the seat in front of me.

"You're going to regret that," Abby said, watching me dial.

"How much could it possibly cost?"

"About three bucks a minute, but I meant calling your mother after two drinks."

"Shh," I said. "She's answering. Hello, Ma?"

"Poppy?" she said. "Don't tell me you're already here. I thought your flight didn't get in until seven-fifteen."

"I'm not there yet. I'm calling from our cruising altitude of thirty-thousand feet or whatever it is."

"Oh. Can you see the Rockies yet?"

"I have no idea. At the moment, I'm enjoying a spectacular view of Abby's right ear. She's got the window seat. How is Hunter? Any change?"

"No change," she said. "He looks just awful. It's pure shocking how much he's aged just in the last few days. You remember how great-grandma looked right at the end? Well, he looks just like her."

"He'd hate that."

"Wouldn't he, though? I'm sorry to be bringing you home for all this, but I'm glad that you're coming, and it's certainly nice of Abby to come with you. I don't know how to talk to these people, these doctors. They speak another language. I also don't know how we're going to pay for all this."

"Medicare will pay, and what they don't cover, the hospital can eat. You're not responsible for his bills."

"I'm his power of attorney," she said.

"I know that," I explained, "but that just means you administer his affairs. It doesn't mean you've opened your wallet to the world."

"I hope not. Last time he was in the hospital, they sent me a bill for forty-three thousand dollars. Did I tell you that?"

"You told me. And I told you to ignore it. You can ignore this one, too. We'll sort everything out when I get there. How's Nana?"

My mother's voice dropped to a whisper. "Strange. Inappropriate. She comes with me to the hospital every day. Sometimes she acts like she's about to be his widow, and other times she interrupts the doctors to ask stupid questions, like whether or not you can cure a bunion with duct tape."

"Duct tape? Is that like using a potato to cure warts?"

"Oh, who knows? Maybe if you put the duct tape over your mouth, you can't complain about your bunions."

"Or ask doctors stupid questions. Look, Nana is probably not sure what her role in this should be. Do ex-wives become ex-widows?"

"I have no idea. I just know that she's driving me crazy." There was a pause and then a sigh. "When should we expect you? Do you want us to wait and have supper together? There's a new restaurant you might like to try, a seafood place. Very inexpensive and they give you a pure platter. Nana and I usually split a meal—it's more than any one person can eat."

"I'll call you," I hedged, knowing my mother's taste for deep-fried, rubbery shrimp. "We have to pick up the rental car and check in at the hotel. It might be late by the time all that's settled."

I looked up to find Mr. Laptop hovering in the aisle, clearly annoyed.

"Sorry," I said, in a failed attempt to appease him. "Look, Ma, I've got to go."

"I'm sure this is costing you an absolute fortune."

"It doesn't matter. I can afford it."

"Must be nice," she said. "Bye."

"Good-bye," I replied in some exasperation. I switched off the phone and snapped it back into the headrest. Mr. Laptop could now be damned. I took my time refolding my jacket, and when he grunted impatiently, I shot him a look that could have shriveled stone fruit.

"Here," Abby said, taking my jacket. "I'll put that under my seat. You hold my drink."

I held my breath until Abby was settled again, then I eased my left leg back onto the edge of her seat, and returned my own seat to the fractionally reclining position.

"I hate when she does that," I said.

"Does what?"

"Says things like 'must be nice' when I tell her I can afford something. I make a reasonable amount of money. My income is right there in the middle between Nelson Rockefeller and skid row." Mr. Laptop snorted. Taking advantage of the fact that I was both taller than he was and not entirely sober, I stretched out in my seat, forcing him to lean into the aisle. "My mother acts like she has to collect cans for a living."

"You've gotten above your raising," Abby replied. "It happens to the best of us. You ought to hear what Edna has to say on the subject of my fine-hairedness. I'm too good to drink instant iced tea. I'm too good to eat macaroni and cheese out of a box. It doesn't matter that no one over the age of seven likes powdered orange cheese, and I have never liked iced tea, period."

"And yet we both go home once a year, like clockwork. It's ritual abuse. Speaking of which, have you called Edna yet to tell her you're coming?"

Abby shook her head, then reached up and rang for the stewardess. I gave her a quizzical look.

"Just made a quick calculation," she said. "One beer plus three more hours of plane ride means I'll be sober enough to drive when we get there."

"Make it two," I agreed. "I'll be the designated drunkard."

Chapter Four

Nana was bad for my self-esteem. Hunter was a bad example.

There were so many ways in which my grandfather was great. At first, he was the anti-Eddie. We went places together, the whole family, to the beach or the mountains. We went to Carowinds and the Tweetsie Railroad—although there were so many flies at the latter that Hunter called it the Tsetse Railroad.

He liked to eat take-out. A couple of nights a week, he brought home fried chicken or pulled pork barbecue. He also liked to cook, a good thing since neither Nana nor my mother had much skill in the kitchen. My grandfather was domestic to a certain extent. He built things, he made repairs. In Michigan, we'd once had to flush our toilet with a bucket for three weeks until my father got around to fixing it.

Hunter wasn't uncritical. He had a sarcastic streak and a temper that in many ways was far worse than my father's. But he was also encouraging. He believed I could do anything I set my mind to. He cleared out a spot in his workshop and let me build things or tinker with little bits of machinery to my heart's content. I could use his tools, as long as I remembered to clean them up afterwards and put them back where I'd found them, and when I was successful, when I fixed the toaster or changed the sprocket on my bicycle, he was genuinely proud.

For my thirteenth birthday, Hunter bought me a motorcycle. It was a fifty-dollar clunker he got from a friend at work. I spent two days disassembling the carburetor, cleaning the screens, and putting it back together. When I was finished, it ran. Not well and not smoothly—white smoke poured from the exhaust pipe—but it would go. Hunter stood on the back porch and grinned from ear to ear.

"Goddamn," he said. "Would you look at that? Goddamn."

My grandfather's problem was that he drank. He was a binger. Every weekend, every holiday, every birthday, every funeral, and every wedding—nothing was sacred and no occasion was safe. Through trial and error and bitter experience, I learned when it was safe to bring people home and when I needed to stay away myself, but in those early days, the first few months after we'd moved to North Carolina, the drinking didn't seem like a problem at all. It seemed like a boon.

August 10 rolled around and Lucky Eddie forgot my birthday. No card, no present, no phone call. My mother was incandescent with rage. I didn't care. As far as I was concerned, being away from my father was present enough. Hunter got drunk that night. He sat at the kitchen table and poured himself beer after beer. At one o'clock that morning, the trashcan was full of empties and the ashtray in front of him was filled with cigarette butts. Nana sat in the living room in the rocking chair. The TV was on, but her eyes were shut and she was snoring loudly through her open mouth. My mother had long since gone to bed.

"It's a goddamn disgrace," Hunter said.

"What is?"

"Forgetting your goddamn birthday. He's got one child." He held up his index finger. "One. And he can't remember her birthday. What kind of son of a bitch is that?"

"A sorry one?" I suggested.

"A sorry son of a bitch," Hunter agreed. He shook his head sadly and brushed the hair out of his eyes. Hunter had a head full of thick white hair, which he wore brushed straight back from his forehead and held in place by Vitalis hair tonic. The first sign of incipient drunkenness was that he would start running his fingers through his hair. When it fell onto his forehead and into his eyes, he was usually close to passing out. "It didn't have to be this way. He didn't appreciate what he had. You and your mama, you're goddamn jewels, you know that? Jewels. Pearls without price."

This was a familiar line. It was also meaningless. One night, he told me I was the baby Jesus come back to earth because I found the bottle opener he'd accidentally thrown into the trashcan.

"Don't tell me about it," I said, yawning. "Tell him."

"Goddamn it, I will! Give me the phone."

This was a new one. I lifted the receiver off the wall and handed it to him, then I watched in dazed and tired amazement as he held the phone at arm's length, trying to focus on the dial.

"What's the number?" he said.

"313-555-4237."

"All right. It's ringing. It's ringing again. Pick up you sorry . . . Hello, there!" My grandfather's voice grew friendly, expansive, and exaggeratedly Southern. It was as if Foghorn Leghorn had suddenly stepped into our kitchen. "Is this Edward T. Koslowski? It is? Well, this is Hunter C. Bartholomew. How the hell are you? You are? Why in the world would you be sleeping?"

The conversation played out in this fashion for several minutes, my father admonishing Hunter for calling him so late, my grandfather pretending not to understand. I could never figure out why Eddie didn't hang up on him, but he never did—and my grandfather called him dozens of times over the next few years. Hunter was a great believer in the telephone. He'd get drunk and call the White House or the president of General Motors and some poor operator would be stuck saying, "Yes, sir," and "No, I'm afraid I can't, sir," while Hunter said, "I tell you this is Hunter C. Bartholomew of Raleigh, N.C. Wake him up—Mr. Reagan will want to talk to *me*."

"All right," Hunter was saying, "all right. You can go back to bed now. I just wanted to tell you something. I've figured out what the T stands for in Edward T. Koslowski—no, it's not that. The T is for turd. You're a goddamn, turd-tapping, toe-sucking son of a bitch. Good night to you."

The next day was Saturday. Hunter and I had a standing date to go out to my great-grandmother's farm. We'd pack my motorcycle in the back of his van, and I would ride while he and Uncle Fred fished. I didn't know if he'd be up for it or not, but in the morning, he was raring to go.

"I've got something for you," he said. "You can use it on your father the next time you see the bastard." He held out a gas-powered BB pistol.

My grandmother pitched a fit. My mother issued dire warnings about loss of sight. I kept quiet for fear that if I danced for joy they'd think I was too immature to be trusted with the gun. I should have gone ahead and danced. The accident proved my mother right and forever shattered my grandmother's slim hope of turning me into a lady.

The pond behind my great-grandmother's house was really just a glorified irrigation ditch. It was full of bug-eyed fish stocked by my grandfather, agricultural run-off, and old junk my Bartholomew kin were too lazy to take to the dump. During drought years, the back end of a '63 Mercury rose from the depths like a rusty-finned Venus.

Though Hunter and Fred went through the motions, they weren't really there to fish. They were there to drink. Nana was a strict Southern Baptist and, consequently, a teetotaler. Drinking at our house took place only after dark.

Hunter was also a Southern Baptist, but he lacked Nana's unquestioning belief in God's benevolent dictatorship. He didn't doubt God's existence, only his intentions. "God is a son of a bitch," he used to say. "Goddamn him." I never knew if it was my grandmother's disapproval or a secret fear of divine retribution in the afterlife for each and every beer, but it was important for Hunter to maintain the fiction that he got drunk only by accident. He always had an alibi—the weather was hot and the beer was cold; someone slipped him a Coke that had bourbon in it; he only had one or two. For the alcoholic Baptist, drinking is like giving a whore a ride to church—if you focus on where you're going, God might overlook what happened on the way.

I couldn't blame Hunter or his drinking for the accident, though both had an effect on the aftermath. If he'd been sober, I'd still be called Frankie.

We arrived at the farm just before noon, and, as usual, we drove right past great-grandma's house and straight to the pond. Miss Agnes was at home. I knew it because I'd seen the curtains in her bedroom twitch as we passed by. She lived in her bedroom during the summer months. It was the only air-conditioned room in the house.

Miss Agnes was a crotchety old woman, and although she was in her eighties, she lived alone. The Bartholomews were a large family, not a close one. My grandfather and his siblings—there were seven of them—paid a woman named Pearl Johnson to look after Miss Agnes. Pearl came in five days a week to do the cooking and housekeeping, and the kids trusted her to let them know if the old lady needed anything. At Nana's insistence, I'd begun sticking my head in on the weekends to check on Miss Agnes. She never seemed particularly pleased to see me. She certainly never invited me into the bedroom to enjoy the air-conditioning.

August 11 was a hot day, about a hundred and four degrees. A dirty miasma rose from the stagnant green water of the fishpond. The tobacco in the sandy fields around us had turned golden yellow, and it smelled sticky and sweet, like raisins. We'd stopped at a bait shop on the way out so Hunter could buy a can of worms and two bamboo fishing poles. The poles rarely survived more than one or two trips. Hunter and Fred dropped them into the pond, or left them on the ground and ran over them when we left. Saving unused bait was also not done—that would've meant we wouldn't need to stop at the bait shop the following week. The bait shop was where Hunter bought the beer. Two six-packs of Budweiser, tucked into the Styrofoam fish cooler.

We parked in the shade of the willow tree, and Fred unloaded the van. Fred always unloaded the van. He was a natural-born flunky. If he'd ever had a thought, he kept it to himself. He answered every question in the negative with "Nope" and in the positive with "Might as well" or "Don't mind if I do." I suspected he was simple-minded, but Nana insisted that he had low cunning. When she and Hunter were first married, they came home from their honeymoon to find that Fred had gone through my grandfather's bedroom at Miss Agnes' house and sold his guitar, his second-best suit, and the quilt off his bed.

Fred set up the lawn chairs and fishing poles and sat down. Then he mopped his face with a dirty red bandanna, a gesture that was alcoholic semaphore for "I need a beer." Hunter took his glasses off, ran a hand across his forehead, and wiped the sweat onto his trousers. This was alcoholic semaphore for "Help's on the way."

Hunter put his glasses back on and squinted up at the sun.

"It's a hot one, ain't it, Fred?"

"It's a hot one," Fred agreed.

"Hot enough for you, Frankie Lou?"

This summertime rhyme was getting to be an old joke. I drew a target on a paper plate and nailed it to the willow tree. "Hotter than the blue gates of hell," I said. "You'd better get yourself something to drink."

This was not part of the game. I'd blown the cover. For my punishment, I had to listen to another five minutes of complaints about the weather.

Finally, Hunter felt the back of his neck. "Look at that," he said, shaking the sweat off his hand. "The water's just pouring off me. I must be getting dehydrated. You want a cold one, Fred?"

"Don't mind if I do."

Fred never said no to a beer. He never said no to anything. According to Hunter, he paid flesh rent to the landlady at his boarding house, an old woman with one leg who looked like a Bonobo monkey. I'd rather have died than picture the two of them together. Fred looked like he routinely slept outdoors in a puddle of urine. His face had the weathered, gnomish look of a hardened street bum, and his eyes were permanently bloodshot. He wore his hair in a greasy black pompadour that was, except for the dandruff, an exact replica of Ronald Reagan's. Deep wrinkles crossed the burnt red skin of his forehead like slashes in a dirty tarpaulin. Why any woman would want him, even the landlady at his boarding house, was beyond me, and yet he claimed to have three ex-wives and a host of children for whom he paid no child support. Hunter said the reason Fred didn't have a driver's license was for fear that one of his ex-wives might track him down and make him pay.

He had a job washing cars at the Chevy dealership where my grandfather worked as a mechanic, and it was entirely thanks to Hunter that Fred kept it from week to week. Hunter picked him up every morning, drove him home every night, and tried to keep an eye out in case anything disappeared from a customer's trunk or glove box. He was his brother's keeper. It was the price he paid for a built-in drinking buddy.

41

I took aim at the paper plate and fired. The BB struck an inch to the right of the bulls-eye, so I adjusted the sight with my Swiss Army knife and fired again.

"Bulls-eye," Hunter said. "You see that, Fred? She's Annie Oakley. She could shoot the balls off a housefly."

I pretended I hadn't heard him, and I tried not to look pleased. Sober, Hunter was sparing with compliments; drunk, he was often effusive. This one meant something. I fired ten more shots into the paper plate and then sat down at the edge of the pond.

"Here," Hunter said, "see if you can shoot the cork on that fishing line."

I tried and missed. So much for Annie Oakley.

"Balance the pistol on your knee," he said. "Here, give it to me, I'll show you."

I handed him the gun and he sat down next to me. Ten shots later, he said, "Goddamn son of a bitch. Throw that in the pond and I'll buy you one that shoots straight."

I took the pistol back from him, took aim at the cork, and fired. This time, I hit it.

"Well I'll be shit," he said. "You see that, Fred?"

Fred nodded and cracked open another beer. I shot several more paper plates, a couple of corks, and an old piece of roofing tin. Then I moved into the shade and whittled a stick with my Swiss Army knife until I put a gash in my thumb. I borrowed the van keys from Hunter and drove the Econoline up and down the dirt road past Miss Agnes' bedroom window. She looked out twice. I didn't stop. When driving lost its charm, I went back to the pond and picked up the now sizeable collection of empty beer cans. These I set up in the branches of the willow tree. The sun was now directly overhead, forcing Fred and my grandfather to abandon their lawn chairs and seek shelter in the back of the van. Hunter whistled to himself: *Once in A While, Deep Purple*, and *You Are My Sunshine*. When he got to *Lady of Spain*, he'd be out of beer.

Checking to make sure that the safety was on, I spun the gun around on my index finger and then rammed it into the pocket of my shorts. I practiced a few more spins and quick draws before closing my left eye and taking aim at a can. The BB hit with a satisfying ping. I turned quickly to my right and shot two more cans.

It was the fourth shot that did the damage. The BB ricocheted off the can and struck my left eye. I dropped the gun and covered my eye with my hand. For a moment, I was afraid to move, afraid the BB was lodged in my eyeball, afraid it had gone straight through to the back of my head. It wasn't until I felt the blood trickling down my palm that I took any action. I picked up the gun and threw it into the pond.

I heard the pop and hiss of two more beers being opened and thought for a moment about throwing myself into the pond as well. In a crisis, my grandfather only had two readily accessible emotions, anger and panic. I decided there was no help for it. With my hand still cupped over my eye, I walked around to the back of the van. Hunter and Fred were sitting on the floor with the cargo doors open, their feet resting on the bumper. Fred had taken off one of his zippered ankle boots and was holding it out for my grandfather's inspection.

Hunter held up his hands to ward it off. "Jesus Christ, Fred. That smells like a fart in a vinegar bottle. Why don't you wear socks?"

Fred shrugged and slipped his bare foot back into the boot. "It's nice, ain't it?"

"I'll give you some goddamn socks," Hunter said.

"I didn't pay but twenty dollars for that boot," continued Fred.

My grandfather shook his head in disgust. "You bought them at that pawn shop, didn't you? What have I told you about that? Somebody might have died in them boots. He might've pissed in them. Why can't you go to a goddamn store . . ."

"Excuse me," I said as calmly as I could. "I think I need some help."

Hunter looked up. He didn't drop his beer can in shock. He didn't even put it down. He said, "What in the sam hell have you done to yourself?"

The pain in my eye had given way to a dull throbbing, so I cleared my throat and took my hand away. When the light hit the pupil, I felt like I'd been stabbed. I put my hand back up quickly and said, "I shot myself."

There was a long pause and then he said, "What did you do that for?"

"It was an accident."

"Goddamn it to hell—what are you doing playing half-assed with that gun?"

I ignored this, as it was a typical five-beer response. There was no logic to it. "Can we go now?" I said. To press home the urgency of my request, I took my hand off my eye again for just a second, making sure Hunter got a good look at the bloody eyelid. He crumpled up his beer can and tossed it into the cooler.

"Come on, Fred," he said. "We have to take this fumble-fingered fart to the hospital."

For the next twenty-two miles, all the way from the farm to Wake Medical Center, Hunter carried on a stream-of-consciousness narrative.

"I told you to be careful when I gave you that thing, and what do you do? You shoot your goddamn eye out. You one-eyed fool— you think you're Sammy Davis, Junior? What the hell were you playing at?"

"I wasn't playing."

"My fanny, you weren't. You want to play something dangerous? Stick a blowtorch up your ass and play Buck Rogers."

Mild stuff coming from Hunter; I didn't interrupt.

"I'll send you to live with your goddamn daddy. You're nothing but a pair of half-assed Polacks. How about I take you out and shoot your other eye? Then you'll match."

I let him carry on the rest of the way without comment. It felt like my eye had been whacked with a hammer.

At the hospital, I learned that the blood came from my eyelid and not from the eye itself. The BB had struck at an angle, done its damage, and fallen onto the ground somewhere. The good news was that I would lose neither my eye nor my sight. The bad news was that my pupil might be permanently dilated. I wouldn't know for a week or so.

This information was delivered by a pretty blonde ophthalmologist with a tiny waist and big boobs. She bandaged me up, gave me a prescription for pain, and told me I was free to go home. When she was out of earshot, Hunter leaned close to me and whispered, "Dolly

Parton says you'll live, but your mama's going to kill us both. You're going to look like a goddamn lizard."

"I won't look like a lizard," I protested, ignoring the more serious concern of what my mother was going to do. "I'll look like David Bowie."

"Like who?"

"David Bowie. He's a singer. From England. He's got one eye just like mine."

Hunter snorted. "You'll look like a pirate. From Poland. A goddamn half-assed Polack Popeye."

Chapter Five

Abby was the first to ask. We met in ninth grade biology class when we were seated at the same lab table, the one in the far back corner, next to the barrel filled with preserved dead cats. At some point during the school year we were supposed to dissect them, but we never got past the fetal pig.

"How did Popeye become Poppy?"

"My grandmother. She believes in making the best of a bad situation. Poppy sounds more feminine than my real name."

"Your real name is Mary Frances."

"Yeah, but no one ever called me that. It was always Frankie or Frank."

"Frank. I can see how Poppy would be more feminine than that." Abby chewed the end of her pencil. All of her pencils and pens had teeth marks in them. Her mother wouldn't let her chew gum because of her braces. "Do you like Poppy?"

"I don't hate it. It's better than Popeye."

"Or Frank," she agreed. "Your eye, you know—it's cool. It doesn't look dilated. It looks like you've got one brown eye and one blue." The bell rang. We shoved our books into our knapsacks and went out into the hallway. "Abby is a nickname, too. My real name is Abia. It's an Arabic word meaning great."

"That's cool."

"My dad was a Muslim. He died before I was born."

"I'm sorry."

"So am I."

The high school we attended was a Magnet GT, the G standing

for gifted and the T for talented. It was called a magnet because it was designed to draw rich white kids into poor, predominantly black neighborhoods. The idea was to create a more appealing system than busing for integrating white and black kids while at the same time serving a specifically academic purpose.

It half-worked. The magnet part worked like a charm; white kids were drawn to the school from all over Wake County. Once they got there, however, the school had its own form of internal segregation. The students in the GT classes were ninety percent white and ninety percent rich. The year we graduated, Abby was one of only ten black students in the Magnet GT class, and she and I were the only ones in our small circle of friends and acquaintances who worked fast-food jobs out of necessity. We moved in a bubble within a bubble. In the academic classes, like English and Math, we rubbed elbows with people who lived in enormous houses in North Raleigh and drove sports cars their parents bought for them. In typing and gym class, we mixed with the general student population, many of whom regarded us with suspicion and resentment as the recipients of special treatment.

Though I didn't realize it at the time, negotiating the various levels of segregation was especially hard on Abby. At the beginning of high school, she had friends on both sides of the aisle, black kids she'd grown up with and white kids, like me, that she'd met in class. As time wore on, it became increasingly difficult to balance these two groups. In ninth grade, she ate lunch with Shalia and Bonita and studied after school with me and Kim DiMarco. In tenth grade, she ate lunch with me and Kim. Abby was good-looking and brilliant, and her expectations were high. She expected to make the long climb to the top on sheer willpower and ability—valedictorian, scholarship, medical school, success. It was an unfair exchange, trading friends for aspirations. Either way, she lost something she valued.

In my ignorance, I thought I knew better. I thought I could take the "I have a dream" speech and smooth it all out for her. One day in the cafeteria, I spied Shalia and Bonita sitting at a table with three empty chairs. They looked up as we came in and waved. Abby and I waved back.

47

"Why don't we sit with them," I said. I'd eaten at their table a couple of times during freshman year. They were funny. We cracked jokes on one another and seemed to get along well.

Abby shook her head and looked away. "No," she said. "They couldn't be themselves with you there. You'd all be playing like you were someone else."

"I'm not a bigot."

"I didn't say you were. But you're also not black." She handed me a tray from the stack at the beginning of the lunch line and took one for herself. "Sometimes," she said, "black people sit together just so they can be black, on their own, without an audience. Do you understand what I'm saying to you?"

"No." We continued moving through the line, choosing the same things, hamburgers with extra pickles, red Jell-O, plain milk. When we came to the cashier, we both paid with reduced-price lunch cards. I hesitated. "Do you want to sit with them? It's okay if you do."

"No," she said. "These days, I make them just as uncomfortable as you do."

We didn't speak about it again. Shalia and I took typing together, and Bonita and I were on the basketball and volleyball teams. Abby and I went on to college, and we didn't see them again. Neither of us attended our ten-year high school reunion.

The traffic on the Durham Highway was a nightmare, bumper to bumper, with cars weaving in and out, speeding along at sixty and seventy miles an hour and then slamming on the brakes, stopping just short of a rear-end collision. I was glad not to be driving.

Twenty cars ahead, the police had a Trans Am pulled onto the shoulder. Abby signaled for a lane change as car after car swung out from behind and passed us. "I wish I had a cigarette."

"You don't smoke."

"I know. I really wish I had a pistol and no fear of consequences."

She gunned the Explorer into the left-hand lane and then slowed back down to the speed limit, causing the car behind us to ride up to within inches of our back window. I watched him in the vanity mirror of the passenger side visor.

"He just called you a stupid fucking bitch," I said. "Should I turn around and give him the finger?"

"No," she said, glancing in the rear view mirror. "No need. A fat guy, about forty-five, tight collar, bright red face. He'll have a heart attack at Fat Daddy's over a plate of biscuits and gravy. Should we check in first or do you want to go straight to the hospital?"

"I don't know. I'm exhausted."

"So am I." We passed Crabtree Valley Mall and negotiated the maze of straight arrows and turn lanes leading to Glenwood Avenue and the Beltline. Abby turned onto the Beltline.

"Hospital it is?" I said.

She nodded. "Let's get really tired. Then, we'll go straight to sleep. Besides, why waste those beers you drank on the plane? You'll be nice and numb for your first family encounter."

I glanced at my watch. "Let's see, it's five o'clock Portland time, which makes it eight o'clock here. Unless my grandfather is in the throes of dying right this minute, Ma and Nana won't be there. They'll have gone home to let the dogs out and settle in for the night. Nana doesn't like to get home after dark."

"I think it's nice of her to go to the hospital at all."

"They were married for nearly forty years."

"That was twenty years ago. It didn't end happily."

"Tell me about it." I closed my eyes and reclined the seat back. "I can't stand watching this traffic. I'm going to pretend I'm back on the airplane, only this time, I'm sitting in first class."

The woman at the reception desk spoke with a thick accent I couldn't identify. It might have been Caribbean or perhaps Gullah. Her voice was low and lilting. "Mr. Hunter C. Bartholomew," she said. "Room 418C, but you'd best be checking at the nurses' station before you go in."

The nurse on duty was a large-breasted bleach blonde with nails that looked too long and too red to be efficient. The nametag clipped to the lapel of her floral print lab coat said she was Marilyn Case, R.N. She looked like a Marilyn. She also looked like a Shirley or a Judy or a Peggy, a short fat woman in her middle forties, a little blowsy and hard-bitten around the edges. Abby and I stopped in front of her desk and she smiled, displaying a mouth full of large crooked teeth.

"May I help you?" She pronounced *help* as *hep*, the true mark of the North Carolina native. She'd also say *cain't* instead of *can't*, call lunch dinner, and use words like *haint* and *nary* and *twern't*. I smiled back at her and then surprised myself by answering in kind, stretching and flattening my vowels.

"I'm here to see Mr. Bartholomew. Would you please tell me his room number?"

Abby gave me a look I couldn't interpret. It might have been, "Why the hell are you talking like that," or "Scratch the surface, find a redneck."

Marilyn stood up. "Why don't I show you? I was just fixing to check on him."

We followed her down a short hallway that seemed too quiet and ill-lit for a busy city hospital. We turned left and then right, winding up in a small alcove with four rooms. Directly in front of us, suspended from a metal arm above the first door, was a computer monitor, on the gray screen of which were four names in yellow followed by four electrocardiograms flashing in green. Bartholomew was the third one down, below Mallard and Bridges.

On the acrylic sleeve marking my grandfather's room number, someone had written *Bartholomew DNR* in heavy black marker. I followed Marilyn in, but Abby paused in the doorway.

"I'll wait out here," she said.

"You don't have to. I mean, I'd rather you . . ."

"I'm going to talk to the nurse when she comes out. I'll find out what's going on, and you can just concentrate on your visit." She reached out for a moment and squeezed my arm. "Go on," she said. "It'll be all right. I'll be here when you need me."

The room was much darker than the hallway, lit only by the glow of medical equipment and a muted television set. My grandfather was lying on a pile of white sheets, his green hospital gown hitched up above his hips. Marilyn quickly tugged it down, but not before I got an unseemly glimpse of his penis and testicles. It wasn't, however, his genitalia that I found shocking—it was his knees and feet. The muscle and flesh had withered away, making the bones and joints seem huge.

As Marilyn moved around the side of the bed to check the IV monitor, I tucked the blankets in tightly around those terrible legs and feet.

"Is it all right if I switch on a light?"

"Yes," said Marilyn. "I don't think it will bother him."

The skin on Hunter's face was a mottled yellow, and the hollows beneath his eyes looked bruised. White stubble covered his cheeks and chin. I wished someone—my mother or one of the nurses—had shaved him. The only time he'd ever allowed his beard to grow was once when he had shingles. He couldn't stand having hair on his face. He said it was nasty. In the summertime, he shaved his armpits as well.

"Deodorant won't work with all that hair," he said. "That's why men stink—men and damn dirty hippie women, off living in the woods."

For some reason, I thought seeing him would be a kind of formality—if not easy, then at least not especially difficult. My grandfather was eighty-two years old. He had multi-infarct dementia, chronic lung disease, and a host of other opportunistic illnesses, the general wear and tear of a long life lived hard. And he'd left us a long time ago, my senior year in high school. He was a ghost from my past. He'd run off with the Avon lady, proving himself no better in the end than Lucky Eddie. I told the story now as a joke. I told it to friends at parties, and they all laughed and said I was making it up. Not your father and your grandfather, they said. It was the old door-to-door salesman tale with the genders reversed.

It was also funny at the time it happened—I could see that, I could appreciate the irony—and yet it wasn't funny at all. It threw my life into complete chaos. He never understood why I was so angry with him, why I couldn't forgive and forget, even long after he'd settled into his new life. I never told him exactly what he'd done, why it had such a profound effect on me.

He reached a reconciliation of sorts with my mother. They'd never entirely lost touch. At first he called regularly, usually drunk. My mother hung up on him. When he called sober, she talked. They began meeting on neutral ground, at Cooper's Barbecue for lunch, or he'd stop by the library during working hours. Five years after he left, Hunter's girlfriend, Jean, was killed in a car wreck. My mother agreed to visit him at home then. Years later, when he needed to go into a nursing home, she made the arrangements. He gave her his power of attorney. She said he'd been a good father to her. Way back when.

Nana had never been as angry as my mother and I were. She'd been disgusted but resigned and, in a way, grateful. She'd grown tired of living with a drunk, but she'd never have left him for that reason. Their divorce became amicable when the Avon lady died, and it fell into casual friendliness as his dementia took hold. She visited him in the nursing home, and they talked about people they'd known and friends they'd shared. They were like old acquaintances. It was as if they'd never been married, as if he'd become just another one of the many unfortunates she visited with her Sunday school class.

I looked at him now, surprised in a way that he was still alive. Except for the jagged, irregular breathing, I'd have thought he was dead. He looked pale and otherworldly. It was hard to reconcile the body before me with what he had once been—a small, lively man with amazingly strong forearms, arms like Popeye the Sailor complete with a couple of homemade tattoos. He was handsome in a rakish sort of way, ready with a joke or a funny story. When I was a child, I thought he knew everyone on earth. He'd strike up a conversation with a stranger and discover that they were distant cousins or that they knew someone in common. Most people liked him. He was a loyal friend, a Good Time Charlie, a hail-fellow-well-met.

He was also ignorant, bigoted, and occasionally violent. Sometimes he went wild with rage. One night I watched him take his fist and smash a windshield in the parking lot of the Jones Street Tavern. My mother thought he was an undiagnosed manic-depressive. My grandmother just thought he was crazy. I never knew what to think. I lived with him for four years. He seemed to be sane when I moved in. Three years later, he was threatening to commit suicide on a regular basis, and threatening to kill other people just as often. Sometimes, I threatened to kill him. One time, I tried. I threw him through the back door and down the concrete steps. I hoped he'd broken his neck, but he just laid there on the ground and cursed at me. His hold on life was tenacious. Despite all the late night phone calls when he said he was going to hang himself or blow his brains out, despite the reckless behavior and the fighting and the bad company he kept, he had no intention of facing God one moment sooner than necessary.

"God is a son of a bitch," I could hear him say. "Goddamn him."

I watched Marilyn change the IV bag and punch buttons on the various machines.

"How long has he been like this? When I talked to my mother— I mean, I knew he was bad, but I didn't know . . ."

She nodded. "My shift started at three. He's opened his eyes a few times since then but that's about it. He still reacts to light and noise. Do you see? His eyelids are fluttering. He hears us talking."

"But he's not really conscious. Is he in a coma?"

Marilyn shrugged. "Not officially. You'll want to talk to the doctor, of course."

"My friend in the hallway, she's a nurse. Would you answer any questions she has? She'll be able to understand the technical stuff and then explain it to me." I smiled, hoping to curry favor. "So, you think he can hear me, then?"

"I believe he can," she said. "Go ahead and talk to him, anyway. It cain't hurt. I'm going to shut this door now and give you some privacy. Leave it open when you go out."

As she pulled the door to behind her, I was suddenly sorry to see her go. There was something reassuring about her bleached hair and red nails, something fat and brassy and alive.

53

I pulled a chair up next to the bed and sat down. There was a local news alert. I didn't recognize the anchor. I missed Charlie Gaddy and Bobbie Battista. She'd gone on to bigger and better things at CNN. He'd retired. All of this had happened since I'd left North Carolina. I switched over to a channel playing country music videos and turned the sound up a little.

"Imagine," I said aloud. "Being nostalgic for old news anchors. Who cares? It's always the same news, a basketball scandal at one of the universities, a wreck on I-40. What was the name of that meteorologist on Channel Five? Bob something." I thought for a moment and then it came to me. Hunter was saying, "If you want to go to the beach tomorrow we'd better check out Bard DeBobeladen. I'm not going if it's raining."

I laughed. "That's it. Bob DeBardelaben." Hunter screwed up names on purpose. He liked movies with Gregory Pecker and Frank Snotistra. He called the Angus Barn restaurant the Heifer House. He called me Popeye the Half-assed Polack.

"You son of a bitch," I said. "I should have knocked your block off."

A woman appeared on the television and sang a song about breathing. I didn't recognize her. She looked like a supermodel.

"Whatever happened to Brenda Lee? She looked like a monkey in a four-foot wig but she could sing the pants off of this hussy."

My grandfather twitched. Was he laughing? I wondered.

"Hunter," I whispered, leaning close to his ear. "Thanks a whole hell of a lot. It's going to be my job to send you to perdition; you know that, don't you? This is it, this is the end. You ready to meet that God you've been pissing off for eighty-odd years?"

"Might as well," my grandfather's voice whispered back. "Don't mind if I do."

It was late and I was dopey. I knew he hadn't spoken and yet I was sure he had.

"Coma, my ass," I said. "If you can hear me, I've got no intention of wasting this opportunity. Just what were you thinking when you ran off with that woman? Can you tell me that? Jesus Christ, why did it have to be her?"

"Do you know what I told your mother when she was pregnant with you?" he whispered.

"Of course I know."

"What was it?"

"You said, 'I don't care what it is as long as it's a girl.' I've heard this story a million times."

"A million and one now, you ill-tempered jackass."

I laughed in spite of myself. "Don't get sassy with me, you old bastard. I flew all the way from Portland to see you. Drove straight from the airport. Ma and Nana don't even know that I'm here."

"Did you come in on the Durham Highway?" he said. "Too many lanes and too many cars. Driving it's like trying to angle a worm up a wild cat's ass."

"Is that really what you want to talk about? Don't you want to know . . .?"

I heard the murmur of voices outside the door.

"Listen," I said quietly. "I don't want to talk about now. Now isn't going very well for me or for you. I want to talk about yesterday."

"Why? Yesterday was a son of a bitch."

He was right, of course. Images from the past flashed by in no particular order, college, junior high, senior high. I'm thirteen again and my grandfather is fifty-nine. He sits at the kitchen table, pouring beer into a glass of tomato juice. He's wearing red-and-white striped pajamas and gesturing broadly as he holds forth about God, the universe, and death. His hair falls forward in a white curtain across his forehead. He looks like a cross between Hitler and Otis Campbell, the drunk on *The Andy Griffith Show.*

"God," he says, "is a lying bastard."

"Really," I reply. "What makes you say that?"

"He told me I was going to live forever."

"Is God a bartender?"

"You blasphemous devil. God said I'd live to be a hundred."

"That's not forever."

He shakes his head sadly. "I'm fifty-nine goddamn years old. Do you know that? Look at my hands, look at them. Do you see it?"

His fingernails are clipped and clean—remarkably clean for an auto mechanic. He scrubs them with Borax and a fingernail brush. On his left hand is a wedding band, on his right, a Masonic ring with a half-carat diamond.

"What am I looking for?"

"That," he says, pointing at a mole about an inch down from the wedding band. "That's goddamn skin cancer."

"No, it isn't."

"Yes, it is."

"No, it isn't. It's a mole. You've had it forever."

He holds his hand up in front of his face, moving it back and forth to keep it in focus. "I have, haven't I? Who told me it was cancer?"

"Jehovah," I say. "He was tending bar at the Jones Street Tavern."

"No, he didn't. He said I was going to live forever. You wait and see."

I opened my eyes again and saw him lying there, shrunken and pathetic.

"It's funny," I said, reaching out to squeeze his cold fingers. "I thought I'd be angry with you forever. I thought I'd be the worst person in the world to decide what happens to you, but that's what I'm going to do. That's why they wanted me to come home, to pull the plug, if necessary."

I looked at the clock on the wall above the sink. It was half past nine Eastern time; I'd been up since four a.m. Pacific. I longed for a hot shower and a warm bed. Abby was waiting for me in the hallway, probably more tired than I was after our harrowing drive from the airport. I wanted to leave, but I couldn't seem to move. I wanted something else—I didn't know what. I closed my eyes and it came to me. I wanted to go back to 1979. I wanted to materialize over that kitchen table and show my grandfather a picture of himself, a cadaver in a hospital bed with tubes hanging out of his arms. I wanted to say, "This is what will happen if you don't stop drinking. This is what will happen if you keep running around."

But I know he wouldn't have listened. If the ghost of Christmas Future had stopped by our kitchen table to take him on a tour of the future, my grandfather would have called him a son of a bitch.

I stood up to leave. "I'll be back tomorrow," I said. "I'm sorry nothing turned out like it was supposed to."

"That's all right," said the voice in my head. "Everything turns from sugar to shit."

Chapter Six

When I was a teenager, I thought the Velvet Cloak Inn was the zenith of luxury. Forget the Ritz and the Waldorf—I'd never seen them. The Velvet Cloak had valet parking. You pulled up to the front door and one man in a red velvet jacket took your luggage from the trunk while another climbed into your car and drove it off to some hidden parking place; it didn't matter where he parked your car because when you were ready to leave, another man would go find it for you. Sometimes, my mother and I took one-day vacations at the Velvet Cloak. She read books and I swam in the pool and we ate dinner in the hotel restaurant. I imagined I was John Lennon, living on the top floor of the Dakota. It was still a very nice hotel. I liked the location, on Hillsborough Street, a few blocks up from the bell tower at N. C. State University. I could wax nostalgic about my campus days without having to put up with the campus noise.

Abby and I checked into our room at a quarter past ten.

"Dibs on the first bath," she said.

"Dibs on the bed by the window," I replied. I threw myself down on the mattress and tested the pillows. Too soft. I stacked one on top of another and tried again. Not perfect, but it would have to do. I should have packed my own pillow.

Abby kicked her shoes off. "I'm not going to call my mom until tomorrow morning. I didn't tell her I was coming, so she won't know I'm blowing her off."

"Lucky dog. I've got to call my mother tonight. Nana's going to be pissed that I went to the hospital first."

"Go on," she said, stripping down to her underwear. "Pay your penance."

"First," I replied, fishing my cell phone out of my hand luggage, "I have to check my voice mail. There might be something urgent. Perhaps George Bush called to ask my advice on Iraq."

"Perhaps Saddam Hussein called to ask your advice on his mustache."

"Close. I have four calls—the first is from Dolores."

"So are the other three." Abby went into the bathroom and turned on the water. "What kind of cop is named Dolores, anyway?"

"A cop in her thirties with a name from the fifties who has five cats, a nicotine habit, and an inability to take no for an answer."

"What?" Abby called over the roar of the bathwater. "You'll have to speak louder."

"She says she knows I'm dodging her and she thought she deserved better than that. She says she's through with me."

"Hooray. She's a lying sack of shit."

"She says this is the last phone call I'm going to get."

"Barring the three that come after this one."

But the next three calls were not from Dolores. The second was from my boss, Clark Hauser of Hauser Designs, an innocuous name for the manufacturer of computer games like *Piping Hot Death* and *Mortuary Mayhem*. I was Hauser Designs' technical writer and editor. I wrote game manuals, translating geek to English, and edited press releases and marketing materials. My favorite were the marketing materials. We had a contract with an advertising agency to write the commercials, but I wrote the copy that appeared on the box.

You're Jack Ripper, Mortician Extraordinaire. You take pride in your work. You can take the hamburger from a car wreck and make it look like Grandma. You make the dead look lifelike. Too lifelike. State-of-the-art graphics and stab and slab action.

We also produced nice, boring stuff like architecture programs and three-dimensional room design suites. I'd taken a six-week leave of absence for my surgery, but I knew I wouldn't be spending those six weeks unmolested by the call of duty. Clark Hauser couldn't write a birthday card to his wife without running it by me.

"*Green Thumb Gardening*," he said. "Gene has worked out the bugs, so we're moving the release date to early January. I need a couple of quick paragraphs for the small trades. A file by Friday—would that be too soon? Oh and how are you doing? Did everything . . . um . . . you know, come out okay?"

Abby turned the water off and settled into the tub with a loud splash.

"Clark is worried that they might have removed the wrong parts. And he wants me to do some work."

"Clark's an ass."

"Clark's a generous ass. Enjoy the luxury of your surrounds, courtesy of Clark's deep-pocket salaries." I went into the bathroom and leaned against the sink. Abby's head floated on a sea of bubbles. "Next is Louise. She took Belvedere to the vet, but it's nothing to worry about. She thought he looked stiff. The vet prescribed a different anti-inflammatory. Rimadyl. Possible side effects include ulcers and death. She doesn't want to give it to him without your permission. Call her back."

"Why didn't she leave a message on my voice mail?"

"She did. And she left one at the hospital. And she sent one by carrier pigeon. You know how she is."

"I know."

"The next call is from . . ." I stopped as a voice stepped out of time and into the hotel bathroom. *Poppy, this is Susan.*

Abby looked at me. "Take it in the other room," she said. "And shut the bathroom door."

I reached the end of the message and punched in the code for repeat.

"Poppy, this is Susan," she said. "Your mother gave me your phone number. I understand you're going to be in town, and I'd like to get together, if you can fit it in. I realize you have a lot on your plate. Maybe we could have dinner? My number is . . . well, my number is the same as it's always been. I'm sure you remember it. I'm staying at my father's house. He'd like to see you, too. He says it's been a long time. Please call. I want to see you."

Please call. I want to see you.

I didn't know which was more disturbing, the assumption that after nearly twenty years I'd still remember the phone number at her father's house, or the fact that I did remember it. I knew it as well as I knew my own.

Two months after my accident with the BB gun, Susan Sava moved into the house next door. It was Saturday, October 13. I wrote it in my diary. Her father, Mike, worked at Bloom's Chevrolet with my grandfather. He was a salesman. Hunter had told me that he had a daughter about my age. He said I'd like her, and so for weeks I'd been looking forward to moving day. When the U-Haul arrived, I got my motorcycle out and rode it in slow circles around our front yard, pretending not to watch the people and furniture going in. I'd been riding for about half an hour when Susan stepped out onto her front porch and waved at me. I waved back. Two seconds later, I ran smack into a hickory nut tree. Thus marked the beginning of the clumsy pratfalls that plagued me whenever I was around her.

Not that I was graceful at the best of times. My depth perception was still slightly off, and I sometimes miscalculated when climbing stairs or reaching for a drink. To add to my general awkwardness, I was self-conscious about my eye. People had a tendency to stare, then catch themselves and look away.

Susan stared that first day as she helped me to my feet. I looked away, embarrassed.

"No, don't," she said, cupping her hand under my chin and forcing me to make eye contact. "That's interesting—the pupil's just dilated. I thought at first that your eyes were two different colors."

"A lot of people make that mistake."

Her own eyes were dark blue, deep set against the rich tan of her skin.

"So, is it permanent, then?"

I nodded.

"I'm Susan," she said, holding out a hand for me to shake. "I understand they call you Poppy, but that's not your real name, is it?"

"It's a nickname. From Popeye. My grandfather—Hunter—he's a

joker. My real name is Mary Frances. People used to call me Frankie. Take your pick. I don't care."

She laughed. "I don't even have a middle name, and here you are spoiled for choice."

"You're welcome to one of mine."

"Thanks," she said. "I believe I'll have Frances. Those were my favorite books when I was a child. Have you read them?"

I shook my head. "Sorry."

"The *Frances* books. They're by Russell Hoban, about a little badger. I'll loan them to you, if you like." She took another shameless look at my eye. "How did it happen, if you don't mind my asking?"

"Mishap with a BB gun. I can still see, so it wasn't a big deal."

"Must've hurt, though."

"It didn't tickle."

She laughed. "Okay, tough girl. I was just going inside for a Coke. Why don't you come with me? You can tell me all about it."

"There's not much to tell."

"You'll have to make something up then. Every scar deserves a good story."

I think I fell in love with her that day. I fell in love on October 13, 1979, and I never quite fell out again. Not even when her mother began selling Avon.

Chapter Seven

My English term paper wasn't due for another two weeks, but I wanted to get it done before Susan came home for Spring Break. She was due back at any time. I reached out to adjust the blinds. Several red cars had driven by, and each time, my heart leapt up for just a moment before I realized it wasn't Susan's Honda. The third time this happened, I gave myself a good shake. Really, I was as bad as a dog panting at traffic.

Nana looked over my shoulder. "What's this essay about?"

"*Oedipus Rex,*" I said irritably. It was the second time she'd asked, and I had to fight the urge to type "Oedipus was a motherfucker" for the next time she looked. Another hour had passed, and Hunter still hadn't come home. My grandmother was chain-smoking, and my mother wore a tight-lipped expression. If I hadn't wanted to sit by the dining room window and keep an eye out for Susan, I'd have taken the typewriter into my bedroom.

Our dining room was actually an extension of the living room. Only imagination and the edge of the carpet divided the space between them. To emphasize what little separation there was, my grandmother had planted an enormous wing chair in the middle of the living room floor with its back to the dining room table. There was only three feet of space between them, but the chair forced us to act as if there were a door. If you didn't slow down when crossing from one room to the other, you risked barking your shins or gouging your ribs.

Both rooms were crowded with furniture. A three-keyboard Wurlitzer organ took up one entire wall, and a sofa, chairs, a stereo cabinet, and a console television filled the rest of the space. It was impossible to walk in a straight line from one side of the room to the other. In order to fit the dining room table into the space available, one side of it had to be shoved against the back wall. Otherwise, the front door wouldn't open.

The noise in the dining room was too much. It was like trying to work in a bus station. My mother had given up reading and was watching *The Andy Griffith Show*. Nana sat down in the wing chair and tried to get our dog, Maurice, to bark along to the tune of Andy's whistling. My mother turned the volume up on the television to drown out the dog. He barked louder.

I closed my eyes and tried to think of something clever to say about *Oedipus*. Nothing came to mind. I checked the window again.

"Stop messing with those blinds," Nana said. "Can't you see the dust you're raising?"

Dust motes caught the light as they billowed over the table. I ran my finger along one of the flat metal blades and then rubbed my fingers together. "How old are these blinds, anyway? Have they ever been dusted?"

My grandmother shook her head in disgust. "When was the last time you did any housework? You ought to be ashamed of yourself, letting me and your mama do it all."

"I mow the grass."

"Once a week."

"All right," I said. "How often do you clean the house?"

Nana turned to my mother. "You raised a terrible smart-mouth, Barbara."

"Don't I know it," she said. Maurice continued to bark.

"Would you please put the dog out? I can't concentrate with all that racket."

"I just let him in. Here, Barbara—Poppy says turn the television down. She can't concentrate on her school work."

My mother sighed heavily and lowered the volume. I wished I'd asked Susan for an exact time. She'd just said Saturday evening when I'd talked to her, and at the time, that had seemed good enough. Now,

I was anxious to get out of the house. Twice, I caught myself typing Opie instead of Oedipus.

I felt something shove against my legs and looked down to find Maurice trying to squeeze between me and the stack of *Reader's Digest* condensed books that propped up the back corner of the table. The Olivetti wobbled precariously, dropping a letter. I advanced the roller and rubbed at it with my typing eraser, scratching a hole in the paper.

"This table has got to go," I said, wadding up the page in disgust. "It's only got three legs, and it's too damn big for this room. It's not as if the leg Maurice chewed off is going to grow back."

"That table was expensive," Nana said, rubbing the mangled arm of the wing chair, which had also been remodeled by Maurice. "I paid three hundred dollars for it."

"It was expensive in 1972. Now it has three legs." I closed the book on *Oedipus Rex* and unplugged the typewriter. "I can't wait to go to college and get out of this mad house. It's like living in the Haney Place."

"The what?"

"The house on *Green Acres* where Oliver and Lisa live. You can't plug the microwave in without unplugging the toaster. If you touch the stove hood while touching anything on the stove, you'll knock yourself into next week."

"This house wasn't wired for that microwave. Your grandfather bought it so you could play with it, baking potatoes and blowing up hot dogs."

"This is the twentieth century. You don't have to heat the oven for an hour-and-a-half to bake a potato. You ought to try it. No heat, no foil, no mess."

"Mess," Nana said. "Talk about mess. You'll miss us when you're gone. You won't have anyone to pick up after you all day long."

"I don't know how you're planning to pay for it," my mother cut in. "Pay for what?"

"College. I don't have that kind of money."

"Financial aid will pay for it."

"Will that cover everything?"

"I was planning to get a part-time job, and I'm going to work this summer."

"As a soda jerk at the flea market, which is only open on Saturday. You need to find a regular job during the week."

"I will."

"Have you filled out any applications?"

"Yes."

"Where?"

"The record store at North Hills Mall and Taco Bell, okay?"

My mother gave me her watch-that-snotty-voice look. "I guess we'll have to work something out with the car, or I suppose you could take the bus."

"I could use Nana's car."

Nana shook her head. "Oh, no, you couldn't. Your driving scares me to death."

"You wouldn't be riding with me."

My mother piped up with mock cheerfulness. "Maybe your dad will give you a new car for graduation. He might win one. Lucky Eddie."

"Ha-ha."

Maurice nuzzled my leg. He was a big, black standard poodle. I cut his hair short every six weeks with a pair of electric clippers. Not a poodle cut, just a simple kennel cut. I thought he looked stupid clipped like someone's hedge, with bald patches here and there and big poufs over his hips and ankles. I kicked off one of my tennis shoes and rubbed his fur with my foot. It felt scratchy against my bare skin. Given my choice of dogs, I would have picked something other than a poodle, something less nervous and over-bred. Maurice was afraid of his own shadow. I stopped rubbing and slipped my shoe back on, prompting him to shove against me with his nose. I reached down and scratched between his ears.

"Come on," I said. "Let's go for a walk."

Maurice jumped up, cracking his head on the bottom of the table. I got up to look for his leash, resigning myself to being dragged all over hell's half-acre. It was then that I saw Susan's car drive past the dining room window. My heart pounded rapidly against the walls of my chest.

"Where are you going?" my grandmother asked.

"Knock it off," I said to Maurice, who was hopping up and down by the front door. "I'll walk you later." To my grandmother, I added, "I'm going next door. I just saw Susan drive by."

She said nothing, though the look she gave me was eloquent enough. Susan was to blame for my wanting to go to UNC, and Nana didn't approve. That look said that it was just a matter of time before I joined the ne'er-do-well hippies of Chapel Hill. I opened the front door.

"I won't be long."

"Hmm," she said. "Just don't forget about AA. Your grandfather wants us to go with him tonight."

"He wants an audience," my mother corrected.

"The meeting's at seven-thirty. I'll be back in plenty of time." I paused to check my hair in the mirror next to the front door. It was still too short. I'd cut it two weeks before with Maurice's dog clippers, hoping I'd look like Annie Lennox. Instead, I looked like an AWOL marine. I gave it a quick brush now with my fingers, making the hairs stand up like the bristles on a scrub brush.

"We need to leave at seven o'clock," Nana reminded me, frowning at my hair. "Why don't you put on a baseball cap and hide that monkey mess on your head?"

"Leave her hair alone," said my mother. "It'll grow."

"Not in time for the meeting."

My mother snorted with derision. "I don't know why you think you'll be going to a meeting. He left three hours ago. I'll bet you dollars to donuts that he's not coming home tonight."

My grandmother said nothing. Maurice, seeing that he wasn't going for a walk, crawled back under the table and gazed at me reproachfully. I turned my back on all of them and slipped out the front door.

Before long, I was spending several afternoons a week at Susan's house, and a good portion of every weekend. She made friends easily. I was in awe of her. She'd moved two months into her senior year of high school, and it didn't seem to matter. It was as if everyone had known her for years. I'd met Abby by that time, but we weren't yet friends. I was still eating lunch in the school cafeteria by myself.

I was devastated when Susan left for college. Her response to my grief was to encourage me to be more outgoing. I'd played sports in Michigan, and Susan pushed me to try out for the junior varsity teams in high school. I made volleyball and basketball, and, my sophomore year, softball.

"Join the French Club, too," she said. "It'll look good on your college applications."

Susan came home for holidays and breaks, and while I looked forward to her visits, I grew less dependent on her as time went by. I developed my own group of friends, Abby, and Kim DiMarco, and a couple of guys who hung around the fringes. Abby's mother, like mine, was single. She was a widow. The apartment they lived in was less than a mile away from my house. We also shared a coincidental connection in that Pearl Johnson, the woman who took care of Miss Agnes, was Abby's aunt. Abby and Susan knew and liked one another. She looked forward to Susan being home almost as much as I did. We rode around in Susan's car, went to the mall or the movies, and ate dinner at the Char-grill Drive-in.

My relationship with Susan gradually changed, and while I wouldn't have described us as equals—as a college student, she seemed too far above me for that—by the time she was a sophomore and I was a high school senior, I no longer felt like her protégée. Susan was the first person to talk to me about going to college, first guiding and then pushing me through the application process. No one in my family had gone beyond high school, and the assumption had always been that I'd graduate and look for a job. They seemed puzzled when I told them I was applying.

There was a world of difference between the Savas and the Bartholomews and Koslowskis. The first time I ever ate butter was at Susan's house. It was spread all over a crusty baguette, and the difference between that sweet, salty flavor and the margarine at my house was a revelation to rival St. Paul's on the road to Damascus. When I suggested that we start buying butter, too, my mother said that as long as she could get eight sticks of margarine for eighty-eight cents, that's what we'd be eating.

As I rang Susan's doorbell, I took note of the two new hammered copper planters on the front porch. Dark green leaves were pushing up through the soil, probably tulips. Mike had been to the Netherlands to scout out new varieties. When he came back, he gave my grandmother a small wooden windmill with the word *groetjes,* greetings, carved on its base.

Susan answered on the third ring, wearing only a red terry cloth bathrobe.

"Groetjes," I said.

She laughed. "Groetjes yourself. Come on in."

Susan had fantastic legs, long and tan beneath the knee-length robe. I was looking at them as I followed her inside. Consequently, I tripped over the edge of the doorframe.

"Walk much?"

"You know how I am. I trip on air."

"It'll get you every time," she agreed, reaching out to hug me. "It's good to see you."

It had taken me a long time to get used to Susan's physical expressiveness—she hugged me, she kissed me, she ruffled my hair. With the exception of my grandfather, who was prone to beer-soaked displays of affection, my family didn't hug. I could count the number of times my mother had embraced me on one hand. I was both thrilled and terrified when Susan touched me, uncertain of how to respond.

"I just saw your car go by. Were you driving around in your bathrobe?"

"No," she laughed. "I came home and stripped first thing. I was just getting ready to take a shower."

"I'm sorry. I didn't mean to interrupt. I could leave and come back later."

"Don't be silly. I'm glad you came."

She kept her arms wrapped lightly around my waist as she pulled back to look up at me. "I like your haircut," she said. "It's kind of edgy. Suits you."

"You don't think it's too short? My ears hang out."

She shook her head. "No, I think it's decisive. I didn't like that long in the back, short in the front cut you got last time. It looked like you couldn't make up your mind what you wanted. This is good. Where did you get it done?"

"Maurice's house of beauty."

"Where's that?"

"It's in our bathroom. I cut it myself with the dog clippers."

"You're kidding."

"Nope. I've been clipping Maurice's hair for years, so I thought, why not? The clippers have these plastic attachments, so you can control just how short you cut it. I used the two-inch attachment. Next time, I'll use the two-and-a-half."

"No, don't. I think two is just fine." She let go of my waist and reached up to cup my chin. After looking into my eyes for a moment or two, she smiled. "You used to flinch when I did that. Now you stare right back at me."

I shrugged. "You do this every time I see you, Susan. What do they call it? Operant conditioning."

She laughed. "You've got the weirdest pockets of knowledge."

"I spend a lot of time at the library."

She continued to look from my left eye to my right, absently stroking my cheek with her index finger. Though she was two inches shorter than I was, she always managed to make me feel as if she were taller—even when, as now, I had shoes on and she didn't.

"Look," she said, "why don't you wait for me in the bedroom? I'll take a quick shower, and then you can chat with me while I get dressed."

"Are you going out?"

"I am, but not for a while yet."

I followed her through the living room and down the hallway. The Savas' house seemed empty in comparison to my own. The ceilings were high and white, and the walls were painted a light buff color, emphasizing the sense of open space. Nothing was crowded or close.

A fat leather sofa and matching chairs sat in a living room completely free of bric-a-brac. Everything in the house matched. The tables went with the chairs, the lamps went with the tables, and the painting over the sofa picked up the brown of the leather upholstery. The only place in the Savas' house that could have been described as cluttered was the wall outside Susan's bedroom, which was filled with photographs. There were some of her parents and grandparents, but most were of Susan, all in matching silver frames. The most recent was her high school senior portrait. She was sitting on a hay bale, smiling against the backdrop of a red barn door. It was the most ridiculous setting imaginable for her.

Susan wasn't pretty by conventional standards. Her nose was too long and too large for her narrow face, and her mouth was too full-lipped and generous. Nevertheless, she was striking. Her hair was light brown, skillfully highlighted with blonde streaks, and she wore it clipped up over her ears, a riot of curls going in every direction on the top of her head. Her skin was smooth and tan, and long lashes ringed her eyes, which were large and expressive. She looked like an actress in a French movie, one with trains and smoke and people wearing raincoats.

I threw myself down on her bed and read a magazine while she took her shower. As promised, she didn't take long. She settled herself in front of the dressing table and slipped a red plastic headband over her hair, pulling it back from her face, and I watched as she made up her eyes. The only makeup Susan wore was mascara and a tricky-looking combination of brown eye shadows. When she was done, the makeup seemed to disappear, and her eyes became bluer and more compelling. I found it just as interesting to watch the process in reverse. She looked younger then, more vulnerable, and I wanted to reach out and ruffle her hair or cup her chin like she did mine. I wondered what she'd do if I reversed our roles in that way.

When she looked at me in the mirror and smiled, I felt the familiar fluttering in the pit of my stomach, followed by a rush of fear and discomfort.

"What are you thinking?" Susan asked.

71

"I don't know. Nothing. I'm glad you're back."

She stood up and slipped off the robe, and I watched her as she shifted hangers back and forth in the closet. When she turned around again, I found myself staring at her breasts, pale pink against the darker skin of her neck and shoulders. "How are things at home?"

"The same as always," I said, looking down quickly. "We don't see him much on the weekends anymore, so that's something."

"Where does he go?"

"Probably down at the shop, getting drunk."

"No," she shook her head. "He's not drinking there. They've cracked down on all that now that Bloom's sons have taken over. No more hanging around on weekends, using the shop as party central, that sort of thing."

I looked up again. She'd put her bra on, and although the back was still unhooked, the cups were tucked under her breasts. My breathing had grown shallow, and I tried to distract myself by looking at the poster on her closet door. It was a blow-up of the album cover of Fleetwood Mac's *Rumours*. Stevie Nicks' leg was draped over Mick Fleetwood's knee, and her arm was extended, waving a length of sheer fabric. He was looking down at her. Two round balls on long strings were attached to his belt and dangling between his legs in a way that was no doubt meant to be suggestive. I just found it puzzling. The contrast between the two of them, Fleetwood, tall and skinny, and Nicks, small and wispy, made it seem strangely sexless. They looked like they were performing a comic dance, something like the Ballet Trockadero.

Susan took the red headband off and began brushing her hair vigorously. "My dad's thinking about quitting. He has an offer from the BMW and Saab dealership. Maybe he'll take your grandfather with him. Dad says he's probably the best mechanic in Raleigh."

That "probably" rankled, but I ignored it. My grandfather didn't like to work on foreign cars, and Susan's father talked a lot about moving over to one of the European dealerships. His customer base was changing. He sold a lot of Oldsmobiles and Cadillacs at Bloom's, but the people who'd bought American luxury cars in the seventies now wanted imports.

"Hunter will never leave Bloom's," I said. "He's been there since World War II. Besides, he hates working on foreign cars."

"He might not have a choice," she said. Susan got up and stood at the edge of the bed with her back to me. "Would you help me fasten this bra?" I reached up carefully and fumbled with the hooks, my fingers brushing against her charged skin.

"There you go," I said, pulling my hands away quickly. "What do you mean he may not have a choice?"

She shrugged into a black shirt, tucking the tails into her jeans. "I mean that he doesn't have the same relationship with the sons that he had with their father. My dad has a hard time taking orders from them, and he's a lot closer to their age than Hunter is. Besides, your grandfather's got to be getting close to retirement."

"He's sixty-three," I said, "but he'll never retire. He'll work till he dies. Or until someone kills him."

"Who would kill him?"

"My mother. She wants to hit him in the head with a brick."

"Oh? I thought you said he wasn't around much."

"He was home last night."

"What happened?"

I shrugged. "He came stumbling in around midnight and started bugging me. When I told him to leave me alone, he grabbed me from behind, wrapped his arms around my chest, and started squeezing."

Susan finished zipping her jeans and sat down on the bed next to me. She put her hand on my shoulder. "What did you do?"

"I told him to stop. When he refused, I stood up, and we sort of reeled around the kitchen for a bit. I finally managed to throw him off, and he fell backwards through the screen door. He bounced down the back steps, rolled a couple of times, and ended up flat on his ass in the middle of the yard. He wasn't very happy about that."

Susan edged closer, her arm dropping from my shoulder to my waist. She knew all about life with my grandfather. Her mother drank. She was a nice woman when she was sober, but hell on wheels after a few martinis. Jean disappeared for days at a time. She'd return on her own or Mike would find her holed up in some flea-bag motel. He'd sent her to rehab half a dozen times. Despite this, Susan's house was more peaceful than my own, perhaps because Jean preferred to do her carousing away from home. When Susan had lived at home, her house had been a refuge for me from Hunter's weekend binges. In the Savas' house, with its tasteful matching furniture, it was hard to believe that anyone ever yelled, much less threw people through screen doors.

"Go on," she said quietly. "What did he do then?"

I tried to focus on my story and ignore the feeling of her hand on my back, warm against the thin cotton of my T-shirt. She upset my equilibrium so much that I was afraid I might pitch forward onto the floor. The only thing that stopped me was the idea that she might think I was upset about fighting with Hunter. He'd gotten more physically aggressive as I'd gotten older, wrestling with me, pushing me around. I wasn't afraid of him. I was eight inches taller and outweighed him by at least twenty pounds, so I could more than hold my own. The thing that bothered me about these battles was the rage I felt afterward. I often felt as if I'd stepped outside myself and become someone else. I was afraid that he'd go too far one day, and I'd bury an axe in his thick skull.

I said, "He sat there for a while, moaning. Then he said that as soon as he got up, he was going to come inside and kill me. So I slammed the back door in his face and locked it. Your parents must have heard the yelling."

She shook her head. "No witnesses, I'm afraid. My folks are at the beach this weekend. They don't even know I'm home. I told them I wasn't coming back until Monday. I thought it might be nice to spend some time by myself."

"I'm sorry," I said, standing up. "I didn't mean to just pounce on you as soon as you arrived. When I saw your car drive by, I . . ."

She put both of her arms around me and pulled me back down, bringing her chin to rest on my shoulder. I caught sight of us then in the dresser mirror—me, my face red and my pulse racing, and Susan with her eyes shut, perfectly comfortable. She filled my view like a solar eclipse.

"I wanted to see you," she said. "When I said alone, I meant I wanted to spend some time at home without my parents. You're an only child. You must know what it's like. Your mother must drive you as crazy as mine drives me. I mean, I love her and everything, but whenever I come home, it's like I'm like her long-lost best friend. She won't let me out of her sight."

I nodded, though my own situation was quite different. I was a second-generation only child on both my father's and my mother's side. It was a disability I considered about as bad as being the offspring of first cousins. They both treated me as if I were a baby sister that had been sprung on them by surprise. My father, when he wasn't being jealous and hostile, acted as if we were bowling buddies, telling me off-color jokes and pointing out women he found attractive. My mother was the more parental of the two, but living with my grandparents made it hard for her to assert her authority. Though she set curfews and limits on my behavior, I often got the feeling that we were partners, united in opposition first to Eddie and then to my grandfather.

"So," Susan went on, "you locked him out, and he sat on the ground and bellowed. What did you do, call the police?"

"Don't make me laugh. Nana was having a fit about what the neighbors might think, so she let him back in. I locked myself in the bedroom, and he spent the next three hours pacing up and down the hall, threatening to beat the door down." Susan, who still had her chin on my shoulder, tightened her arms around my waist. I twisted until she was forced to loosen her grasp.

"Don't worry," I said lightly. "He started drinking again and passed out, but not before playing a long serenade on the Wurlitzer. Some Lawrence Welk sort of thing. I think it was *Harbor Lights*."

I sang a few bars until she laughed, which forced her to take her chin off my shoulder. She kept her arms around my waist.

"I shouldn't laugh," she said. "It's really not funny. Now, changing the subject, have you mailed your applications?"

"Yeah. UNC and N. C. State."

"You'll get into UNC," she announced. "No thanks to your . . ."

"No thanks to my what?"

"Nothing."

"You were going to say no thanks to my family. They don't want me to go to college."

"Of course they do," she said, avoiding my gaze. "I'm sure your family's very proud of you."

I shook my head. "No, your family is proud of you. Your dad couldn't be happier that you're off studying to be a doctor. My family thinks I'm a freak. Nana made me take typing this semester so I'll have something to fall back on."

Susan stretched her arms above her head and shifted on the bed so that she was leaning against the wall behind us. "What does your mother say about you going to college?"

"My mother says I should do what I like. If I want to go to college, that's fine with her."

"There you go then," she replied, as if everything were settled.

"She also says that two of the women in her office have college degrees, and they're doing the same job she does. She thinks it's a big waste of money."

"She won't be paying for it," Susan said sharply. "You've sent in your financial aid forms, haven't you?"

"Of course. I got my mother to do her taxes early so I could send all that stuff off last month. But look, Susan, will they give me enough to go? What if it's only half of what I actually need?"

"They won't do that," she replied. "They'll come up with some combination of grants and loans, and it will be enough. If you need spending money, you can get a part-time job. There are plenty of student jobs on campus. You're not getting out of this, Poppy. Next fall, you're coming to UNC with me."

"That's what I want."

She smiled. "Good. My work here is done." She glanced at the alarm clock on the bedside table. "Do you want to hang out here while I'm gone? You can spend the night."

I made a wry face. "Oh? And what about your boyfriend, Brad? I assume he's the reason you're getting dressed and putting on makeup."

She sighed and got up, slipping on a pair of black loafers. "Don't talk to me about Brad. I told you that wasn't serious. Anyway, I'm done with him after tonight. This is a courtesy date."

"You're dumping Brad?" I tried to sound nonchalant.

"Yes, if he'll shut up long enough to let me get a word in edgewise. He wanted to go to dinner and a movie, but I think just dinner will be enough. I'll be back by nine at the latest, plenty of time to sit up and gossip."

"What are we going to gossip about?"

"You. I want to hear all about what's been happening since the last time I saw you."

"There's nothing to tell."

"I doubt that. Are you still going out with Dave?"

"I was never going out with Dave. He gives me a lift from time to time when I can't borrow the car."

"Are you going out with anyone else?"

"No."

"Interested in anyone?"

"Could we talk about something else?"

She cocked her head to one side and regarded me intently. "Of course. What do you want to talk about?"

"I don't know."

"Uh huh," she said, her voice carefully neutral. "Maybe you'll think of something while I'm gone. I'd call and cancel, but I think breaking up with people over the telephone is wimpy."

"People?" I asked. "As in plural? More than one?"

She smiled enigmatically. "That's something we can talk about."

"Sounds very mysterious. Are you keeping secrets?"

"Sure, aren't you?"

Dangerous territory. I stood up and handed her the jean jacket that had been hanging on the back of the door. "I hang out with a lot of guys. Dave is just one of them. It's nothing. Really."

"I know." She gave herself one final check in the mirror, screwing her face up in response to what she saw. She always did this before she went out; she called it her ritual grimace. "So will you stay? You can watch television. We have MTV."

77

"I can't. I have to go to an AA meeting. The great pretender has announced that he's collecting a white chip tonight. It was the only way he could get out of last night's debacle without actually having to apologize."

"AA again? How many white chips does this make?"

"I've lost count. Four, I think. Soon he'll have a full house."

"Stop making me laugh," she said. "It isn't funny. Come over after the meeting. I'll leave the kitchen door unlocked for you."

Chapter Eight

"What are you thinking about?" Abby asked.

"Oddly enough, I was thinking about my name."

"I see. Do you need to do that with the light on?"

"No. I'm sorry." I reached over to the bedside table between us and switched off the lamp. The curtains were open and the moon was full, so the room wasn't entirely dark. I stared up at the ceiling, allowing my eyes to adjust to the reflected glow.

"I'll never get used to sleeping alone," she said.

"You're not alone. I'm two feet away."

"You know what I mean. Or," she added dryly, "maybe you don't."

"I sleep alone plenty. Why do you always make out like I'm the lesbian equivalent of Warren Beatty?"

"Envy."

I waited for a moment, trying to gauge how far I should go. We had only recently begun to discuss the subject of Abby dating again. Her partner, Rosalyn, had been dead for five years. I considered the topic taboo and commented only if she brought it up first. Since the lights were out, I decided to be brave.

"You could do something about that, Abby. The world is full of women who would jump at the chance to have you as a bed-mate."

"Right," she said. "As evidenced by the fact that I'm in a hotel room with you and we're sleeping in separate beds like Lucy and Ricky Ricardo."

"Come on over. One half of my spacious queen-sized bed is at your disposal."

"No thanks, Warren. I'd rather not end up on Dolores's hit list.

Do you mind if I close the curtains? I'll never get to sleep with that full moon."

"The moon's always full in the South, didn't you know? That's why we're all so crazy. Lunatics."

"I was just thinking," she said. "It does seem to get closer here than it does in Portland, and yet Oregon's not that much farther north. Why were you thinking about your name?"

"I have no idea. Random association of thoughts in a tired mind."

She yawned. "Too much beer and not enough dinner. Goodnight, Poppy."

"Goodnight."

Despite my exhaustion, or maybe because of it, I was awake for a long time after. When the sound of Abby's breathing grew heavy and regular, I climbed out of bed and walked across to the window. I opened the curtains an inch or two, just enough to let a small shaft of moonlight shine across the room and onto the foot of my bed. I loved moonlight. As a child, I used to sneak out of my bed and meet Jack Leinweber in the cornfield behind our subdivision. We'd chase one another along the rows of stalks, or bend the stalks over to make huts and fortresses. The farmer must have hated us. We used his field to make elaborate crop structures.

I watched the shaft of moonlight until I fell asleep, sometime after midnight. I dreamed about field corn, and Abby, and my name.

"For heaven's sake," my mother said, "it's not that bad. You're lucky you weren't blinded, or worse."

"What could be worse?"

"A glass eye. An empty socket. Your eyelids sewn shut over a gaping hole."

"Here now," my grandmother interrupted, "there's no need for that." She sat at the dining room table shelling field peas. "Just tell Hunter to stop calling you Popeye. If you kick up enough fuss . . ."

"If I kick up any fuss, he'll never stop. You know how he is."

"It's your own fault," Nana said. "You'll answer to any awful nickname. You ought to insist on your given name."

"I hate Mary Frances."

"Well, I don't know why. Mary Frances is a pretty name."

"I'm not pretty."

"You're not when you flop on a chair like that with your legs all splayed out. You want to sit up straight, stop hunching over, and cross your legs at the ankle. It's high time you started acting like a lady."

I remained where I was. Unless she got up to pinch me—and she'd been known to—I didn't bother to correct myself.

"And while I'm thinking about it," she went on, "I will pay you to take off those raggedy old cut-offs and put on something decent. People will think you don't have any better."

"No one cares about my shorts."

"I care. They have a hole in them. I can see clear to Chattanooga. You make me wish I had a long stick with a pin on it—then you'd learn to sit right." A line of peas rolled into the metal mixing bowl. "Your mistake was letting people call you anything other than the name you were born with. No one has ever called me anything but Myrtle."

"Not true. Hunter calls you Dolly."

"He calls every woman with big boobs Dolly," my mother observed.

"It's disgusting and sexist." I sat up in the chair, not to correct my posture but to better make my point. "Why don't you object to that?"

Nana dismissed this with the wave of a pea pod. "It's just nicknaming," she said. "Why should you mind? *You* were called Mary Frances until you went to school. *You* started letting people call you Frankie, and Fran, and I don't know what all . . ."

"Frank," I said.

Nana rolled her eyes. "Frank. You shouldn't have been allowed to get away with that." She cast a pointed look at my mother. "If they're calling her Popeye at school, someone should call her teacher and tell her . . ."

"She's in high school now," my mother said calmly. "She has more than one teacher. She can sort out for herself what she wants to be called. If that's Popeye, Frank, or Rosy Red Ringbaum, it's not up to me to decide. I'll abide by her wishes, but she'll have to enforce

81

them at school. As for Daddy, no one can make him do anything."

"Poppy," Nana said. "That's like Popeye, only it's nice. It's a flower. Very feminine. What about that?"

"Good God," I said.

"You know I hate it when you talk like that, Poppy. It's common and trashy."

"Poppy," Nana said, hugging me. "It's so good to see you. Have you lost weight?" She spun me around and examined me from all angles. "I believe you have. Look how skinny she is, Barbara. You're too skinny. Is everything all right?"

"It's the surgery. I lost weight before, and then I wasn't hungry after, and, all in all, I'm down about fifteen pounds. I've got my appetite back now."

"Good," my mother said. I hugged her, too. She and my grandmother both seemed to have shrunk since I'd last seen them, though it had been only a couple of years. My mother was five foot five, and my grandmother an inch or so taller, and yet I towered over them like Shaquille O'Neal. "You're not too skinny. You look fine, unlike me. I could do with six months on a desert island, living off the fat of the land, so to speak." She patted her stomach.

"You always say that, Ma, but you look great."

"I'm so glad to hear you say that because I'm starving. Where would you like to eat?"

I laughed. Then I said, "Don't we need to go to the hospital first?"

She shook her head. "We've already been, first thing this morning. There's no change. Dr. Adkins—that's the doctor who's treating him—wants us to come back at noon to talk about his options. I told her I wanted to wait until you could be there."

"I'm ready whenever. So, how about Fat Daddy's?"

"Well," my mother hesitated. "I don't really like Fat Daddy's. Too greasy. Is there anywhere else?"

"I don't know. I haven't been in Raleigh for a while. What about Courtney's, is that still open?"

"It is, but we just ate there day before yesterday."

I turned to my grandmother. "Where would you like to go, Nana?"

"Oh, I don't know," she said. "You decide."

"How about Gregory's?"

"I prefer Big Ed's in the City Market," she said.

"Big Ed's," my mother agreed. "That's good. Have you been to Big Ed's?"

"No."

"You'd like it. They have good food."

By that point, I didn't care if they served French fried toe-nail clippings. Five minutes in the bosom of my family, and I found myself playing the Great Magnifico, breakfast mind reader. It was an old pattern, and it drove me crazy. It also felt welcoming and familiar. I could fly to the moon or sail the seven seas, but when I finally got back home, I'd have to stand around in a parking lot guessing where it was Nana and my mother wanted me to say I wanted to eat.

We walked up Hillsborough Street to where my mother had parked her ancient Datsun. It was a faded, rusty yellow and it burned oil, but she'd managed to get nearly three hundred thousand miles out of it.

"You could have used the valet parking," I said. "All you had to do was give them my room number."

"My car would have died of shock. Or the valet would have." My mother unlocked the passenger side door, and I was faced with the age-old dilemma, Granny in the front or the back? Nana was a notorious backseat driver. She'd be better able to shout instructions from the co-pilot's chair. Also, she was eighty years old. It would take her twenty minutes to climb over the front seat and into the back. On the other hand, there were the questions of knee-room and stitches.

"I'm torn," I said. "Politeness tells me to let you have the front, but my hysterectomy says, 'Be rude to your granny.'"

"I'll get in the back," Nana said. "You can ride up front with your mama."

"Actually," my mother said, "I was going to let Poppy drive."

"Oh lord." Nana's hand fluttered up to her chest. "Then I am definitely riding in the back. With my eyes shut."

Once again, I was a fifteen-year-old with a learner's permit. My grandmother sat in the back seat and screeched and gasped at every opportunity, nearly causing more wrecks than she prevented.

"No thanks," I said, swallowing my irritation. "I'm not supposed to be driving yet. That's why Abby took the car this morning."

Abby had actually taken the car on the grounds that she needed a getaway vehicle more than I did. Edna had expressed a restrained pleasure when Abby had called her that morning. It quickly faded when she said that she'd come with me. When Edna was feeling charitable, she referred to me as 'that white girl.' This morning, I was 'that crazy white girl.' She blamed me for Abby being a 'bull-dagger.' Never mind that I had nothing directly to do with it. I was gay first, Abby and I were friends, ergo I led Abby astray. Edna was perfectly polite to me the times I'd been to her house, she could even have been described as cordial, but you could have cut the air with a knife.

"How is Abby?" my mother asked. "Is she still working at the same place?"

"Still working trauma at Emanuel. That hospital would fall apart without her."

"It's good of her to come home with you."

"It's good of you to let her use your rental car," said Nana, fumbling with her seat belt. "I think she takes advantage."

I looked at my mother. "I wish they made seatbelts for mouths," I said.

Abby met Rosalyn Bodie in the English Department at N. C. State. Rosalyn was a returning student, about forty-five, in the final year of her Master's program. Abby was in Rosalyn's survey of American literature class. It was not love at first sight. Rosalyn was a terror, a brick shithouse of a woman, nearly as wide as she was tall, with a loud booming laugh and a reputation for flunking science and engineering students. Abby was pre-med, and she had a four-point she wanted to maintain. She had no problem with biology, physics, or chemistry, organic and inorganic, but she resented having to take any English classes at all.

"I understand what the white whale represents for Captain Ahab," she said. "I read the book. Ask me any question, any factual question, and I will tell you the answer. I deserve an A. I have A-level knowledge. But Rosalyn Damn Bodie doesn't like my essay about the white whale and Captain Ahab. She says that I'm missing the subtle point. She says that literature is not plug and chug, and she accuses me of using Cliff's Notes. How can you stand being an English major? It's all so fucking subjective."

When Rosalyn Bodie finished her Master's degree, she went on to UNC-Chapel Hill for a Ph. D. That same year, Abby dropped out of pre-med and transferred to UNC's nursing program. She said she was less interested in driving a Porsche and more interested in patient care. I knew she was more interested in Rosalyn. They moved in together, and Abby learned to tolerate Moby Dick, though her literary tastes still ran to murder mysteries and Looney Tunes. Rosalyn named their cats Starbuck and Queequeg. Abby named the dog Belvedere.

I finished my Bachelor's and a Master's at N. C. State, and then I spent several months working at a bookstore in Chapel Hill. I lived in Abby and Rosalyn's spare bedroom and paid them a ridiculously low rent. Rosalyn got a teaching position at Case Western Reserve in Cleveland, Ohio. Abby moved with her and enrolled in the Master's in Nursing program, and I went on for a Ph. D. at Ohio State University in Columbus. A year later, Rosalyn was diagnosed with colon cancer. Two years after that, she was dead.

Abby fell apart. She didn't eat, and she didn't sleep. She emptied their apartment and sent everything to Good Will. She gave Belvedere to a farmer and Starbuck and Queequeg to a friend in nursing school. She slept in a sleeping bag on the bare floor and stopped answering her phone.

I had a friend who'd left Ohio State to take a job at Hauser Designs in Portland, Oregon. When a technical writing position came open, he thought of me. He said I never did anything but complain about graduate school and the frauds and lame-shits who passed for intellectuals, so I might as well get out in the world and earn some actual money. Did I really want to spend the rest of my life teaching middle-class morons to appreciate sonnets?

I took the job, and I took Abby. I retrieved as much of her furniture as I could find at the Good Will and I loaded it, my own stuff, and her into a U-Haul. I got Belvedere back from the farmer. Starbuck and Queequeg stayed with the nurse friend. Abby and I lived together for three months. When I left in the morning, she was still asleep. When I came home in the evening, she went to bed. One day, I found supper waiting for me on the table at five-thirty. Abby told me she'd applied for and gotten a job. Though I asked her to stay, she and Belvedere moved out within the week. We had a fight about whether or not she was going to pay me back rent. I won.

I'd never been as afraid as I was during the months after Rosalyn died. I thought I'd lost Abby, but as far as I could tell, she was nearly herself again. Or at least a reasonable facsimile.

Chapter Nine

I sat back down in front of the typewriter, yawning. The afternoon sun was streaming through the window blinds, casting slatted rays over the dining room table. I guessed that it was about four—my view of the mantle clock was obscured by an enormous jar full of plastic flowers. I switched on the typewriter. My grandmother appeared in the kitchen doorway as if by magic.

"What are you up to?" she asked.

"Just typing my essay."

"Oedipus still?" she said, pursing her lips.

"The very same."

"Don't be sassy with me. You're not too old to whip."

I laughed and rolled a sheet of onionskin into the typewriter. As a tool of art, the Olivetti was a sacred object. It belonged to my grandmother, who was an occasional poet. From birth to death, every significant life event was invariably marked by four verses of doggerel. She wrote poems for birthdays and weddings, retirements and funerals. She wrote a poem to celebrate each presidential inauguration and dutifully mailed it to the White House. The letters on White House stationary that she received in reply were framed and hung on a wall in our hallway.

For a time, I was on typewriter probation, having been caught using the Olivetti in the commission of a crime. I'd slipped an extra couplet into my grandmother's birthday poem for one of her childhood friends, Rosarita Callahan. The poem began, "No one is sweet-ah than dear Rosarita." My addition was, "Rosarita was born in Durham, nine months after egg met sper-um." I thought it was funny. Nana did not.

She stood in the doorway, watching me. I yawned again. "I'm fixing to make me a grilled cheese," she said, her face softening a little. "Do you want one?"

"No, thanks."

"You have to eat something. You didn't eat breakfast or lunch."

"I'm not hungry."

"If you sleep all day, you lose your appetite," my mother said. She sat cross-legged on the sofa, watching television with one eye and reading a book with the other. "She's on the vampire diet. Up all night, in her coffin by dawn."

"I'm on the drunk diet," I replied. "I'm going to put a stake in *his* heart. Where is he, anyway?"

"He went to get a haircut and then to the hardware store," Nana said. "He said he might stop by the shop to do something."

My mother shot me a disgusted look. The only thing Hunter ever did at the shop on the weekend was drink. Bloom's Chevrolet seemed to employ only alcoholic mechanics. I hoped Susan was right about old man Bloom's sons; I hoped they were putting a stop to the garage parties.

"How long has he been gone?" I asked my mother. She held up two fingers. Two hours. That might or might not be all right. Hunter's barber didn't take appointments; he was first come, first serve. Including the wait, the hair cut could take anywhere from forty-five minutes to an hour. Depending on what he needed at the hardware store, and whether or not he had to go to more than one, two hours was within the realm of possibility.

"Did he say what time he'd be back, Nana?"

"In time for the AA meeting."

"AA meeting, my ass," my mother said. "I've heard that one before. Listen; let's disable this damned Wurlitzer while we've got the chance. I can't take any more of his midnight serenades."

"It wasn't midnight," I pointed out, "it was two a.m."

"Why didn't you hit him in the head with a brick?"

"If you want him dead, you'll have to kill him yourself."

"Who was that he was calling last night?"

"Lucky Eddie."

"Eddie?" my grandmother called out from the kitchen. "I don't want to see that phone bill. He's called from one end of the country to the other this month."

"It's always after midnight," I said, "so at least the rates are low."

"Eddie," my mother smiled. "Really?"

"Really. You shouldn't have told him about Eddie's new car."

"I don't know why not," she said. "Your father owes me nearly five thousand dollars in back child support. If I had that money, maybe I could have a new car, too."

"You probably got Jane in trouble. Now Eddie knows she told you. She's going to stop calling to report on his acquisitions."

"Nonsense," my mother replied. "Jane hates your father. She's got her house up for sale, you know. Says the old neighborhood has gone to hell in a hand basket. So, what did Eddie say? Did he have any explanation for the car?"

"He said he won it."

She laughed grimly. "What was it this time, the lottery? Las Vegas?"

"Tenth caller on the Hot Ten at Ten. How should I know?"

"When we were living in Detroit, radio stations gave away certificates for free pizza. That lying sack of shit. What did Hunter say?"

"He said that since Eddie was so goddamn lucky, he had a bet for him. He said, 'I'll bet a pig turd against your chin, and if you win, I'll roll it in.'"

"Ha! Serves him right."

"He also offered to stomp a mud-hole in him and walk it dry. It was a colorful night. Unfortunately, he ruined the overall effect by winding up in tears, telling Eddie that he'd always loved him like a son. He said that if Eddie asked you, he was sure that even now you'd give him a second chance."

My mother slammed her book down on the arm of the sofa. "I'll kill him!"

"Don't worry. I talked to Eddie before he hung up. He's about as likely to remember that conversation as Hunter is. He was stoned out of his mind."

"He's as bad as your grandfather. They're six of one and half a dozen of the other."

"Hunter's not so lucky," I said, starting to work on my essay. "He told Eddie he'd never won anything, not so much as a goddamn piece of Eisenhower Ethiopian pewter."

"I don't know why he says that," my grandmother observed from the kitchen. "He voted for Eisenhower."

Hunter came home about an hour later. What's more, he was sober. Of course, that was no guarantee that he'd actually go and get his fourth white chip. He'd announced his intention to go back to AA last night just before passing out. There was every chance that he'd forgotten all about it.

I was not a fan of Alcoholics Anonymous. I wasn't sure I believed in God, so I was skeptical of the whole "surrendering one's life to a higher power" thing. At AA, they said that it didn't matter, that your higher power could be a Greyhound bus, but no one ever stood up in a meeting and thanked the old gray dog for the gift of sobriety.

My grandfather believed in a petty, cantankerous God, one who took a perverse interest in the minutiae of everyday life. God was to blame for everything from bouncing checks to athlete's foot, and he had a sick sense of humor. It struck Him as funny when you stubbed your toe or lost your car keys. My grandfather's favorite hymns, all of which he could play on the Wurlitzer, sketched out a bleak theology. *Angel Band, I'll Fly Away,* and *Rock of Ages* were all about laying down your earthly burdens and trading in God's schadenfreude for his eternal smothering affection. In AA, my grandfather's thinking developed a grim, predestinational twist—if God had the power to make you quit drinking, then God was probably the one who made you start drinking in the first place. The gospel according to Hunter C. Bartholomew was that he'd already surrendered his life to a higher power. That was why he was knee-deep in the shit pile.

My grandmother, on the other hand, was a Freewill Baptist. She believed in volition and strength of character. Her favorite hymn was *What a Friend We Have in Jesus.* She was a regular attendee of Al-Anon, the spousal support group, and often led the meetings. Hunter alternated long spells of belligerent denial with occasional episodes of blubbering repentance, but Nana was a true believer. She maintained that if he could just get with the program, he could stop drinking.

He was sitting in the wing chair when I came in, reading the funny pages. My mother was on the sofa, still reading her book. I sat down next to her. No one spoke. I tried to catch Nana's eye, but she was darting around nervously—bustling, as she called it. This involved picking things up at random and dropping them somewhere else for no apparent purpose. She sorted through stacks of magazines and then put them right back on the floor where she'd found them; she picked up full ashtrays and failed to empty them; she shifted the china figurines on the shelf above the television and then shifted them back. When she pulled all the coats out of the coat closet to get out the vacuum cleaner, my grandfather sighed, folded the funny pages in half, and tossed them onto the coffee table.

"Goddamn it, Myrtle, stop buzzing around like a blue-assed fly."

"I can't help it," she replied. "My nerves are shot."

"I'm going to shoot you if you don't sit down."

She glanced at her wristwatch and then at me.

"It must be about six-thirty," I said, standing up and stretching. "Let's get while the getting's good."

Hunter stared at his shoes.

"Would you hand me my pocketbook?" Nana said.

"Sure." I picked it up off the coffee table and walked it over to her, passing in front of my grandfather. He didn't look up.

Nana pulled out a pack of Virginia Slims and tapped it on the dining room table. When she wasn't smoking, she seemed to have no idea what to do with her hands. She drummed her fingernails on the table or patted her hair, her fingers twitching restlessly. Her hands fluttered up to her face like moths to a porch light. We had fifteen minutes before we absolutely had to leave, time enough for three cigarettes.

I wasn't looking forward to the night ahead, but neither did I dread it. Storytelling was the foundation of every AA meeting, and, at the very least, a drunk's story has entertainment value. Most of the men in my grandfather's group were old white Southerners who'd been born and bred on the tall tale. They knew how to milk misery for laughs.

I quickly learned that there was a fundamental structure to the Southern drunk story. It usually began with a disclaimer along the lines of "Mama didn't approve of drinking" before moving on to the good part. I never knew why it was so important to establish Mama's innocence, but, unless the storyteller was an orphan, that's how the story began. Once Mama was in the clear, the budding young drunk was safe to start narrating his journey. Most began drinking beer and graduated to bourbon. At first, the drunk's only problem is the old two-hands-but-only-one-mouth dilemma. Then—and no one's ever really sure how this happens—the young drunk becomes an old drunk. He finds himself plastered every night and hung over every morning. He's suddenly skipping work, or he's drunk at work. He's unemployed, he's lost his driver's license, and he can't remember his kid's names, his wife's birthday, or where he parked that stolen car.

This might or might not constitute what AA calls rock bottom, the miserable nadir that forces a drunk to stop drinking. Usually, rock bottom involves a trip to jail, financial ruin, or a car wreck; in the best stories, it's all three.

Finally, through some miracle of divine intervention, the drunk finds AA. He finds God. He surrenders his life to a higher power. He takes it one day at a time.

I hated one day at a time. It wasn't a philosophy; it was a threat. One day at a time meant that sobriety wasn't something you could count on. It meant the drunk in your life might start drinking again at any time. It meant signing on for a ceaseless vigil. You had to be more involved in a drunk's sobriety than you ever were in his alcoholism.

And that, it seemed to me, was the point. Rock bottom might be the moral of the story, but the drunk's favorite part, the one he told with the most relish, described those final moments just before rock bottom. His wife has emptied every bottle she can find and hidden his wallet and the car keys; he still manages to get drunk because he's taped a bottle of booze inside the toilet tank. The drunk is locked up in jail. Somehow, he makes wine in the jail toilet out of canned peaches and bread mold. The drunk's ingenuity is endless at this point. He's on top of the world.

And then he's not. His wife has left him. His friends and family cut him dead. He doesn't have a pot to piss in or a window to throw it out of. He is sorry now, just as sorry as he can be. Every drunk in AA is sorry. That's when he finds the light. Hallelujah. His confession is done. Sorry is dropped on this amazing story of catastrophe and resilience like the cherry on top of an ice cream sundae. Sorry is an anti-climax. Thank God for one day at a time—it keeps the dramatic tension alive.

My mother wouldn't go to AA or Al-Anon. She said it was a steaming load of bullshit. I went. My grandmother went. My grandfather went in a Jimmy Swaggart sort of way, only after a night of weeping and wailing and 'I have sinned.' He enjoyed the occasional whiff of the revival tent, as long as it didn't interfere with his drinking.

My grandmother stubbed out cigarette number three, put the pack in her pocketbook, and snapped it shut. It was the moment of truth.

"All right," Hunter said. "Let's go."

Nana and I followed him to the door. My mother continued to sit on the sofa with her legs tucked beneath her, reading.

"Are you coming?" Hunter said.

My mother didn't look up, and she didn't answer.

"In Al-Anon, they teach us that alcoholism is a disease," Nana said. "A disease that affects the whole family."

My mother turned the page in her book. "Cancer is a disease," she said. "He doesn't have cancer."

Nana took a compact out of her purse and checked her lipstick. My mother had been to exactly one AA meeting during the four years we'd lived with my grandparents. That was the one at which Hunter collected his first white chip. When he started drinking again, she said she'd never go back.

Hunter ran a hand through his hair. "If I had some goddamn support," he said. "I don't ask for much."

My mother looked up then, and I had to suppress a desire to laugh. She and Hunter looked so much alike—same nose, same eyes, same expression. Both of them had pronounced underbites and a tendency to lead with their chins.

"Support?" said my mother in a voice that could wilt lettuce. "You don't want support; you want an audience. I've already seen this show. I give it two thumbs down."

The AA meeting we attended was in the basement of the United Methodist Church. As the crow flies, it was about five miles across town from where we lived. There were AA meetings just down the street from us in the Baptist church Nana attended, but my grandparents wouldn't have been caught dead at those. It reminded me of that old joke about the difference between Methodists and Baptists—Methodists say hello to each another when they meet in the liquor store.

The drive across town was quiet. Up Old Wake Forest Road, under the bridge, and left at the hotdog stand. A few more turns and up a winding road through an old neighborhood of cracker box houses, their front yards enclosed by chain link fences. The church was on a street Hunter called Varicose Vein Lane. It didn't seem to have any residents under the age of seventy. We pulled into the parking lot and parked the van. Across the street, old people sat in lawn chairs and porch swings, watching us. We were clearly the Saturday night entertainment. I waved at them as we got out of the van.

"Here now," Nana said, grabbing my arm. "What's the matter with you?"

Hunter walked quickly into the building. We followed at a more leisurely pace. I'd heard him tell his AA story. The second time he quit drinking, he stayed sober for three months. He told his story as well as he told jokes, switching on like a neon sign. His eyes twinkled and his teeth flashed. He looked like the living embodiment of a damn good time.

Hunter picked a chair on the back row against the wall where he sat with his arms folded across his chest. I sat down next to him. Nana milled around for a few minutes, chatting with friends and acquaintances from Al-Anon. Of the thirty or so people in the room, I was by far the youngest. My grandmother must have noticed this at about the same time I did because she came over and whispered, "Are you sure you don't want to go next door to Alateen?"

"No," I said firmly.

"You'll meet people your own age."

"And the only thing I have in common with them is that we all live with a drunk. I'd rather pick my friends some other way."

In order to put an end to the conversation, I stood up and made my way over to the coffee urn. Everyone drank coffee at AA. Everyone smoked. One vice at a time. I filled a Styrofoam cup, stirred in two packets of sugar, and sat down to watch the show.

The speaker was a tall, skinny man with a nose like a bloodshot cauliflower. His hair was curly and red and he'd attempted to comb it back and grease it into submission. He looked like Uncle Fred, right down to the zippered dress boots. Somewhere in the City of Raleigh, there must have been a Fashion Bug for drunks.

The speaker began by telling us he was Ronny and he was an alcoholic. "Hello, Ronny," we all replied in unison. The bonhomie of AA always drove me crazy. I was prepared to be entertained; I wasn't prepared to be friendly. I recognized many of the men from previous visits. There were only three women present—Nana and I and a woman named Margaret. Margaret was married to Bill, the only man in Nana's Al-Anon meeting. The Al-Anon women all felt sorry for Bill, much sorrier, it seemed to me, than they felt for themselves. He was a soft-spoken man who looked like Mr. Rogers, and judging from the stories he told, his wife was a cross between Dean Martin and Yosemite Sam. They'd been married for thirty years. The Al-Anon women wondered aloud why he didn't divorce her. It never seemed to occur to them that he might stay in his marriage for the same reasons they stayed in theirs.

Ronny was slow to warm up. He told a couple of stories about his teenage experiences with moonshine that might have been cribbed from *The Dukes of Hazzard*. Hunter suppressed a yawn, and several people shifted in their chairs. His narrative soon picked up steam, however. In his early twenties, he moved north to work in a ball-bearing plant in Cleveland. He got drunk after work one night with some of his co-workers, who made fun of his accent and called him a hillbilly. He beat the shit out of them so decisively that it led to a career as a bare-knuckles boxer. After seven years of this, he'd broken all of his ribs and most of the bones in his hands, and he'd destroyed the cartilage in his nose and ears. He drank to numb the pain, and he fought because he liked to hurt people. The end of the fighting came when he killed someone. He spent nine years in prison for manslaughter. That wasn't the end of his drinking, of course.

"There's nothing you can't get in prison," he said. "Nothing."

Ronny was covered in tattoos, several of which he'd done himself with a razor blade and cigarette ash. Despite this, he didn't look particularly menacing. Perhaps it was because of his hair—as his story progressed and he became more animated, his hair tonic began to fail. Red curls sprang up on the sides of his head. Between the hair and his nose, there was something cartoonish, clownlike about him.

One month after he was paroled, he got into a bar brawl and stabbed someone to death with a broken beer bottle. Altogether, he spent more than twenty years behind bars. He said he was forty-nine. He looked ten years older than Hunter.

The other drunks shifted uncomfortably in their seats. Hunter checked his watch a couple of times. Time in jail on a DUI was not the same as two decades in prison. Ronny had killed two people. He talked about older prisoners sizing up new ones—they called them new fish—and he came perilously close to telling a prison rape story. Someone cleared his throat and Ronny paused and looked around the room. His eyes came to rest on me, and I found myself mesmerized, unable to look away. The contact wasn't broken until he blinked. He'd stopped in mid-sentence with him and two of the other older prisoners cornering a new fish in his cell. Now he moved on smoothly to his first experience with AA.

His was a "Jesus saved me" story. He got out of prison and fell back into his old habits. He was drunk all the time, fighting, and unable to find work. The miracle happened one night at a bar when he found a flyer for AA taped to the door of a toilet stall. He'd been hearing voices for years, but this time he was sure it was God. He went to a meeting and surrendered his life to a higher power on the spot. He joined the local Baptist church and met a woman in Sunday school. They got married, moved back down South, and the first thing he did was find himself an AA meeting. He looked around the room again, raised his eyes to heaven, and lifted his hands as if he were about to pray.

That's when he blew it. He said he'd been sober for a year and married for a month. He began talking about Jesus and his wife and his stepchildren, and it wasn't ordinary talk, it was drunk talk, the sort of stuff Hunter said whenever he was three sheets to the wind. According to Ronny, his step-kids were angels sent from above. His wife was the Virgin Mary. I could have kicked myself for buying his story. I'd been swept up by the gritty tales of prison life, but I knew all about all that over-the-top praise and 'Baby, I love you' crap. It was only a matter of time before his kids began to disappoint him and his wife failed to be perfect. Then it would be back to the bottle for Ronny the Red Head.

At the end of the meeting, Hunter stepped forward to pick up his white chip. He grinned broadly when everyone clapped, but afterwards, he was out of there like a shot. No one said anything on the ride home. My grandmother stared out the window, and Hunter tapped out a tune with his wedding ring on the steering wheel. I knew what was coming long before we pulled into the driveway.

Nana and I got out of the van. Hunter stayed in with the engine running.

"Aren't you coming in?" Nana asked.

"I'm out of cigarettes," he said, looking anywhere but at the two of us. "I'm just going to run to the IGA and pick up a pack. I'll be right back."

Nana and I looked at each other. We needn't have bothered. If speech wasn't necessary for communication, neither was eye contact. He'd surrendered his life to a higher power, all right—Budweiser, the King of Beers.

Chapter Ten

I should have gone straight over to Susan's house.

At ten o'clock, Hunter still hadn't come home. My mother finished her book and went to bed. Nana put her hair up in pin curls and slathered cold cream all over her face. Now I was stuck. I couldn't leave my grandmother. If Hunter called, too drunk to drive, she'd go pick him up; it didn't matter where he was or how late he called. Nana was a terrible driver. She'd learned out of necessity at forty-five when my grandfather lost his license for a year. She did everything by the book. Her hands gripped the wheel at ten and two. She signaled for lane changes in heavy traffic. She checked her mirrors constantly. It took her half an hour to drive the three miles from our house to downtown.

Reluctantly, I called Susan. She was still out, so I left a message on her answering machine. I apologized for standing her up and said that I'd see her on Sunday night since I had to work on Sunday morning.

I pulled up a chair and sat down next to Nana.

She pushed her glasses up on her nose and stared at the glowing end of her cigarette. Whenever I suggested that she quit smoking, she said that she didn't want to get fat. Fat chance. She was at least twenty pounds underweight. The only thing round was her face. The women in my grandmother's family didn't wrinkle; instead, their cheeks fell into what my mother called the Abernathy jowls.

Nana had been beautiful as a young woman. She was still beautiful at sixty-four. I had a picture of her in my bedroom that was taken in 1941, not long after she married Hunter. Nana was posed in front of a paper moon, smiling broadly. She was only twenty. I tried to imagine what it would be like to be married at twenty with a high school diploma, no college, and, in two more years, a baby. The idea of it gave me the creeps.

"Why are you waiting up for him?" I asked. "Go to bed."

"He might come home. Someone's got to let him in."

"He's got a key."

"He won't use it, or he won't be able to use it. He'd rather beat the door down."

"In which case you'll hear him when he gets here, so there's no need to wait up."

"I have to get to him before the neighbors call the police," she replied irritably.

"Why? Let him beat the door down. Let the police pick him up. He's out there somewhere right now, probably driving around drunk. Why don't I call the sheriff's department and give them his license tag number?"

She grabbed my arm. "Sit down," she said, "and behave. I've got enough to worry about without you acting up."

"So much for all that stuff they tell you in Al-Anon about Let Go and Let God. As long as you keep saving him from the consequences of his own actions . . ."

"I don't want him arrested on my doorstep," she said, making swirls in the ashtray with the end of her cigarette. "And I don't want you to provoke him."

"I don't provoke him."

"You do. You always want to argue with him."

"He's always wrong."

"Turn on the TV," she said. "See if you can find something worth watching."

The dog and I were curled up together asleep on the sofa when the front door opened and Hunter fell in with a crash and a moan.

"Goddamn carpet. Son of a bitch tripped me on purpose!"

"Come in," Nana hissed, looking around as if she feared the neighbors were all on their front porches, watching. "It's after midnight. For heaven's sake, close the door!"

Maurice growled. My grandfather, still lying on the floor, pointed a finger at him. "You shut up, you sawhorse son of a bitch."

I put an arm around the dog, hooking a finger through his collar. Maurice was an idiot. At five years old, he couldn't sit, stay, or be counted on not to pee in the house. He had only one talent—he could smell booze on the breath at twenty paces. The dog was infallible, better than a Breathalyzer bag.

Hunter got up on all fours and crawled through the front door, which my grandmother closed and locked behind him. She reached a hand down to help him up, but he waved her away.

"You know why I'm down here, don't you?" he said sadly, shaking his head. "I am down here because God threw me down, down on the dirty floor." For emphasis, he slapped the carpet with the palm of his hand, raising a stir of dust and dog hairs. He glared up at Nana. "Is the vacuum cleaner broken?"

"Why would God throw you down?" I said, tightening my hold on Maurice's collar.

"Because he's a selfish son of a bitch! I get something, and he takes it away. I can't have anything."

"Your god is a jealous god."

Nana gave me a sharp look. "Get up," she said, reaching down to take Hunter by the elbow. "You need to go to bed."

"Not a goddamn thing," he repeated. "Nothing. Do you know what?"

He was looking at me, so I said, "What?"

"I lost my Masonic ring." He held up his right hand and pointed to his ring finger. "He reached down and snatched it right off my goddamn finger."

"Who did?"

"God did, goddamn it! What the hell's the matter with you, are you deaf? He took my Masonic ring." He shook off my grandmother's hand and dropped back down onto the carpet. "I don't know where it is."

"It's in heaven," I said. "I don't know why God would want it, of course. His fingers are probably bigger than yours."

That did it. He staggered to his feet and pointed at me, panting

101

with the effort. "You've got enough mouth for another row of teeth. And you," he shook his fist at the dog, "stop growling at me. I'll get a shotgun and blow your ugly head off. How would you like that?"

"Come to bed, Hunter," Nana said, taking his arm. "We'll find your ring in the morning. You probably dropped it out in the yard somewhere. Come on now."

He shook her off a couple of times, but she persisted, and soon he was leaning against her as if the bones in his legs had melted away. They began a slow shuffle toward the bedroom, my grandmother cajoling, my grandfather muttering. Maurice had begun to growl again, so I tightened my grip on his collar.

Hunter paused at the end of the sofa and stared at us, his head cocked to one side.

"Go on," I said quickly. "I've got him."

Maurice put on a good display. He bared his fangs, but I could feel him shaking. Hunter stuck his hands in his pockets and stood there, jiggling his change.

"You going to bite me?" He reached into his pocket and pulled out his cigarette lighter. He flipped the lid back and leaned over the edge of the sofa, running his thumb across the sparking wheel.

I blew the flame out. "Do you want me to let the dog go? I'd be more than happy to let him bite your hand off."

Maurice strained at his collar, twisting my fingers in his attempt to pull himself backward off the sofa. Hunter grinned. He flicked the lighter again and lunged at Maurice, waving the flame in his face.

"How do you like that? I'll burn you up, you crazy son of a bitch!"

That was it for my fingers. Maurice gave a violent twist and pulled out of his collar. He ran across the room and dove beneath the dining room table, where he backed into the far corner, snarling.

"Ha!" Hunter yelled. "Where you going, boy?"

He dropped down on all fours and crawled towards the dog.

Nana grabbed at the back of his shirt. "Stop it, do you hear me? Hunter, stop it!"

My mother appeared in the door to the hallway and stood blinking at the light. The left side of her nylon nightgown was tucked into the waistband of her underwear.

"What the hell is going on?" she said. "I can't find my glasses."

Hunter was stuck. He'd managed to get halfway under the table, but my grandmother had him by the belt and was hauling him backwards for all she was worth. He still held the lighter, the flame on it about three inches high. Every time Nana gave a yank on the belt, the flame scorched the bottom of the table.

"Come out from under there," she said.

"Let go of me, goddamn it!"

"Go find your glasses," I told my mother. "The dog and I are going to make a break for it. If I can get Maurice out of here, we'll be at Susan's."

She squinted at me for a moment before heading back to the bedroom.

My grandmother had lost her grip on Hunter's belt and been obliged to take hold of his ankle. He'd managed to edge forward so that he was only a foot or so from Maurice's nose. The dog was in a panic, trying to back up and knocking his head against the bottom of the table. On the side with the missing leg, the stack of books wobbled precariously.

I unlocked the front door and opened it wide behind me. I grabbed Hunter's other ankle. "On the count of three," I said to my grandmother. "One, two, three. Maurice! Here boy!"

We pulled a little too hard. The dog slipped between two dining room chairs and ran outside, but my grandfather was farther out than I'd planned. If he'd been a bit quicker, he could have turned over and grabbed us both. Instead, he tried to stand up. I heard rather than saw his head hit the bottom of the table. Hunter had dislodged the stack of books and the table was sloping dramatically. The Olivetti slid towards the far wall of the dining room.

I didn't wait to find out what happened next. I slammed the front door shut behind me and followed Maurice out into the night.

Chapter Eleven

"Tell me about your visit with your mother," I said.

"First you tell me what the doctor said." Abby reclined on the bed with her hands behind her head. She looked as tired as I felt.

"There's an unidentified mass in his left lung. Could be cancer. The lung specialist wanted to do a biopsy."

"What for? Your grandfather smoked for, what, sixty years?"

"Longer. He told me he started smoking cigarettes at fourteen. Before that, he and his brothers used to roll up something called rabbit weed and smoke that."

"Nice. Don't tell Joe Camel about rabbit weed. So, I'm assuming you said no to the biopsy."

"I did. If it is cancer, they can't treat it. He'd never survive radiation and chemo. He's not going to survive the week; that's perfectly clear. I told the doctor we wanted palliative care only. I said we wanted him to be comfortable and in no pain at all. Morphine sulfate PNR."

"That's PRN," she said, "but you could have just said 'as needed.' You don't really give morphine PRN. You give it every two-and-a-half or three hours."

"Shit." I sat down on the foot of the bed. "I tried to remember everything you told me. I wanted to sound like I knew what I was talking about. Do you think they thought I was just some idiot who's been watching too much *ER*?"

She smiled and sat up, edging closer to me. "No," she said, rubbing my shoulder. "They didn't think you were some idiot. They thought you wanted to do what was right for your grandfather. They thought you were making a hard but realistic decision. How is your mother taking it?"

"She didn't say anything. She was just . . . quiet. She has a problem with authority figures—doctors, teachers, cops. They make her nervous. She doesn't like to be talked down to."

"Quite rightly," Abby said. "That's why nurses are better than doctors. You know the old joke, what's the difference between God and a doctor? God knows he's not a doctor."

"This one, Adkins, seemed okay. The lung specialist was a bit of an ass. Why in the hell would he even suggest a biopsy on someone like Hunter?"

"Some doctors like to cut on people." She shrugged. "Who knows? Maybe he was concerned about liability. Maybe he thought you'd want to take heroic measures to save your grandfather's life. Some people want us to do absolutely everything, even when there's no hope."

"Nana won't take a dog to the vet to have it put to sleep. She didn't take Maurice. One day, he just fell over dead in the backyard, riddled with tumors and lumps and arthritis."

Abby flinched, and I knew I'd said the wrong thing. I put my arm around her. She rested her head on my shoulder and we comforted each other.

I said, "Louise called, Abby. She said Belvedere's doing fine. The Rimadyl is already working wonders."

"It won't turn back time."

"Nothing will. How was your visit with your mother?"

She lifted her head and laughed, a genuine, amused, unforced laugh. She said, "How have I failed her? Let me count the ways. My visit was the usual. What am I doing out in ass-end Egypt? Why do I spend all my free time with a crazy white girl? There are jobs in hospitals in Raleigh. There are rich black doctors for nice nurses to marry, even nurses like me who are no spring chickens."

"Hmm," I said. "Are there a lot of rich black doctors in Raleigh or, to be fair, the world in general?"

"She didn't say I'd be spoiled for choice. It was more of a . . . what's the word?"

"A threat? A carrot on a stick? A remote possibility?"

"That's it. A possibility. Our conversation ended on a sour note, as it always does. I told her something she didn't like, she got mad, and I left. Goodbye."

"More like au revoir. What did you tell her that she didn't like?"

"The truth."

I'd arranged to meet Susan for dinner at The Irregardless. The restaurant was a mutual favorite and one I could walk to from my hotel. I'd first eaten at The Irregardless in high school, with Susan, while a three-piece chamber ensemble played a selection of Bach. The menu featured a lot of vegetarian dishes that didn't interest me and a unique salad dressing that did. Though I'd learned to make a version of lemon tahini at home, it never tasted quite the same.

I arrived first and was seated at table against the far wall facing the door. I ordered a glass of merlot. I would have preferred a domestic beer, but wine seemed more grown-up. I'd last seen Susan when I was a teenager. Sitting in the restaurant waiting for her, I felt like a teenager again. It wasn't a good feeling. I didn't want to feel like the same person I'd been then; I wanted to feel dramatically different, older and wiser, a jaded sophisticate who'd lived an interesting, exciting, titillating life. I wanted to be the human equivalent of lemon tahini dressing.

Instead, I could sum up my life in three short sentences. I'd dated a lot, rarely seriously. I'd failed to become a professor of English. I'd recently lost my uterus.

Pathetic. I ordered another glass of merlot. I don't know what the vintage was, but it tasted like paint thinner.

Susan walked in the front door. I realized with a start that she was thirty-six now. She looked thirty-six. She looked great. Her hair was pulled back into a clever chignon and was just as carefully and expensively blonde as ever. She wore a flax-colored linen sheath with a matching jacket and a necklace of brown and ivory beads. It looked African, like something from one of those non-profit shops that sends all of the proceeds back to Gabon or Cameroon. She spoke to the woman at the front desk, who pointed in my direction. Susan caught my eye and smiled. I smiled back.

Chapter Twelve

Susan's back door was unlocked. I could hear Hunter on the front porch, bellowing. I shut Maurice in the laundry room and stuck my head out into the hallway. The light was on in Susan's bedroom and *Bella Donna* was playing on the stereo.

"Susan? It's me."

"I know," she called. "I'm in the bedroom."

She was sitting up in bed, propped against the pillows.

"I'm sorry. I know I said I wasn't coming, but . . ."

She shook her head. "It's all right. I unlocked the back door when I heard all the yelling. I guessed you might change your mind. Is everything okay?"

I hesitated. "I think so. He cracked his head on the dining room table. For all I know, he might have a concussion."

"I doubt it. His head's too hard." She climbed out of bed and rummaged through her dresser. "Here," she said, handing me a pair of striped cotton pajamas. "The pants on these should be long enough."

I looked at the pajamas and then at her. "These are men's pajamas."

"So?"

"Where did you get them?"

"Hudson-Belk's. If you want proof, I'm afraid I didn't save the receipt. Do you want to wear something else?"

"No, I . . . no, these are fine."

"Wait," she said, smiling. "You think these belong to Brad. You think he left them behind after spending the night."

I glanced at the white tank top and bikini underwear Susan wore

108

and shrugged. "I can't picture you wearing these. You're not exactly known for your modest night attire."

She laughed. "Even I get cold from time to time. Are you going to put them on or not? You don't have to. I only got them out for the sake of your modesty. You're welcome to strip down to your underwear and climb into bed."

"I'll put them on," I said. "In the bathroom."

She shook her head. "Suit yourself. Why don't you have a shower as well? Use the jet massage. It'll relax you."

A relaxing shower was that last thing I wanted. Susan's lack of modesty was going to be the death of me. I shut the bathroom door behind me and locked it. Then I took my clothes off, folded them neatly, and laid them on top of the toilet. I stood for a moment looking from the pajamas to the smooth green tiles of the shower surround. Wanting a shower and needing one were two different things. Perhaps Susan was giving me a hint—I was sure I reeked of cigarette smoke and frantic standard poodle. I turned the water on as hot as I could stand it and stepped in.

I tried three different settings on the showerhead before choosing the one labeled Chopping. The water pounded my neck and shoulders. I pressed my hands against the green tiles on the back of the shower and let hot streams of water cascade down my back. I'd nearly forgotten my own name when I heard Susan knocking on the door and calling to me. I turned the water off and reached for a towel. There wasn't one. The closest thing I could find was an embroidered hand towel, which meant I could cover my crotch or my chest, but not both. She knocked again.

"Just a second. I can't seem to find a towel."

"That's because they were all in the laundry room," she said. "I've brought you one hot from the dryer. Why did you lock the door?"

"Fear of burglars." I shook off as best I could and dripped my way across the floor. I turned the lock, and, being careful to keep myself completely behind the door and out of view, I opened it just wide enough to allow her to slip a towel through the crack.

"What do you think I'm going to do?" she laughed. "Faint? I've seen naked women before."

"You haven't seen me."

"Haven't I?"

Our eyes met in the bathroom mirror. It was fog-free. Susan could see from Newport News to Chattanooga, as my grandmother would say. I snatched the towel from her hand and shut the door quickly. Much to my relief, there was no giggling in the hall, and her footsteps gradually receded. I wondered what she was thinking.

I looked pretty good with my clothes on. I looked long and lean and physically fit. But like most people, I looked better with my clothes on than off. My mother and Nana were master illusionists, hiding figure flaws with padded shoulders and girdles. I was equally skilled. I was built like a man, so I wore men's clothes, men's jeans and shirts. I was obliged to wear women's underwear, jackets, and shoes because my grandmother, like the vice cops of old, insisted that I wear at least three items of women's clothing at all times. I didn't examine myself in the mirror very often because I found my body so appalling. It wasn't a man's body. True, I had no hips to speak of, and my straight, flat waist dropped down without contour to my legs. But I did have breasts. They weren't large, but there they were, tacked onto my chest like an afterthought.

I wasn't the sort of woman other women admired. I wasn't pretty or delicate. I had strong features, good muscles, and straight, white teeth. There was a word for me—mannish. I didn't want to be a man. Sometimes, I thought it might be easier if I were.

I put the pajamas on and hung the towel over the shower rail. The towel was the same green as the tiles in the shower. I wondered which came first, the tiles or the towel.

Susan pulled the covers back and motioned for me to climb over her so that I could sleep with my back to the wall. I was flattered that she remembered. If something came after me in the middle of the night, Dracula or Hunter and his cigarette lighter, I wanted to face it head-on. I wriggled down beneath the sheets, and Susan slipped in beside me. Stevie Nicks was still singing softly in the background.

"Lights out?" she asked. I nodded.

110

I was used to falling asleep with music playing. I often left the radio on in a vain attempt to drown out Hunter's midnight serenades on the organ. This felt different. Susan was lying very still, breathing softly, and I began to get the feeling that I wasn't supposed to fall asleep. Then I remembered what she had said about gossiping together. Perhaps she was waiting for me to start.

I said, "How did it go with Brad tonight?"

"Okay."

"He didn't burst into tears or anything?"

She laughed. "No, I think he was relieved."

"I find that hard to believe."

"Why?"

I didn't know what to say. Susan wasn't completely on her side of the bed, and between that, the dark, and the music, I was nervous.

"Are you going to leave the stereo on?"

"I thought I would. You don't mind, do you?"

"No."

"Poppy," she said seriously. "I want to tell you something about Brad."

"What?"

She rolled over to face me, her breath blowing warm and moist across my cheek. "He's gay. I've dated three gay men since high school. I don't want to do that anymore."

Anymore? I didn't know why she'd have wanted to do it in the first place. I said, "Three gay men? Did you know, or was it just bad luck or something?"

"I knew."

"If you knew, then why did you . . ."

"Shh." She put her hand on my arm, silencing me. "Did you hear that noise?"

"What noise?"

"It's coming from the kitchen." She sat up. "It sounds like someone scratching on the door."

I heard the noise now, too. "I'm sorry. That's Maurice. I put him in your laundry room. I'd better let him out before he tears down the door."

111

"Wait a second—why did you bring Maurice with you?"

"Because Hunter tried to set him on fire."

The light was suddenly switched on, and Susan loomed in front of me, her face only an inch or two from mine. "He did what?"

I blinked. "He didn't actually light him up or anything. The dog growled at him, so he chased him around the room, waving a lighter in his face. You heard the noise. We had to leave in a hurry, so I brought him here. You don't mind, do you?"

She shook her head. I tried to get up, but she pulled me down. "Forget about the dog. You can let him out in a minute. I want you to listen to me, Poppy. You can't live there anymore. You've got to get out."

I sank back down onto the pillow and stared at the ceiling. My mother had made this announcement about five hundred times over the last four years. She wanted to leave. She wanted my grandmother to divorce Hunter. She didn't make enough money to pay rent on an apartment. In the end, my mother and I would talk about it, decide that Hunter wasn't really that bad, or at any rate he wasn't bad all that often, and we'd stay.

I said, "I'm leaving for college in the fall, but maybe I can get a job or something this summer and move early. I'll be fine until then."

She gazed at me sadly. "Your mother should have gotten an apartment years ago and moved you out of there."

I felt a surge of irritation. Susan's house looked like a fucking palace. She had a massaging showerhead and a green tiled tub with matching towels. Her family never had to subtract, they just added. "She can't afford it. My mother doesn't sell Cadillacs for a living, she files library cards."

"My father," she began, in a voice that reflected the anger of my own. Then she stopped herself, waited three beats, and started over. "My father doesn't have anything to do with this, Poppy. We're talking about you. When are you going to stop taking responsibility for everyone except yourself?"

This was a bolt from the blue. "I do take responsibility for myself."

"Listen to me," she continued. "I'm talking about getting what you need out of your family, instead of them taking what they need out of you."

I flipped the covers off my legs and climbed out of bed.

"Where are you going?"

"I've got to let Maurice out."

"You don't like me talking about your family, do you?"

"No. And you don't like me talking about yours."

She let me pass. The kitchen tile was cold on my bare feet. I ignored it. I let Maurice run around the Savas' back yard for ten minutes. As usual, he didn't need to go out for any particular reason, and I spent another five minutes trudging through the wet grass, trying to catch him and make him go back in. The kitchen and dining room lights were still on at my house, but the blinds were down and the curtains were drawn. That meant that Hunter was awake but quiet, no doubt nursing a head wound and a grievance.

I wiped Maurice's feet on the doormat and shut him up again in the laundry room. He whined for a moment or two before throwing himself down with a thud and a sigh. There was nothing subtle about Maurice's emotions. I thought about flinging myself on the floor of Susan's bedroom and doing the same thing. I owed her an apology. There was no point in being angry with her for having a rich family. Besides, she only said what I'd often thought. She didn't have any idea what it was like to not have enough money. Her solutions made sense to her. That wasn't what aggravated me—what I didn't like was the idea that I needed rescuing. It made me feel weak and stupid.

I schooled my face into a proper expression of chagrin and went back into the bedroom. Susan smiled at me. I relaxed. She'd changed the music on the stereo, as if she wanted to wipe out the last half-hour as much as I did. She said nothing as she slid out of bed to let me back in. She propped herself up on one elbow and looked down at me.

"*Rumours*," I said. "You love that damn Stevie Nicks, don't you?"

"I do. You don't mind?"

"Of course not. She's kind of a hippie, but . . . Susan, I'm sorry. I don't want to fight with you."

She brushed this aside with an impatient gesture. "Do you want to pick up where we left off?"

"Sure. I wish you'd lie down." My eyes were level with her breasts. There was nowhere to look but across at them or up at her eyes, and the intensity of her gaze was making me uncomfortable. She obliged by dropping onto the pillow beside me, her head only a few inches from mine. She continued to look at me, however, until my skin began to tingle.

"Why did you lock the bathroom door?" she asked.

"Why do you date gay men?" I countered.

"Past tense, why *did* I date gay men. When will you be eighteen?"

"In five months. Are we going to keep asking each other questions?"

"No," she said, and she kissed me. I never saw it coming. Her lips were soft but insistent, and I could feel every muscle beneath the skin, moving against me, forcing my mouth open. I wasn't aware that I'd reached out for her until I found that my fingers were tangled in her hair, pulling her head down. Then she was above me, her hands on my shoulders, her knee pressing down between my legs.

"Poppy," she whispered, fumbling with the buttons on my pajama top. I panicked, covering her hand with my own, tightly grasping her fingers. She looked at me for a moment and then sat up, pulling the tank top up over her head and tossing it onto the floor. She kissed me again. This time when she began to unbutton my top, I didn't stop her.

I closed my eyes and pressed my lips against her ear. "I don't know what to do," I said softly, not sure I wanted her to hear me.

"Yes, you do," she said. "Yes, you do."

And I found that I did know. In a moment, my lips were on her breast, and the blood was pounding in my ears. I swam up only once, in that amazing moment when she pressed hard against my fingers, but I was soon lost again in the rhythmic motion as she rocked back and forth against the heel of my hand.

Hours later, I fell asleep with her face pressed against my shoulder, her arms wrapped tightly around my waist. *Rumours* played on the stereo in an endless loop, and I dreamt about women in gauzy white skirts dancing around a bonfire on a foggy mountaintop.

Chapter Thirteen

I woke up with my head on her chest. The sun was streaming through the window blinds, bathing us in horizontal lines of light and dark. I held very still, not wanting to wake her but wondering how I might contrive to put my pajamas back on. Everything was different at night. There, it was our secret, and it all seemed right. In the morning, it was a fact to be examined and analyzed. What would she say when she woke up? Would we talk about it? What did it mean? Did it mean anything?

I knew what it meant to me. Confirmation. Affirmation. Joy and fear.

From the other end of the house, I heard a scratching sound followed by a whine. Maurice. If I didn't get up and let him out soon, he'd destroy the laundry room door. Then Susan would have to tell her parents what he was doing in there, and they'd wonder what we were doing in here, and why I didn't just get up and let him out. Maybe they'd talk to my mother, and she'd suspect, she'd know, she'd see it in my face. I couldn't hide it. If I didn't grin like an idiot, I'd weep. All my suspicions and clues, my half-dreamed awareness, it was all there for everyone to see.

Beside me, Susan moved slightly, shifting into a more comfortable position. I lifted my head, and she rolled over, facing me, but she didn't open her eyes. I watched the light move through the blinds from her shoulder to her elbow. Slowly, carefully, I slid off the end of the bed and made my way to the bathroom. I put my clothes on quickly and quietly and tiptoed down the hall. I opened the back door and let Maurice out of the laundry room, pausing only long enough to check for damage. There was none. I closed the door behind me, walked across the wet grass, and hopped the fence into my own backyard.

The house was quiet. I sat on the back porch and put my shoes and socks on. Over in the Savas' yard, the sprinkler switched on, scaring seven kinds of hell out of Maurice. It scared the hell out of me, too, until I remembered that it was on a timer. Maurice, trapped between the jets of water, was running back and forth, trying to find a way out. Any minute now, he would start barking and wake up the whole neighborhood. I crossed the yard again and whistled for him. He couldn't figure out how to get around the sprinkler. I had to go in, pick him up, and lift him over the fence. I got drenched in the process.

I checked Susan's window to make sure she wasn't watching. Then, I leaned my head over the sprinkler and let the cold water blast me in the face.

My mother was the only one up. She sat at the kitchen table, eating a fried bologna sandwich and reading the Sunday paper.

"Your hair's all wet," she said. "You're all wet."

I nodded quickly and turned my back on her to open the refrigerator door. "I got caught in the automatic sprinkler. Do we have any orange juice?"

"You'll have to make some. There's a can in the freezer. I wish I'd gone with you last night."

I knocked the butter dish to the floor, shattering the glass lid.

"Careful," my mother said. "You're as jumpy as a cat. What time did you blow out of here last night? Was it before or after he lit the drapes?"

"Before," I said, picking up the pieces of the butter dish and dropping them into the trash can. I sniffed. "Is that what I smell? I left when he tried to light the dog. How long were you up?"

"I haven't gone to bed yet," she replied, taking another bite of her English muffin. "He passed out about four-thirty. Mama and I dragged him off to bed. If it had been up to me, I'd have left him on the living room floor, wrapped in burnt chintz."

I wiped the butter off the floor with the dishcloth. I'd been planning to make a big production number out of yawning and surprised myself by doing it for real. "I think I'm going to go to bed now myself. I'm really tired."

"Didn't you and Susan sleep?"

My heart pounded up into my throat. "No, no, no, we slept."

"Oh. I thought you spent the night catching up on gossip. I assume you took the dog with you. I hope her parents didn't mind."

"They weren't . . . ," I began, and then stopped myself. "They don't care. It wasn't a problem."

"I think we should get rid of him," my mother went on. "This is no kind of life for that poor dog. We need to find him a good home."

"We should keep the dog and find Hunter a home."

"There's no pound for drunks." She folded up her newspaper and took her reading glasses off. "Poppy," she said, looking at me closely, "I've been thinking. You graduate in two months. I know you want to go to college . . ."

"I want to go to UNC," I said firmly.

"I know that, but I was thinking if you went to N. C. State, you could live at home. Not here. You and I could get an apartment together, someplace near campus."

I turned on the tap and let the cold water run. "An apartment? But what about Nana? We can't just leave her here with Hunter, not by herself."

"She's married to him," my mother said. "That's her choice. She could divorce him if she wanted to. I can't live here anymore, and I don't want you to, either. If you go to UNC, you'll have to pay for room and board. It'll be cheaper to live with me and go to State. Besides, I don't know that I want you off in Chapel Hill."

I stopped chopping at the frozen lump of orange juice I'd dropped into the pitcher and looked up. "Why not?"

My mother sighed and shook her head. "Because it's full of weirdoes."

"It is not!"

"It is. Just think what happened to your cousin Sammy when

she went. She had a full-ride scholarship, books, tuition, everything. They even gave her spending money. She wasn't there a year before she dropped out and became a dirty pot-smoking hippie. Next thing we knew, she was living in a shack with ten other dirty pot-smoking hippies."

"There aren't any hippies anymore, Mom. It's 1984."

"Try telling that to your father," she replied. "He doesn't know what year it is."

"Lucky Eddie's not a hippie. According to Hunter, he's a greasy bohunk."

"Are you going to invite him to your graduation?"

"No way."

"He's expecting it."

"How do you know?"

"He called this morning, just before you got home. Don't ask me why he was up, and on a Sunday as well. He asked when your graduation was, so I told him."

"I don't want Lucky Eddie at my graduation. I don't want anyone to meet him."

"Well," she shrugged, "he says he's coming. I'll tell you what else— he also says he's bringing you a car for your graduation present. I asked how he could afford it when he was so far behind in his child support. He said that's why he's behind. Can you believe it?"

"No, I can't believe it, and I won't count on the car."

"That would be wise." She put her reading glasses back on and picked up the newspaper. I saw now that she was scanning the classifieds, apartments for rent.

"I want you to think about N. C. State," she said. "Together, I think we could afford a nice two-bedroom apartment. You're planning to work part-time, right?"

"Poppy." Susan draped her jacket over the back of the chair. "You're here. What are you drinking?"

"Merlot. It's not very good."

"I'm sorry I kept you waiting. I had to change after my rounds. I should have said eight-thirty instead of eight." The waitress came over and Susan ordered a glass of white Bordeaux. I looked at the stains on the tablecloth where I'd sloshed my glass and wished I'd ordered white Bordeaux. "Poppy, how have you been? You look great."

"Thanks. I've been fine. Busy. Well, not busy. I had surgery recently."

"Really? Your mother didn't mention that."

"Must've slipped her mind. What with . . . you know."

She reached across the table and held out her hand. After a moment's hesitation, I reached back, upsetting my wine glass. "Leave it," she said. "Let the tablecloth soak it up. It's only a drop. Poppy, I'm sorry about your grandfather. I'm sorry he's dying, and that you've had to come back home to deal with this. I want you to know that we can talk about him tonight. We can talk about my mother, too. We can talk about anyone and anything, about what they did to everyone with their affair. What they did to us, you and me."

I held her hand for a moment, savoring the sensation. Then I let it go.

"What's the matter?"

"I want to know why we can talk about it now," I said. "We couldn't talk about it then. I wanted to talk to you. I tried." She was watching me with concern. I looked away. "I don't think I can do this. I can't sit here and eat dinner with you and pretend like this is the happy reunion of old friends. I feel seventeen years old. I don't feel like I'm another minute older than I was back then."

"Funny," she said. "I feel ancient."

"I'll get it!" I yelled, nearly yanking the phone out of the kitchen wall. "Hello?"

"Poppy?" Susan spoke in the same quiet, confident voice she always had. I felt a vague sense of resentment. I was a nervous wreck, and she sounded like she was placing an order at the McDonald's drive-through. "Why did you leave this morning?"

I felt my mother watching me. "I had to let the dog out. He was tearing up your laundry room. Hunter set fire to the drapes last night."

"We need to talk," she said, ignoring the non sequitur. "Can you come over?"

"I don't know."

"I want to see you."

I wanted to see her, too, more than anything. I wanted to tell her about Lucky Eddie, that he was coming to my graduation, and that he might give me a car. I wanted to ask her how I could get out of going to N. C. State and sharing an apartment with my mother. I wanted to know if she loved me as much I loved her. I wanted to know if she was a lesbian for life or just for last night.

Instead, I closed my eyes and repeated, "I don't know."

There was a long pause, and then, "Is this going to ruin everything?"

"No, it's just . . ."

"Yes or no, will you see me?"

I couldn't tell if my mother was listening or not. She seemed to be absorbed in her newspaper, circling apartment prospects with a blue magic marker. "Yes."

"Good. How about tonight? My parents won't be home until to-morrow. I called them at the beach house and told them they should stay another day because I was held up at school. Six o'clock. I'll cook dinner, what do you say?"

I said yes. It was what I wanted to say. I wished I could tell my family to stay away and actually have them do it. Instead, my mother was planning to become my college roommate, and my father was coming to wreck my graduation.

I hung up the phone. "I'm having supper with Susan tonight. In the meantime, I'm going to bed."

"You can't," she said. "You have to be at the flea market in half an hour. Cookie's expecting you to open the concession stand. Go change your clothes and I'll drop you off on my way to K-Mart."

"Why are you going to K-Mart?"

She pointed at the charred fabric soaking in a dishpan on the kitchen counter.

"To buy some new drapes. And a fire extinguisher."

120

The light in The Irregardless was dim and intimate. A lone cellist played somewhere out of sight around the corner from our table. I didn't recognize the piece.

"What kind of surgery did you have?" Susan asked.

"A hysterectomy."

"Complete?"

"Simple, or rather, halfway complete. They took my uterus and one ovary. One is all you need, they tell me. At least I won't have to take estrogen to keep from growing a mustache."

"When was this?"

"Let's see." I looked at my watch. "Eleven days ago."

"Good heavens," she said. "Why are you here? You shouldn't be up and around yet. You ought to be at home, taking it easy. How do you feel?"

"Tired and sore," I admitted. "But I was tired and sore at home. It's not any worse here, and here is where I need to be."

She opened her mouth to say something, but I spoke first.

"Tell me about Yugoslavia."

She took a sip of her wine. "What do you want to know?"

"Everything. What was it like? Why did you go?"

"I went because my father's family was from Belgrade," she said. "His father, my grandfather, came to the U. S. in 1919 or 1920, just after the First World War. I never met him. He died before I was born. He was some sort of radical—a bomb-throwing anarchist, my dad says. He spent most of the war in an Austrian prison."

"Your grandfather was Gavrilo Princip?"

She laughed. "Not exactly. He didn't shoot Archduke Francis Ferdinand." She tapped her fingers on the side of her wine glass. "Imagine remembering something like that. We have strange pockets of knowledge, don't we?"

"It's the by-product of a liberal education. I can't remember where I put my car keys, but I remember all sorts of pointless things, like who started World War I, or who wrote *London Labour and the London Poor.*

I don't know what use it is, unless you're playing *Trivial Pursuit*."

"It's useful for other reasons," she said. "The people I work with at the hospital only want to talk about their investments and their Hummers. Physicians can be very dull. All of our light conversation is either boring or macabre."

"That's what Abby says. They're apparently really sick in the Trauma ICU—I mean they make sick jokes. The nurses in her unit are pretty jaded."

"They would be," she agreed. "That's one of the reasons I like working ER. It's very real. The general population has no idea. They suspect that certain people exist, gang members, murderers, drug addicts, self-mutilators, psychotics. They read about them or see them on the nightly news, but they don't interact with them in the course of everyday life."

"And you do."

"And I do."

Susan had ordered a vegetarian entrée, and for reasons I couldn't explain, I'd followed suit. It was good, a Portobello mushroom cap stuffed with tomatoes, garlic, and provolone, and at the same time unsatisfying. What I really wanted was a steak.

"So, you went to Yugoslavia because of Gavrilo Princip."

"I went to Yugoslavia to be of some use to someone. I had a distant connection to the people and skills I felt were being wasted here. I realized that I've been very selfish all of my life, Poppy. My father paid for college and medical school. I never had to work a part-time job or worry about a thing. I finished my general residency and then spent two years training to be a surgeon. I did it because I wanted to make a lot of money. I thought I'd do plastic work, tummy tucks and eye lifts. I'd cater to the vain."

"I thought you wanted to be a general practitioner, doing the Mother Teresa thing among the poor and needy."

"That was my high school plan," she said. "When Jean died . . . I got calloused."

I chewed the last of my Portobello. Susan ordered dessert, a crème brûlée.

"What changed, Susan?" It was a loaded question. She took it to refer to her change in career plans, which it did, in part.

"I don't know. It might have been a gradual realization that I was on the wrong track, but it didn't feel that way. It felt sudden. I woke up one morning and decided to do something different. I resigned my surgical residency and contacted Médecins sans Frontières. I knew they worked in the scattered parts of the former Yugoslavia, and I said I wanted to volunteer. I treated people in refugee camps—flu, diarrhea, gunshot wounds, bomb victims, you name it. When I came back home, I wanted to keep some of that connection to the real. I also wanted to go home at night and leave the war behind me."

"Do you leave the war behind?"

"Some days, yes. Others, no."

We finished our meal. I had a bite of her dessert. I liked the crème brûlée—it was crunchy and creamy and just the right amount of sweet. She offered to drive me back to my hotel, and I said yes. She asked if she could come in for coffee. I said that Abby was probably in the room asleep and suggested that we have coffee in the hotel restaurant. The look she gave me was inscrutable.

"I know you're busy," she said, "but would you like to come to dinner tomorrow night? I think we have more to talk about. My house this time. I'll cook."

"It depends on how my grandfather's doing," I said. "I think it'll be okay."

"I'll pick you up. You shouldn't drive."

"I know. Abby's seized control of the rental car. So far this week, she's been *Driving Miss Daisy*."

"Abby," she said musingly. "You two were always inseparable. I'm glad that hasn't changed."

"'Those friends thou hast, and their adoption tried, grapple them to thy soul with hoops of steel.' *Hamlet*."

"If I were Abby, I'd be extremely flattered."

I laughed. "Abby would say that it was the least I could do. I have half of a Ph. D. in English. If I couldn't summon up the occasional quotation from Shakespeare, I'd have wasted several years and several thousands of dollars."

"Still," she said.

"Still," I agreed. I opened the car door. The overhead light illuminated Susan's face for a moment. She suddenly looked older. There were dark shadows beneath her eyes and fine lines above the bridge of her nose. It occurred to me that however young I felt, I certainly didn't look it. It might have been thanks to her highlights, but I had more visible gray in my hair than Susan.

"Six o'clock tomorrow night?" she said.

"Six o'clock. Don't bother to come up. I'll meet you down here." I eased myself out of the car's bucket seat. Susan drove a Honda Civic, small and low to the ground. Not the most comfortable ride for the recent hysterectomy patient.

"Poppy . . ."

"Yes?"

"I wish I knew something Shakespearean to say to you."

"You have until tomorrow night to brush up," I replied lightly. "Goodnight."

I was unsteady on my feet as I walked down the thickly carpeted hallway of the Velvet Cloak. To be funny, Nick Stybak had always called it the Velvet Cloaca. I fumbled in my jacket pocket for the electronic card that unlocked the door. It was missing, so I knocked. Abby opened the door. "And?" she asked, her voice portentous.

"'What wound did ever heal but by degrees?'" I said. "*Othello.*"

"I told you to wash it out with peroxide," she replied.

Chapter Fourteen

"I thought I'd go to Durham tomorrow," Abby said. "Do you need me to drive you anywhere?"

"Just drop me off at Nana's in the morning. They want to go to the hospital and then the flea market. If Hunter's dead when we get to the hospital, I might be spared the flea market."

"Everyone does appear to be taking this in stride," Abby observed.

"That's how we take everything," I replied. "Life, death, marriage, divorce—never mind us, we're just window shopping."

I was on the verge of being drunk. I was simultaneously loquacious and resentful at having to talk. I had that tipsy feeling behind my eyes, as if the room were going to start spinning at any moment. I could have used a walk in the night air.

"How was your dinner with Susan?"

"It was . . . inconclusive."

"You mean she didn't throw you down on the table and say, 'God, I have dreamed of this moment'?"

"No. And I didn't do that to her, though that strikes me as the more likely scenario. We sat, we ordered, we ate our meal. I talked about you and about living in Portland. She talked about Yugoslavia. She worked with Doctors without Borders, Médecins sans Frontières. Ever heard of them?" She nodded. "Well, you're better than I am. We talked a little about the past, not a lot. We only broached the subject of Jean and my grandfather long enough to agree that it was now an okay subject to talk about."

"Why did you talk about me?" Abby asked.

"I said you were here with me. She asked how you were."

"God, she probably thought we were a couple."

I rolled onto my back and stared at the ceiling. "Yeah, so what? We are a couple. We've lived together off and on for sixteen years. You're as serious as I get about anyone. Just ask Dolores. And Carol. And Leesa, Lisa, and Tracy."

"Stop," she said. "You're running out of fingers. And names."

"Do you mind if I watch TV?"

She shook her head and tossed me the remote control. I sat up and flipped through the channels. I rejected reruns of *Seinfeld* and *Friends* in favor of an episode of *Buffy the Vampire Slayer.*

After a few minutes, I said, "I wish someone would stick a stake through my heart. No, wait. Someone already has." I fell back and feigned writhing in agony until I felt the room shift beneath me. I held very still until the walls stopped moving.

"Just how much did you have to drink tonight?" Abby said. "You're not usually this maudlin."

"No, but I do suffer the occasional bout of feeling sorry for myself."

I tried wallowing in despair for a moment or two, but even drunk, despair was a stretch. What I was suffering from was acute nostalgia, the recognition that time had passed and things had changed, and still yesterday was always more clear to me than today. It was certainly more comfortable; I knew what was going to happen.

"I had two glasses of horse-piss merlot, and then we split a bottle of something which might have been better. I don't know. My taste buds were already shot by then."

"Are you going to see her again?"

"Yep. Barring the immediate demise of my grandfather, she's asked me to come to her house tomorrow night. Her dad's going to be up in Virginia, delivering a new Lexus to a customer—now isn't that a ridiculous sentence? 'Come on over. My dad's out of town.' At our age. Do you want to know my theory?"

"Do I have a choice?" Abby seized the remote control. "Let's watch something without stakes. I had steak for dinner." She switched channels to VH1.

"Ha-ha. This is my theory—I just thought of it, lying here on this fabulous hotel bed. My theory is that time isn't linear. It isn't even circular. It's a big, amorphous, overlapping blob. Different times exist simultaneously, and you're a different age depending on who you're with. For example, with my grandmother, I'm fifteen. I've just learned to drive a car, and I'm still working out the kinks. I'm kind of headstrong and annoying but appealing in a gawky and awkward sort of way. She doesn't know what to do with me. With my mother—that's trickier—with my mother, it's not about my age, it's about hers. We're both still teenagers. We're the same age, though she might be a little older. She's my slightly older sister. We get along well. We'll be friends when we grow up."

Abby propped herself up on her elbow and looked at me. "That's an interesting theory. You stole some of it from Einstein and the rest from Buddha."

"Wrong. I stole it all from a guy named Crazy Charlie. We used to ride together on public transit."

"When was that?"

"1982, I think. I didn't say it was a new theory, I said I just thought of it."

"Tell me," she said seriously. "How old are *we*? I mean you and me, together?"

I thought about it for a moment. How old were we? I didn't feel young with Abby, and I didn't feel old. I felt thirty-four and not thirty-four. Time didn't stand still; it moved and we moved with it, not sweeping us along or smothering us, just going along day by day. Abby seemed the same to me, and yet I knew she was profoundly different. She wasn't older, she wasn't younger; she just was. Even when she had her breakdown after Rosalyn died, she didn't regress. She just disappeared.

"We're the same age," I said finally. "And that's whatever age we are."

She said nothing. Her eyes had a faraway look, as if she weren't at the Velvet Cloak or anywhere else in Raleigh, North Carolina. She might have been time traveling.

"Day after tomorrow," she said, coming back to earth, "I'm having

127

lunch with Kim DiMarco at the Rathskellar. You want to come? We can find out how old she is."

"I know how old Kim is. She's the same age she was in high school. She's a thirty-five year-old divorcée. She has two kids, two ex-husbands, and two boyfriends, one named Sven and the other named Bob. The future stretches out before her like the smorgasbord at the Ikea. She might get married, she might win a Nobel prize, or she might take a ceramics class. Who knows?"

"I gather you have other plans."

"On the contrary. I wouldn't miss it for the world."

Perhaps it was the wine. I fell asleep with my clothes on and dreamt about my grandfather's second wife, Tammy Carter. Until I was thirteen, I didn't know she existed. No one ever mentioned her. No one ever mentioned my grandparents' first divorce. I knew they'd been married twice, but I'd assumed that the second ceremony was a renewal of vows. There was a picture in our living room of Hunter in a dark blue suit and Nana in a cream-colored sheath with a short damask jacket. They stood together in my Aunt Dot's formal dining room, hands clasped on the handle of a silver server, slicing into a white sheet cake. It was June 5, 1971, which, had there been no interruption, would have been their thirtieth anniversary.

I learned about Tammy Carter by accident. I was shocked, not that Hunter had had an affair—I suspected he'd had many—but that he'd gone so far as to divorce my grandmother and marry the other woman. That suggested a degree of intent, of seriousness, that I wouldn't have guessed he had. Hunter was good-looking in an impish sort of way. Women liked him, and he liked them. He flirted constantly. He wasn't fussy. He found women in general appealing. Pretty and not-so-pretty, high-toned or trashy, it didn't seem to make any difference to him. Hunter made passes at girls who wore glasses; he made passes at girls with fat asses. My mother said he'd flirt with a cadaver if she wore a tight shroud.

Hunter left on New Year's Day, 1967, having spent New Year's

Eve, 1966, pouring his heart out in drunken confession. Nana packed his bags and told him to get out. I was five months old. Tammy Carter was two years younger than my mother. There was quite a hullabaloo. North Carolina had archaic divorce laws. My grandparents had to be legally separated for a year before they could file. They also had to make an attempt at counseling and reconciliation. That was a farce—Hunter showed up at the sessions drunk, or he brought his girlfriend along and made her wait out in the car. After twelve months of merry hell, my grandmother sued him for abandonment and alienation of affection, and she named the girlfriend as a correspondent.

Hunter married Tammy Carter as soon as the ink was dry on the final decree. They had a big church wedding with him in a tuxedo and her in a white dress. He was immediately sorry, or so he claimed. Tammy didn't like his drinking any better than Nana had, and she was considerably less tolerant. One fight led to another, and six months later, he found himself filing for separation once again. A year-and-a-half after that, he remarried my grandmother.

Throughout all of this, my mother and I lived with Nana. The first four years of my parents' marriage were conducted in Nana's house. My parents met when my father was stationed at Fort Bragg. He came up to Raleigh one weekend, a fresh graduate from basic training, looking for a hot time in the state capital. He met my mother at a fast food restaurant called the Piggy Park. He introduced himself, bought her a hamburger, and four months later, they were married. Four months after that, she was pregnant with me. They lived with my grandparents because they knew my father was due to be sent to Vietnam at any time. They also lived there because my mother had begun to suspect that she'd made a terrible mistake. My grandparents and their problems acted as both a buffer and a mask. Lucky Eddie shipped out to Vietnam on December 27, 1966, and four days later, Hunter dropped his bomb.

Eddie got out of the Army at the same time my grandfather got out of his second marriage. We moved to Michigan and Hunter moved back in with Nana. I was too young to remember that he'd ever left, and no one thought to mention it to me.

It was my Aunt Dot, my grandfather's youngest sister, who let the cat out of the bag. We'd gone shopping at a Kerr Drug Store east of town, a new one that had just been built. As we turned the corner from one aisle to another, we ran into a short fat woman with dark curly hair. She had two little girls who looked to be about seven and five. "Excuse me," she said, and I think she would have walked on without noticing us if Dot hadn't spoken.

"Tammy Carter?" she said. "Is that you? I'll bet you don't remember me."

The woman looked up, startled. She stared at my aunt for a moment, and her daughters stared at me. All three of them had pale blue eyes, the edges of their irises washing out to near white.

"Dot Bartholomew," she said in a low, flat voice. "How are you?"

"Just fine," my aunt replied cheerfully. "And how are you? Are these your little girls?"

The woman nodded. The girls continued to stare, so I stared back.

"This is Poppy," said my aunt. "You won't have seen her since she was a little baby. They called her Frankie, then. She's tall, just like her daddy. I don't suppose you knew him?"

"No," said the woman, "I didn't."

"Well, no matter. He and Barbara separated earlier this year, and she and Poppy moved back to Raleigh. They're living with Hunter and Myrtle. Same old house, you know. It's a tight squeeze with three bedrooms, but I guess it's only temporary. I see that you've remarried. How long has it been?"

I wasn't surprised by this litany of family business or the sheer nosiness of the questions that followed. Aunt Dot was famous for talking to hear her head roar. She plowed through conversations like a bull through a china shop, saying too much and listening too little. There was no point in taking offense, as Dot never meant any.

Tammy Carter looked dazed. "Y-yes," she stammered. "My husband, Pete, is around here somewhere." She glanced around a little desperately, clearly hoping that Pete would materialize.

Dot glanced around, too. "Would you like us to help you look for him? What's he look like? Poppy, go find Pete."

"No!" Tammy snapped. "I mean there's no need. We'll probably run up on him in the checkout line. It was nice seeing you, Dot, and . . . um . . ."

"Poppy," I said. "Pleased to meet you."

"Yes," she replied, looking away. "Come along, girls. Let's go find Daddy."

As soon as she was out of earshot, Dot leaned over and whispered, "Would you look at that? She's as broad as an ax handle, isn't she? And to think she was such a little thing once upon a time. Hunter ought to see her now—she looks like a bale of hay with legs!"

"Hush," I said. "She'll hear you. Who is she, anyway?"

"Tammy Carter. Didn't you hear me say?"

"I heard you. Is she one of our cousins?"

"Cousin?" my aunt declared, forgetting to whisper. "Tammy Carter was your grandfather's second wife. Don't tell me you don't know."

"His what? I've never heard of Tammy Carter in my life. How could she be his second wife? What's Nana, his third?"

"Now who's being loud?" she said. "Here, let's get out to the car. I can't believe you don't know all this."

I followed Aunt Dot to the exit, my gaze firmly fixed on a spot in the middle of her back. The last thing I wanted was another look at Tammy Carter and her two glassy-eyed children. When we reached the parking lot, it was all I could do not to break into a run. As soon as I was safely ensconced in the passenger seat, I slammed the car door shut and locked it.

"Do you think she's going to get you?" laughed Aunt Dot. "What in the world would she want with you?"

"I didn't know she existed."

"Well, I didn't realize it was a deep, dark secret, though I don't suppose your grandmother would care to be reminded. Tammy Carter was Hunter's midlife crisis. Lots of men have them. He made a fool of himself for a while, and then everything worked out for the best. You were just a little thing when it happened."

"I don't believe this. My grandparents have been married for forty years."

"Give or take a few," she agreed.

"And no one ever said anything—you never said anything."

"Tammy Carter was just a hiccup. She wasn't important. It's the oldest story in the world. Men have been stupid since the days of Adam. Are you ready to go home?"

I shook my head. "I want to get another look at her. Let's wait until she comes out of the store."

"Fine," she said. "We'll sit here in the parking lot like a pair of dirty gumshoes and hope no one calls the police. If I'd known you were going to take on like this, I'd never have told you."

It was only a minute or two before they came out, Tammy Carter, the kids, and a skinny red-haired man in a dirty blue boiler suit. I stared without blinking as they walked across the parking lot, amazed by the thought that my grandfather had slept with this strange woman. It was as if a whole host of synapses connected in my brain all at once—my grandfather wasn't just my grandfather. He was a man, a stranger, a person with a life outside of my purview. He had a past, a present, and a future that had nothing to do with me. And so did my mother, and my grandmother, and Aunt Dot and my father. I felt like a fool.

Tammy Carter and her husband stopped by a two-door Chevelle. He put their shopping bags into the trunk, and she bent over to help their daughters into the back seat.

"As broad as an ax handle," said Aunt Dot, turning the key in the ignition. "I wouldn't have recognized her if I'd seen her from behind."

Chapter Fifteen

Quit bitching about your garden. Get up off your ass and do something.
I tried again.
Pull your thumb out. Is it green?
"Now I know why Hauser pays you the big bucks," Abby said. "Put that laptop away and wait until you're in a better mood."

"When will that be?"

"When we're on the airplane heading back to Portland. You can be like that guy who sat next to you on the way here, grumble, grumble, tap, tap, tap."

I closed the file and logged onto the Internet.

"Hey," Abby said, "would you check my email when you're done with yours? You don't have to read it, just tell me if there's anything interesting. You know my password."

Her password was *belvedere1*. I'd tried many times to get her to change it to something less easy to crack. "I will. Oh, shit. There's a message from Dolores."

Abby looked over my shoulder. "There she is. Triple-X Ladykiller5. What frightens me is that there were four *other* people who wanted to be triple-x ladykiller."

"Yeah? What frightens *me* is that I dated number five, for however short a time. What was I thinking?"

Abby pretended to consider. "Oh, I don't know. She's about five-foot eight, blonde hair, blue eyes, a couple of years older than you. I wonder who she looks like? Sister, wake up and smell the déjà vu. Have you ever gone out with a brunette?"

"Yes."

"More than once?"

"Shut up." I opened Dolores's message. "She's sent an attached file. It's a jpeg. It's . . . oh Jesus."

There stood Dolores in her shiny black cop shoes, her shiny black shoulder harness, and her shiny black service revolver. And that was it. All the rest was shiny hiney. "Do you really want to kiss this goodbye?" was written on the bottom of the picture.

"She's not a real blonde," Abby said.

"She's a real fucking nut." I logged out of my email and onto a switchboard site.

"What are you doing?"

"I'm looking up the name and email address of her immediate supervisor. I've had enough."

"Oh no." Abby squinted at the screen. "You can't send him—excuse me, her—that picture. Okay, this is sick, but . . . what will they do to her? Fire her?"

"I hope they paste her photo up in the cops' locker room. I hope they mail it to her mother. I hope she's cop of the month in *The Oregonian.*"

"Poppy . . ."

"I'm not sending the picture to her boss, Abby. I'm sending a formal complaint. I'm telling her that Dolores James has gone beyond the call of duty. Far beyond. I'm glad they found the fifteen year-old bad-ass who stole my CD player and my copy of *A Charlie Brown Christmas,* but now I want to be left alone. I'm also going to email Dolores and tell her I've emailed her boss. I'm going to say 'fuck-off, you loony,' in no uncertain terms."

"Oh," said Abby.

"Oh," I replied.

I finished typing. Abby backed away and sat down at the desk. She filled out the 'How was your stay' questionnaire. I hit the send key, checked Abby's email—three messages from Louise about how happy Belvedere was, even though Louise was sure that deep down he really missed Abby—and logged off. I put the computer back in my suitcase and put the suitcase in the closet.

"It's a quarter past eight," she said.

"I know, time to go. They won't be ready when I get there. My grandmother won't be dressed yet and my mother will be curling her hair. It takes me five minutes to get ready in the morning."

"You're low maintenance. Some women like to do a bit more to themselves than shower and brush their teeth. Come on, I think we've missed the worst of the rush hour traffic."

I tied my shoes and then sat for a moment on the edge of the bed.

"Are you ready for this?" I asked seriously. "Going to Durham and everything?"

She nodded. "I'm ready. I've already put it off for far too long."

You had to pay to park in the Wake Medical Center parking lot.

"I can't believe this. It's not as if we're downtown. Space is not at a premium."

"You're in the big city now," Nana said. "Raleigh has grown so much, I can't believe it. There are houses springing up everywhere."

"And shopping malls," my mother agreed. "They're building an outer loop to the beltline for all that traffic to and from RTP."

"The Research Triangle Park," I mused. "Who would've thought thirty years ago that a few buildings out in the middle of nowhere would become such a huge economic center? You remember what Eddie said about North Carolina?"

"He said they ought to build a fence around it and make it a zoo. He had a job offer from a company in RTP, after he got out of the Army. If he'd taken it, he might have made something of himself. Instead, we went up to Michigan so he could work on the factory floor at Ford's. He said the future was there."

"He just wanted to be closer to his family," Nana said. "Down here, he was a long way from home."

"Being a long way from home was a family tradition," I said. "His parents were from Warsaw."

My father's parents, Bernice and Walter, had begun life as Bronislawa and Wojcek. They escaped from Poland shortly before the Second World War and went to live with relatives in Detroit. They had a small house now in Tampa, Florida. Even after thirteen years of marriage, eight of which were spent living less than five miles from them, they remained as mysterious to my mother as she was to them. They spoke very little English, attended Mass seven days a week, and kept their furniture entombed in protective plastic covers. They still sent my mother birthday and Christmas cards, the pre-printed messages within written in flowing Cyrillic script. They asked about me from time to time, wanting to know if I was still 'that way.' My mother assured them that I was.

"He wouldn't listen," my mother said. "He was stubborn. He's still stubborn. Has he tried to contact you at all?"

"Not in the last five years. It wouldn't do him any good if he did. I won't have anything to do with him—I made that clear to him. I gave up on Lucky Eddie a long time ago. If I need a father, I'll go to confession."

An emaciated man in a wheelchair sat just outside the automatic glass doors of the hospital. He was smoking a cigarette. A woman who could have been his daughter or his granddaughter stood next to him, looking bored. There was an oxygen tank mounted on the back of his chair; the plastic face mask attached to it dangled from a clear tube wrapped around the valve.

"Tobacco is king," I said to my mother.

"That reminds me," she said. "Uncle Fred has emphysema. He's in a nursing home down in Selma."

"Why Selma?"

"They had a space open. On Medicare, you go where they send you."

"He's the only white one there," said Nana.

"Lucky black people," I replied. "A lifetime of dealing with white people's shit, and then they get to spend their declining years with Uncle Fred."

"There aren't any all-white nursing homes," my grandmother went on. "Not that anyone can afford."

I took a deep breath. "I know," I said evenly. "And no all-white lunch counters or drinking fountains. I've even heard tell that black people get to sit wherever they want to on the buses nowadays. Imagine."

"All right," Nana said. "You always were a sass-box."

"Where's Abby today?" my mother asked.

"Speaking of which?"

"I suppose so," she said mildly. "I thought she might come with you today."

"She's gone to Durham to visit Rosalyn's sister."

"Rosalyn," said Nana. "She's the one that died, isn't she? That was sad. I just read about her in *The News and Observer*. Some of her old students have set up a memorial for her at N. C. State. It's a scholarship for older women who want to go back to school. I saved the clipping, if you think Abby would like it."

I stared at her for a moment, open-mouthed. "I don't get you at all. Rosalyn Bodie was the biggest, blackest woman on earth. If you met her on the street, you'd cross to the other side."

"I'd do no such thing. I know what you think, but I am not prejudiced. I treat everybody the same."

"You just said Uncle Fred . . ."

"Ya'll stop it," my mother interrupted. "We're not going to settle this in the hallway, and we ought to have some pleasant conversation for Hunter's sake."

"Why?" I asked. "I think we should try to make him feel like he's back home. If I'd have been thinking, I'd have brought him a six-pack and a CD of organ music."

My mother laughed. "Add a couple of fast women. He'd get up out of that hospital bed and dance."

"He pulled his feeding tube out," Dr. Adkins said. "Sometime in the night." She was a small woman, about the same size as my mother, with round wire-rimmed glasses and short dark hair. "Would you like us to try and reinsert it?"

I looked at my mother, who shrugged. Nana sat in the room's only chair, her pocketbook on the floor next to her, her hands folded primly on her lap. She was looking around the room as if sizing it for new wallpaper.

"No," I said. "Don't. You're absolutely certain he's in no pain at all?"

"I'm certain," she replied.

Abby had told me that thanks to the morphine, he was on the best drunk of his life. I hoped that was so. His breathing was so labored I thought every exhalation would be his last.

"We could also take him off the antibiotics," she suggested.

"Yes, please do that."

She gave me an encouraging nod. "It won't be long now," she said. "Please be assured that he's comfortable and well cared for. Is he called Hunter or does he go by some other name?"

I smiled. "You've lived in the South for a while, haven't you? No one ever seems to go by their actual name. They call me Poppy, but yes, he was Hunter."

"He called me Dolly," my grandmother said. "We were married for forty years. Then he up and left me for the Avon lady. Can you imagine? And he called, two weeks after he left, and he said that my order for some lipstick and a bottle of moisturizer had arrived and asked did I still want it. I told him to put it where the sun doesn't shine."

My mother bit her lip. I couldn't tell if she wanted to choke Nana or laugh.

Dr. Adkins said, "Really. It's very good of you to visit him and help your daughter and granddaughter."

"Oh, I helped Barbara put him in the nursing home. He had senile dementia. Crazy as a bedbug, poor thing."

I caught my mother's eye. It was choke, not laugh.

"Nana," I said. "I think we'd better go. Let's have lunch somewhere."

"There's the hotdog stand at the flea market. We could eat there. Of course, it's not as good since Cookie died. And they've doubled the prices on everything."

"That's okay. Mama," I said. "If you'll give me the keys, I'll take Nana on down to the car. You can spend a minute or two up here by yourself."

She nodded and handed me her purse. I ushered Nana out and closed the door behind us. I checked the monitor on the wall in the corner. The patient named Mallard was gone, but Bridges was still there. His green EKG line showed a steady heartbeat. So, for that matter, did Hunter's.

"What happened to Mallard?" I asked Dr. Adkins.

"I'm afraid Mr. Mallard passed away," she said.

"I'm sorry to hear that."

Nana and I made our way down the hall. I pressed the elevator button and we stood there, waiting.

"This is the slowest elevator on earth," she said. "I'd feel funny having a woman doctor, wouldn't you?"

"What are you talking about?" I asked, exasperated. "I only have woman doctors. A woman surgeon took out my uterus."

"It's like having a woman minister," Nana went on. "It just doesn't seem right. If a woman married me, I wouldn't feel married."

"Don't worry," I replied. "There's no woman on earth who wants to marry you."

"This is your old stomping grounds," my grandmother said. "Don't you miss it?"

"No. I don't miss the yellow jackets, either."

The flea market at the state fairgrounds had expanded in the seventeen years since I'd worked there. In addition to the indoor booths, which were leased by vendors on long-term contracts, there were now two rows of outdoor stalls. These were operated week to week on a first-come, first-serve basis. Some were run by serious vendors, but most sold yard sale junk. We passed tables covered with rusty tools, empty picture frames, and children's toys. The day had turned out fine. The temperature was in the mid-seventies and the sky was clear blue, not a cloud in sight. My mother stopped at a table displaying chipped china and boxes full of old silverware.

"Look," she said, picking up a blue-and-white Staffordshire tea cup. "No saucer, a crack in the handle, and they want five dollars for it. They're crazy."

"Let's go inside," I said. "That's where the good stuff is."

Nana was examining a three-foot porcelain statue of a black poodle.

"You don't need it," my mother said.

"Doesn't it look like Maurice," Nana mused. "They only want forty-five dollars for it."

"Only?"

The proprietor of the stall, a tall skinny man in his late fifties, addressed himself to Nana. "That's bone china, ma'am. Made in England, not Japan."

"Really?" Nana said, growing fluttery. "Is there a match to it? It looks like one of those things you put on either side of the fireplace. What are they called?"

"Andirons," I said. "That isn't an andiron."

"It just might be," the man said, carefully ignoring me. "That one doesn't have a mate. I bought it at an estate sale from a woman who lived in a fine old house out in Cary. I tell you what; you can have it for forty. We'll call it a sunny day special." He grinned, showing off a mouth full of yellow teeth.

"In Cary, you say," Nana began. "I know some folks in Cary. My sister and her husband live there. You might know them, Len and Thelma Price?"

The man stopped to ponder. Whether he knew them or not, if he were smart, he'd say he did. My grandmother was a sucker for sales patter.

"Do something," my mother whispered. "We don't need anymore junk."

"What do you want me to do?"

"Interrupt."

"Nana," I said. "Maurice was a standard poodle. That looks to me like a toy."

"You think so?"

"I don't know," the man said. "It looks to me . . ."

"I know," I said firmly. "We had a standard poodle once upon a time. A great big one. Let's go inside, Nana. If the candy shop's still there, I'll buy you a pound of pecan fudge."

"Oh," she said, now thoroughly distracted. She smiled vaguely at the man. "I shouldn't eat nuts with my dentures."

"Then we'll get plain chocolate," I replied. "That's my favorite, anyway."

Nana put the dog down and led the way inside.

"Good work," my mother said. "What a sweet tooth. She puts sugar on her sugar."

I laughed. "Mom," I said, holding the door open for her to pass through, "do you ever think about Tammy Carter?"

"Not if I can help it. What brought that up?"

"A dream I had last night."

"Must've been a nightmare."

"Who had a nightmare?" Nana asked.

"Me," I said. "About the fact that you gave Hunter a second chance after the whole Tammy Carter business, and he blew that one, too."

"Let that be a lesson to you," my grandmother replied. "Never let the same dog bite you twice."

Chapter Sixteen

I came home from the flea market every weekend with my fingers covered with yellow jacket stings. Yellow jackets were an occupational hazard at the outdoor concession stand. They clustered around the soft drink spigot, falling into the Cokes that I served. I'd gotten to be an expert at the surreptitious flick, knocking the bug out of the cup and snapping on the plastic lid before the customer noticed. There was no pouring drinks down the drain just because of a few floating hornets. My boss, Cookie Turnipseed, didn't believe in waste. "What they don't know won't hurt 'em," he said.

Cookie was one of my grandfather's customers at Bloom's. He and his wife both drove brand new Cadillacs, so there must have been money to be made in hot dog stands and flea market junk stalls. Alva Turnipseed, Cookie's wife, ran a booth that sold antiques, mostly old bedsteads and washstands she picked up at estate sales. She was a pinched and unpleasant woman, but I loved Cookie. He paid me in cash, five bucks an hour, with an extra twenty on top if business had been brisk.

The downside of work was that it left me tired. And stung.

Cookie gave me a ride home at five. He lived around the block from us in one of the brightly renovated houses in our rapidly gentrifying neighborhood. Our house was beginning to stand out for all the wrong reasons. We lived in an area called Oakwood. It had been nice in the Victorian era, grown dumpy after World War II, and was beginning to be nice again. First, people had moved in and begun restoring the Painted Ladies. Now there was an Oakwood Tour at Christmastime. Cookie's house, a purpled majesty with a gingerbread turret, was on the tour; the Savas' house could have been, but it wasn't. Jean wasn't reliable enough to risk it. She might be just fine, greeting her guests with grace and charm, and then again, she might be falling down drunk.

Dotted among the big houses with gentrification potential were smaller houses, like ours. We had hardwood floors and a sizable yard, but in the last few years, my grandfather had lost interest in keeping the place in good repair. The paint was flaking on the front of the house, and the fence listed out of true. During the sober work week, Hunter made occasional noises about fixing things, promises he forgot on the drunken weekends.

Cookie pulled into our driveway, and I felt the contrast between his prosperous car and our shabby house.

"Thanks for the ride, Cookie," I said. He was always Cookie. Alva was always Mrs. Turnipseed.

"You're welcome." I opened the car door. "Wait," he said. "You're graduating soon, aren't you?"

"Yes."

"I'd like to give you something." Cookie was generous with his cash. He'd put a hundred dollar bill in my Christmas card. I'd expected he'd do something similar for graduation. Instead, he said, "Mrs. Turnipseed and I have a little beach cottage down on Topsail Island. It's nothing fancy. I like to fish. We aren't using it the first week of June, and I don't have anybody to rent it. I thought you might like to go down there with some of your friends."

"Thank you, Cookie, but I probably can't afford . . ."

"Free of charge," he said, patting me on the knee. "That's my present."

"I don't know what to say." I did know what to say. Hot damn.

"I'll give you a key at the end of May. You're planning to go to college, aren't you?" I nodded. "Good," he said. "I wished I'd have gone. I might have spent my life doing something better for a living than flinging boiled hot dogs."

I looked at him. He was the picture of success, the proverbial jolly fat man. Everyone loved him. He laughed a lot and told jokes on himself about his not quite undetectable toupee.

"Cookie, you couldn't be more perfect if you had a Ph. D. from Harvard."

He laughed. "I'll have to tell Mrs. Turnipseed I have an admirer. See you next weekend. Put some meat tenderizer on those bee stings."

I skipped the meat tenderizer. It always left a smell on my hands for hours afterward. Instead, I went straight in and took a long shower, letting the hot water pound on my back until the temperature grew tepid. It took me twice as long as usual to dress because I couldn't decide what to wear. I finally settled on a black turtleneck, a shirt my grandmother hated because she thought it made me look older. The only pants I owned were jeans. I dug out the cleanest pair with the fewest holes and searched through the bottom of my closet for something other than my old Nikes. Faced with a choice between cowboy boots, sandals, and a pair of in-case-of-funeral pumps, I went for the boots. Satisfied that I looked nearly nineteen and maybe even twenty, I wandered into the living room to wait a seemly ten minutes before I went to Susan's.

Everyone was out. My mother had left me a note on the dining room table saying that she and Nana had gone to the K & W Cafeteria for supper. My grandfather had disappeared at noon without a word to anyone, so if I wanted to stay at Susan's again, that would be fine with her.

Maurice gazed at me expectantly. I dumped a can of Alpo into his food bowl. I sat down, flipped through a magazine, watched a minute and a half of *The Andy Griffith Show,* and paced the rest of my time away. Maurice stared at me balefully. I ignored him. He threw up on the carpet.

Still smelling of pine cleaner, I knocked on Susan's door.

"Why did you leave this morning?" she said.

I was no longer afraid to look at her. Lying there naked, she was still marvelous to me. I couldn't believe that I'd touched her, kissed her, held her close. Afterward, I'd tried to cover us both with a blanket, but she'd taken my hand and held it. She'd looked at me until I thought I was going to melt or burst into flames. She stroked my hair, pushing it back off my forehead.

"I don't know."

"Yes, you do."

I didn't answer. I wrapped my arms more tightly around her waist.

"I didn't mean to frighten you," she said.

"I wasn't frightened."

"Right," she laughed. "That's why you snuck out and ran back home."

"I didn't," I began, but I stopped. "All right, I did."

"It's okay."

"Is it?"

"Of course."

Her skin was warm and slightly damp.

"Are you . . ." I tried to think of the best way to form the question I most wanted to ask. We'd said nothing until now, not a word from the moment she'd closed the front door behind me until we'd had to pull away from one another or fly into pieces.

Her eyes were dark blue. I met her gaze for a moment. Then I looked away. "You can't say it, can you?"

"I can."

"Then do it."

I felt myself tensing up. I took a deep breath, willing my muscles to relax. "The guys you've dated. Did you do this with any of them?"

"Not this exactly."

"You know what I mean."

"Yes, I know what you mean. Yes. Once. That was enough. For me and for him."

"What about . . ." I paused. For God's sake, I thought, out with it. "Has there been anyone like me?"

"Never like you. A woman, yes. My roommate freshman year. It didn't last long. Do you remember her?"

"Vaguely. She came home with you once. A redhead with an English accent."

"That's the one."

"What happened?"

"She went home to England."

"Were you sad?"

"For a while. I missed her. She called for a few months, and then she met someone else."

"Another woman?"

She nodded, and I sat up. I was surprised to see my reflection in the mirror on her dressing table. My cheeks were flushed, my eyes bright, my hair sticking out in every direction. My lips were swollen and red. I pulled the covers up to hide my bare chest.

Susan laughed. She put her hands behind her head and stared up at the ceiling. "Cheryl and I were together constantly. After she went home, I thought about going to England. A visit or a student exchange program, maybe."

"Why didn't you?"

"You ought to know. My mother. I can't leave my dad to handle her on his own. I can live exactly as far away as Chapel Hill, where I'm out of the house and away from the everyday annoyance but can drive home at a moment's notice. I can pour her into bed or take her off to another pointless spa to try and dry out."

"What about . . ."

"Say it, Poppy."

She took my hand and rested it in the hollow between her breasts. I felt her heartbeat and the rise and fall of her chest. Her breasts, like my own, were covered with red marks, a map of every place visited by mouth or hand.

"What about us, Susan? Why me?"

"Last night, everything seemed to fall into place. It was like the music of the spheres. Do you know what I'm talking about?"

"I don't have a clue." She pulled me back down and put her arms around me. "Unless you're talking about those spheres Mick Fleetwood's wearing in that poster."

She laughed until I grew embarrassed and kissed her.

"You'll be eighteen in August," she said.

"And you'll be twenty in November."

146

She nodded. "In two years, I'll graduate. Then four years of medical school, two years of residency, and I'll be a doctor."

"You'll be twenty-eight."

"I suppose so. What will you be, Poppy?"

"Twenty-six."

"I know that. I mean what are your plans? You're going to major in English."

"I want to be a professor. I like to write. I think I'd like to teach."

"So, that's four years of college, two years for a Master's, and four for a Ph.D. That'll make you . . ."

"Twenty-eight," I said. "Same as you."

"Except that I'll be thirty," she laughed. One of her hands began tracing a path up my arm and over my right shoulder. "You have such a strong back. The muscles in your shoulders . . ."

"What about them?"

"They're bigger than Brad's." I had moved my hand down to the curve of her hip, but this made me pull it back. "Stop that," she said, replacing my hand. "That was a compliment. I'm glad you're strong. You're tall but you're not bony. You're not all knees and elbows."

"I'm not feminine."

"No," she agreed, "you're not. With your clothes and this new hair cut, you could pass for a boy."

"Thanks," I said. "Thanks a lot."

"Well, what did you want to be? Scarlett O'Hara?"

"That would make my grandmother happy."

She laughed. "Scarlett in bed with Melanie, I like that idea. Relax, Poppy. You're perfect. You just need to get used to your own skin, stop listening to people who want to make a regular girl out of you. There are all sorts of ways to be a woman."

"Not in my family, there aren't."

"Oh yes, there are. Your mother's not exactly Scarlett herself." Her fingers, which had been tracing small circles on my shoulder, stopped now and grabbed my arm. She gave me a shake. "You'll never be a Southern belle, but you're very attractive. Now stop fishing for compliments."

Tomorrow, her parents would be back, and at the end of the week, she'd go back to Chapel Hill. There was something more I wanted to hear, something I wanted to ask her about. She traced her hand up the length of my spine, and I forgot what it was.

Chapter Seventeen

Ever since I'd gotten my driver's license, my mother had let me drop her off at work in the morning and take her car to school. It saved her the cost of a parking space downtown and me the shame and horror of riding the bus. I loved driving. Most of my friends were still nervous and tentative behind the wheel, but not me. I'd driven Hunter's van up and down the dirt road at great-grandma's farm since I was thirteen. The license examiner who gave me my test told my mother that I was the only sixteen-year-old he'd ever seen who already had bad driving habits.

At dawn, I'd left Susan's house reluctantly and gone home to shower and change. If her parents hadn't been due back from the beach, I'd have fabricated an illness and skipped school. My mother didn't mention the apartment on the ride to town. I hoped it was just a passing fancy. My mother had talked before about moving out of my grandparents' house, but it never amounted to anything.

I missed my turn on Jones Street and had to weave my way through the traffic on Edenton to get to New Bern Avenue, past the state capital, to drop my mother off at the back door of Olivia Raney. Some afternoons, I went straight downtown after school and waited for my mother to get off work, feeding the birds or just wandering around. Today, I had other plans. I was going to skip softball practice, go home, and finish all of my homework for the entire week. My mother had agreed to take the bus home.

I could have taken New Bern Avenue all the way to school, but I turned left on North Bloodworth, and then right on Oakwood. I liked to drive backstreets whenever I could, taking the true Raleigh resident's pride in knowing at least five different ways to get anywhere. I especially liked the Oakwood Avenue route to school, which took me past the Oakwood Cemetery and St. Augustine's College. The proximity of a Confederate graveyard to an excellent black college seemed to sum up what people called the New South. The old white bones buried beneath those enormous leaning monuments couldn't have imagined a world in which black people were allowed to read, much less get college degrees. I wondered if their spirits were restless and thwarted, or if death really did lead to enlightenment.

I drove past the front gates of St. Augustine's, turned right onto a small, crowded street, and stopped at a shabby duplex with white paint flecking off its clapboard siding. I parked in front of number twenty-two and waited. I made this stop five days a week and knew better than to blow the horn. The curtains twitched in the front window and a minute later Abby came tripping down the front walk in a starched white blouse and a pair of dark blue jeans with crisp creases ironed down the front of the legs.

Unlike me, Abby never looked like a bum. She always looked like she'd just stepped out of an advertisement for laundry detergent. My shirts were perpetual magnets for pizza sauce; Abby wore white with impunity. It suited her, a dramatic contrast to her warm brown skin. She was extraordinarily pretty. Her hair was combed into a perfect black cap, and she wore some hair care product that smelled like coconuts. I loved that smell. I found myself leaning toward her sometimes, sniffing. Abby thought that was funny. She said my hair smelled like grapefruit.

"You're early," she said, slinging an enormous backpack into the front seat and climbing in beside it. "Edna's having a fit. She wants to know why I'm in such a hurry, am I meeting some boy?"

I laughed. "I'm not early. You're late. Please note, however, that I didn't blow the horn. I didn't even get out and knock."

"Am I late?" She looked at the enormous watch on her wrist. It had a bright purple band and a barrage of buttons, all calling up useful features like an alarm clock or a calculator that could do square roots. "You lie like a rug. I'm not late. Don't be tripping me out like that, Poppy."

"I'm sorry." I smacked the tan vinyl dashboard of my mother's ancient Oldsmobile. "You know this piece of shit doesn't have a clock. I hate just sitting here every morning. People are going to think I'm planting a bomb or something."

"If you knock on the door when my mother's home, she'll blow us both up."

"Buckle up." I checked my rearview mirror and pulled out into the road. "She knows I drive you to school every day."

"That doesn't mean she wants folks seeing you on the doorstep."

"Jesus, Abby, we've been friends for four years."

"I know that, but don't tell Edna. She thinks you're a recent development."

"When do I get a chance to tell your mama anything?"

"What did you do this weekend?" she said, and when I didn't answer, "Girl, what's your deal? You're as red as a beet."

"Nothing. What did you do?"

Abby's eyes narrowed. I tried to focus on my driving.

"What did I do? I really did do nothing. Let's get back to you."

I shrugged. I'd had occasion several times to wonder if Abby could read minds. Now was my chance to find out. "Let's see. On Friday night, I threw my grandfather through the back door. On Saturday, I threw myself through the front. I also attended an AA meeting, practiced some fire prevention, and walked the dog. How about you?"

She just nodded, choosing for the time being neither to believe nor disbelieve. "I did my homework this weekend. I hope you did yours. They're going to throw you out of the National Honor Society if you flunk Calculus."

"No, they won't. I can flunk this semester and still pass for the year. Besides, N. C. State has already accepted me. I'm just waiting to hear from UNC."

"You better hope UNC decides before they get your final grades."

"God, they will, won't they?"

She patted my arm kindly. "They will. I'm just flipping you shit. Listen up, have you thought any more about, you know, rooming together?"

"If I go to State," I hedged, "sure. But you know I want to go to UNC." I told her about my mother's evil scheme.

Abby was gratifyingly outraged. "There is no way you are going to college and living with your mama. What's the point of that? If I listened to Edna, I'd be going to St. Augustine's and sleeping on her sofa for the rest of my life. Girl, you've got to get up and get out. You've got to make it happen."

"I don't want to live with her," I agreed, "but if I go to State, how am I going to get out of it? And what makes you think Edna is going to let you room with me? She hates me."

"She doesn't hate you in particular; she just hates white people generally."

"That's shocking," I said. We both laughed.

We found a parking place directly across from the school and made our way over to a group hanging around by the steps at the west end of the building. Five faces, four male and one female, looked up at us. They were all wearing glasses. Kim DiMarco pushed her pink plastic frames up on her nose. She gave us a quick wave but was deep in a tête à tête with Alan Marshall and clearly didn't want to be interrupted. Alan was the Cary Grant of the geek crowd. Abby said he was kind of cute if you caught him on a good day, meaning a day when he'd remembered to comb his hair and put on a clean T-shirt. She also said it helped if you squinted a lot.

The other three—John Wilder, Joe Chang, and Nick Stybak— were huddled around a Rubik's Cube, which John was rapidly spinning back into order. The Rubik's Cube had been all the rage two years before. John was the first person in our class to solve it. Having tasted that glory, he couldn't let it go. He kept Rubik's Cubes everywhere, in his backpack, in his locker—he even had one on his key chain.

"If she's hoping for a prom date, she's wasting her breath on Alan," Abby whispered to me. "He doesn't like girls; he likes cosines and tangents. But look over there. See how Count Stybak is staring at her? I think he wants her. He's going to take her back to Gdansk and make her eat cabbage."

I tried not to laugh. Sure enough, Nick was gazing at Kim with puppy dog admiration. He was a small guy with enormous glasses perched on an enormous nose. His black curly hair stood straight up on the top of his head, like Albert Einstein's. Nick was smart, but the hair and the accent always made people think he was brilliant. I liked him. Kim wouldn't give him the time of day. She liked to think she wasn't nearly as big a nerd as the rest of us. She was wrong—she'd already been accepted at MIT and half a dozen other places to study mathematics.

"Not cabbage, surely," I whispered to Abby.

"Cabbage. He's the red menace. Don't look now," she hissed, grabbing my arm. "Dorky Dave is making his move."

Dave Wilson was the last person I wanted to see. Nevertheless, I turned around to find him bearing down on me with a smile on his face and two fatal prom tickets in his wallet. He was nice-looking in a bland sort of way. His hair was a coarse sandy brown, with no discernible part in it. He combed it in a swirl with his bangs dropping down low over his left eye. He had the added advantage of being taller than me. As far as I knew, he always wore the same outfit, a gray T-shirt underneath a zippered blue sweatshirt with a hood. There were minor variations— sometimes the T-shirt was blue and the sweatshirt gray. Dave was a creature of habit. In the wider world, he would have blended in with the rest of the young, white, male population; in high school, he was a standout. At eighteen, he had a full mustache, thick and brown and very useful for not getting carded at the liquor store. He wasn't much of a drinker himself, but he could always be counted on to supply the beer for Kim DiMarco's parties.

I'd been out with Dave a couple of times. He was a nice guy, sweet-natured and funny, and he didn't seem to want anything from me. A trip to the movies or out to Pullen Park, with no goodnight kiss at the end. Just the threat of one. He'd leaned toward me once or twice, but I'd always managed to get out of the car before it ever came to the crux. Now that I'd kissed Susan, I couldn't imagine letting Dave and his mustache get anywhere near me. It would be a kind of sacrilege.

He had been after me for at least a week to go with him to the prom. I didn't want to. I'd tried to explain it to him. "It's not you," I'd said. "It's the dress. And the heels. And having to dance."

153

I didn't know if Abby was going to the prom or not. Probably not. Her idea of a good time was a sleepover at Kim's house, just the three of us, watching MTV all night long. I don't know why Kim was acceptable to Edna and I wasn't—perhaps it was because Edna had never met Kim.

Kim was definitely going to the prom, but not with poor Nick. She wasn't going with Alan, either. Kim had a date with a guy named Kevin, who went to another high school across town. God only knew how she met him. Kim wouldn't say. Looking at Dave's eager face made me feel guilty. I knew he'd already paid for the tickets. He didn't say so when he asked me; one of his friends told me later.

"I'll make myself scarce," Abby said as he drew near.

"Oh no, you don't," I said, holding her in place with the force of my glare.

"Hi, Poppy." Dave grinned. I noticed that he'd trimmed his mustache too close on one side, emphasizing the crookedness of his smile.

"Hi, Dave. What's up?"

He was bouncing from foot to foot like a kangaroo. He bounced like that only when he was nervous. It still made me want to shoot him. I thought about Susan and her calm, careful movements. Of course, thinking of Susan made me blush, and this, once again, was not lost on Abby. Despite my glare, she made herself scarce.

"So," Dave said, looking at the ground, the concrete wall, anywhere but at me. "Have you maybe thought about changing your mind and going to the prom?"

"No," I said carefully. I'd been thinking for a long time about this, so I wanted to get it exactly right. "It's not you, or that I don't want to go with you. I just don't want to go to the prom. I've never wanted to go. Ever."

"What, have you taken a sacred vow?" He laughed.

"No." I decided that honesty was the best policy. Or partial honesty, anyway. "Look, Dave, I don't want to spend a bunch of money on a stupid dress that I'll only wear once. I hate dresses. I look stupid in them."

"No, you don't."

"How would you know? Have you ever seen me in one?"

He thought for a moment. "I guess not. But you'll have to wear a dress to graduation."

"No, I won't!"

"Yes, you will. You can't wear jeans, they won't let you."

Great, first Lucky Eddie, and now a dress. I began to wonder if it were possible to just skip graduation and go straight on to college.

"I can't go to the prom," I said firmly. "I just can't. I'm really sorry."

"Okay," Dave said amiably. "I've got another idea. I'll give the prom tickets to Alan. He can take Kim or whoever. Can I take you out to dinner? Someplace really nice, like a French restaurant. There's one over in Chapel Hill that my parents go to."

Chapel Hill. Susan. I was eating dinner with her in a French restaurant. I was wearing a tuxedo; she was wearing a strapless gown. We drank toasts to one another from tall crystal flutes.

"So," Dave said. "How about it?"

I said yes because I couldn't think of a graceful way to say no. After all, I'd told him it wasn't personal, and in a way, it wasn't. I felt like I'd been torn apart and reassembled. Some of the old pieces were gone forever, and new ones had taken their place. What would it be like, being in love with someone I couldn't tell anyone about? Not Abby, not Kim. Certainly not Dave.

I felt giddy with the possibilities of tragic romance.

"I can't believe you'll let an Avon lady into this house," I said.

"It's only Jean," my mother said. "I like Avon. The company's not tainted. And I never blamed what's-her-face for what your father did."

"Avon's not tainted? What about Glenda Norris?"

Glenda Norris had been my grandmother's Avon lady for years. She claimed to be forty-five, but she looked like she'd spent twice that many years as a warden in a women's prison. Glenda was rough. She chain-smoked filterless Pall Malls and told stories about her husband Jimmy which made me feel grateful to be living with Hunter. Jimmy hadn't worked since 1975. He had a bad back, a bad temper, and a sebaceous gland problem that made him smell like dead dog. Avon wasn't a sideline for Glenda. It paid all the bills not covered by social services. On my more generous days, I felt sorry for her. I imagined going door to door, peddling cologne in bottles shaped like eagles or Betsy Ross, all so a stinking mean drunk could lie on a sofa in his underwear and call you a bitch.

Of course, Glenda gave as good as she got. The last time she came over, she had six stitches in her forehead marking the spot where Jimmy had beaned her with a beer bottle. Jimmy had a broken arm because she'd taken her revenge with a two-by-four. Nana, who would've bought cutlery from Jack the Ripper, ordered at least forty dollars' worth that day.

Glenda could outmaneuver Jimmy, but there was no escape from the Pall Malls. She'd gone coughing and gasping to her final reward, the heavenly version of World Wide Wrestling, and now Jean was taking her place. It was part of Jean's occupational therapy—her therapist said she had to find an occupation. Her work history was spotty at best. She showed up at a job, worked like a charm for a month or two, stopped showing up or showed up drunk, and got fired. Sales was the best she could hope for. She was cheerful about it, cheerful and enthusiastic. She'd chosen Avon and Cutco Knives in order to maximize her options. I gave it two weeks.

"Jean is such a sweet woman," Nana said. "You wouldn't believe she could act like she does. I've heard tell that alcoholism might be an allergy."

"An allergy to not being the center of attention," my mother said.

Jean rang the doorbell, and Nana let her in with a flurry of offers—a chair, a glass of iced tea, a Little Debbie's snack cake. Jean waved away all but the chair.

There was a resemblance between Susan and her mother. Jean, however, was naturally blonde. Her hair was pale yellow, shot through with streaks of silver gray. She and Susan shared the same slender build, and there was something about the way they carried themselves—they both vibrated with energy, Susan's quiet and self-contained; Jean's nervous and bursting. Jean's hands shook when she talked, and she talked a lot. She aggravated my mother, who said Jean reminded her of a parakeet she'd had as a child. One day, my mother had flung the cover off its cage, said 'Good morning,' and the bird had fallen over dead.

Jean always wore brightly colored, wildly patterned clothes. Today, she had on a long, flowing, purple paisley skirt and a yellow peasant blouse. She liked gauzy stuff that billowed out and around her in wispy strips. That was the way she wore her hair as well, in a blonde sweep that flowed over her ears and cascaded down her back.

"That hair's too long and too wild on a woman her age," Nana said, her tone suggesting ribald nights of long-haired passion. It was the same tone she and my mother used when they talked about my hippie cousin Sammy, who had dropped out of UNC to live in a commune.

Jean's shoes were another sore trial for Nana. In the winter, she wore knee-high leather boots that zipped up the inside of the calf. In summer, she wore platform sandals of a kind that hadn't been fashionable since about 1976. Susan told me that her mother owned five pairs each of those boots and sandals. I wondered what she was going to do when they wore out.

Nana cast a baleful eye at my T-shirt and jeans. I sent a stern glance back: I'm not going to dress up for the Avon lady. I'd reconciled myself to the visits from Glenda by thinking of them as White Trash Theater. I tried to picture sales conventions featuring motivational speeches by Daisy Duke and Billy Carter. There was no way to enjoy this visit. Jean was visibly shaking, whether with excitement or the delirium tremens, I couldn't say.

"Why don't you come have a seat, Poppy," Nana said sweetly, patting the chair beside her. "Jean might have something you'd like."

"Sorry," I waved breezily. "I'm on my way to Kim DiMarco's. I'm spending the night."

"You need some makeup of your own," Nana observed. "Time to start doing a little something with yourself."

"I am doing something with myself. I'm taking myself to Kim's."

"We have a line just for the younger woman," Jean said. She arrayed sample packets of lotion, miniature lipsticks, and plastic vials of perfume before her like a hand of cards. "Skin care products, lip glosses, eye shadow."

"Thank you," I smiled politely, "but I don't need anything."

"Every woman needs a little enhancement." Jean spoke in a shaky Blue Ridge Mountain drawl that must, at one time, have been seductive. "You're a pretty girl when you smile."

"Well," I said, smiling now like Miss America with a gun to her head, "I suppose I could use a bottle of Skin So Soft. We've used it for years to repel fleas."

That made my mother laugh. Nana scowled at both of us.

"A sixteen-ounce bottle?" Jean said.

"I use it, too," Nana said quickly. "I've always loved the way it smells."

"Makes your skin feel like a soft chamois," Jean agreed. "Would you maybe like two bottles, so you don't get your personal moisturizer and the dawg's bottle mixed up?"

At that moment, the dawg had two feet on the stovetop and was eating leftover hamburger out of a frying pan. "Bad boy!" Nana said. "Maurice, get down!" And then to Jean, "Yes, why don't we do that. I'll keep his in the laundry room."

"Write his name on it with a Sharpie Marker," Jean suggested.

The squeak of the back door followed by a low growl from Maurice told me that Hunter had come in. He'd been out looking for Fred, who had disappeared from work on Friday shortly after getting his paycheck.

"Find Fred under any bar stools?" I asked.

My grandmother stiffened. Hunter, however, was all smiles. He'd caught sight of Jean and was delighted to find a fresh female audience. The charm was switched on and ratcheted up to insulin-provoking levels.

"Hello, Ms. Jean," he said, drawing the words out to their maximum length. "What brings you over here?"

"Avon," Jean croaked. "My new job. How are you today, Hunter?"

"I'm just as fine as frog's hair," he replied. "It's the damnedest thing, though. I can't find my brother or my Masonic ring. I lost the one on

Friday and the other about a week ago. I have been over hell's half acre looking for both of them."

"White gold with a three-quarter carat diamond," Nana said, shaking her head sadly. "I hate to think where something that valuable might have gotten to."

"Have you reported your brother as a missing person?" Jean asked.

"No," I said, "but we've called the dog catcher."

My mother laughed. Jean winced, perhaps thinking of her expertise in *being* a missing person. Hunter pulled up a chair at the dining room table and drummed out the William Tell Overture with his fingertips. He treated Jean to a wide-lipped grin.

"I might just do that, Ms. Jean. I might just."

In Hunter's scheme of things, women fell into two categories, damn relatives and sweet things. Sometimes the two crossed over. When he was happy with us, he called us honey, sugar, and babe. I hated the way both of my grandparents interacted with members of the opposite sex. Hunter became Sir Goofus Gallant, fawning and obsequious. Nana grew flustered and helpless, batting her eyelashes and fanning herself with one limp hand.

Jean wrote down our order and stood up to leave. "I have five more stops today," she said brightly. "If ya'll know anyone who might appreciate a catalog or a visit from Avon, ya'll let me know."

"We'll do that," Hunter said. "Here now, let me help you with all of that." All of that was a bag of samples weighing less than a pound.

"I'm going too," I told my mother. "I'll be back sometime tomorrow afternoon."

"Do me a favor," my mother said, eyeing my grandfather. "Take the dog with you. The DiMarcos have a fenced yard, don't they?"

I nodded and snapped a leash onto Maurice's collar. I followed Hunter and Jean outside. Her car, a navy blue Cutlass Supreme, was parked next to my mother's battered old Cadillac. As I opened the back door for Maurice, Hunter opened Jean's door. He dropped the sample bag onto her back seat. Then he paused. I watched as he bent over and picked up something shiny from the blue carpeting behind the driver's seat.

Jean climbed in and waved at us both. I closed the door on Maurice and leaned against it, watching Hunter. When Jean was out of the driveway and up the street, I said, "What was that thing you picked up?"

He kicked a piece of gravel with the toe of his leather work shoe. "An eighth-inch socket," he said. "One of the mechanics must have dropped it when he was working on her car."

"She had her car in for repairs?"

"Those '83 Cutlasses aren't worth the shit on a shit-ass's shoe," he said. "It's always something."

I climbed into my mother's car and started the engine. Hunter came around the front and tapped on my window.

"Here," he said, fishing his wallet out of his back pocket and handing me a twenty-dollar bill. "Buy you and your friends some pizza tonight."

Just then, I wasn't clever enough to put two and two together. All I knew was that what he'd picked up from the back of Jean's car was no socket, it was his Masonic ring, and that twenty bucks wasn't a gift, it was a bribe.

Early Sunday morning, the Capitol Area Police found Uncle Fred passed out beneath the statue of Sir Walter Raleigh. Fred's pants were down around his ankles. Someone had stolen his wallet and his new Florsheim Imperial dress boots. That afternoon, I went with Hunter to retrieve him from the drunk tank.

Hunter berated him all the way to his boarding house. Fred didn't say a word. He was still drunk. Mrs. Jones met him at the top of the steps, her artificial leg shining pink beneath her tan support hose. She took his arm and they walked together into the house.

When we got home, my mother said, "Well?"

"The cops loaned him a pair of pants, and a pair of shoes," I said. "Did you know that they keep old clothes and stuff that the prisoners leave behind? It was like a flea market in there."

"No," said my mother. "I didn't know that. Too bad. He deserved to ride home naked."

I agreed. "He'd cashed his entire pay check. What he didn't drink up was stolen."

"I suppose we'll have to feed him all next week," Nana said.

"So what else is new?" my mother asked.

I sat up late that night, trying to write an essay about *Henry IV, Part One.* From Sophocles to Shakespeare in one week's time was quite a leap. Our English teacher, Mr. Reynolds, had decided to cram us full of random classics in the final quarter in order to make up for his dawdling approach during the first thirty weeks. The GT Magnet program ate first-year teachers for breakfast.

I tried to concentrate, but every time the phone rang, I ran to answer it. It was never Susan. Lucky Eddie called to confirm that May 23 was my graduation date and to say that he was looking forward to meeting all my friends. I wondered if he'd had a religious conversion, some late night experience at a tent revival that made him pretend to be nice.

At midnight, I gave up on *Henry IV* and went to bed. I didn't think Falstaff was funny at all, just another fat bastard drinking wine and eating chicken.

My father had visited only once during the first year after we left Michigan. He'd shown up at Thanksgiving with divorce papers for my mother to sign and a wad of twenties held together with a gold money clip shaped like a dollar sign. My mother reminded him that he hadn't sent her any child support yet. He told her the check was in the mail. Then he insisted on taking us all out to dinner at the Kanki Japanese Steak House.

He didn't notice my eye until Nana pointed it out to him. He looked at it for a moment before stuffing another piece of steak in his mouth.

"That's nothing," he said. "One day at work, I got a metal sliver lodged under my right eyelid. Hurt like hell, but I taped the eye shut with two strips of electrical tape and then drove myself to the hospital."

My mother rolled her eyes. "What a load of . . ."

"Amazing," I interrupted.

161

"Unbelievable," my mother corrected.

When we dropped Eddie off at his hotel room, my grandfather asked if he could come in for a moment to use the bathroom. Eddie said sure. Hunter was gone for about ten minutes.

When he came back out, my grandmother asked, "What in the world were you doing in there?"

"Pissing knee-deep in his shampoo bottle," Hunter said.

Chapter Eighteen

Kim DiMarco's family was moderately rich. Her father was a retired IBM executive, and her mother sold high-end real estate. In high school, it seemed to me that she was filthy, stinking, beyond-the-dreams-of-avarice rich. At the entrance to her neighborhood—a collection of monstrously large houses, each with a great circular driveway planted on an acre of lushly maintained lawn—was a small stone gatehouse. It sat unoccupied on the grass median, shaded by an old oak tree. I was both fascinated and repulsed by that gatehouse. It had been built purely for effect, a folly for those who looked to *Masterpiece Theatre* as an arbiter of taste. "I'm the lodge," it said. "Welcome to the manor. Please doff your cap to the occupants within."

The effect, thankfully, was spoiled by the DiMarcos themselves. Kim's father, Vince, looked more like Chef Boyardee than to the manor born. He was a short, fat man with a bushy gray mustache and a wide, waddling gait. Her mother, Norma, was a heavy-breasted woman with slapdash hair, who always looked as if she'd thrown on her clothes while running to escape a house fire. Had the DiMarcos been more polished nouveau riche, or more attentive to their daughter, it would have been easy to envy Kim. As it was, I only resented the breezy assurance with which she contemplated the future. Kim couldn't imagine not getting what she wanted out of life—an education at an Ivy League college, a junior year abroad, and big, easy piles of money.

"I don't understand why you don't want to go to the prom," she said, pinching off a string of mozzarella and chewing it thoughtfully. "You only get one chance. Then we all graduate and high school is over."

"You don't believe all that bullshit about high school being the best years of our lives, do you? I'm looking forward to college. And graduate school. And getting a job and an apartment and a dog who isn't Maurice." I softened this blow by reaching out to scratch behind Maurice's left ear. He sighed and stretched out a lazy paw.

Kim laughed, a low gurgling sound. "Okay, it's true that the prom isn't important in the great scheme of things, but it is one of those quintessential high school experiences. It's a Hallmark moment. Do you want to miss a Hallmark moment?"

"I do if it means dancing and wearing a ball gown."

"I like to dance," Abby said. She sat on the floor, reclining against the front of the sofa. Five slices of pepperoni pizza had forced her to unbutton the top of her jeans. "Too bad I don't know anyone who knows how."

"How about you, Kim?" I asked. "Are you up on all your groovy moves?"

"Oh, yeah." Kim closed her eyes and folded her hands behind her head, stretching out full length on the brown carpet of her parents' rec room. Annie Lennox flashed up on the console television behind her, singing, "Here comes the rain again." Kim assumed a look of concentrated bliss and turned the sound up with the remote control. "I love this song. I wish I looked like Annie Lennox."

"I have the haircut," I said. "But it's not enough."

She curled her lip in disgust. Kim was all hips and breasts, with a narrow waist that emphasized both. "You lie. You've got that whole androgynous thing going on; what with your hair and your eyes and your whole . . . I don't know what."

"Your whole way of being," Abby supplied. "You could go to the prom in a tux, Poppy. That would be very Annie Lennox."

"Picture me doing that with Dave," I said, turning away to hide my blush.

Abby made a wry face. "Can't see it," she agreed.

"You should go to the prom, Abby," Kim said. "John and Joe have both asked you."

This was news to me. I looked at Abby, who shrugged. "I don't want to go with them."

"You're both weird," Kim said. "An invitation to the prom is not a marriage proposal. It's one night out on the town. It's somewhere to go and something to do."

Kim lived her life in constant search of social stimulation. She was extraordinarily smart. She whizzed through complex math problems with such ease that she'd exhausted the advanced classes at our high school by the time she was a sophomore. For the past two years, she'd been leaving campus in the afternoons to take courses at N. C. State. She made up for academic boredom with an excess of personal excitement. She was a man-magnet. I never asked and she never told, but I suspected she'd been sexually active since junior high.

Abby struggled to rebutton her pants. She soon gave up and dropped the zipper down an inch instead. "Where are your parents this weekend, Kimmy? Timbuktu?"

"Atlanta, visiting my brother and his wife. They won't be back until next week. Then they're off for a month in France."

"Must be nice," Abby and I said in unison.

Kim was the youngest of five. Her parents were at least twenty years older than my mother and Edna. One of Kim's sisters was in her thirties, and her youngest brother was twenty-four. It was like being an only child, only better. Kim's parents practiced a form of benign neglect. It didn't matter what she did—drink, smoke, or stay out all night—they'd seen it all before. She didn't have a long leash; from the time she was sixteen, she had no leash at all. Vince and Norma seemed to regard her as little more than a handy house-sitter.

"Dad's retired," Kim said, "and my mother might as well be. Why should they hang around Raleigh?"

"To make sure you graduate," Abby replied. "MIT might be holding a spot for you, but if you flunk English, you'll find yourself in summer school. You're as bad as this one," she jerked her thumb in my direction. "Can't think about Calculus because she's too busy thinking about you know what."

"What?"

"Boys. Sex."

"I am not!"

"You forgot your locker combination twice this week. You drift around, not paying attention when people are talking to you. Like me. Are you going to dish with the dirt or what?"

"There's no dirt to dish," I said.

"If you don't want to share, that's fine." Kim pushed her glasses up on her nose and reached for another slice of pizza. "We're your best friends, but why should you tell us anything?"

"She's not acting like this about Dave," Abby observed. "No one would act like this about Dave. It's got to be someone else."

"Tell us about him," Kim whispered conspiratorially. "I'll tell you about my prom date. I met him at State."

"There is no him. Tell us about your date."

"Right," Abby said. "She's lying." She turned to Kim. "You tell first. Show her how it's done."

"His name is Kevin. I helped him with some differential equations. Very cute, tall with green eyes. He's got curly brown hair with this kind of wayward piece that keeps falling into his eyes. I want to reach out and brush it back for him."

"Okay," said Abby, "the picture I'm getting is messy. Another one of those math nerds in dirty jeans and worn out loafers with no socks. Just like . . . what's his name?"

"André," I said. "He wasn't messy. He was French."

"That's not nice," Kim said. "Who else am I going to meet except math nerds? *I'm* a math nerd."

"Not entirely," Abby said. "You're on the volleyball team."

"I'm the worst player on the team. They keep me out of pity for my nerdiness."

"We actually keep you because you help us with our homework."

She reached out and pinched me on the arm. "Fine. Where did you meet your mystery man? We're the only people you hang out with besides the volleyball team. Wait—it's not one of our teammates, is it? I know. It's Patty Abbott. She's tall, dark, and handsome, and you sat next to her on the way to the Millbrook game."

Lesbian jokes were common on all the teams on which I played.

166

Homophobia and women's sports went hand in hand. We accused one another of being gay in order to prove that we weren't, and we accused our opponents because we thought they probably were. Nevertheless, I stared at her in blank astonishment. A hot flush stole up my cheeks, and I could feel Abby's shrewd brown eyes appraising me.

Kim laughed. "Don't get bent out of shape. I was just kidding."

At that moment, the doorbell rang. Maurice jumped up, barking, and followed Kim up the basement steps.

Abby poked an experimental finger at the last slice of pizza before firmly slamming down the cardboard lid. "No. If I eat one more bite, I'll explode."

Upstairs, Kim was laughing loudly while several male voices fought to be heard over top of one another. I recognized Alan, Joe, and the inevitable Dave. The rest, no doubt, were on their way.

"Damn," I said, gesturing at the ceiling. "It sounds like a party."

Abby frowned. "It's Saturday night and Kim's parents are out of town. I told my mother I was staying over, but if she finds out there were guys here, she'll skin me alive."

"Don't tell her."

"I won't, but that doesn't mean she won't know. The woman is psychic." Abby stood up and, after a brief struggle, finally succeeded in fastening her jeans. "Here," she said, looking down at me. "I saw your face when Kim said that thing earlier. When you're ready to talk, I'll be there."

I couldn't pretend I didn't know what she meant. I looked at her squarely. One thing I'd learned about having a permanently dilated eye was that people found it disconcerting when you deliberately stared at them. "Until I'm ready to talk about what? Is there something you want to hear?"

Abby stood her ground. "I thought there was. Maybe I was wrong."

I sighed and looked away. Cyndi Lauper danced across the television screen. Lying to my best friend was the next best thing to lying to myself. I didn't want to do either.

"You're not wrong," I said, "but we've got to get out of this rec room. I can't talk about this while Cyndi screams 'Girls just want to have fun.'"

I couldn't see Abby's face in the darkness. She sat next to me on the wooden swing at the bottom of Kim's parents' garden. Above our heads, a cool breeze shook the needles on the pine trees. They made a whispering sound. Something scuttled through the grass a few feet away. It was after midnight. More people had arrived during the course of the evening, and we'd left them in the rec room, dancing the *Time Warp* to the soundtrack of *The Rocky Horror Picture Show*.

"I'm glad you told me," she said at last. "You know it doesn't matter to me."

"You don't think I'm going to hell?"

"I don't believe in hell. Even if I did, why would I think you'd end up there?"

A siren sounded in the distance, a few miles from where we sat in the semi-wilderness. Probably a wreck on the Beltline. The freeway circled downtown Raleigh and separated my home and Abby's from the rich suburbs on the outside. I could feel the hard thump of the music resonating behind the concrete wall of the rec room.

"That's some shitty music," Abby said.

"And those boys can't dance. I know. You're my best friend, Abby. Do you still feel . . . you know . . . comfortable around me?"

She laughed. "Of course I do. So far, you seem to be resisting your desire to throw me down and have your wicked lesbian way with me."

"Abby," I warned.

"It was just a joke, Poppy. Lighten up. If you're happy, then I'm happy for you."

The cloud that had been covering the moon blew away, and the yard was suddenly illuminated. The gray and black forms of trees and bushes took shape, and the thing that was rustling through the grass turned out to be an enormous black cat.

"Here, kitty, kitty," I called. The cat stared at me with its bright yellow eyes for a second or two. Then it hissed and ran beneath an azalea bush.

"That pussy doesn't like you," Abby observed. We sat for a moment in silence. Then Abby began laughing. She laughed so hard that she knocked us both out of the swing. I helped her up and we sat cross-legged on the grass.

"I suppose I'm setting myself up for a lifetime of your pathetic jokes."

"Of course you are," she said. "I'm not going to stop cracking on you now. You don't have a disability or a fatal illness. You like girls. That'll freak some people out, but so what?"

"How'd you get to be so enlightened?"

"Look at me. In case you haven't noticed, I look a little different than all your other friends. I look a little different than all of my friends. While you puzzle that one out, why don't you tell me how you came to make this discovery about yourself?"

At the bottom of the DiMarcos' garden was a path leading to Shelley Lake and the Greenway Trail. "Do you want to take a walk?"

"What, in the dark?"

"The moon's out."

"It won't be out for long," she said. "Look at the clouds."

"Would you rather go back inside and do the *Time Warp*?"

She stood up. "Let's walk. If I fall in the lake, you better jump in and save me."

"We'll drown together," I promised.

The Hokstra Center didn't look like an abortion clinic. It was an unassuming building on Old Wake Forest Road, nicely landscaped with flowers and juniper bushes. There were no protestors out front the day I took Kim DiMarco in to terminate her pregnancy. We were both relieved. Kim had had nightmares about running into an Operation Rescue blockade.

"But I'll do it," she said. "I can't have a baby. I can't. Not now."

"It's okay," I told her. "We'll call in advance. If there are protestors, we'll work something out. Maybe they have a back door."

She didn't say who the father was, and I didn't ask. It might have been Jack Leinweber, or Alan, or even Nick Stybak. He'd gotten contact lenses for graduation and suddenly looked eccentrically handsome rather than hopelessly geeky. The name of the father didn't matter. Kim was seven weeks pregnant, which put the conception date squarely in the middle of our week at Cookie's beach house.

Hunter and Jean dropped their bombshell on Tuesday, June 5. Hunter busted Jean out of her rehab at Hilton Head. Susan went home, I went crazy, and Kim took a midnight walk through the sand dunes with Jack. They were gone for hours. I felt responsible. I didn't care what went on in the house after Susan left. I didn't care if they burned it down around me. I sat on Abby's bed and cried. It was hard not to feel as if Kim were paying the price for my inability to pull myself together.

Under other circumstances, my mother might have insisted we all come home, or she might have come out to join us. Instead she said she was glad that I was gone. I was spared some of the worst scenes Hunter had ever staged, and also the sight of Mike Sava weeping for hours on end at our three-legged dining room table.

The staff at the Hokstra Center were uniformly kind and soft-spoken. Kim and I had an hour-long session with a counselor before her surgery. We met in a room with dim lights and multi-colored floor pillows. The counselor asked questions about how Kim felt, what her plans for the future were, and whether or not she had anyone to take care of her when she went home. I said I'd be staying with her over the weekend, and longer, if necessary.

The counselor went with Kim into the operating room. Kim said she held her hand and talked to her during the procedure. Afterwards, I went in and sat with her in recovery. She was reclining on what looked like a dentist's chair. There were two other patients in the room. Both appeared to be in their twenties. One had her husband or boyfriend with her. They spoke quietly to one another, the woman crying, the husband-boyfriend making reassuring noises. The other woman was alone. She sat with a heating pad on her stomach and listened to music on a pair of headphones.

After an hour or so, Kim was released with a list of instructions and a prescription for tetracycline. I helped her to the car. We were driving her mother's cast-off Volvo, a pumpkin orange station wagon. They'd given it to Kim in lieu of a new car, theoretically to teach her the value of a dollar. Since they also gave her a four-hundred-dollar-a-month allowance, she couldn't see the point, and neither could I.

"Are you okay?" I said.

"I'm okay. It wasn't as bad as I thought it would be. The doctor was very nice."

"Good." I tried and failed to think of something comforting to say. "Good."

Her parents were on the first week of a six-week tour of England, Scotland, and Wales. I collected their mail from the box and put it on the kitchen table. Kim sat down in a recliner in the living room. I made iced tea, and we watched television.

"What I feel," she said quietly, "is relieved. Is that wrong?"

"How you feel is how you feel. It's not right or wrong."

"You got that from the counselor," she said. "What do you really think?"

"I think . . . that I don't know. I wouldn't want to have a baby right now. I don't know if I ever want to have one."

"I want one," she said. "Someday. Maybe more than one."

"You can have as many kids as you want, when you're ready. And you'll be a good parent."

"Better than Vince and Norma. Jesus."

I could offer no answer to this, so I waited. The painting over the fireplace in the DiMarco living room was an Italian seascape, a watercolor Norma had painted during a month's stay on the Riviera. It was all in bright, primary colors, the sea, the sky, even the people basking on the shore. It was executed with some skill, but it didn't go with the room's heavy, dark furniture. It was a painting for a sunny piazza, not a mock Tudor morgue. If Abby had been there, she'd have taken Kim's hand. She'd have held her close until she felt better. It was the middle of summer, and I didn't feel warm enough to comfort anyone. I felt cold and confused, and so I sat and silently ruminated on Norma DiMarco's strange decorating taste.

171

"I have a follow-up appointment with the counselor in two weeks," Kim said.

"Do you want me to come?"

"No." She took a sip of her iced tea and adjusted the heating pad on her belly. "I think I can handle that on my own."

I was born in Raleigh's old Rex Hospital in the same room where my mother had been born twenty-two years earlier. This, coupled with the fact that the Abernathys and the Bartholomews had lived in North Carolina since it was a colony, should have been enough to qualify me as a true Southern woman. But it wasn't.

Those eight formative years in Michigan were one strike against me. Another was my mother herself. She wasn't antebellum; she was anti-belle. Instead of being a hard-bitten beauty full of ruthless charm and feminine wiles, she was a quiet and self-contained woman. She never flirted with any man, my father included. She wore big, thick glasses and preferred reading books to batting her eyelids, and she had no interest in hiding the fact that she was smart. I grew up believing that the Southern woman was the gold standard of femininity. She was the Coca-Cola, Q-Tip, Band-Aid original against which all others were judged. It didn't matter if she were slinging hash or shoveling shit, the ghost of a hoop skirt hovered around her hips. Susan Sava's ethnic makeup was just the same as my own. We were hybrids, the product of WASP mothers and Eastern European fathers, and yet she conveyed the very essence of Southern woman. She was all woman, all the time.

My mother used to say, usually in reference to my father, that she wished there were a third sex to choose from. I wondered how she could be so blind. I *was* the third sex, large as life and twice as ugly, to quote Hunter C. Bartholomew.

I pulled the waistband of my underwear down and considered my reflection in the bathroom's full-length mirror. My hysterectomy scar was still angry and red.

"I'm halfway to a sex change," I said experimentally to Abby.

"What're you talking about?" She was tired after her visit with Vivian and aggravated with me. I was late. After my dinner with Susan, I'd spent the night in my old bedroom at Nana's house. We'd visited Hunter in the morning, and then my mother had dropped me off at the hotel. I'd asked Abby about her visit, and she'd said "fine" in that clipped tone she usually reserved for the particularly stupid.

"No uterus, only one ovary. If I started taking testosterone, I could be Frank Koslowski in six months' time. For real, this time."

"What do you mean this time?"

"Some kids in Michigan had started calling me Frank, just before we moved. No doubt sensing the butch-to-be."

"Hmm," she said. Her hair was freshly braided. The beads on the ends were bright blue. I knew the braiding process took about six hours. Perhaps she and Vivian had spent part of the day at a salon together. That seemed odd, considering.

"You'd need a double mastectomy," she continued. "Not to mention chest reconstruction and a phalloplasty. It would take a hell of a lot longer than six months to make a man out of you." She finished buttoning her blouse and tucked it into the top of her pants. The blouse was new, silk I thought, and the exact same color as the beads. If it weren't for her expression, exasperation mingled with some emotion that I couldn't read seething just below the surface, the overall effect would have been almost cheerful. She turned to me and sighed.

"You're grieving. For a lot of things. Just at the moment, we don't have time to talk about any of them. We're going to be late meeting Kim. She's been at the Rathskellar—" she looked at her watch—"for the past ten minutes."

I pulled my pants on and slipped into my shoes. "I'm sorry I was late. We left the hospital in plenty of time. My mother just drives slowly."

"I'm not angry that you were late. You have to spend time with your grandfather. That's why we're here, or some of why we're here. We can talk about all of this when we get back this afternoon. Maybe we could go out tonight, have a quiet dinner somewhere."

I grimaced.

"Or not. Susan again?"

"No, not Susan again. It's Nana and my mother. We're having dinner tonight at the Kanki."

Her face relaxed, and the transformation was remarkable. She did look cheerful. In fact, she looked happy. I realized suddenly that I'd been waiting for this look to reappear ever since Rosalyn died.

"What are you grinning at?" she said.

"Sorry, I just . . . you're coming with us. To the Kanki. My mother specifically invited you."

Abby smiled. "You, me, your mother, and your grandmother. All at the same table?"

"You know it. Unless, that is, you'll let me sit somewhere else."

"Not a chance. You'll be my garlic necklace."

I buckled my belt and walked through the door Abby held open for me.

"Poppy," she said. "I'm sorry. I was kind of on edge when you came in this morning."

"It's all right."

"You let me get away with murder. But you don't need to. Not anymore."

"We *do* have a lot to talk about," I said. "But first, we must dine with the lovely Kim DiMarco. Shall we walk or ride?"

"Walk, I think. If you're up to it."

"Lead on. I feel like a million bucks."

For the fit and healthy, it was a five-minute stroll to the Rathskellar. At our steady but relaxed pace, it took us ten.

"Kim can order a drink," Abby said. "Noon is not too early for Ms. DiMarco to have a cocktail."

"She always liked a cocktail," I agreed. "So, for that matter, do I. About tonight, Abby. My grandmother—she has blind spots. Big, huge, honking blind spots. Some of it's generational and some of it's, well, I don't make excuses. Nana was wonderful to me when I was a small child. She was my rescuer. When Lucky Eddie was a bastard to me, which was most of the time, I could always count on Nana to do or say something that let me know that I was okay, that the problem was him. She wrote me letters, she called me on the phone, she . . ."

"You don't need to explain or defend," Abby said. "Your grandmother has flaws. We all do. No one is perfect." She opened the door to the Rathskellar. "But if she pretends like she doesn't know who the hell I am, I'm going to knock her block off."

Kim had three ex-husbands, not two, and no boyfriends on the horizon.

"It's so great to see you guys," she said. "I'm sorry you're here for such a sad reason, though."

She reached a pudgy hand across the table and patted me kindly. She'd put on about twenty pounds since high school, most of it in her breasts and hips. As far as I was concerned, it only made her more attractive. Kim DiMarco, now DiMarco-Andrews-Stewart-Cooke, had a pleasant, open face. Her bright green eyes, no longer masked by corrective lenses, were framed by long dark lashes. She'd had laser eye surgery—best four thousand dollars she'd ever spent, she said. As I watched her, I felt a familiar wave of attraction sweep up from the pit of my stomach. Kim could have seduced the chair she was sitting on. She pulsed with good humor and charm, and she interacted with everything and everyone with an animal sexuality that wasn't so much aggressive as inevitable. I reacted to it the same way I reacted to a warm, sunny day, soaking it up and enjoying it for what it was, a gift of nature.

"It must be hard," she went on. "I know you and your grandfather were estranged."

Estranged. Were we? I'd seen him twice during the last ten years, once when I was delegated to make sure that he arrived on time and sober to my cousin Sammy's wedding, and then again a few years later when I went with my mother and Nana to visit him in the nursing home. We took him out to lunch, to some barbecue place about half a mile down the road. I asked him what he wanted, and he mumbled something that my mother interpreted as fried chicken. He'd lost his false teeth, having wrapped them in a Kleenex one night and thrown them away, but that didn't stop him from tearing into a drumstick and gnawing it down to the bone. I didn't ask any more questions. He knew who I was—he seemed mildly pleased to see me—but the spark of personality was gone. My grandfather, the Hunter Bartholomew I'd known, had been dead for much longer than a decade. I tried and failed to pinpoint the exact moment when he'd died. He'd died drop by drop, like Chinese water torture, drowning my awareness of him as a separate, sentient human being. Now he seemed like someone I'd dreamt up.

I made each decision about his care as it became necessary, and I had nothing but support from my mother and Nana. I was here for a reason. I was here to pull the plug. Everyone approved—Abby, the doctors, my mother, and Aunt Dot. Dot had trooped into the hospital room just a few hours ago, patted Hunter's leg, and said, "Well, I guess it's his time." We were all agreed; he was going to die. If I'd said, "Now it's time to put the pillow over his face," I don't think anyone would have stopped me.

"We had a complicated relationship," I said.

Kim laughed. "Is there any other kind? My oldest is thirteen and precocious as hell. She's had little boyfriends since she was in kindergarten. Now, she wants to date. I tell her she can date when she has her Ph. D. and not before."

The waitress came to take our order. She didn't look old enough to drive a car, much less work in a restaurant that served alcohol. I wondered when I'd gotten old enough to notice how young other people looked.

"The Greek burger, please. And could I have a side salad instead of fries?"

"The same for me," Abby said. "Only I want the fries and the salad."

"I'll have the Mousetrap," Kim said. "I never eat anything else here," she told us when the waitress had gone. "In all the years I've been coming here, I always think, this time I'll have the Greek burger or the Provençal sandwich, but I never do. I get the Mousetrap, which is basically just an overpriced grilled cheese. Force of habit, I suppose."

"I love this place," Abby said. "I think I've sat at every table in here and had every kind of conversation. We were having dinner here when Rosalyn asked me to live with her. I was eating seafood fettuccine and she was drinking this ridiculous drink called a Scarlett O'Hara, bourbon and cranberry juice with a maraschino cherry. I had a sip. It tasted like cough medicine."

Abby and I rarely spoke about Rosalyn. We didn't avoid the subject—if she came up naturally in the course of conversation, we didn't flinch or begin talking about something else—but neither of us mentioned her death or its aftermath with any apparent deliberation. Sometimes I wanted to make a point of talking about Rosalyn. I wanted to say something that would let Abby know that I no longer believed that she was going to crack up and step aside, that I knew she was healthy again, changed but intact.

"How was your visit with her sister yesterday?" Kim asked.

"Good," Abby said. "They were close. Vivian was the only one of her sisters Rosalyn could talk to about the cancer. She listened, she didn't turn away or, worse, put on a happy face. This is the first time I've seen her since the funeral. We went to Duke Gardens and walked around. Some of the plants were in bloom. Most were just beginning to bud out. Vivian has Rosalyn's ashes. She wants me to take them."

The waitress brought our sandwiches. She'd given Abby and me both French fries and forgotten our salads. Abby didn't seem to notice. I poured ketchup onto my plate and made the best of it.

"What are you going to do?" I asked.

"I think I'll take them," she said.

"You could sprinkle them somewhere pretty," Kim suggested. "Somewhere that meant a lot to the two of you."

"But not here," Abby replied. "I don't think the Rathskellar would go for that."

Chapter Nineteen

Kim told us about her daughter, Tory, and her son, Justin. Tory was a freshman at our high school alma mater.

"She's terrible in math," Kim said. "Even simple algebra. She wants to be a poet, dresses in black with white makeup all over her face. She looks like that guy from The Cure. What was his name?"

"Robert Smith."

"That's it. Although I suppose she's trying to look like someone else, God knows who. I feel so out of it sometimes. When did we switch from MTV to VH1?"

I laughed. "It sneaks up on you. Abby and I were watching VH1 the other night. They had some nostalgia show on, and what it was nostalgic for was the eighties."

"I'm not ready for nostalgia," Kim said. "I'm not old enough. Not nearly."

"Tell us about your son," Abby said.

"Oh, Justin, he's a sweetheart. Well, to be fair, he's at that sweetheart age. He just turned six. He wants to be a cowboy, and he thinks his sister is just wonderful. As far as he's concerned, she can do no wrong."

"I suppose it's the difference in their ages. You've escaped sibling rivalry."

"To some extent," she agreed. "The harmony won't last forever, though. Tory's father—that's Tony, my second husband—takes a real interest in her. He's never missed a birthday or a school performance. He's great, and we've remained friends. Justin's father, total opposite. He can't be bothered. Birthday parties, soccer games—Justin calls to invite him, and he never shows up."

"That's a shame," I said.

Kim said lightly, "Oh, I think it's all for the best. Chris was a real bastard."

Abby polished off her last French fry and wiped her fingers on her napkin. "That's not what you really think, Kim. That's not what you think at all."

Kim sighed. "You're right. Sometimes I see Justin's face, I see how disappointed he is, and I'd like to shoot his fucking father."

"It must be awful."

"You can't imagine," she said. "When someone hurts your child—it's far worse than anything they could ever do to you."

The week passed slowly. It rained three times and, despite Kim's tutoring, I failed a Calculus quiz. On Wednesday, Susan called, but she didn't talk long. Dave told me he'd made reservations for April 30 at the French restaurant. Eight o'clock. He asked if I'd ever eaten snails. I said no.

On Saturday, the sun was shining, not a cloud in the sky. By ten o'clock in the morning, it was eighty degrees. It was my great-grandmother's eighty-fifth birthday, and the entire Bartholomew clan was set to turn out in force. Hunter's brothers and sisters and their children were coming from all over the country to mark the occasion. Not because they loved her, and certainly not because she loved them. They were coming because my great-aunt Lucy had decided that they ought to do something to mark the passage of time. My grandmother's family, the Abernathys, had family reunions every year. They liked one another. The Bartholomews got together only for weddings, funerals, and birthdays they hoped would soon be leading to a funeral.

Lucy was the second oldest child after my grandfather. She lived in Florida with her bejeweled husband Oscar. They both sold real estate. She'd called several times over the past few years to say that Miss Agnes ought to move into a nursing home.

"She can't live out there by herself forever," Lucy said. "Anything could happen to her."

"A nice nigger lady comes five days a week to clean and cook and do for her," Hunter answered.

"If only I lived closer," Lucy opined, "she could come live with me."

"My ass," Hunter said after he'd hung up the phone. "She moved out at sixteen, and we didn't see her for dust."

Abby's aunt, Pearl Johnson, looked after my great-grandmother. Pearl had a stable of old ladies she checked on, taking them food, making sure they hadn't fallen and broken a hip, making sure they had heat and electricity. My grandfather and his siblings paid her a pittance every month, about two hundred dollars. She spent at least two hours a day with my great-grandmother, which meant she was only averaging five dollars an hour.

"You ought to pay Pearl a living wage," I said. "And it doesn't soften the blow of 'nigger lady' if you add the word 'nice.'"

"If I want any shit out of you," Hunter replied, "I'll knock it out."

At noon, we stopped by Fred's boarding house and blew the horn. Hunter was driving my grandmother's car, which was of a slightly more recent vintage than his van. None of us wanted to sit next to Fred, so Nana, my mother, and I were squished together in the back seat. We waited while Fred came stumbling down the front steps. He'd gotten himself a new pair of shoes, black wing-tips. Still no socks.

Mrs. Jones appeared in the doorway behind him, leaning on a cane and waving jauntily. Hunter rolled down the window and called out, "How you doing, Ms. Jones?"

"I'm just fine," she hollered back. "How about yourself, Mr. Bartholomew? Isn't this a beautiful day?"

Hunter grinned. "It feels so good out, Ms. Jones, I think I'll leave it out!"

"Hunter!" my grandmother hissed, but I could see that Mrs. Jones was laughing. Fred climbed into the front seat, and we headed east on Highway 64, stopping at the bait store so Fred could run in for a pack of cigarettes. He came out with a bag of beer.

Nana lit up a Virginia Slim and stared out the window. My mother cracked open a Harlequin Romance. A sultry redhead in a

180

low-cut blouse lounged provocatively on the cover, her pouty pink lips promising a-hundred-and-fifty pages of formulaic titillation.

My great-grandmother's house was across the road from the First Baptist Church of Knightdale. It sat on a hard patch of red clay with its kitchen window looking across to the cemetery where her husband and two infant children were buried. Past the house a rutted dirt track led through the tobacco fields to the pond. Two barns and a derelict sharecropper's house, all covered in green tar-paper, sat at right angles to one another on the far side of the first tobacco field.

No one had lived in the sharecropper's house since the 1940s. The roof over the porch had caved in, and there was a dry well lost somewhere in the tall weeds. In the early days of my weekend jaunts to the pond with Hunter, I could never resist climbing through a window and wandering around the sharecropper's house. I found old bottles, cigarette papers, and a black button shoe, which I took home and polished. Abby said it probably belonged to one of her ancestors.

The party was under a large green tent set up by the pond. There were too many people—and Miss Agnes would have objected—to have it in the house. Lucy had flown up from Florida to do the organizing. The tent was her idea. She'd rented it from the Mile End Funeral Home. I had hoped it would have the funeral home's logo on it, but in this I was disappointed.

We parked on the edge of the dirt track behind a long line of cars. Of great-grandma's nine children, seven had made it to adulthood, and six were at this birthday party: Hunter, Lucy, Alice, Allard, Dot, and Fred. Many of Miss Agnes' grandchildren, great-grandchildren, and nieces and nephews were also in attendance. Great-grandma owned two hundred acres of prime farm land, and no one knew if she'd made a will or not. Whenever anyone asked her, she always said, "Wait and see."

I could count the number of people I recognized on one hand. Lucy and her husband, Oscar, stood next to my great-grandmother's chair, looking Florida-tanned and prosperous. Oscar liked chunky gold jewelry, and he wore a lot of it. He had fat rings on both hands, a thick bracelet, a gold watch, and two heavy chains nestled in his curly gray chest hair. My grandfather wore his Masonic ring. He said he'd found it behind the toilet.

"Our toilet?" I asked.

"Yes, our toilet," he replied testily. "Does it matter?"

"Not at all," I said. "But I thought you said God stole it from you. If God's going to use our toilet, I'm going to start locking the bathroom door."

I spotted my mother's nemesis, Linda, standing next to an enormous bowl of potato salad. Linda was Lucy and Oscar's daughter, and, like my mother, she was an only child. Linda was a tiny, dried-up raisin of a woman, though I'm sure she thought of herself as petite and tan. She was two years younger than my mother and had been a bridesmaid in my parents' wedding. She herself had married a doctor, as she and Aunt Lucy never tired of reminding everyone. They had a Mercedes and houses in Palm Beach and Charlotte. They also had two exceptionally hideous children, Jake and Nancy. It didn't take me long to spot Jake. He was standing at the edge of the pond holding something under the water with a stick, probably Nancy.

I took my mother's arm and whispered in her ear, "Don't look now, it's Linda the Cinder and the awful Jake."

My mother grimaced. "I see her. Where's Dr. Crippen?"

Linda's husband's name was actually Brown, but my mother always called him Crippen or Mengele. I scanned the crowd. "Don't see him. I spy Nancy. She's over there in a black dress and sunglasses."

"Do you think she's anorexic? She looks like Karen Carpenter, only breathing."

Linda waved and tottered over on her spindly legs.

"Hello, Barbara Jo," she said. She turned and smiled up at me. "This must be Mary Frances. My goodness, what a big girl you are!"

"Five foot ten," my mother replied equably. "But I think she's done growing."

"And so muscular," Linda went on, feeling my arm with her hard brown fingers. "Is she one of those lady weightlifters, Barbara Jo?"

"No, she's a trapeze artist," my mother said. "We're sending her off to Ringling Brothers after graduation. How's Jake? Is he enjoying military school?"

My cue to skedaddle. While it might have been fun to watch my mother fence with Linda, I didn't care to be a foil. At twelve, Jake was already an evil delinquent, and word had blown through the family grapevine that Nancy had been busted for marijuana possession. I was sure that my musculature would not bring undue shame upon our branch of the family. I weighed 155 pounds, and at my height, I thought that was pretty reasonable. It meant that I would never look wispy in crepe and tulle, but I was fit and trim in my 501s, and Linda "I shit fruit salad" Brown could put that in Nancy's hash pipe and smoke it.

For lack of anything better to do, I wandered over to the pond to see what Jake was drowning. A small calico kitten, as it turned out. I snatched the stick from his hand and cuffed him on the back of the head.

"Hey," he said, his beady eyes watering from the smart.

"Hey, yourself," I replied. "I suppose you'd like my foot up your ass?"

Jake didn't have any fight in him. He turned tail and ran, leaving me free to pull the kitten out of the slimy water. She was a homely thing, half-starved and misbegotten, like all of the cats that hung around Miss Agnes' place. My great-grandmother didn't believe spaying or neutering her cats, relying instead on the road traffic and malnutrition to keep the population in check. I grabbed a handful of napkins off the buffet table and wiped the algae off the kitten as best I could. Then I fed her a piece of fried chicken. She bit me for my pains, a sharp pinch between my thumb and index finger.

"It'll turn septic," said an old voice behind me. I turned around to see Miss Agnes leaning on her walker. She was chewing a piece of bubble gum—or mashing it, rather. She refused to wear her false teeth. Pearl puréed meals for her in the blender.

"I'll pour some peroxide on it. Happy birthday, grandma."

She pushed the gum to the front of her mouth and poked at it with her tongue. Hunter said she'd been a redhead in her youth. Her hair was white now, and she wore it in two thin braids coiled on top of her head.

Her face was as wrinkled and brown as a dried apple doll, but the watery blue eyes behind the gold-framed glasses were sharp and alert.

"You want to put that kitten down and help me with my plate? Use some of them wet wipes to clean your hands."

I hesitated. "I'm afraid she'll fall into the wrong hands. I caught Jake holding her under the pond with a stick."

She cocked her head to one side and regarded me like a vulture sizing up a carcass. "I told him to drown her," she said. "Got too many cats around here. Didn't think he'd mind."

"I'm sure he didn't," I agreed, "but I did."

"You fixing to take it home with you?"

"I guess I'd better."

She laughed at that and edged her walker closer to the table. I dropped the kitten into a large cardboard box marked "Bread Rolls." She scuttled around from side to side, clawing at the cardboard. Miss Agnes handed me a wet wipe and placed her food order.

She pulled her gum out, stuck it on the edge of the plate, and dug in. For a woman with no teeth she managed to eat an astonishing number of chewy foods—a slice of ham, a chicken breast, macaroni salad, and a rock hard biscuit courtesy of Aunt Alice, the kitchen terror. I had a ham sandwich but decided to avoid anything with mayonnaise in it, as the temperature had crept up to ninety degrees.

I pulled a chair up next to great-grandma's and played with the kitten. On closer inspection, I could see that it was older than I'd thought. It might even have been fully grown, just small and malformed. Its face was long and pointy, and its eyes were crossed.

"Probably retarded," I said.

"Her mother's a moron," Miss Agnes agreed, pronouncing moron with a long O. "Had fourteen litters. I used to drown 'em in a bucket, but they've gotten too hard for me to catch."

"It's like *The Grapes of Wrath* out here, isn't it?" I said.

She laughed.

"You've read *The Grapes of Wrath*?"

"Of course," she said. "I used to read a lot, before my eyes got too bad. Pearl reads to me now. She reads better than she cooks."

"It can't be easy to cook for the blender. What sort of books do you like?"

She pulled the wad of chewing gum off her plate and stuck it back in her mouth. "Some of everything," she said. "History, romance, biography. We just finished one by Kitty Kelley about Elizabeth Taylor. She was no better than a common whore."

"I suppose not."

"Where's your grandfather? He hasn't wished me a happy birthday."

The last time I'd seen Hunter, he was drinking something out of a paper bag. I decided the conversation was too interesting for a pointless lie, so I told her so.

Miss Agnes nodded. "I always said that if I'd been a man, I'd have been a drunk."

This surprised me. I said, "Why would you have to be a man?"

"Because women always have work to do," she said.

By five o'clock, only the die-hards remained. Fred, Allard, Oscar, and Howard sat in lawn chairs at the edge of the pond, drinking out in the open now. Linda had taken Jake and Nancy, who looked like she'd been in possession of something a lot harder than pot, back to the Holiday Inn. She informed us that they had tickets to hear the North Carolina Symphony perform Beethoven's Ninth.

"As if she could tell the difference between the Ninth and a fifth," my mother hissed. She had finished her Harlequin and was flipping through a battered copy of *Chariots of the Gods*. "What are you planning to do with that kitten?"

"I thought I'd name her Jezebel."

"She looks more like Boo Radley." She reached over and picked the kitten up off my lap. "We might not be able to find an apartment that allows pets."

I didn't want to have this conversation with my mother now anymore than I had two weeks ago. "If Jezebel stays out here, you know how she'll end up, knocked down or knocked up. I'm going to rescue her. I'll find her a home."

185

My mother pursed her lips. "We'll see. When Fonzie died, I told you that was it. I don't want to spend the next twenty years cleaning out a litter box."

"Look at her. Do you think she'll live to be twenty?"

"You'd be surprised," my mother said. "I brought a kitten home from this place in 1946. She lived until the year your father and I got married. I'm about ready to go home. Any sign of Hunter?"

"Oh, yeah. He's right over there, laughing like a hyena."

"Great." She looked at her watch. "He's got till six o'clock. Then, I'm taking us home, and he can stay here with his mother."

"I don't want him," Miss Agnes said. She lowered herself onto the padded wing chair Lucy had transported from the house to act as a birthday throne. "I told Myrtle when she married him that she'd have to keep him."

Nana pulled up another lawn chair. "I believe your exact words were 'You've made your bed and now you'll have to lie in it.' I should've taken that as a warning."

As if on cue, Hunter wandered over.

"Uncle Robert was a sorry son of a bitch," he said.

"Stop it, Hunter," my grandmother said.

Miss Agnes stared off into the distance, her hands folded primly on her lap. I thought it was about time for someone to take her home. The mosquito coils had burned down to nothing, and the flies had long since taken over the buffet table.

"He was tighter than a bull's ass in fly time," Hunter went on. "A worthless cheating bastard in a shiny two-dollar suit."

Nana put her head in her hands. I couldn't tell if she was miserable or just tired. My mother closed her book and retreated to the car.

Hunter flung his head back and wailed, "Why did you do it, mother?"

Jezebel, who'd been asleep in my lap, opened one crossed eye.

"I don't know what you mean," Miss Agnes said.

"I saw you through the kitchen window," Hunter wailed. "Daddy was gone, and I was riding my tricycle on the side porch. I saw you letting Uncle Robert play with your titties." He knelt beside her chair and ran his hands through his hair several times.

186

Miss Agnes shook her head. "You're only saying this to hurt me, Hunter."

"Uncle Robert, your baby sister's husband," he went on mournfully. "You ruined my life. My entire goddamned life. I hope Daddy never knew."

I looked at my great-grandmother. The titties Uncle Robert had apparently been so fond of were tucked somewhere beneath the waistband of her flowered dress. Had she been good-looking once upon a time? She'd been a redhead, and like as not, the blue eyes weren't always watery. She wanted Hunter to shut up and stop wrecking her birthday. So did I.

"You should have kept the kittens and drowned him in a bucket," I said.

She didn't disagree with me.

Chapter Twenty

Mr. Chisholm, the Vocational Ed teacher, also served as the lunchroom monitor. He didn't like GT students. He'd written several letters to the Raleigh paper saying that the Magnet program was a waste of taxpayer money. He stopped Abby and me at the doorway to the cafeteria.

"Five per table," he said, glowering at us. "No more." The hand he held up to demonstrate this number had only three fingers and half a thumb.

"Those who can't do, teach," I whispered to Abby. She laughed so hard she swallowed her gum.

We waited in line for our helpings of Salisbury steak and industrial strength mashed potatoes. A tired woman in a white coat and hairnet slapped the potatoes onto a tray. "Gravy?"

Abby hesitated.

"Go on," I urged. "You're holding up the line."

"Gravy?" the woman asked again.

"Let's find Dave," Abby suggested. "His dad owns the Hardee's on New Bern Avenue. Maybe he'll extend us some credit."

I shook my head emphatically. "No way. She'll have gravy," I said to the woman with the hairnet, "and so will I."

She pushed two trays over the steam shield. Abby sighed heavily. We both passed on the chocolate pudding. The skin on top was so thick it looked like the outer casing of a Nerf ball. Abby snapped the lid on a cup of Pepsi and shoved a straw through the hole.

"What's the matter with you," she said. "Do you want to eat this stuff?"

"No. I also don't want to go to lunch with Dave."

"You're going to dinner with him. You've got his hopes up."

We threaded our way through the crowded tables, finally settling in a secluded spot next to the fire exit, as far as out of Mr. Chisholm's line of sight as possible.

"We're not on the barter system. One dinner doesn't equal a relationship."

"What does equal a relationship?"

I frowned, thinking.

"Don't pull a muscle," she said. "I was just wondering."

I spotted Kim, Alan, Joe, and Nick and waved to them.

"Five per table," I said, holding up my right hand with the index and middle fingers folded down. Everyone laughed except Abby, who was busy using her fork to make a gravy moat for her castle of mashed potatoes.

Ten minutes later, Dave came waltzing in with a bag from Hardee's. Abby shot me an evil glare. Fortunately, there was no room on either side of us, so he pulled up a chair between Nick and Joe.

"I hope you're happy," Abby whispered after a minute or two. She waved a piece of Salisbury steak at me, shaking congealed drops of gravy onto the table. "I could've had a hamburger."

"Why don't you go out with him, then?" I whispered. I took the fork from her hand and put it down on her tray. "Stop threatening me with that toxic waste."

I looked out the window. The table next to the fire exit overlooked the students' smoking lounge, which was where the kids in black Judas Priest T-shirts hung out. A girl in a motorcycle jacket caught my eye. Though I didn't realize it at the time, she had all the hallmarks of the classic butch bar dyke, aggressive posture, shag haircut, and a bored expression. All she needed was a pool cue. We stared at one another for a moment. Then she leaned forward and thrust her head at me in a fuck-you gesture. I looked away.

"Abby," I said. "Don't look up, but that girl . . ."

I was interrupted by the ubiquitous Mr. Chisholm.

"You kids are blocking the fire exit," he said. "There should be no more than five students sitting at this table. Five."

Kim and Alan jumped apart as if they'd been shocked with a cattle prod. Nick and Joe stopped playing quarters with their soda cups. Abby and I tried to look innocent.

Mr. Chisholm glared at us. "I warned you. For kids who are supposed to be so smart, you're pretty stupid. Five," he said again, holding up his right hand.

"How many was that?" I asked Abby.

"Three and a half," she replied.

We spent the next hour in the Principal's office, trying to explain why we thought it was appropriate to mock the victims of Vocational Ed.

It was half past seven when Susan called, and I had to spend fifteen minutes arguing with my mother about whether or not I could go out on a Monday. I won, but only after promising to be back by eleven. It was eight before we actually pulled out of the driveway. We arrived at the drive-in forty-five minutes into *Terms of Endearment*.

I watched enough of the movie to know that Debra Winger died and Jack Nicholson drove Shirley Maclaine up a beach while steering the car with his feet. It was a cloudy night with no moon. Susan turned the volume on the speaker down. Pictures flashed on the screen. Two hours after my curfew, I went home to face the wrath of Barbara Koslowski. It was worth it.

Susan was squinting at me in the dim light. She'd given me a choice between an Indian restaurant and an Irish Pub on Franklin Street. I'd gone for the Pub. Though she'd only had half a glass of wine, her cheeks were flushed. Of necessity, I was drinking coffee. The only thing worse than being too young to drink, I decided, was having a girlfriend who was just old enough. I felt so obvious ordering a Coke or a glass of water. Coffee was the next best thing to beer or wine. It was the sophisticated choice. For emphasis, I ordered it black, though I preferred it with cream.

"Do you believe that story about your great-grandmother?"

I nodded, taking a bite of dill pickle. "Yes. People had extra-marital affairs in 1923, just like they do now."

Susan speared a piece of fried cod on the end of her fork and dipped it in tartar sauce. I'd finished everything but my pickle ten minutes before, but Susan was a more contemplative eater. I was contemplating my parsley when she finally pushed her plate away.

"Let's walk," she said. "I'll show you the sights of Franklin Street."

The sights were an ice cream parlor, a movie theater, and several shops of one kind or another. I loved it anyway. The trees on the UNC campus were old and mysterious; their roots shoved up huge mounds of dirt and grass. Susan and I found a secluded gnarl on an enormous oak and sat down with our backs against it. The sun had set, but there was still light in the sky. I reached through the evening shadows to take her hand, lacing my fingers with hers.

"My mother is having an affair," she said.

"What are you talking about?"

"I know the signs. She's furtive. She calls me up and wants to do mother-daughter things. She wants to drive over and take me out to lunch. She'll disappear soon. My father will wait forty-eight hours, and then he'll call the police. They'll find her and bring her home."

"I didn't know . . ."

"I've never talked about it," she said. "Not with anyone; not my mother, not Dad. Just you."

"I'm sorry." I put my arm around her and she rested her head on my shoulder.

"My mother has affairs," she said. "Always with someone awful, some low-life she picked up in a bar. Young, old, it doesn't matter. She goes off with them, and then my dad brings her back."

I waited. Whatever I said, I didn't want to sound shocked. The problem was that I was shocked.

"Why?" I asked at last. "Why does your father bring her back?"

"He loves her," she said. "He says she's mentally ill."

"Your father's a good man."

"My father's a fool. Sometimes, I think he's the one who's mentally ill. How long is he going to let her go on wrecking his life? She's not

191

going to wreck mine," she said firmly. "I'm done. When she's clean and sober, I'll see her, but no more helping my dad pretend like everything is fine and normal when it's not."

"My grandfather had an affair once," I said. "When I was a baby. He left my grandmother and married some woman who was younger than my mother. My mother said having a grandchild made him feel old."

Susan lifted her head. "Like it was your fault?"

"Not like that. She was just trying to explain."

"It sounds more like an excuse."

We sat in silence. Then we went back to her apartment and climbed silently into bed. Sometime in the night, she turned to me, and without a word, she undressed us both. The next morning, the sun rose red in a nest of mare's tales spun along the horizon of a pale blue sky.

April 30 bore down upon me with a dreadful inevitability. On the 29th, I told my mother and Nana about dinner at the French restaurant in Chapel Hill.

"Instead of the prom," I explained.

"Are you going to eat snails?" Nana asked.

"Maybe."

"Your grandfather ate them in France during World War II, didn't you, Hunter?"

He nodded. "You won't catch me eating them again. They'd gag a dog off a gut wagon."

"You're going to need a dress," my mother said, frowning.

"What for?"

"Are you planning to wear jeans and a T-shirt to a French restaurant?"

"No, khakis."

Nana gasped. "You are not wearing pants! Barbara, put that magazine down. We're taking this child to Belk's."

"She's got the funeral dress," my mother said.

"That dress is four years old and she is two inches taller. It will not do."

192

"I don't need a dress. No one expects me to wear a dress."

"Poppy," my mother explained, "you've never been to this kind of restaurant. I know the place you're talking about. You have to have reservations."

Half an hour later, I found myself standing in Crabtree Valley Mall, forced once again to choose between the devil and a deep blue dress.

"I'm not wearing that."

"Then how about this?" Nana held up a floral print dress with capped sleeves.

My mother laughed. "She can't wear that. That looks like Aunt Lucy's bedroom curtains."

"It'll have to be the blue, then." Nana sighed. "I'll loan you my diamond necklace and teardrop earrings, that'll dress it up. What do you want to do about shoes?"

"I want to outlaw them."

"Little Miss Smarty had a party, and nobody came but Little Miss Smarty. The shoes are on the first floor, aren't they, Barbara?"

I ended up in a pair of dark blue pumps with a one-inch heel. I rejected the two-inch heels with the open toes, and Nana rejected the sandals with the ankle straps.

"I don't know what Belk's is coming to," Nana said. "What kind of salesgirl brings out white before Memorial Day? And you in a size ten, you couldn't wear white if it was the Fourth of July."

I finished tying my torn and duct-taped tennis shoes. "Do we have time for a visit to the foot binder? I'm sure if I chopped off a few toes I could squeeze into a seven."

My mother gave me a thorough appraising look. "A visit to the beauty parlor might not be amiss. Let's see if one of the salons has a walk-in available."

A girl with two-inch long red fingernails did the best she could with my three-inch long hair, giving me a spiky Sheena Easton kind of look. Nana and my mother loved it, so much so that they bought me a bottle of salon shampoo and a can of mousse. My reward for not killing myself or anyone else was dinner in the Belk's cafeteria.

"Just this once," my mother said, "you can break your curfew.

193

Chapel Hill is a long drive, and a good French dinner can take hours to eat. Let yourself in with your key, and we won't wait up for you."

"You might not have a choice if Hunter is home." A new and horrible thought occurred to me. "My god, he might meet Dave at the front door!"

Nana paused with a spoonful of banana pudding halfway to her mouth.

"That's true," my mother said thoughtfully. "I'll tell you what—I'll put a light under the curtain in the dining room window. If it's switched on, don't let Dave walk you to the door. Just say goodnight when he pulls into the driveway."

My grandmother giggled. "She can't do that. She has to give him a goodnight kiss."

I pushed away the plate of half-eaten roast beef and covered it with my napkin.

"Mama, stop that," my mother said firmly. "You tormented me in high school. You're not going to do that to Poppy."

"I'm only teasing." Nana stabbed at a slice of banana. "She's practically grown-up now. I wasn't much older than she was when I got married."

"Let that be a warning to you," my mother said.

Chapter Twenty-One

We emerged from the Rathskellar to find that the day had taken on a mellow cast. A few large, white clouds had appeared, and the bright glare of noon had softened into the warm light of mid-afternoon.

"I'm sorry to rush," Kim said. "I promised to take Tory to the mall to meet some of her friends. It was a babysitting bribe. I can trust Justin to her care for about three hours without fear of fratricide."

I hugged her and promised to keep in touch, wishing that meant more than Christmas cards and email jokes. I missed Kim; or rather I missed the Kim I'd known, the one who was on her way to MIT, who had absentee parents and parties in her rec room. I wanted to know the mature Kim, the mother, the ex-wife, the woman who'd dropped out of MIT. Years later, after Tory was born and her divorce was final, she'd gone back to school and become an accountant. She had her own business now. By all reckoning she was very successful. I knew the bare details of her life, and yet I could catch only glimpses of the adult Kim through the prism of the teenaged girl who'd been my friend.

She climbed into a convertible Saab and drove off, waving to us in the rearview mirror. In high school, her dream car was a Datsun 280ZX, and she'd dated at least three guys who drove that make of car.

"Do you remember Kim's car in high school?"

"The Great Pumpkin," Abby said. "I remember pushing it." A slight breeze ruffled Abby's silk shirt, causing the sleeves and chest to billow out. She put her hands in her pockets and tucked her elbows to her sides. "Where to now?"

"Let's walk across the brickyard and down through Free Expression Tunnel. We can visit the dorms and then stop at the bookstore and buy some of that overpriced alumni crap. Kim looks good, doesn't she?"

"She does. It's funny to see her without a man in tow."

"Men," I corrected. "There was always more than one. Kim liked to hedge her bets. Do you think she likes being an accountant?"

"Instead of an unemployed mathematical genius? I think so. She seems happy enough with her life. She was depressed as hell when she came back from Boston. I thought she should have been hospitalized."

"If her parents could have abandoned their goddamn travel schedule for five minutes," I said. "I don't think they stuck around long enough to notice that she'd come home permanently."

"She left MIT and saved them god knows how much in tuition. More money for Germany or Thailand or wherever the hell they wanted to gallivant off to next. She nearly died after that second abortion, a hemorrhage like you wouldn't believe. If I'd gone home that night like she asked me to . . ."

"I know. Rosalyn insisted you stay."

Abby shivered. I handed her my jacket.

"Clever Rosalyn. I should have known. What kind of nurse was I?"

"One who didn't have any training yet. That was the fall you started at UNC, remember?"

"Okay, then what kind of friend was I? I didn't want to spend a minute away from Rosalyn. I wanted to be with her twenty-four seven. Kim should've asked you."

"Me. Kim *told* me. I would have gone with her again, but she didn't want me to. She wanted you, Abby. She said it was too humiliating to have me go twice—once was a mistake. She could be forgiven for once. Twice was careless. Twice was a sin. The DiMarcos practiced a weird form of Catholicism: once-a-year visits to midnight mass, and the rest they made up as they went along."

"Thanks for the jacket. Aren't you cold?"

"No. Remind me—why didn't Kim go back to the Hokstra Center?"

"It was closed. The doctor who founded it died or moved or something. We went to some place on the edge of town, I forget the name. It was no better than a mill. The waiting room was full of women sitting on hard plastic chairs. A hatchet-faced nurse called out names as their turn came up. Take a number. No counselors, no soft cushions, just a cold steel table in the operating room."

"Did she tell you that?"

Abby nodded. "She said she deserved it. She said the experience was just as awful as she'd hoped it would be. She should have sued that fucking doctor. The anesthetic didn't work—she felt the whole thing. I should've gone into surgery with her. I should have insisted. You would have . . ."

"I would have what? I wouldn't have done a single thing that you didn't do. Kim lived, Abby, thanks to you. You took her to the hospital. You remained calm. She wanted you because you're better in a crisis than I am. You're warm and generous and competent. I'm not. Don't tear yourself to pieces over what might have been."

She took a deep breath. We'd crossed Hillsborough Street and stopped to lean against the low brick wall that separated the back of D. H. Hill Library from the brickyard. Students who would have been toddlers when Abby and I were freshmen here walked past us, backpacks slung over their shoulders. For some reason, it seemed strange to think that anyone who had been born during the Reagan administration could possibly be old enough to attend college.

"How are you, Poppy?" she asked.

I opened my mouth to say, "What do you mean," but I knew what she meant.

"I don't know. I feel better than I've felt in a long time. Except for some lingering soreness, I'm pain-free. That's good. But I'm sad, Abby. Really sad. This stuff with my grandfather, and Susan, and—it all seems like nothing compared to the fact that I'll never be anyone's mother. I'll never be pregnant. I don't know what to think about that. I don't know why I feel like this. Maybe it's seeing Kim. I associate her with pregnancy, terrible disastrous pregnancy. I know that's not fair."

Abby was silent for a long time. Then she took my hand.

"Come on," she said. "Let's walk."

197

Hand in hand, we crossed the brickyard. We passed Harrelson Hall, Cox, and Dabney, and we walked down through the Free Expression Tunnel. It was painted with the usual assortment of messages—announcements for fraternity parties and campus meetings, slogans supporting the basketball team, slogans attacking the basketball team, and, at the fringes, cryptic notes like *Free the White Panties* and *Don't be a Pussy*. Periodically, the university painted the tunnel walls white, which was an invitation to the campus graffiti artists to turn out in force and once again make it their own.

We emerged on the other side and, by some psychic common consent, skipped my proposed tour of our old dormitory. Instead, we went straight to the snack bar tucked into the side of the campus bookstore. Abby bought a cup of coffee. I bought a large Pepsi and two Ho-Hos.

"Dessert," I explained. We sat at one of the plastic and metal tables outside. Once upon a time, we'd eaten breakfast at these tables five days out of seven.

"It's not uncommon to feel grief after a hysterectomy," Abby said. "Most women do. I've got to tell you, though—that wasn't what I expected you to say."

"What did you expect?"

"Something else."

A group of skateboarders was practicing jumping off the wall behind us. Abby turned around and gave them the eye. "Sorry," one of them muttered, "Come on, guys."

Abby turned back to me. "What makes you think you're not warm?"

"What?"

"Back there on the brickyard. You said that I was warm and you weren't. That's not true, you know. You're not a cold person. You're very warm."

"I don't feel warm."

"How do you feel?"

I thought for a moment. "Aloof. Detached."

"You'd like to be aloof, but you're not. You don't detach yourself from anything. You feel it all, even when it's not yours to feel."

"What's that supposed to mean?"

Instead of answering my question, she said, "This morning, I was angry with you. Do you know why?"

"Because I was late."

She shook her head. "I was angry because you stayed out all night. You went to dinner at Susan's house, and you didn't come back. You spent the night with her."

"I spent the night," I said, biting into my first Ho-Ho, "in my old bedroom, which is once again my grandmother's sewing room. She shifted her ironing pile, and I curled up on a musty single bed beneath a fluffy pink duvet. I'm sorry. I should've called you."

Abby squinted at me. "You didn't have sex with Susan Sava?"

"I didn't say that," I replied. "But no, I didn't."

"Huh."

"Huh, yourself."

"Did you want to?"

I laughed. "Of course. She's one of the women on my list."

"On your what?"

"My list. Come on, don't tell me you don't have one—the Impossible Women list. You fantasize about sleeping with them, but you know you won't. Sharon Stone, Gillian Anderson, Hillary Clinton, that English teacher we had in the tenth grade."

"Mrs. Ferguson?"

"That's the one. Sigourney Weaver, Sandra Bullock, Barbara Jordan . . ."

"Hold on a second." Abby reached out and stole my second Ho-Ho. "Barbara Jordan. I'm not getting that."

"What do you mean you're not getting that? Barbara Jordan is . . ." I struggled for a moment to explain Barbara Jordan. Then I gave up. "Barbara Jordan is god. What a woman, what a voice. Why wouldn't she be on my list?"

"*One of these things is not like the other,*" Abby sang.

"Oh, Jesus. You mean because she's black? I know I was raised by crackers, but I'd like to think that doesn't limit my libido."

"God knows," Abby agreed. "Nothing else seems to." Before I could object, she said, "Tell me something. Whose idea was it to invite me to dinner tonight?"

"My mother invited you."

"Did you suggest it to her?"

"You ate my Ho-Ho."

"I thought so," Abby continued. "But that's okay. I'll come. First, however, I want you to tell me what happened during your dinner with Susan. Everything. Spare no small detail. Then . . ."

"Then what?"

Abby took the lid off her coffee and blew on it. Tendrils of steam rose from the black surface. She took a sip. "Complete crap," she pronounced.

"We're not in Portland anymore, sister. This is not a coffee town. Then what?"

"Edna doesn't like my braids," she said. "Specifically, she used the words *unprofessional* and *pickaninny*."

"Edna doesn't like anything."

"True. But I want to know what you think."

"About what?"

"About my braids."

I stared at her for a moment. Somewhere along the way, a sea change had taken place between us. I wondered where I'd been when the tide had turned.

"Okay," I said tentatively. "But you'll have to buy me another Ho-Ho."

I'd driven myself to Susan's house over Abby's objections. She'd offered to drop me off and pick me up, but I said I didn't want her to be my chauffeur. I'd also called Susan and asked her not to pick me up. I wanted the freedom to come and go as I pleased. I wanted to be able to escape, if need be. If the evening went poorly, I planned to tell Susan a lie, like Abby was waiting for me at Edna's at thus and such a time, so I was sorry, but I had to go. Thank you and good night. I don't know what I expected. A scene perhaps, some longed-for and yet dreaded emotional confrontation. I didn't get it. We had a quiet dinner and a long talk. We cleared the air, or at least rendered it a little less opaque. Nothing is ever transparent between ex-lovers. Once you've seen someone naked, your vision is forever fogged.

Susan met me at the door in a terry cloth bathrobe. She said that dinner was on the stove—coq au vin, an old favorite—and that she'd be dressed in a moment. I should sit down and make myself at home. There was wine on the buffet and beer in the refrigerator.

The living room was smaller than I remembered, smaller, in fact, than my own living room in Portland. A new cream-colored leather sofa had replaced the old brown one, and the room was tastefully redecorated in what I now recognized as straight-from-Martha Stewart. The Savas had more money than the Bartholomews and the Koslowskis. They didn't have more unaided good taste.

"You can come back here if you like," Susan called. "Or are you still painfully modest?"

"Still modest," I called back, "though not painfully. I'll wait here. Does anything on the stove need stirring?"

"Nothing. I'll be there in a second."

She came out in a pair of jeans and a lilac turtleneck, her hair pulled back into a loose ponytail. She poured herself a glass of wine and sat down on the sofa next to me with her feet tucked up beneath her.

"What should we talk about?" she said. "I don't know where to begin."

"Me neither," I admitted. "Perhaps we should start with the obvious."

"My mother and your grandfather." She finished her wine and then reached over to take my glass. "After dinner," she said. "Let's not keep the coq au vin waiting."

Dave had impeccable timing. Hunter had no sooner driven off for the proverbial pack of cigarettes than he pulled into the driveway. I'd planned on going out to meet him, but since the coast was clear my mother insisted on my waiting until he came up and knocked on the door. He was obliged to make polite conversation with her and Nana while Maurice sniffed his crotch.

I was pleased to see that his mustache was even once again. He was wearing a white turtleneck, khaki trousers, and a navy blue blazer with gold buttons. Between the blazer and the turtleneck, he looked like Thurston Howell on *Gilligan's Island.*

Once we were alone, Dave talked about the weather and about the much-anticipated release of the third Star Wars film, *Return of the Jedi.* He said Kim had mentioned getting a big group together and skipping school the afternoon it came out. I agreed that sounded like fun.

"Abby's been dying to see it," I lied. "It's nice of you to offer us a ride."

The French restaurant was called Jack's, not Jacques, and it was only a block or two from the Irish pub where I'd eaten dinner with Susan. Dave parked on the street outside and then insisted on opening my car door for me. Thanks to my stupid blue pumps, I was obliged to take his arm to pull myself up out of the plush bucket seat of his dad's red Monte Carlo.

The maitre d' wore a black tuxedo with a thin satin collar. He was only a few years older than we were, probably a student at UNC. He stood next to a lectern between two enormous palms in hammered copper pots.

"Reservation for two," Dave said. "Wilson."

Our table was in the back, next to the double swinging doors of the kitchen and as far away as possible from the chamber quartet playing on a dais in the front of the restaurant. The violinist was a tall thin blonde in a long black dress, but it was the cellist who really caught my eye. She was a substantial redhead with a fabulous cleavage tucked into a forest green gown. She had on a black velvet choker with a small silver medallion. Her eyes were closed with the passion of her playing.

"It's nice, isn't it?" Dave said.

"It is," I agreed.

"Bach?"

"Mozart, I think."

The waiter, who was even younger than the maitre d', arrived with two menus. Dave's had a small wine list tucked inside. Mine featured a list of dishes with no prices.

"Have whatever you like," he suggested. "I'm starting with escargot."

"Hmm," I said, noncommittally.

My starter was a pâté that tasted like liverwurst. I pushed it around the plate and ended up trying one of Dave's snails. It was like eating an eraser soaked in garlic butter, but I smiled and pronounced it delicious. This, unfortunately, prompted Dave to offer to switch appetizers with me. When I had a napkin full of surreptitiously discarded escargot, the waiter brought out our entrées. I had coq au vin, chicken in wine sauce, and Dave had coquilles St. Jacques, which he also thought was chicken. The waiter explained that coquilles were scallops. "Oh," said Dave.

We finished with two salads and a cheese plate. One of the cheeses was wrapped in oak leaves and tasted like a creamy Danish blue. I liked it. Dave took one taste and stuck to the Camembert. Two cafés au lait later, the waiter brought out our bill, and Dave tucked four twenty-dollar bills into the brown leather folder.

"Will that be all?" the waiter asked, taking the folder.

"Yes," Dave said.

"Well then, good evening." The waiter smiled.

"No change?" I whispered.

Dave tucked his wallet back into his pants. "Gratuity. My dad says you tip twenty percent in a place like this."

He'd spent as much on dinner as my mother and Nana had on my dress, hair, and shoes. I'd done his pocket no favors by refusing to go to the prom.

We left the restaurant and walked up Franklin Street, retracing the route I'd taken with Susan the weekend before. We even finished up at the same oak tree, though neither of us cared to sit down in the space by the gnarled root. I didn't want him to spoil his khakis, and I had to think about funerals I might someday attend.

On the way back to the car, he reached out to take my hand. I hesitated; then I thought about the bill for dinner. His hand was hot and damp.

"Poppy," he said. "I know you don't like to dance and everything, but there's a band playing up at the Cat's Cradle. I read about them in *The Spectator*. Do you want to go?"

"I don't know. What kind of music do they play?"

"Rockabilly and techno punk."

I laughed. "A kind of Stray Cats meets the Talking Heads sort of thing?"

"Something like that."

"Okay, but on one condition."

"What's that?"

"You let me buy the tickets."

The band was called The Chattering Classes. They weren't bad. I'd seen The Police and Phil Collins in concert. This was my first local band.

Dave had looked embarrassed when I paid at the door. We flashed our driver's licenses and the bouncer stamped "No drinks" onto the backs of our hands in glow-in-the-dark green ink. I felt that I was, if not even, then at least no longer under an obligation. I didn't have to hold his hand on the way back to the car.

"Mustache didn't help you," I yelled over the noise of the crowd inside. "You still got carded."

"They're sophisticated over here in Chapel Hill," he shouted back.

It was standing room only. Between the walk and the new blue shoes, my feet were killing me. Halfway through the concert, I excused myself and pushed my way through the crowd to the women's bathroom. The line stretched all the way back to the bar, so I had another ten minutes to wait before I finally got into a stall.

Once inside, I put the lid down on the toilet, sat down, and pulled my pantyhose off. I started to stuff them into my purse, borrowed from my mother's collection of thrift store finds, but I thought better of it and put them in the stainless steel container marked Sanitary Napkin Disposal instead. I pressed my bare feet against the back of the stall door and felt the cold spread up through my soles and into my legs. I had a blister on the little toe of my right foot. I thought it was a shame I hadn't borrowed my grandmother's purse, as she always carried an assortment of Band-aids. When I began to feel sorry for the beer drinkers lined up outside, I put my shoes back on, flushed the empty toilet, and washed my hands in one of the sinks. There were no paper towels, so I ran my wet fingers through my hair. The water felt good on my hot scalp.

The bathroom was in a short hallway that ran to one side of the stage. There were a couple of concrete pillars with circular plywood benches built around them between me and the spot where I'd left Dave. I was threading my way past one of them when I spotted Susan, or rather, we spotted one another. There was a moment's hesitation, during which neither of us seemed to know what to do. Me because I was with Dave, and Susan because she had her arm around an attractive redhead.

The redhead looked like a younger, thinner version of the cellist at Jack's. Despite the heat, which had forced Dave to take off his blazer within the first five minutes, she was wearing a black leather jacket. Susan broke the impasse. She said something in the woman's ear and made her way over to me.

"A friend," she said.

"A good friend."

"Yes."

The Chattering Classes were playing something reminiscent of *Rock This Town*, and people danced around us. The room stank of stale beer and sweat and cigarette smoke. The redhead was smoking. Susan laid a cool dry hand on my arm and leaned in close. Her breath smelled like beer and cigarettes.

"Poppy."

I shook my head. "I can't talk right now. I'm here with my friend, Dave. He's waiting for me."

She kept her hand on my arm. "I'll call you."

"Yeah."

"I will."

I meant to walk away in quiet dignity. I meant to go straight back to Dave and ask him to take me home. Instead, I stunned Susan and myself. In the sight of God, the Chattering Classes, and Susan's red-headed friend, I took her face between my hands and kissed her right on the lips. Her eyes were bright when I pulled away, and she was laughing.

"Jealous?" she asked.

"Goddamn you," I said. "I've got to go."

I pushed my way over to Dave, who was propped up against a wall, yawning.

"I'm tired," I yelled. "Would you take me home?"

The electric candle was in the dining room window when we pulled into the driveway. Hunter was home. I told Dave there was no need to walk me to the door. He put the car into park and leaned over. I braced myself, but all he did was pull the door handle.

"If you don't pull it just right, it sticks," he explained. "Thanks for coming to dinner with me."

"Thank you for asking me."

"Don't forget about *Return of the Jedi*." He cupped his hand over his mouth. "Luke," he growled. "I'm your father, Luke."

"Dave," I said, also in a Darth Vader voice. "You're such a nerd."

Chapter Twenty-Two

"Good?" Susan asked.

"Witness the evidence." I gestured at the small pile of chicken bones on my plate. "It was delicious. Thank you."

"You're welcome. Shall we retire to the living room? Bring your wine glass."

I sat down on the sofa, and Susan put Diana Krall on the CD player. The lights were dim, the music was right, and a full bottle of wine sat before us on the coffee table. At another time, under other circumstances, I might have kissed her while Diana sang *Peel Me a Grape*. The staging would have been irresistible.

"My mother," Susan mused. "I feel like I should begin at the end and go backwards."

"I've been doing that a lot lately," I said. "Beginning at the end or in the middle. You begin wherever you like."

She leaned back against the sofa cushions and made herself comfortable. I fought an urge to put my feet up on the coffee table. It was lightly stained mission oak and sported no visible heel marks.

"When my mother died," Susan said, "I didn't mourn. At the time, I didn't feel much grief. I felt relieved, glad that she didn't take anyone with her. The post mortem showed that my mother's blood alcohol level was point three. The woman she hit had two kids in the car. They were both injured. One had a broken arm and the other needed six stitches on her forehead. They could have been killed. I couldn't get that out of my mind. I don't think my mother deserved to die, but those kids—what if one or both of them . . . what if they'd lost their mother?"

"They didn't, Susan. It didn't happen. Don't borrow trouble."

"What happened was bad, Poppy."

"I know that. What happened was awful, but there's no point in . . ." I stopped. "I'm sorry. I sound condescending, don't I? I don't mean to."

She shook her head. "You're not condescending."

I was beginning to feel the effects of a heavy dinner and a good deal of wine, and even though it meant the risk of falling asleep mid-sentence, I wanted to be more comfortable.

"This coffee table," I said. "If I take my shoes off, would you mind?"

"Put your feet up," she said. "Shoes on or off. I don't care."

"Off, I think." I unlaced my oxfords and tucked them under the edge of the sofa. I'd worn a ridiculous pair of socks, thick rag wool suitable for Portland in the wintertime but not Raleigh in the spring. I gazed down at the rest of my attire, brown chamois shirt, flannel-lined jeans, and realized I wasn't dressed for a coq au vin dinner but for a trek up Mount Hood. That's it, I thought. My problem in a nutshell. I was just Southern enough to know I wasn't dressed right, but not Southern enough to catch the mistake before I made it. A day late and a dollar short, my grandfather would have said.

"You were saying," Susan prompted.

"Sorry. What I was going to say is that there's no point in hashing out every possible scenario and wondering 'what if.' We torture ourselves with 'what if.' I wonder what if Hunter had stopped drinking, what if AA had actually done the trick, what if . . ."

"What if he and my mother had never gotten together?"

"Exactly. I've spent so much time on 'what ifs' past that I've blinded myself to 'what ifs' present. Somewhere along the way, I stopped making choices and just began careening along. I'm not going to do that anymore. I'm going to try not to, anyway." I held up my wine glass in mock salute. "Wisdom courtesy of Ernest and Julio Gallo. With the aid of Jack Daniels, I'm a regular sphinx."

Susan said, "One of my most persistent 'what ifs' is what if I'm an alcoholic? I know I'm not, but I don't know why I'm not. I like a glass of wine, but I can always put the bottle down. I wonder if that will ever change."

"I don't know," I said. "When I was in college, I experimented, trying to see if I was an alcoholic. I went to a lot of parties, stayed out all night. It didn't last long. I was never able to drink until I passed out. I always got sick first, and then I was hungover. I hated that feeling. Now I find that the older I get, the less I can tolerate. I've had more alcohol since I got here three days ago than I drink in a year in Portland."

We were silent for a while after that. I finished the wine in my glass and waved away Susan's offer of a refill. I was definitely getting sleepy, another sign, I thought, of incipient old age.

Susan shook me out of my reverie. "I saw you at my mother's funeral," she said. "And at the wake. You didn't speak."

"I was avoiding you," I admitted. "I wasn't sure I was welcome, being, as it were, from the enemy's camp."

"You were never the enemy," she said. "Never."

"I came to run interference. I don't suppose you knew that. Hunter was a wreck after Jean died. He called us at all hours of the day and night, Nana included, and wept and wailed and acted like a lunatic. He said he was going to kill himself because he didn't have anything left to live for. I was sorry for him—not as sorry as I was for you and your dad, but that was different. Part of Hunter's grief was genuine, and part of it was self-indulgent. He was going to milk it for all it was worth. I wasn't certain who was going to handle the funeral. I thought if he couldn't pull himself together, then I might have to organize something . . ."

Susan sat forward, interrupting me. "You would have planned my mother's funeral? After what she did to you and your family?"

"Susan, she didn't do anything to *me*. I realized that not long after she and my grandfather did what they did. I tried to look at it from their point of view."

"Their point of view?"

"I'm not saying what they did was right. But if you're a hardened alcoholic, who are you going to be happier with, a teetotaler like my grandmother or another alcoholic? There was a perverse logic to their affair. Your mother didn't want to go to another clinic to dry out. She wanted to drink. How many relationships are based on enabling?"

"I hate to think," she said.

"Exactly. Anyhow, when Jean died, it was long after all the up-roar. I was in graduate school. Nana and my mother had settled down, and Nana—after the initial shock, I think Nana was grateful. A few months after he moved out, Hunter called to ask if he could have the Wurlitzer organ. My grandmother played it too, but he'd paid for it, and she didn't care all that much about it. Do you know what she told him? 'Fine,' she said, 'Tell Jean she can have both my old organs.'"

Susan laughed. "Not an unmitigated disaster for your grandmother, then."

"Not at all, not in the long run. A month after Hunter left, Nana stopped smoking. She quit cold turkey. She'd been a chain smoker for thirty years, lighting one after another. Now, suddenly, she could sleep at night. She wasn't going to get any of those 'I'm too drunk, come pick me up' calls. Jean took those along with Hunter, the Wurlitzer, and Uncle Fred. Nana's troubles were gone, bag and baggage."

Susan refilled her wine glass. Then she offered me the bottle.

"No, thanks," I said again. "I really have hit my limit. When your dad stepped in to make the funeral arrangements, I was surprised."

"They never divorced," Susan said. "Legally, he was still her husband."

"I know. But I still wasn't expecting him to do that. And my grand-father—I knew he'd show up at the wake and the funeral, and I knew he wouldn't be sober. I didn't come to mourn. I came to patrol the perimeters. I was sorry Jean was dead. I was sorry that your father didn't have the same reaction as Nana; that he didn't see your mother's leaving as a chance to get on with his life."

"He was hurt," she said. "He loved my mother. If you'll forgive me, her leaving with your grandfather was what the AA people call rock bottom. She didn't leave my dad for a stranger. She left him for a mechanic from Bloom's, a man who worked under my father. And she wouldn't come back, not like she had before. He tried. He humiliated himself begging her to come home. She said she was happy, and she stayed. There was nothing he could do."

I took a deep breath. There, in the midst of the old grief and anger, was the thing that had come between us in the past and would come between us for as long as Susan and I chose to remain friends. We'd never be equals. It didn't matter how much money I made. It didn't matter if I won the lottery. The pattern of our relationship was set in stone. At some point we'd tacitly agreed that the Savas were a hop above my family. They drove better cars, they lived in a better house, and they didn't get their fingernails dirty with manual labor.

I felt the old twinge of inferiority, the sense that I was sitting on the sofa, drinking the wine, and enjoying the company of a superior being. For a fleeting moment, I thought I ought to be grateful. Then, I got angry, angry with myself as much as with Susan. I'd always accepted my role without question. Why? Hunter and Jean were both drunken sluts. They ran off together. Didn't that make them equal? And what, really, was the difference between a man who sold cars and a man who fixed them?

"You're not the Queen of England," I said.

"What?"

My anger dissipated, replaced by embarrassment. "I'm sorry. I was just thinking aloud. Sometimes, I think I have Tourette's." I sat up and yawned to hide my blush. "Must be getting tired."

"Don't go," she said, putting her hand on my arm. "You're welcome to stay here. We have a guest room."

I shook my head. "I can always go next door. My old bed is still available, if Nana will move the ironing pile."

"We'll cross that bridge when we come to it," she said. "Why don't you finish your story?"

"Yes, I will. I don't know if you saw Hunter at the wake. It was just luck that I caught him. It was getting late, and I'd decided to go home. I was having a hard time avoiding you. Whenever you came into a room, I left it, all the while keeping an eye out for my grandfather. Just after nine, I slipped out the back door and ran straight into Hunter. He'd just arrived with Fred in tow. It was like something out of the Three Stooges. Fred had his shoes on the wrong feet, and Hunter was so drunk he fell up the back steps of the funeral home."

211

To my surprise, Susan laughed. She laughed hard. "Oh hell," she said, putting her wine glass down. "I'm spilling this all over myself." She covered her mouth with her hand and laughed again.

"It was funny," I agreed. "In a macabre sort of way."

"It's okay, Poppy," she laughed. "It's okay to laugh now."

"I laughed then, Susan. I laughed right there in the Neal-Allen Funeral Home. I laughed after I'd poured them into my car and driven them home, and I laughed again when I told my mother about it. My grandfather's shirt was buttoned up crooked, and Fred wasn't wearing any socks. They seemed to me a fitting pair of mourners for the third wheel in their alcoholic comedy act—Falstaff and Bardolph mourn Mistress Quickly."

She stopped laughing then and looked at me. I could tell that she didn't like what I'd said. I also knew that she wasn't exactly certain why that was. I let my observations marinate for a moment. Then I said, "From the Henry plays. *Henry IV*, parts one and two, and *Henry V*. In point of fact, it's Mistress Quickly who announces Falstaff's death. It's a great tragic-comic scene."

When she spoke, her smooth tone was at odds with the flinty look in her eyes. "Last night you told me to brush up my Shakespeare," she said. "Do you ever think about brushing up yours?"

"How do you mean?"

"Going back. Finishing your Ph. D. You wanted to be a college professor."

"Once upon a time. Now I write technical manuals and the ad copy for game boxes. I agree that it's not a noble profession. I don't have an imposing title and a gothic office in an ivy-covered hall."

"I didn't mean to suggest . . ."

"Yes, you did. And yes, I've thought about it. Someday, I might even do it. The only thing that stands between me and the shabby prestige of minor academia is my dissertation. The problem is, I don't care. I can't work up any enthusiasm for a Foucauldian analysis of power relationships in the history plays. I could write it, but who would read it?"

"Don't you think you're selling yourself short?"

I laughed. "No. The world is full of half-assed academics. I don't want to be one of them. Hauser Designs pays me well. I'm the envy of countless teenaged boys—I get to play games like *Slaughterhouse Dozen* and *Zodiac Attack* long before they come onto the market. That won't always be enough, but for now, it is."

"And are you happy personally? Are you seeing anyone?"

Trust Susan to keep probing until she knocked the wind out of my sails. I felt deflated and mean-spirited. I thought I'd been insightful when perhaps I'd just been defensive. Susan relaxed again as she waited for my answer.

"I was seeing someone. I stopped. Recently."

"And the happy part?"

I shrugged. "I'm not unhappy. My surgery is behind me. I have friends, books, family. I laugh a lot. And I have Abby and Belvedere— he's Abby's dog. I have them."

I wished fervently that I was with Abby at that moment, but she was with Vivian, and they were talking about Rosalyn. I had only a small part of Abby. I had what was left after Rosalyn died. In truth, it wasn't even half of the Abby I'd known.

"Poppy," Susan said. "What happened to us?"

"What happened?" I repeated dumbly.

"Why did we let anything come between us?"

"Anything?"

"Hunter and Jean," she said. "What they did shouldn't have mattered."

"Susan, it didn't matter. It didn't matter at all. *You* mattered. *You* came between us. Don't you remember?"

"I don't remember it like that," she said. "You stopped speaking to me."

"My father can only handle one disaster at a time," I quoted. "You don't remember saying that?"

"No. When did I say that, and why?"

"Good grief. I don't believe this. You said that to me when you started dating Brad again. That summer—I asked you why you were going out with him, why you couldn't be with me. You said,

'My father can only handle one disaster at a time.' Do you have any idea how I felt?"

"Poppy," she said. "Please don't be angry. I don't remember it that way."

"I'm not angry. I just feel stupid. I remember it vividly. For years, I've thought of that remark as 'The End.' You have no idea how long I've spent brooding over something that you've clearly forgotten."

"I'm sorry."

"Don't be." I shook my head. "Don't be. It doesn't matter."

"It does," she said. "Tell me how you remember it. I've wanted to mend fences for a long time, but I never knew how."

"They're mended," I assured her. "Really."

"Tell me anyway. Please."

"Do you remember Kim DiMarco's graduation party?"

"Of course." She thought for a moment and then looked at me, her eyebrows raised. "Your father . . ."

"My father. That's as good a place to start as any."

The day before my graduation, Lucky Eddie called from the Brentwood Motor Inn to say that he'd arrived and that he had a surprise for me. I knew that Jack Leinweber was with him, and I knew about the car, so I wondered what the surprise could be.

"Perhaps he's taking you to the Foxy Mama for your graduation dinner," my mother suggested.

"That wouldn't be surprising," I replied.

No one nice stayed at the Brentwood Motor Inn. It was infamous, not so much for its dirty decor and sleazy clientele as for its restaurant and lounge, the Foxy Mama Nite Club. Raleigh had its fair share of seedy clubs, but the Foxy Mama was the only one that featured an amateur night. On Wednesdays, any woman with knockers bigger than her inhibitions was invited to climb on stage and strip for prize money. Lucky Eddie was probably paying for his room by the hour.

I refused to meet him at the Brentwood, suggesting instead that we meet for dinner at a Chinese restaurant called the Hang Chow.

I told him that my mother and Nana would be coming with me.

"Sure," he said. "Bring everyone. Bring your grandfather, too. It'll be Old Home Day."

"Yeah," I agreed. "That would be better than Old Home Week."

When dinnertime rolled around, Hunter was nowhere to be found. I was relieved. He'd been particularly erratic of late, getting drunk during the week and missing work. He was only three months from retirement, and I knew Nana dreaded the freedom he would soon have. I was counting the hours myself. I just wanted to get through graduation, get a summer job, and move out of the house before all the constraints of his work life disappeared. I'd received a financial aid package from N. C. State that would be more than adequate to cover my expenses in the fall, but I was still waiting to hear from UNC. Until I did, I couldn't make my final arrangements, and though my mother had backed off from talking about her apartment plans, I knew she was waiting, too.

Lucky Eddie was late. We'd been in the Hang Chow for twenty minutes and drunk a pot of tea before he sauntered in, Jack behind him, and, bringing up the rear, a woman in her mid-forties with long black hair. She was dressed like the seventies Cher, complete with flared hip-hugger jeans and a fringed pocketbook.

"Frankie," Eddie said, looking around the table as if trying to spot me in a large crowd. "Ah, there you are. Stand up. I want you to meet Shirley Chantrell. She's a friend of mine from Parents without Partners."

"Parents without Partners," my mother said slowly. "What in the world . . ."

I stood up. "Hi, Shirley. Please, have a seat."

She gave me a limp handshake and a vague smile. Eddie pulled out a chair for her and she sat down. My mother and grandmother introduced themselves. I avoided my mother's eye and caught Jack's instead. He shrugged. There was a story there, but I was going to have to wait to hear it.

"Dinner's on me," Eddie said. "Whatever you want. Where's your grandfather?"

"He's, um, busy."

215

"Working late," he observed equably. "He's getting kind of long in the bone to be working those hours, isn't he?"

"Tooth," I corrected automatically.

"Yeah." Eddie examined the menu. "So, what's good here?"

"Everything except the Mongolian Beef," I replied. "Too many green onions."

"I like green onions," Eddie boomed. "I'll have that."

We ordered family style. My mother ate in complete silence. Nana kept up a cheerful patter about absolutely nothing, and Jack nodded and answered my questions about Jane and his plans to join the Marine Corps. Shirley spoke very little, just enough to say that she had two teenaged girls who were spending the week with their father in California, and that she was glad to be able to make the trip to Raleigh with Eddie.

My father, meanwhile, shoveled rice into his mouth like a third-world orphan. Food flying, he kept up a running commentary about the drive, how much work was being done on the West Virginia Turnpike, how quickly they'd managed to get from Detroit to Raleigh, and how much the roads had changed, particularly around Research Triangle Park.

"I wouldn't have known the place," he said. "Who'd have thought? This used to be a haystack town."

"Hayseed?" I suggested.

He squinted in a fashion reminiscent of the old Eddie. Then he smiled.

"She might be smarter than her old man," he said to Shirley. "But we'll see if she does as well in college as I did."

Eddie had taken two drafting classes at Henry Ford Community College in the mid-nineteen seventies. He'd gotten an A in both, but over the years this experience had transformed in the telling. First, it became an associate's degree and then a bachelor's. Sometimes, he claimed to be an engineer at Ford's. On other occasions he said he was a computer programmer. According to my mother, when we lived in Michigan he operated a stamping machine that pressed sheet metal into car doors.

"Have you decided where you're going?" he asked. "You were thinking about N. C. State and Duke."

"Carolina," I said. "University of North Carolina at Chapel Hill."

"Going to be an engineer like your old man?"

"No, I'm going to be an English major."

He grimaced. "What're you going to do with that? Teach?"

I nodded. "College. I want to be a professor."

"I always thought I'd make a good highway patrolman," he said. "A motorcycle cop. They like tall guys for that job. I passed the height test."

"What happened?" Shirley asked.

"Too smart on the aptitude test," he said. "I'd have had to go in at a higher rank than usual. The cops' union didn't like that."

Shirley looked as if she really believed him. Jack grinned at me. I looked into my teacup to keep from laughing. My mother glowered, and Nana came to our rescue.

"So you're going to be a sailor," she said, patting Jack's arm. "All the nice girls love a sailor!"

"A marine," Jack replied. "Not a sailor."

"A marine," Nana pondered. "I don't know how the girls feel about them. Poppy, how do you feel about marines?"

That wiped the smile from my face. Jack looked away, and I felt the blush begin in my cheeks and creep down to my neck. It was then that my mother spoke up for the first time since we'd ordered dinner.

"When I was a girl," she said, "we called Marines jar-heads. No offense, Jack."

"None taken."

"Now," she continued, "does anyone mind if I finish the General Tso's chicken? It's hard work listening to bullshit. It makes me hungry."

Chapter Twenty-Three

Hunter came home at three o'clock that night, three sheets to the wind. It was no surprise. He'd been displaying all the usual signs of an impending binge. That morning, none of us could do anything right. When my mother failed to laugh at one of his jokes, he said she was a Friday fart at a Saturday market. Nana, he accused, was buzzing around like a fart in a windstorm, and for no reason that I could discern, he called me a dried apple fart. He said we all drove him crazy. I said that was because he was a miserable old fart himself. That did it—I'd summoned the devil. A crack, a sizzle, a whiff of bourbon, and he was off.

I had time to lock Maurice in my bedroom before Hunter stomped back in, a six-pack in one hand and a can of tomato juice in the other. It was going to be a long night. Hunter diluted his beer when he wanted to stay drunk but not pass out.

"He doesn't know shit from Shinola," he muttered. He got a glass from the kitchen and flopped himself onto a dining room chair. "The sorry son of a bitch. Thirty-four thousand goddamn dollars."

Nana sat yawning in the rocking chair. I sat yawning on the sofa. My mother had long since gone to bed. Hunter poured himself a beer and tomato juice and stared at the glass as if it were about to spew forth some oracular wisdom.

"Sorry," he said again. "Sorry son of a bitch."

According to time-honored family practice, it was my job to ask him who the sorry son of a bitch was. Instead, I kept mum. I thought about Susan and my pending escape. She'd assured me that the woman at the Cat's Cradle was just a friend. She seemed pleased that I'd been jealous and was inclined to tease me about it. I didn't mind. I took the reassurance at face value. We had a real relationship, something that would continue into the future, something that would last. We'd be together, no matter what. Hunter had to repeat himself twice more before I finally said, "All right, who in the hell are you talking about?"

He frowned at me and took a sip of his drink. The new drapes on the window behind him were ugly, but they were fireproof. I wondered idly if flame-retardant had to mean beige.

"Larry Wisniewski," he said. "That's who."

"Wisniewski?"

"Wisniewski-ski," he stuttered deliberately. "Another goddamn Polack. We've got a plague of Polacks, don't you know? They fall from the sky like shit-brown rain."

"It's raining shit and Polacks," I agreed, looking at my watch. "You missed dinner with Lucky Eddie and his new squeeze."

"His what?"

"He brought his girlfriend with him. Shirley Chantrell. They met in Parents without Partners."

"Chantrell," he said, as if testing the name for flavor. "Chantrell, hell. Parents without what?"

"Partners. I'm guessing they didn't have a chapter of Parents without Children, so he had to join this other group. Jack said he did it to pick up chicks."

"Chicks," Hunter replied. "More like chicken shits. Ha! You hear that? Chicken shits." He laughed, and unless I laughed too, he was bound to repeat the punch line.

"Ha-ha," I said. "What's the problem with Larry Wisniewski?"

Hunter fixed me with a glassy stare. "He makes six thousand dollars a year more than I do, that's what's wrong. That sorry son of a bitch. Where's Eddie staying with this Parents without Pussy?"

"The Brentwood. How do you know Larry makes more money?"

"Why's he staying at the goddamn Brentwood?"

"Because he can't stay here. How do you know Larry makes more money?"

219

"Fred saw his goddamn paycheck, that's how. I'd sleep in a god-damned ditch before I slept at the fucking Brentwood. There's no telling what's in those sheets."

"How do you know they have sheets?" I didn't bother to ask how Fred had gotten hold of someone else's paycheck. Found it, no doubt. He was probably out trying to cash it.

My grandfather dropped the subject of Lucky Eddie for the time being. "I trained that son of a bitch, Wisniewski-ski. He didn't know his ass from a hole in the ground. I taught him, and they pay him five hundred dollars a month more than they pay me. I've been there forty years, since 1944." He waved four fingers in the air for emphasis. "Since 1944, and they piss in my goddamn face."

I propped my feet up on the glass-topped coffee table and picked a book from my mother's library pile. It was *Rubyfruit Jungle* by Rita Mae Brown. I'd never heard of it.

"Have you talked to Mike about it?" Nana asked.

"That dried up little shit? Hell, no!"

"Mike's your friend," Nana said. "He's always looked out for you."

"Well, not anymore," Hunter replied. "Not anymore. He's been referring his customers to Larry Wisniewski. He tells them Larry's the best goddamn mechanic in Raleigh. Wisniewski-ski. Son of a bitch."

"Why would he do that?"

"Hell if I know."

"Does Wisniewski-ski drink?" I asked.

Hunter held his hand in the shape of a gun. "Bang," he said. "Don't you start with me, goddamn it."

"Have you talked to either of the Bloom boys?" Nana interrupted. "Rob or Fletcher?"

"Fletcher T. Bloom." Hunter held his lips in the O shape. "Fletcher T. Bloom, the Third. The third, the turd. Fletcher T. Bloom, the Turd. He's a turd-tapping son of a bitch. You know that? Just like that other turd-tapping son of a bitch."

I put *Rubyfruit Jungle* back on the book pile. "Which turd-tapping son of a bitch would that be? I'm losing track."

"Your dear sweet daddy, that's who. You just let me know his room number." He made the gun shape with his hand again and took aim. "I'm going to load up my pistol. I'm going to shoot him full of shit and then kill him for stinking." He put his finger gun down and picked up his glass. "You know what's wrong with this world?" he asked, beer and tomato juice slopping out of the glass and cascading over the edge of the table.

I walked over and handed him a napkin. "You've got a drinking problem," I suggested. "What's wrong is that your mouth is open but nothing's going in."

Hunter grinned broadly and dabbed at the tomato juice. "Thank you, honey. Thank you very much. You are perfect, you know that? A perfect goddamn Polack. What's wrong with this world is that Richard Nixon resigned. He shouldn't have done that. Not in a million years."

"For heaven's sake," Nana said. "That happened ten years ago."

Hunter slammed his fist down on the table, shattering the glass. "It doesn't matter when it was! He shouldn't have done it. What I'm trying to tell you is that Nixon didn't do anything wrong. Not like that son of a bitch from Texas—what was his goddamn name?"

"Lyndon Johnson. Look what you've done to the coffee table! Did you cut yourself?"

"Fuck the coffee table! I'm trying to tell you something. That bastard, Lyndon Baines Johnson, he tape-recorded everybody." He waved a hand to include the White House, the Congress, the broken coffee table, and the people in our living room. "He had machines all over the goddamn place. No one gave a damn, but Nixon shit in his white hat, you know why? Because he lied about it. All he had to do was say I'm sorry. Admit it, and say I'm sorry. We would have forgiven him!"

"My coffee table," Nana wailed. "I paid good money for that."

"We would have forgiven Nixon," Hunter said firmly. "I'm sorry. That's all he had to say. That's all you ever have to say. I'm sorry. Dolly," he turned to my grandmother, "I'm sorry. I'm just as sorry as I can be."

"For what?" she said. She looked exhausted, and she was out of cigarettes. For the past ten minutes she'd been tapping her fingers on the arm of her chair.

221

Hunter closed his eyes and stuck his chin out. "For nothing," he said. "Never mind."

"What about my coffee table?"

"Forget the coffee table," I interrupted. "It's toast. Hunter C. Bartholomew, you've got plenty to be sorry for. You can be a pretty sorry son of a bitch when you put your mind to it."

Hunter gazed at me slyly. "I'm not the only one who's sorry. Do you know where your daddy was the night you were born?"

It wasn't a question but a challenge. My father had disappeared the minute my mother went into labor, leaving Hunter and Nana to drive her to the hospital. It was an old scandal that had long since lost its power to shock. It didn't take a rocket scientist to figure out that my father had been less than enthusiastic about parenthood, but Hunter seemed to regard it as proof that no matter what, he was better than Lucky Eddie. He'd driven my mother to the hospital, and he'd waited to get drunk until after he knew my mother and I were okay.

"No," I said, rolling my eyes. "Should I care?"

"I don't give a damn whether you care or not. He didn't show up until the day after you were born, the drunkest son of a bitch you've ever seen. He made your mama get up out of the hospital bed so that he could lie down on it."

"I know all of this," I interrupted. "What's your point?"

"You don't know a goddamn thing. I should've killed the son of a bitch!"

"Hunter!" Nana snapped. "That's enough."

"He was in jail for soliciting!" Hunter cried triumphantly. "Got picked up behind the Church of the Good Shepherd trying to get some hooker to polish his pecker. I had to go and bail him out."

Nana groaned and covered her face with her hands. Hunter reared back in his chair, a nasty self-satisfied grin plastered across his face. He and Nana both seemed to be under the impression that Lucky Eddie's true nature had been a mystery to me, and that this news was a shocking revelation.

I wasn't shocked. My mother had never mentioned it, but I'd long since guessed that there was something more to the story than "Eddie got drunk the night you were born." My mother had never described what it was like to be married to him. She talked about the overdue child support, the lying, and the fights. She didn't talk about their sex life, or Eddie's weirdness, but I knew. In our garage in Michigan were stacks of pornography far more graphic than the copies of *Playboy* Eddie occasionally forgot in the bathroom. Sex was a taboo subject with my mother and with my grandparents as well. It was the unnamed horror. If we had to talk about it at all, we used euphemisms like "ran around" or "acted up." We said Hunter ran around with Tammy Carter, never Hunter had sex with her. We said he acted up. That he fucked a woman younger than his daughter was understood.

I waited, wanting to compose my response perfectly. "And what," I said at last, "does a seventeen-year-old blow job have to do with the many things for which you should be sorry?"

I waited for an explosion that never came. Nana gasped, and Hunter lost his shit-eating grin. He contemplated the broken glass floating in the pool of beer and tomato juice.

"Did you think this would devastate me? Lucky Eddie would screw a snake if someone held it still for him. The fact that he's a bastard doesn't get you off the hook. Just what have you been up to, Hunter? You're never home, you're skipping work. You're falling to pieces. This is rock bottom, and you know it. Mike Sava knows it. Larry Wisniewski knows it. We all know it."

"You're crazy," he muttered. "A crazy, crazy Polack. It's sad to be crazy."

"Tell me about it," I agreed. "It's sad to go from perfect to crazy in less than five minutes. I'm glad to know that at least I'm still a Polack."

"A crazy half-assed Polack."

"A crazy half-assed popeyed Polack. I graduate tomorrow, Hunter, and then I'm moving out. Don't you come to my graduation, though. Stay away. At the moment, I'd rather have Lucky Eddie there than you."

He didn't come. My mother and grandmother came. Mike Sava came with Susan. Lucky Eddie, Shirley, and Jack Leinweber were there.

223

Hunter disappeared for three days, which turned out to be a dress rehearsal for the big vanishing act he pulled two weeks later.

Graduation was held in the Civic Center downtown. I got out of wearing a dress by wearing a pair of shorts under my gown. My legs were tan enough that I could get away with not wearing panty hose. The only down side was that my feet felt damp and sticky in the blue pumps. I couldn't wait for the whole thing to be over so I could get into the normal clothes I'd left in a bag on the back seat of my mother's car.

Nana sat next to Jack, who sat next to my mother. Susan sat bravely between my parents. Mike sat on the other side of Shirley and made polite, one-sided conversation. When the principal called for the students in my row to step forward, I saw Lucky Eddie lean over and whisper something to Susan. I prayed that it wasn't lewd or obscene, but judging from Susan's reaction, I was praying in vain. She edged closer to my mother.

My father had outdone himself in stylish attire. In the three years since I'd last seen him, he'd abandoned the disco look in favor of the urban cowboy. He wore a western-style suit made of gray polyester and a pair of black cowboy boots. His thin dark hair, balding on top, was pulled back into a ponytail, and despite the fact that it was night and we were indoors, he wore a pair of mirrored sunglasses. He didn't look like a motorcycle cop. He looked like someone who'd been busted by the vice squad.

I felt pretty clever about my shorts trick until I stepped onto the stage. A roar went up from the crowd, and, too late, I realized that the floodlights behind the podium were shining through the thin acetate of my gown. Susan, my family, and two thousand other people now knew that I wasn't wearing my navy blue funeral dress. My shorts were so short that they looked like underwear.

My classmates, thank God, assumed it was a deliberate joke. I got several pats on the back and a smile or two from some of the teachers. I thought it was pretty funny myself when I caught sight of Mr. Chisholm. He looked like he was ready to bite off one or two of his remaining fingers.

Abby whispered, "Nice one," when we returned to our row, and then, "They'll probably take your diploma back." Beneath her gown, she was wearing an emerald green dress that fit so well I thought I might have to beat Nick, Joe, and John off with a stick.

"Can I get a ride with you to Kim's party?" she asked.

"Sure. Susan's coming," I added, not looking at her.

"She's here then?"

"Yes. Sitting over there with my mother."

Abby scanned the crowd until she found them. "Get a load of Willie Nelson," she laughed, pointing at my father.

"That's Lucky Eddie."

"No way!"

"Yes way."

She laughed again, adding kindly, "You don't look anything like him."

"Thanks. The milkman's my real father."

Outside, we posed for a million pictures, most of them taken by Kim's parents. They planned to leave for Florida that night in order to absent themselves from Kim's party. As a consequence, Abby and I considered it essential that Vince and Norma not have a chance to talk to our parents. As soon as I spotted Edna Johnson making her way over to us, I gave Abby a poke in the ribs, and she hurried off to intercept her. Lucky Eddie, unfortunately, proved to be more elusive. His thin ponytail bounced in my peripheral vision as Kim and I posed for a shot beneath a banner that said "Everything and More, The Class of '84."

"Frankie!" Eddie held out his arms, leaving me no choice but to hug him. The hug didn't last long. We both pulled away quickly. He smelled like cigarettes and Brut by Fabergé.

Susan stood a few feet behind Eddie, looking uncomfortable. The rest of my family stood behind her. Mike and Jack stared at their shoes, my grandmother smiled happily, and my mother looked as if a change in the wind would crack her face. Thanks to graduation rehearsal, staging, and a host of other cleverly made-up excuses, I'd avoided seeing Eddie at all between dinner at the Hang Chow and graduation itself. Mercifully soon, I'd be taking off for Kim's party. Eddie and Shirley were going back to Detroit tomorrow, leaving Jack with us to be delivered safely to Camp Lejeune. Eddie hadn't mentioned it, but I assumed he and Shirley were flying back. The car Eddie had driven up was supposedly my graduation present. It was a nice present—a new Ford Escort. Perhaps I'd have to drive them to the airport.

My mind wandered over the prospect of owning a car just long enough for Kim DiMarco's father to step forward and introduce himself to Lucky Eddie.

"Vince DiMarco," he said, holding out his hand. "This is my daughter, Kim. She and Poppy are old friends."

Eddie put his mirrored shades up on top of his head and shook Vince's hand. "So this is your daughter," he said, gazing at Kim through red-rimmed eyes. "Very pretty. I see Frankie here has her old man's taste in girlfriends."

Susan blanched. I held my breath. Then I realized that he meant "girl" friend, not "girlfriend." I exhaled. My father looked his age, but he refused to act it. Eddie liked to convey the impression that he was a man on the make. He was quick off the mark with the dreadful, inappropriate, and frequently inaccurate double entendre. If I were looking for something to admire, I might have admired Lucky Eddie's unshakable belief that he was witty, attractive, and charming. Unlike me, he didn't seem to lack self-confidence, and if he insisted on keeping up this new father-daughter relationship, I suspected that he'd soon be asking me to introduce him to my single friends.

Vince DiMarco gazed at him, puzzled. My father must have looked even more like a space alien to the DiMarcos than he did to me. Vince and Norma were dressed like rich tourists in casual linen suits and sandals. They both wore chunky gold rings and leather-banded watches, and they each carried a camera, an expensive thirty-five millimeter with a telephoto lens.

"So," Eddie said, turning to me. "What was that trick with the underwear under the gown? You do it on a bet?"

"Yeah," I said. "That was it. Look, Dad, we've got to go . . ."

"Pretty good joke. Of course, at my graduation . . ."

Oh God, I thought, wait for it. Lucky Eddie had a captive audience.

226

He wouldn't be able to resist the urge to one-up me with a big fat lie. The worst part was that it would be an obvious big fat lie, a stupid whopper, and he'd tell as if it were gospel truth.

"I streaked," he said. "Did it on a dare. Stripped off and ran naked across the stage."

My father had graduated from a Catholic high school in 1961. He was an altar boy. Beatrice and Walter's den was filled with pictures of him in all stages of childhood, infancy, adolescence, and high school graduation. There was a prominent photo of him shaking the priest's hand as he received his diploma. Fully clothed.

"Really. I never heard that one before."

"Can't believe I never told you. They revoked my diploma. Your grandmother had to beg the principal to give it back."

"The priest, you mean. I hope he spoke Polish."

Vince DiMarco had backed away gracefully and begun conversing with my mother and Norma. I couldn't hear what they were saying. Perhaps my mother was telling him to ignore Lucky Eddie, or explaining that he was an escaped mental patient.

My father opened his mouth, whether to argue with me or expand upon his lie, I didn't know and didn't care. "Excuse me," I said, before he could speak. "I need to go over there and talk to some people."

"Poppy," said Mike Sava, enveloping me in a bear hug. He was a large man, six feet tall and about 250 pounds. He'd been a football player in high school and had some of that muscle-gone-to-fat look. He was very much the successful salesman, exuding professional charm. Still, I liked him, even when I suspected, as I did now, that he was making a conscious effort to come across as warm and genuine. He smiled at me brightly with his very white teeth. "Congratulations. High school graduation, a red letter day."

"I didn't expect to see you here, Mike. Thank you for coming."

"Wouldn't have missed it." He slipped an envelope into my hand and winked. "A little something for your college fund. Did your grandfather not make it tonight?"

"No. Something came up."

"I see," he said, and I could tell that he did see.

227

"I'm sorry."

"Not your fault," he replied. He looked at Susan and cleared his throat.

"My cue," Susan said. She laughed easily and handed him a set of car keys. "I told Dad I'd get a ride with you to the party. Is that all right?"

I nodded happily. "I have my mother's chariot for the evening. It's at your disposal."

"Well, that's settled," said Mike. "I'm sorry to watch you graduate and then run, but I've got another engagement. Will you be home tonight, Susan?"

"Probably not." She kissed her father on the cheek. "I'll call you this weekend, though, about that other thing."

"Gotcha," he said. "Good night."

We waved to him as he walked out the door.

"What's that other thing?" I whispered.

"My mother," she said. "Another detox. He's found a place down in Hilton Head, South Carolina. He's taking her there weekend after next. It's a forty-five day treatment, no family contact. She won't like it."

"What if she refuses to go?"

"She can't. This is an ultimatum. Dry out, or else."

"Oh." I wasn't sure what to say, so I said, "What did my father say to you? You know, when they called my row to come up and get our diplomas. I saw him lean over."

"It was nothing."

"You lie. What was it?"

"He said—as your class walked by—he said there were a lot of hot girls out there. He said he wouldn't mind meeting a few."

"Gross but typical. What did you say?"

"I said that one of them was his daughter, and that perhaps he should pay more attention to the solemnity of the occasion."

I laughed. "If we weren't in public, I'd kiss you."

"The Cat's Cradle," she said. "That was public."

I didn't know what coming out was, so I couldn't consider whether

228

or not I was going to do it at that moment on that night in the lobby of the Raleigh Civic Center. We stared at one another, and I felt my breathing grow shallow.

In the next moment, the moment was lost. When I'd walked away to join Mike and Susan, Lucky Eddie had descended on the hapless Kim. Now he said loudly, "Hey, a party. Great idea! Poppy can ride with Shirley and me and show us the way."

I was speechless, so Susan spoke for me.

"Oh, fuck," she said quietly.

And so it was that we wound up sitting in the DiMarco's basement rec room with my father and his girlfriend, listening to a tape of the Doobie Brothers that Eddie insisted on bringing in from the car.

I said, "I wish I were dead."

"Me, too," Susan replied.

"Me, three," added Abby.

Eddie was holding court on the sofa, with the spaced-out Shirley sitting quietly by his side. Kim didn't seem particularly bothered by their presence. She'd discovered Jack Leinweber, and they were ensconced in the far corner, talking intently. John, Joe, and Alan were playing pool. Dave Wilson had brought his younger brother, Tom, and they were taking turns shot-gunning cans of Diet Coke. Nick was stuck on the sofa next to my father, nodding politely like the nice Polish boy he was. There were several other people milling about the room, girls from the volleyball team, friends of Kim's from the neighborhood, and people from high school that I scarcely knew.

Abby, Susan, and I propped up the far wall, as far away from Lucky Eddie as we could get without actually leaving the room—though Abby had suggested that leaving might be the better part of valor.

"Didn't you say someone else from the volleyball team was having a party?"

"Lisa Branch. Two girls from the basketball team are having one as well, but it doesn't matter. We can't leave."

"Why not?" Abby asked.

"Look around." I gestured vaguely at the room in general rather than at my father. I didn't want to draw his attention at all if I could avoid it. "I can't leave him here. God knows what he'll do. I can't stick Kim with that."

"And again I say, why not? She was the idiot who told him about the party."

"She couldn't know that he'd invite himself."

"So now what?"

"We pray for a snarl in that Doobie Brothers tape," Susan suggested. I leaned my head on her shoulder.

Abby reached over and patted me kindly on the leg. "High school graduation," she said. "Glory days."

Eddie was gesturing broadly, describing something to Nick that was apparently enormous. His idiocy, perhaps. He reached into his jacket pocket and pulled out a Ziploc bag.

"Hey," Abby said, tapping me on the arm. "What's he doing?"

From the bag, Eddie extracted the largest joint I'd ever seen, not that my experience was especially broad. My crowd of nerds did little more than drink beer, and precious little of that. I'd never been drunk. I'd never been more than slightly tipsy. My father's joint looked like something Bob Marley might smoke in Rastafarian heaven.

He pulled out a lighter and fired it up. Time seemed to stop.

"Here," he said, passing it to the bemused Nick. "Have a hit."

"Oh, fuck," Abby, Susan, and I said in unison.

Chapter Twenty-Four

My grandfather claimed that he'd never read a book. He read the newspaper but only because he liked the cartoons. He hated Bermuda shorts, Elvis, and men in sandals. He'd grown a mustache once but never a beard. He wouldn't eat tacos. He said they looked like something somebody already ate.

I stepped into the weird hospital elevator with its facing doors and pressed the button for the fourth floor.

He loved Ava Gardner. They shared a birthday, December 24. I sat up late with him one night watching *The Snows of Kilimanjaro*. At the end he said, "I love that movie—except for that goddamn Gregory Pecker."

He played several instruments, the guitar, the harmonica, and that goddamned organ. He could bang out Baptist hymns, Jerry Lee Lewis-style, on the piano. He was always making some kind of noise—he whistled, he jangled the change in his pocket, and he tapped out rhythms on the steering wheel with his wedding ring. He had a wide assortment of annoying habits, cleaning his fingernails with his pocketknife and poking in his ears with his car keys. And, of course, the beer.

I met with Dr. Adkins for five minutes, and I sat with Hunter for another ten. He'd curled up into the fetal position, his hands and feet drawn up like a desiccated mummy's. The white stubble on his face had grown longer. He had his first beard.

Here was a man who was going to disappear from the face of the earth in the next twelve to twenty-four hours. A crazy, alcoholic, bastard of a man who had somehow managed to marry three times, raise a family, and elope in his sixties with a woman in her forties. He'd lived, outrageously, for eighty-two years.

"I love you," I told him. "Goddamn you."

Abby was waiting for me in the hospital lobby. She'd changed into a more subdued color back at the hotel, trading the blue silk blouse for a black turtleneck. She had on black pants and black loafers, and her contact lenses had begun to itch, so she was also wearing her glasses. The overall effect was very Malcolm X.

"How is he?"

"Dying. It all seems so strange. I feel like I should be up there, sitting a vigil. Instead, I'm meeting friends for lunch and dinner. I'm shopping at the flea market and reclining in the Jacuzzi tub at the Velvet Cloak. Nana and my mother, they're in holiday mode. It's like I'm just here for a visit, when I'm here to help my grandfather die."

"You're here to do both," she said. "Visit the living and aid the sick. This is what happens when someone gets old, honey. With your grandfather, it's all about waiting. You don't need to do that waiting here in the hospital. It's better if you don't."

We walked to the car through the cool night air. The breeze felt slightly damp. In the summer there would be no cool nights. Raleigh would turn into a twenty-four-hour-a-day steam bath.

"Thank you," I said.

"For what?"

"For pretending like my family is normal."

"Speaking of which," she said, "are you ready for dinner at the Kanki?"

"Only if burning at the stake is not an option."

Susan and I gave Abby a ride home from the party. We invited her to come with us to Chapel Hill, but she declined. She said she'd told her mother that she was going to spend the night at Kim's. Now she was afraid that Edna would call to check up on her and Nick, or Joe, or someone else who'd taken a hit off of Lucky Eddie's joint would answer the phone.

"If she smells reefer on me, I'm a dead woman," Abby said. "She sniffs me for evidence, reefer, sex . . . she's like a bloodhound."

"It's okay," I assured her. "You don't smell like pot. You smell like Lysol."

"Good. I sprayed the hell out of myself with the bathroom air freshener."

"You're all right. She'll never know."

"I hope not. *You* better hope not. She won't be satisfied just killing *me*."

"Abby, I'm sorry."

"No," she sighed. "Don't be. It's not your fault."

I opened the car door and pushed the lever on the front seat so she could get out. We hesitated for a moment, standing there beneath the broken street lamp in front of her mother's apartment. Susan had left the engine running, and I imagined Edna peering at us through the curtains. Abby must have imagined it too. She glanced quickly at the house and shivered. Then, unexpectedly, she leaned forward and hugged me.

"I love you," she said. "You're my best friend."

"I love you, too. You're still coming to the beach, right?"

"Yeah. I just need to think of something to tell Edna."

"Tell her you're eighteen."

"I might as well tell her to kiss my ass." When I laughed, she said, "Shh. Poppy, will you call me tomorrow?"

"I will. First thing."

"Do it," she said seriously. "Please."

She waved good-bye to Susan and me and let herself in the front door. There were no lights on inside, so I hoped the coast was clear. The drive to Chapel Hill was long and for the most part silent. I was exhausted. Susan was contemplative. Back at her apartment, we undressed and climbed into bed. I held her tightly, my arm around her waist, her back pressed against my chest.

"Poppy," she said. "Do you mind if we just go to sleep?"

"I don't mind. I'm tired."

"Me too. About the beach trip," she began. "We need to talk . . ."

I didn't hear what she said next. I was asleep as soon as my head hit the pillow.

"If my mother refuses to go to Hilton Head, I'll have to go home and help my father. You see that, don't you?"

I did see. I just didn't want to. Susan sat on the bed hugging her knees to her chest. I sat across the room with my back against the door, trying very hard to look cool and aloof rather than immature and sulky.

"Tell me you understand."

"I understand."

"Thanks for saying it like you really mean it," she replied sarcastically. "I don't know why you're being like this. I could come down to the beach a day or two later, as soon as my mother is settled. It's not a big deal."

"I suppose it's not," I admitted, relenting. I could finesse Susan's late arrival with my mother. I could tell her about Hilton Head and that Susan would meet us down there. A day or two unsupervised by our so-called chaperone wasn't the end of the world. My mother would probably be okay with that. Abby and I had been planning to ride with Susan, but I supposed we could ride with Kim and Jack.

What I didn't know how to deal with was the real issue at hand, Susan's physical withdrawal. We'd both been tired the night before, and I'd been content just to sleep. In the morning, however, I thought things would be different. They weren't. First I'd waited, and then I'd asked. The look I received in response told me that I'd stepped across some invisible barrier into forbidden territory. I realized then that Susan had always initiated sexual contact. I'd never asked; I'd only been available. I wanted that to change. I wanted to be an initiator, an equal, not merely on tap.

"I'm sorry," I said. "I didn't mean to be juvenile."

"You weren't."

"Susan . . ."

"What?"

I stood up and walked over to the bed. She remained in the same position, knees still tight against her chest. I held out my hands. After what seemed to me a very long time, she reached up and took them, allowing me to pull her to a standing position. I looked down at her. She refused to make eye contact.

"You're angry."

She shook her head. "I'm not."

"Then what is it?"

"I don't like to argue. And," she looked at me now, "I don't like feeling guilty."

"Did I make you feel guilty?"

"You did," she said. "You do. Sometimes."

"For what?"

"For a lot of things. For not meeting your expectations."

I stepped back. "When have I ever . . ."

"I can tell when you're disappointed," she said. "I can tell when you don't understand, or when you don't want to understand."

"We're not talking about the beach anymore," I said. "Are we?"

"The issues are related."

"My expectations. Should I not have any?"

"It's just . . . sometimes this is too close," she said. "Too confined."

I tried to make a joke out of it. "Is this where you say, 'Don't fence me in,' or something like that?"

"It might be."

The right thing to do would have been to agree, to say that I didn't want anything from her that she didn't want to give. I should have played it cool and asked her to drive me home. I should have been older than seventeen.

Instead, I kissed her. I kissed her until she kissed me back, until she put her arms around my neck and pulled me close, no more interested in letting go of me than I was in letting her feel unconfined. When I pushed her back onto the bed, she went without hesitation. I undressed her quickly and made love to her aggressively, surprised by

235

my own actions and thrilled by her response, which was enthusiastic and voluble.

I'd solved one of my problems. I could initiate. I could push past her resistance and my reticence and take us to a new level of awareness and intimacy. The result was better than gratifying. As I held her afterwards, compliant and clinging, I felt triumphant. She loves me, I thought. More than she knows.

It might have been true. Susan never said that she loved me. She only sighed and smiled and let me believe. It was only later, through trial and error, that I learned to separate sex and love. I got used to the idea that they weren't one and the same. I just never managed to grow callous enough to like that.

My father left the party shortly after midnight. He was completely wasted. Shirley drove him back to the Brentwood in the Ford Escort, and, the next day, they drove my graduation present back to Michigan. Eddie left me a card with a hundred bucks in it. I found it in our mailbox when I came home from Chapel Hill.

"I wasn't really counting on the car," I told Jack. "He lies like a rug."

"Still," Jack said. "If your dad promised . . ."

"He didn't. He told me on the phone that he was going to give me a car. It was just some of that blah-blah-blah he does. I don't think he hears what he's saying half the time, or maybe he does hear it and because the words sound good he says them. They don't have any meaning. I'm surprised that he came to my graduation. I don't know why he bothered."

"Shirley has a daughter the same age as you. Eddie's probably trying to make her think he likes kids."

"So why is he going to Parents without Partners?"

"I know that," he said. "They were talking about it on the way down here. Shirley was a member. He met her somewhere else, and she invited him to join. Man, it was a strange trip riding with them. Too weird. He tells her stuff like, 'I was an assassin for the CIA,' and she goes all gooey-eyed and says, 'Really?'"

"Is she stoned all the time?"

"As near as I can tell. She used to be in some rock band, or hang out with some guys who were. So, can you give me a ride to Kim's house? She's invited me over tonight. We're going to watch videos and stuff."

"Yeah, but I'll have to borrow my grandmother's car. Fuck Lucky Eddie."

I apologized to Abby for calling so late. It was a quarter past nine, and Edna had answered. She was polite, as always, and called Abby to the phone with no trace of irritation in her voice. I knew better, of course. Non-emergency phone calls to the Johnson house were restricted to the hours between eight a.m. and eight p.m.

"She'll give me a lecture on your phone manners," Abby said. "So what? I've heard it before."

"I'm sorry," I said again. "I got back from Chapel Hill late this afternoon, and I had to drive Jack to Kim's house. I'll probably have to pick him up, too. Otherwise, Kim will just keep him there all night, and my mom will have a fit. Two nights in a row is out. It's that curfew thing—while Jack's staying here, it applies to him, too."

"I know. I keep telling my mother that there's nothing I can do after midnight that I can't do before. Maybe she thinks I'm going to turn into a pumpkin."

"Speaking of which," I said, "we may have to ride down to the beach in the Great Pumpkin. Susan might have something she needs to do with her father next Saturday. This is a maybe, not a definite. If she has to do it, she'll join us later, Sunday or Monday."

"Poppy," Abby said, her tone serious, "there's something I want to talk to you about, but I don't want to do it over the phone."

"Do the walls have ears?"

"My mother has ears."

"Do you want me to come get you? We can walk around Shelley Lake and then stop at Kim's to pick up Jack. I'd rather not go over there by myself anyway, if you know what I mean."

"Come get me," she said. "I'll bring a bucket."

"Why?"

"We can fill it with cold lake water. It might come in handy."

"Why do we always end up walking around this lake in the dark?"

"We like the excitement."

Abby tripped over some invisible object on the dark path, and I grabbed her arm to keep her from falling. "I'd like some lights," she said.

"Don't misinterpret this," I replied, "but would you like to hold my hand? I see better in the dark than you do. It must be my magic lemur eye."

"That's a handy disability you got there."

"I know." I squeezed her hand. "And believe me, I work it."

"Knock that off. Are you trying to make a convert?"

"Never. So, what did you want to talk to me about?"

"I need to know if you're going to N. C. State or not. I've listed you as my preferred roommate. Edna thinks it's a done deal."

I believed that, given the chance, I should go to Chapel Hill. I was an English major, and UNC was the premier liberal arts school. I also wanted to be with Susan. The answer seemed clear and yet I hesitated, surprised by how much I didn't want to tell Abby no. "I still haven't heard from the financial aid office," I hedged. "I don't know if I'll be able to afford UNC."

"You have aid from State. You'll get aid from UNC. It's all the same."

"I filed my application late. For some reason, UNC seemed out of reach last fall. Probably because I was doing such crappy work in Calculus. I'm sorry. If I'd filed it sooner, I could tell you for certain . . ."

"I don't want to put pressure on you," she said, "but I want to room with you. I just thought I'd tell you that."

We walked along in silence for several minutes, hand in hand. I could picture rooming with Abby. I was certain we'd be happy living together. She'd be good for my discipline, and I'd be good for her—I stopped, suddenly realizing that I didn't know what I'd be good for.

"Why do you want to room with me?" I asked. "I mean, I know why you'd be great to live with, but I can't think what I'd bring to this equation."

She stopped walking. "Are you serious or are you just fishing?"

"Fishing for what?"

"Compliments. Listen," she said firmly, "because I'm only going to say this once. It'll probably come out all corny, and I hate that, which is why I never want to have to say it again. Okay?"

"Okay," I agreed.

She took a deep breath. "You're smart, you're decent, and you're funny. You're kind, and you're generous. There is no one I like as much as I like you. I like you better than any other person on the planet. I want to room with you because I think it would make us both happy—I know it would make me happy, and I hope it would make you happy. I also think that we could help each other. This is a big deal for me, and it's the same kind of big deal for you. We're the first people in our families to go to college. That scares me. You make me less afraid."

"Wow."

"Speech over. Don't get a big head."

I made a whooshing sound.

"What's that?" she asked.

"That's me, letting the air out. You do know that that's the nicest thing anyone has ever said to me?"

She didn't answer. She said, "I suppose if you go to UNC, you'll live with Susan."

"I don't know. She hasn't asked me."

"She's lucky to have you. There—that's your last compliment of the evening."

"Thanks. Now I'm set for life."

We reached the end of the trail and had to turn back. I waited until we were out from beneath the canopy of trees where the moon cast enough light that I could see her face.

"Give me a week," I said. "Whether I hear from UNC or not, I'll give you a definite answer then. Does that sound reasonable?"

"Yeah."

"And Abby . . ."

"What?"

"Thanks." I hugged her and, because I thought I'd never have the opportunity again, kissed her lightly on the mouth. She held very still for a moment and then kissed me back. We pulled away at the same time, both breathing unsteadily. Abby was the first to speak.

"Well, that's done it," she said, laughing. "Now I'm a great big honking dyke. Edna's going to kill you."

Hunter still hadn't come home. My mother was in favor of calling the police.

"It's been more than forty-eight hours," she said. "We can file a missing person's report. It would serve him right to have the police drag him home."

"No." Nana opened a fresh pack of Virginia Slims, her second of the day. "I don't want the embarrassment. He's off with Fred somewhere. He'll be back."

"Unfortunately," I said.

"You shouldn't provoke him," she told me. "It only makes things worse."

"How do I provoke him?"

"You argue with him. You get him started. You . . ."

"You," my mother interrupted. "Did you get the keys to Cookie's beach house?"

"Yes."

"I'm still not sure that Susan is a suitable chaperone for a mixed party."

"Boys and girls, all together in a beach house, no adults anywhere in sight," Nana clucked. "What will people think? In my day, that sort of thing wasn't done."

"In your day, people wore bathing suits down to their knees."

"We did no such thing," Nana snapped. "We . . ."

"Ya'll stop," my mother said. She eyed me closely. "I trust you,

Poppy. It's the others I worry about. That Kim—she's a little too fast for my taste. Her parents let her run pure wild. No curfews, the house all to herself most of the time."

"It'll be okay," I assured. "Susan will be there."

"Susan's not yet twenty. Is there a phone down there?"

"I think so."

"Phone or not, you are to call home every single night. Get yourself to a pay phone if you have to. I want a full report on the day's shenanigans. You remember—it's not just a question of me trusting you, it's Cookie. You don't want to let him down."

"Be sure to call collect," Nana added. "Don't you run up Cookie's phone bill."

"When have I ever run up anyone's phone bill? That's Hunter's department. Ma, you've met everyone who's going—Abby, Kim, the nerd boys, and Jack. Not exactly a rollicking crowd. Every night, I promise, we will separate into same sex sleeping groups. No co-ed. Cookie says there are five bedrooms. Some of them might even have locks."

"Keep cracking the jokes," she replied, "and you'll find me coming with you. Just like your father. Ha!"

"Not funny," I said. My mother only knew half the story. I'd kept the part about the pot-smoking to myself.

"I know," she went on. "I'm not nearly as much fun as Eddie is. Now remind me, just how long is Jack Leinweber going to be sleeping on our sofa?"

"Until beach week. He has to report at Camp Lejeune on June the 6th."

"Fine," she said. "I'm not his mother, and Jane didn't ask me to baby-sit him—she just seems to have sent him down here for a free vacation. I'm also not Kim DiMarco's mother. If I were, she wouldn't be going to the beach with Jack Leinweber. I'm sure you know that there is something going on there. I'm not asking you to be the nookie police, but I don't want you held responsible should that situation get out of hand. Do you understand?"

"You ought to go with her," Nana said. "Can't you get some time off from the library?"

"No," my mother and I said simultaneously. My no was a little too vehement, so I added, "She doesn't need to do that. We're not animals. This won't be a beach blanket orgy."

"I'm sure it won't," my mother said. "What worries me is what state Hunter will be in after disappearing for three days."

"Mental state or geographical?" I asked.

"It's not funny," Nana said, puffing nervously. "He's missing work. This is the rock bottom they talk about in AA. He's been warned, time and again. There's no telling what he'll do when he comes back. No telling."

"Another reason I'm sorry we've got Jack staying here," my mother observed.

"Don't worry about him," I said. "He grew up next door to Lucky Eddie. He's already seen the worst this family has to offer."

"So when Hunter came home," Abby said, "he brought you a car."

She turned right onto Raleigh Boulevard. We drove for two blocks and then she turned to the left, passing through her old neighborhood. When we were in high school, Raleigh Boulevard was a line of demarcation. It separated a predominantly black neighborhood to the west from a predominantly white one to the east. Though the line had blurred, it had never been erased. Black advancement led sadly but inexorably to white flight. Abby's aunt, Pearl, now lived in one of the eastern houses, sandwiched between two elderly white women who eyed her with suspicion and yet relied on her as heavily as my great-grandmother had.

"He wouldn't say where he'd been. He just showed up, driving that alligator green Pinto. Lucky Eddie didn't come through, so he did. He was like that, Abby—nothing was ever simple. The car was a bribe and it wasn't a bribe. He wanted me to have it. He wanted me to like it. I could never hate him like I did Eddie. My father had no redeeming characteristics. He was all ego. Hunter—Hunter was a martyr to the id."

"You drove that car until graduate school," she said.

"I drove that car for eight years. It didn't die until my first year in the Ph. D. program at Ohio State. It ground to a halt on the freeway just outside of Yellow Springs."

"What were you doing in Yellow Springs?"

"What do you think? Throw a rock in Yellow Springs, hit a lesbian. I thought I might meet a better class of woman if I prowled somewhere other than the Columbus gay bars."

"And did you?"

"I met Leesa. Remember her?"

"Do I ever. Vegan, pagan, insisted you throw out all of your aluminum cookware because she thought it would give her Alzheimer's. I assumed you'd met her in that yoga class you were taking—back when you were pretending to be flexible."

"I am flexible. Sort of. What I learned from my Yellow Springs experience is that there's something to be said for meeting women in bars. If she's drinking straight bourbon and her hand is permanently curved in the shape of a pool cue, she's probably not for you. If you meet a woman while you're both shopping for natural fiber clothing, you think, 'She's okay, she likes cotton.' It's very misleading."

"Instead of exchanging phone numbers," Abby said wryly, "you ought to ask for letters of reference. There's a pattern here, if you would but look."

"I see it all right. I just don't know what to do about it."

"Why don't you think long and hard," she replied. "Ask yourself why it is that all of your relationships come to grief."

"'This grief is crowned with consolation.' *Antony and Cleopatra.*"

"Don't you Shakespeare me. I'm wise to your tricks."

She pulled into the driveway of my grandmother's house and turned off the engine. The yard was immaculate, masking the chaos within. How my mother and Nana could keep the sidewalks edged and the borders trimmed while packing the interior like a pair of wharf rats was a mystery to me.

I hesitated, my hand on the door handle. "I warn you, it's like threading your way through the ruins of Pompeii."

"You've warned me. Now lead the way."

I looked at my watch. "We told them we'd be here at seven. It's

243

now a quarter past. That doesn't matter because they'll still need another forty-five minutes to get ready. We'll have to sit and wait."

"Okay," Abby said, "what's the problem? Do you want me to blow the horn and give them time to take down the Confederate flag?"

"Don't be a jackass. I just . . . I never thanked Hunter for that car, Abby. I just took it. All I said was something rude about it being a death trap. His response was to tell me that all of that stuff about the Pinto being dangerous was horseshit. He said if you drove one car up the ass of any other car, of course it was going to catch fire. We had a fight about a car he gave me. I fought with the man over a present."

"You were angry. He drank too much. You were getting ready to move out. He was getting ready to leave. You were both trying to pull away."

"He did leave. And I left. We pulled away from each other, but all I can remember now is fighting with him. It's the last thing I can remember us doing together. I didn't stop fighting with him until he was too senile and too demented to fight back. There was never any kiss and make up with us. I fought with him the day my mother and I had him involuntarily committed. I fought with him at Jean's wake, for God's sake."

Abby put her hand out and waited.

"No," I said. "I don't want any human contact right now. I want to wallow in guilt and self-pity."

"Too bad. Take my hand." I took her hand. "Now listen to me. A man who was like a father to you—a better father than the rotten one you had, anyway—is dying. He wasn't perfect. He wasn't even close. But when you didn't want to kill him, you loved him. Dying is absolute hell on the living. The feelings you have, they won't stop until you kick the bucket yourself, but they will fade. Over time."

I hesitated. "What are you going to do with Rosalyn's ashes?"

"Hell if I know," she said. "Maybe I'll put them on the fireplace mantle. Maybe I'll sprinkle them on Mount Hood. I might put them in the back of a closet and try to forget about them. They're not Rosalyn. Rosalyn's gone."

244

We sat there and waited. I laced my fingers with hers and she gave me a reassuring squeeze. Finally, I let go and opened the door.

"There's no Confederate flag," I said, "but my grandmother does have a set of Mammy salt and pepper shakers."

"I knew it," she replied.

Chapter Twenty-Five

It was the Friday before we were due to leave for the beach. I was mowing the grass again. In the summer, it had to be mowed at least twice a week, and, if the weather had been particularly humid, three times. I'd finished the back yard and was starting on the front. I began on the outside edge, next to the sidewalk, and worked my way around in decreasing circles, blowing the green onions, dandelions, and grass clippings into the center of the yard. My grandmother's azaleas—pink, red, and white—were the envy of our neighborhood. Our grass was not. The Savas used a lawn service that sprayed a terrifying concoction of chemicals onto their grass every month. It looked great, smooth, uniform, and entirely weed-free, but I wouldn't have walked on it barefoot for any amount of money. Besides, I liked the smell of the onions. Mowing the grass had a cumulative, heady effect, like walking an aromatic labyrinth. I let my mind wander, lulled by the smells and the rhythmic drone of the lawnmower engine.

It was nearly halfway done when I saw Jean. She was down on her hands and knees, poking around at the bottom of one of the juniper bushes that marked the boundary between our yard and her driveway.

"Hi, Jean," I called.

She'd always been Jean to me rather than Mrs. Sava, and even my grandmother didn't consider this a shocking lapse of manners. Mike insisted on being called by his first name as a matter of professional habit—no one wanted to buy a car from someone they called mister—and Cookie Turnipseed was Cookie because he hated formality. I called Jean by her first name because, despite the fact that she was forty-four, she didn't seem old enough to be addressed by anything else. She was perpetually jejune. Sober, she was nervous and scatty. When drunk, she was bumptious.

I liked her anyway. I often found her ingenuous and engaging. She assumed a casual friendship with everyone she met. She hoped you'd like her—she thought you probably would—and she hoped you'd help her. Jean was utterly without shame. She'd ask anyone for anything, a ride home, a kidney, or help tying her shoe. Whatever she asked, she presented it as a reasonable request, and most people seemed to find it hard to refuse her. My mother was one of the few exceptions, but then, my mother had been vaccinated against charm.

I stopped and switched the mower off. "Are you looking for something?"

Jean rocked back on her heels as if the juniper bush had spoken to her. "Oh, honey, I've lost one of my diamond earrings. Mike gave them to me for my fortieth birthday. They were antiques, and I'll just die if I can't find it. Would you help me look?"

I had hoped to finish mowing the grass before the sun reached high noon. It was nearing its apex now. "I'll help," I said. "Must be an epidemic. Hunter lost his Masonic ring a few weeks ago."

"No!" This was delivered in tones of deepest horror, though it didn't escape my notice that the instant I crouched down to look, Jean stood up.

"Don't worry. We found it behind the toilet."

"The bathroom!" she cried. "I didn't even look there."

"When did you first notice it was missing?"

She closed her eyes and thought. The sun was beating down on the top of my head and beads of sweat were rolling down my forehead. Fresh as a daisy, Jean took her time. "Just now," she said. "The phone rang and when I reached up to take my earring out, it was already gone. As soon as I hung up, I looked all around in the house, and then I came out here."

"Okay, where else have you been?"

"Well, I went to the Winn Dixie to buy some steaks for dinner— you don't think it fell out there? Anyone could have picked it up!"

"I don't know. Why don't we retrace your steps?"

"What a good idea!" More thinking. "Okay. I came home and put away the groceries. I pottered around in the kitchen for a while, and then I came out here to get something out of the car, something I'd forgotten. That's when the phone rang. I ran inside to get it and then . . . what was it I forgot out here in the car? I don't believe I got it. That phone distracted me."

I opened the door to her car. "I'm guessing that what you forgot was your pocket book. It's here on the driver's seat. And here's your earring, right beside it."

She flung her arms around my onion-smelling, sweaty, grass-stained self and hugged me as if I'd just saved her life. "Good heavens," she said, drawing back, "you're hotter than a fritter. Come inside right this minute and have a glass of iced tea."

It felt nice to sit in the cool, air-conditioned kitchen, and Jean made good tea. She made it the Southern way, dissolving the sugar in it while it was hot and then diluting the resulting syrup with ice and water. No lemon. I drank two glasses while she moved around the kitchen, pounding steaks with a little metal hammer and mixing up some kind of marinade that took at least a cup of bourbon. Inevitably, she also filled a glass with ice and poured another half-cup of bourbon into it.

"Susan says she's going to the beach with you next week," she said. "That's nice, isn't it?"

I nodded. "Yes, yes it is." She was leaving for the Hilton Head detox the next day, and not a moment too soon. I didn't want to hang around any longer. I finished off my iced tea and stood up.

"Don't go," she said. "I get so bored cooking all by myself. Stay and talk to me. Have some more tea."

"If I drink any more, I'll float away."

She laughed and sipped her bourbon. "It's so nice to have a young person around the house. Susan doesn't have any time for me anymore. She's always busy, always off doing something with somebody. She doesn't come home on the weekends like she used to. I wish I'd had more than one child, I really do. Mike only wanted the one, though. 'Only children have all the advantages,' he said. He's one of six—did you know that? His mother wouldn't stop having them. Just kept on and on until she wore herself out."

"I need to finish mowing the grass, Jean . . ."

"Only children are lonely, don't you think? No one to confide in, no built-in playmates. I was an only child. I had an older brother, but he died in infancy. Polio—this was before the vaccine—if he'd lived, he might have been crippled or in an iron lung. You don't see people in an iron lung anymore, do you? Still, he would have been someone to talk to, someone to share things with. It would have been even better if I'd had a sister. I would have loved a sister."

She sighed and took another drink. I had no intention of keeping Susan's mother company while she got plastered.

"Thanks for the tea. I really have to get going. The sun's already so hot, and the grass . . ."

"It's a dangerous business falling in love with your best friend," she said suddenly.

I stood there, dumbstruck. Condensation from the glass in my hand dripped down my arm. Jean finished her drink and poured another.

"That's not what they tell you," she went on, gesturing emphatically with her drink. "It's supposed to be a good idea. My mother said, 'Marry your best friend, and you'll always be happy.' Mike and I met in college, at Appalachian State. He was getting a business degree, and I was studying to be a schoolteacher. I wanted to teach elementary school. Can you picture that? Me, surrounded by five year-olds."

"Yes," I said, exhaling slowly. "I can picture that."

Jean laughed. "I would have loved it, I think. I love children. Their little sticky hands and faces. Susan was the cutest little thing. You've seen the pictures of her in the hallway? Our hall of fame, Mike calls it. Are you sure you don't want another glass of tea? You're awfully red in the face."

"No, no thank you."

"Well, I'll take your glass, then." She took my glass and put it in the sink. Then she sighed. "Mike. He dotes on Susan. He dotes on me, too." She shook her head. "When I met him, he swept me right off my feet. We spent every waking moment together. I stopped spending time with my girlfriends, quit my sorority and all of my clubs. I put all of my eggs in one basket, and now see what's happened. He's off at work six days a week, sometimes until nine o'clock at night, and here I am. No more children to raise, no grandchildren on the horizon."

"You have your job," I said. "Avon and Cutco."

"Sales." She rolled her eyes and polished off her second drink. "Going into people's houses, abusing their hospitality, and then asking for their money. Can you feature it? When I visit people, I want to *talk* to them."

Hilton Head, I thought. I planned to call Susan that night and warn her. All we needed was Jean disappearing on another wild bender. Then Susan would have to cancel and the beach trip would be off, or, worse yet, my mother would come.

"I'm going to go now," I said. "Thanks again for the tea."

She shook her head sadly. "If the marriage doesn't ruin the friendship, the friendship ruins the marriage. It really does. You cut yourself off from everyone else, and then where are you? Sad and lonely."

"You didn't warn me," Susan said.

"I got distracted. By Hunter. That was the night he came back, bringing me a car. He'd been AWOL for three days, remember? He came sailing home as if he'd just been out to the grocery store, all smiles, and handed me the keys to that Pinto."

"I don't suppose it would have done any good. Nothing I could have done would have stopped her."

"I know. I've been thinking about that a lot lately, you know, the old time machine question. I can't change anyone now, so why do I think I could have changed them then?"

She yawned.

"It's getting late," I said, yawning in response. "I should probably go."

"Don't. You still haven't told me why it was that my going out with

250

Brad again upset you so much. You knew about him—it didn't mean anything."

"I don't suppose it did."

She slid down the couch and sat beside me. When she put her arm around me, I didn't move away. I didn't move at all.

"I wasn't ready to come out," she said softly. "You must understand that. Think of what my father was going through. I didn't want to be something else for him to worry about. I know I didn't express that to you properly. I didn't say the right thing. But we hadn't talked for more than a month."

"Not since the night you left the beach house, after your father called to tell you what had happened."

"I shouldn't have run out like that. I should have stayed to talk to you, to tell you that it didn't matter, that we'd work it out between us."

"But it did matter," I said, pulling away slightly. "Not to me, I've told you—but it mattered a lot to you. I left messages on your answering machine. I wrote to you. I drove over to Chapel Hill and knocked on your door. I made a complete fool out of myself, and when I finally saw you, you were with Brad. You were on your way out. I asked what you were doing and why you were doing it. I was angry."

"That's when I said . . ."

"That your father could only handle one disaster at a time. I was another disaster to you."

She winced. "I don't remember it that way," she said. "I don't mean that you're wrong—I'm sure that's what I said, but I didn't mean to suggest . . . you weren't a disaster to me. Our relationship wasn't a disaster. Never. I meant coming out, telling my father that I was a lesbian. Surely you can see that now. It was a misunderstanding."

"A misunderstanding that's gone on for seventeen years?" I shook my head. "I'm sure you didn't mean to hurt me. We were having problems before all that happened. I didn't see it very clearly at the time. I was walling you in. I was possessive, jealous. I was young. You were looking for a way out, and Hunter and your mother blasted a hole big enough to drive a truck through."

251

"We might have worked it out."

"I was seventeen. You were nineteen. Not good ages for a lifetime commitment."

She sighed. "I've never been good at commitment."

I laughed. "You and me both. Tell me, before you left for Yugoslavia, were you seeing anyone?"

She gazed at me shrewdly and then smiled. "How insightful," she said. "But then you always were. Yes, I was seeing someone. We'd been together for nearly a year. She wanted to move in with me."

"And you didn't want that."

"In the end, no."

"Yugoslavia?"

"It seemed like a good idea at the time. I meant what I said the other night about wanting to do something useful."

"I believe you. Did you love her?"

"Not enough."

"That's always the problem, isn't it?"

She took her arm from behind my back and sat forward. "I think I'm going to put the rest of this wine in the kitchen. If you don't want any more, that is."

"No, I've had enough." She stood up. I reached under the sofa and retrieved my shoes. I was tying them when she came back into the living room.

"Are you okay to drive back to your hotel?"

"No, but that's okay. I'll crash with Nana tonight."

She hesitated. Then she said, "You could stay here."

"No, I couldn't."

"I meant the guest room."

"I know."

She stepped closer and waited. I held out my hands, and she took them. I pulled her to me and embraced her.

"Tell me," she said, leaning back to look at me. "Have *you* ever loved anyone enough to live with them? I mean to really commit."

The answer came easily. "Yes," I said.

"What happened?"

252

"I don't know yet. I haven't asked her."

"You mean there's someone now?"

I nodded dumbly. Susan stepped back. Had I been blind? There had always been someone. I relied on her, I couldn't live without her, I loved her.

"You might have told me," Susan said, a slight sulkiness in her tone.

"I've only just realized," I said. "My god, I'm stupid."

Susan didn't disagree.

"So this was your bedroom," Abby said. "Has it changed much or is it an untouched shrine to your youth?"

"Apart from the fact that someone's taken down all my posters of The Police, it's an untouched shrine, but not to my youth. This is a shrine to my grandmother's optimism. She really believes she'll get around to ironing that pile of clothes. It was there when I first moved here back in 1979." I looked around. "Same bed, same dresser, same carpet. You can see less of all three now, thanks to the assortment of accumulated shit. What the hell is this?" I picked a doll up off the dresser.

"It looks suspiciously like Shirley Temple."

"It has one eye that doesn't quite work. It looks suspiciously like me."

Abby negotiated a path through my grandmother's stacks of *Life* magazine to examine a framed poem. "Hey, what's this? *For Poppy on her Graduation, May 23, 1984. By Myrtle Abernathy Bartholomew.*"

"Oh, for God's sake, please don't read that."

"*When Poppy was born, she was little and sweet, from the top of her head, to her tiny pink feet.*"

"Okay, please don't read it aloud."

"*She soon grew tall, and strong and fair, with Polish cheekbones, and short brown hair.*" She paused to consider my cheekbones. "So far, so good. I suppose those are Polish cheekbones, anyway. *She looked like a countess, from old Warsaw, with a brave Roman nose, and eyebrows like the Shah.* Eyebrows like the Shah?"

"In some universe, Shah rhymes with Warsaw. You have to

253

admit, my eyebrows are rather Shah-esque." I waggled them at her for emphasis.

"More Groucho than Shah. Why is your nose brave?"

"I'm not afraid to stick it into other people's business."

"Ain't that the truth. *She's graduating today, and we feel so proud, we're telling the world, we're shouting out loud!*"

"Oh, the shame."

"Oh, my ass. I think it's nice. Your grandma was proud of you. She wrote you a poem. So it's not your damn Shakespeare, so what? Your family loves you. You have no business complaining."

"No," I agreed. "And yes, they do. However, as long as you're passing out pearls of wisdom, here's one for your treasure trove. Edna loves you, too."

"Right."

"I have proof. Remember when we needed jobs the summer after graduation?"

"Yeah?"

"Edna got us jobs—you and me both. She didn't have to help me. She didn't want to help me. She did it because you asked her."

Abby sat down on the bed and looked under Shirley Temple's skirt. "No underwear," she said. "Perhaps she should change her name to Dolores."

"Perhaps you should stop violating the Littlest Rebel."

I took the doll from her and put it back on the dresser. Across the hall, the bathroom door opened. My mother stood there, holding a curling iron.

"I'm sorry," she said. "I told her at six o'clock to start getting ready, but you know how she is. She stayed in the tub for so long, she nearly melted."

"It's all right," I said. I glanced at my watch. "The Kanki is open for another couple of hours. If we don't make it, we can always go to the Waffle House. They're open all night."

"Yuck." My mother addressed Abby. "She was always a smart ass, you know. Even as a small child."

"I can believe it," Abby replied.

254

"You have the patience of a saint." She closed the bathroom door. I could hear Nana pottering around in the living room. I couldn't tell what she was doing. From the sound of it, she was kicking over the stack of books that still propped up the dining room table.

I picked up a *Life* magazine and sat next to Abby on the bed. "Can I offer you some reading material? This is all about Jackie Kennedy."

"Oh, thank you," she replied. Her stomach growled. "Mind if I just eat this?"

"I warned you."

"I know."

"You *are* a saint."

"Oh no, I'm not. No one's ever written a poem about my nose."

Return of the Jedi was both better and worse than I'd hoped. Better because the special effects were amazing, worse because I was too old for ewoks. Abby and I agreed that whoever had come up with them needed to be strangled.

We sat in the back of the theater, behind the rest of our friends, sharing a giant tub of buttered popcorn and a Pepsi. In front of us, Kim sat huddled up next to John Wilder. Joe and Nick sat on either side of them, and Alan sat next to Nick, casting the occasional baleful look in Kim's direction. Dave and his brother sat down on the front row. They said they were experimenting to see which seats were the best for viewing the forest chase scene. They'd all seen the movie twice before, once on opening night, and then again on the Sunday after we came back from the beach. Two weeks had gone by since then, and this was the first day that Abby had managed to coax me into leaving my house.

Hunter hadn't yet been by to pick up the rest of his things. He and Jean had taken up residence in a trailer in the Stonybrook trailer park. My mother and Nana had driven by late one night to look at it. The lights were on and his van was parked out front, but they didn't see anyone, and they certainly didn't stop.

255

"It's a nice park," my mother said. "Lots of trees and landscaping. It's better than he deserves."

"Did you want him to live in a hovel?"

"Yes," she said. "That's where he belongs, he and that idiot blonde parakeet."

When the credits rolled on *Return of the Jedi*, Abby asked me if I'd found a job for the summer yet. "Are you picking tobacco for that third cousin of yours again?"

"First cousin once removed, and the answer is no. I haven't done that since I was fourteen, and I only did it for a week then. It was hot and it was gross."

"Uh-uh," she said. "Like working at the flea market is better. Why don't you come with me and put in an application at the DMV? Mama says they're hiring temps for the summer. The pay's okay, and it's nice and air-conditioned."

"What would I do?"

"You'd do whatever. Filing, typing, opening boxes of license plates."

"I wouldn't be making the license plates?"

"Prisoners make the license plates, so unless you're incarcerated, no."

The credits ended and the lights went on. Joe Chang turned around in his seat and gave us the thumbs down. "Sappy ending. Gag me."

"'Your father was dead, in a manner of speaking,'" Nick said, his impersonation of Alec Guinness somewhat marred by his Polish accent. "Crappy. Totally unbelievable."

"I liked it," Kim said. "I thought it was sweet."

John nodded in agreement, smiling stupidly at her.

Abby and I laughed. Alan gazed at them mournfully.

"If you think it's stupid," I asked Nick and Joe, "then why have you seen it three times?"

"Cool special effects," Joe said.

"Really cool," Nick agreed.

Before we went to the personnel office at the Division of Motor Vehicles, we stopped by the file room where Abby's mother worked.

We found her sitting in the ninth row of a room full of cabinets. Edna sat in what looked like an old elementary school desk. It was a small chair with a flat top attached to it. She had a long file drawer filled with index cards in front of her and rubber finger cots on the thumb and index finger of her right hand. She looked up without smiling.

"Hi, Mama," Abby said. "We're here to apply for temp jobs."

"We?"

"Poppy gave me a ride. She needs a summer job, too."

"I don't know how many they're hiring."

"Could you show us where we need to go?"

Edna extracted herself from the small chair. She was an attractive woman, not especially tall, but muscular and well built, like Abby.

"Let me tell the boss lady where I'm going," she said. "I'll be right back."

She entered an office a few rows away. There was a hushed conversation and someone said, "Sure. You can use your break time." When she came back, she plucked the rubber finger cots off and laid them next to the file drawer.

Abby and her mother walked side by side down the hall with me bringing up the rear. The less attention I drew to myself, the better. Edna was a broad-shouldered woman, and her hair was short and no nonsense. I knew that she was younger than my own mother by several years. She'd had Abby when she was eighteen, which made her thirty-five or thirty-six. Other than that, I knew very little about her, except that she didn't like white people, particularly me. She and Abby fought constantly, though it was clear that Abby loved her mother, or at least felt a strong sense of obligation to her.

"My mother works hard," she said. "She never buys herself anything."

"Don't you wish she would?"

"All the time."

In the personnel office, Edna spoke to a gray-haired woman in gold-rimmed glasses who, according to her nameplate, was Marcella Rockway.

"This is my daughter that I told you about, Abia."

Marcella nodded. "And you're looking for summer work? Can you type?"

"Yes, ma'am," Abby said. "My friend is looking, too." She turned around and dragged me forward. "She took typing last fall. She can do sixty words a minute."

Edna gave me a brief, curdled look. Then she mastered her features and smiled at Marcella. "Her name is Frances Koslowski."

"But everyone calls me Poppy," I said.

Marcella gave me an imperious nod. "Is that right? And can you type sixty words a minute?"

"I can. So can Abby. She's more accurate than I am, though."

"You're not . . ." she paused. "Can you see out of that eye?"

I nodded. Abby bristled, and I saw Edna put a hand on her arm.

"You'll need to fill out these applications," Marcella said. "You can sit over there and fill them out now, if you like."

Abby and I took the applications and sat down on a short vinyl sofa.

"I've got to get back to the file room," Edna said. "Will you be home for dinner tonight?"

"Yeah," Abby said. "I'll cook, if you like."

"Sounds good." She turned to walk out the door, and then she stopped and looked back over her shoulder. "Goodbye, Poppy. Thanks for giving Abby a ride down here today. I know she appreciates it."

Abby and I looked at one another and, without saying a word, began filling out our applications. Abby listed our high school typing teacher, our principal, and her old shift manager at McDonald's as her references. I listed the typing teacher, Cookie Turnipseed, and Edna Johnson. We both got jobs.

Chapter Twenty-Six

After years of steadfastly refusing to try anything more exotic than Chinese almond chicken, my grandmother had, at the age of seventy-five, discovered the Kanki Japanese Steak House when a Sunday school friend insisted on taking her there for her birthday. There were no tables at the Kanki. Instead, there were chef stations where you sat at a wooden counter, in the middle of which was a stainless steel griddle. A waitress took your order, and, a few minutes later, the chef for your station came out, wheeling a cart filled with kitchen tools. The thrill of the Kanki was watching the chef—usually a man and always Japanese or Japanese-American—prepare your food. Rapid slicing, knife flipping, and intricate juggling of the salt and pepper shakers were all standard features in the chef's floorshow.

I liked the Kanki, though I felt rather ashamed by that. It was hopelessly corny, not truly Japanese cuisine, and yet the chef's knife work was always amazing. Every chef in the place, from the most senior to the ones who were clearly still in training, could clean and butterfly a shrimp in a second, all the while keeping up a steady banter with the customers. Many of them spoke English as a second language. I tried to imagine myself cracking jokes in Japanese while tossing sharp knives into the air.

Nana loved it. She laughed when our chef, whose English seemed limited to the names of ingredients, took a squirt bottle full of oil and made a smiley face on the hot griddle. She laughed even more when he took the spatula and smeared the eyes to make them slanted.

"My God," I whispered to Abby. "It's worse than a minstrel show."

"Enjoy your white privilege," she whispered back. "I think this one's going to have to stick to the visual jokes."

He tossed off four quick shrimp appetizers and flipped them onto our plates.

My mother, who was sitting to Abby's right, leaned over and said, "Forget what I told you about playing with your food. These shrimp are delicious, aren't they? I especially like this ginger sauce."

"What's that?" Nana asked from my left. "I can't hear a thing way down here."

"Why didn't you sit next to Mama?"

"Because you got in the middle," she said. "Did you think I was going to bite your friend?"

Before I could answer, the chef interrupted us.

"Steak?" he asked. "How done?"

Nana and my mother wanted well done. The chef, who had just made a tower out of rings of raw onion, poured a jigger of alcohol into the small hole at the top and set it alight. He offered to cook their steaks on top of this volcano. Abby and I requested rare. He offered us each a slab of raw meat.

"Will the fun never end?" I muttered.

"Relax," Abby said. "There's nothing wrong with being silly every now and again. So it's not Shakespeare. So what? Try to enjoy it anyway."

"You're really on poor old William's case these days, aren't you? I'm sure I could enjoy this if I had a drink. Or two."

"What's that?" Nana asked.

"You need to get the doctor to clean your ears out," my mother observed loudly. "Quit poking in them with a Q-Tip and jamming all the wax down inside." To me she added, "I'd tell you to order yourself a glass of wine, but your grandmother would have a fit. She thinks sniffing the cork will make you an alcoholic."

"You think that, too."

"I do not."

"You don't drink."

"I've never wanted to. That doesn't mean I think *you're* an alcoholic. I've got a little more perspective than some people."

"Thanks. I didn't realize the topic had come up."

She speared a piece of zucchini on the end of her fork. "You know how Nana is. She was bound to say something when you came over from Susan's the other night and said you didn't want to drive back to the hotel."

"Oh, yeah? What?"

"She said she bet it wasn't a case of 'didn't want to.' More like 'couldn't.'"

I looked at Nana. She was on her fifth container of ginger sauce. From the moment the appetizers had dropped onto her plate, she'd been using up sauce faster than the chef could refill it. She poured at least two onto her fried rice.

"I'm not an alcoholic."

"That's what your grandfather always said," she replied.

"I'm not a cannibal, either. That's what Jeffrey Dahmer always said."

I felt Abby squeeze my leg. "You're not an alcoholic," she breathed into my ear. "Remember what I said about trying to have fun?"

"Okay," I said. "Let's go all out."

I asked the chef for a martini and a pair of chopsticks. He gazed at me for a moment, puzzled. With my left-hand, I shook a pretend drink; with my right, I made a pinching motion with my thumb and forefingers. He handed me the chopsticks and signaled to the waitress.

"A dirty martini," I said. "Three olives, please."

After I'd dropped the fourth piece of steak onto the front of my shirt, I began to regret my joie de vivre.

"She was always like that," Nana told Abby. "Contrary as the day is long, and couldn't go five minutes without dropping this or spilling that. When she was a little tiny thing, just learning to walk, I had to follow her all over the house with a broom in one hand and a mop in the other."

"It's true," my mother agreed. "While I was cleaning up the powder she'd spilled in the bathroom, she'd be off in the kitchen, playing in the flour bin. I couldn't keep up with her. None of us could."

"Pure wild," Nana said. "It was because she spent too much time in the playpen. That makes them wild, you know. Caging them in like that."

261

"Nonsense," said my mother. "If it weren't for the playpen, we'd never have had a moment's peace. She'd have gotten into the knives or drunk bleach or who knows what all."

"Hello," I said. "I'm sitting right here."

Abby laughed. "I was a very calm child, or so I'm told. No colic. Slept through the night as soon as I came home from the hospital."

"Wasn't your mother lucky!" Nana exclaimed. "I don't believe we got a wink of sleep until Poppy was two years old. We used to put her in the back of the car and drive all over Raleigh, trying to get her to fall asleep."

My mother picked up the narrative. "And about half the time, she'd wake up just as soon as we pulled into the driveway. Then we'd have to start all over again."

"Do you want to hear more?" I asked Abby. "Or would you like to eat your dinner?"

"I can eat and listen."

"Thanks. You're no help at all."

Nana poked at my steak with her fork. "I don't know how in the world you can eat that so bloody. It would make me pure sick."

"Well, I don't know how you can eat a steak cooked to the consistency of shoe leather. No wonder you have dentures. You wore out your real teeth."

"Sass-box. Goodness—that blood has run all into your fried rice."

"Don't look if it bothers you. You eat your dinner and I'll eat mine. We have different tastes."

"Hmmph." She gave my plate a disgusted look and went back to sawing her own steak. "What do you suppose is happening at the hospital?"

"Nothing, I hope," my mother replied.

"I don't know. The doctor said it could be any time now. He sure looked awful when we went to see him this afternoon. Did you go by, Poppy? Didn't he look awful?"

"He looked like he was dying."

"It's a terrible shame, but I warned him. I always said he'd wind up either dead or crazy."

"We all wind up dead," I pointed out. "That's not really an either/or. The only variable part is the crazy."

"Poppy's grandfather drank himself into Dorothea Dix Hospital," Nana explained to Abby. "He had to be committed."

"The washing machine was talking to him," my mother said. "He blew a hole in it with a shotgun. Neighbors called the police."

"We all tried to tell him," Nana said, "but he would never listen to anyone. I said, 'Hunter, if you keep drinking, you'll wind up dead in a ditch.' But he knew better. He said we were crazy. One time . . ."

"Abby knows all of this, Nana. The only part of my life she's missed was that locked in the playpen bit."

"Don't you wonder if alcoholism is an allergy, like they say? Do you know anything about that, Abby? You're a nurse, aren't you?"

"I don't know anything about it, I'm afraid."

"I think it's a form of narcissism," my mother said. "It's about wanting to be the center of attention. No one could be sick in our house, except him. I remember one time when I had bronchitis. He laid down on the floor next to my bed and wheezed louder than I did. It was ridiculous."

"Have you thought any about the funeral arrangements?" Nana asked. "We could ask my preacher. He's such a nice man."

My mother sighed. "I don't know. I suppose we might could."

"Do we have to talk about this in the Kanki?" I said. Everyone looked at me as if I'd ordered a second martini. "It's just . . . I don't know. He's not dead yet, and here we are." I pointed to the station next to us, where the chef's show had just started. "That guy is balancing an egg on a spatula, and we're talking about Hunter's funeral. And besides, what would your preacher say about him? Hunter never went to church. He said God was a son of a bitch."

"Wash your mouth out with soap," Nana said.

"You know what he thought of God," I continued. "I don't want to hear a sermon from someone who didn't even know him. Who would do the eulogy? What would they say?"

"He liked wine, women, and song?" my mother suggested.

"He liked beer, whores, and the Wurlitzer organ."

"We couldn't say that," my mother agreed. "You can't tell the truth at a funeral."

"Well, we have to do something," Nana said. "He had a lot of friends."

"Most of whom are dead."

"A lot of them are doing just fine. And the people he worked with—they'll be expecting something," she went on. "And his family. Dot and Lucy and Allard . . ."

"Oh, for God's sake, we don't have to have Lucy, do we? And Nancy and Jake and their nasty little weasel children."

"Don't forget Fred," my mother said. "I suppose someone will have to get him out of the nursing home in Selma. Maybe Dot can do that. Or Linda." She giggled. "Definitely Linda, having to show up there and tell everyone that Fred's her uncle."

Abby cleared her throat. "This is none of my business," she said, "but you might want to call a funeral home. They could take care of the arrangements for you. You'd just need to give them a general idea of what you want."

"He wants to be cremated," my mother said. "He left a note somewhere about it. I found it in his papers when we emptied out the trailer. It was in a strong box along with his will."

"Hunter had a will?"

"Yes. He wrote it a few years before he ran off with Jean. I thought he'd probably changed it, but there wasn't anything more recent. He left you and me everything."

"And what about Nana? If they were still married when he wrote it . . ."

"I had everything I wanted," Nana said. "I got the house after the first divorce, and I kept it in my name, even after we remarried."

"I didn't know that. I'll bet he didn't like it."

"He said something to me one time, but I set him straight, and he never said another word about it."

I stared at her in amazement. Nana could be stubborn, but I'd never known her to stand up to my grandfather so firmly that he backed down.

"I had no intention of giving him back his half of the house," she said. "I had to fight for it the first time. He wanted to sell it out from under me and buy something nice for him and that little miss he married. Once bitten, twice shy is what I say. I learned my lesson."

Abby brought us back to the point. "Why don't Poppy and I call around to funeral homes tomorrow morning?"

"Would you?" My mother looked relieved. "That would be so nice of you, Abby. I've been worried about what to do. I just hate this sort of thing."

"We'll take care of it," Abby said. "We'll see what's available and find out what your options are."

"And what it costs," said my mother.

I opened my mouth to say I didn't care what it cost. Abby put her hand on my leg again. She shook her head slightly.

"Of course," she said. "That's certainly important, although since he's being cremated, I don't think it'll be too outrageous."

"He has a five thousand dollar burial policy," my mother said. "That's it. We had to cash out every one of his life insurance policies and use up all but ten thousand dollars of his savings when he went into the nursing home. We had to spend his assets before the government would pay for anything. It doesn't seem right, does it? But I didn't know how to work the system."

Ordinarily, this would be the point where Nana said, "Well, some do. The blacks know how to get all of the money. They know how to work it." I'd heard her say it a dozen times, whenever my mother told the story of having to spend Hunter's savings. It was an automatic response, like the dogs drooling when Pavlov rang his bell. I felt myself tensing up.

"Brace yourself," I whispered to Abby.

Nana pursed her lips. "I wonder what's in this sauce," she said, gazing at the again empty container. "It's a little bit sweet, isn't it? I believe I could drink it with a straw."

ଔ   ଔ   ଔ

Hunter died while we sat in the Kanki Japanese Steak House, watching the chef at the next station flip the egg he'd balanced on his spatula into his hat.

That was my estimate of the time, anyway. When we left the restaurant, my mother suggested we stop by the hospital.

"I have a funny feeling," she said. "I think we'd better check."

We got to the hospital just after ten. One look at the face of the nurse on duty and I knew. Abby knew, too. She reached out and took my hand.

"Are you Mr. Bartholomew's family?" the nurse asked. He was a short, fat man with a neat black goatee.

"Yes," my mother said. "His room is dark and the monitor over the door—you've turned it off."

"I'm sorry," he said. "Mr. Bartholomew died about an hour ago. We called you at home, but there was no answer."

"We went to dinner," my mother said. She shook her head. "What should I do?"

Abby stepped forward. "You should go see him, Ms. Koslowski. All of you, Poppy, Ms. Bartholomew—go be with him. I'll stay here and talk to . . ." She glanced at the nurse's nametag. "Steve. Y'all take as long as you need."

"No. I'll stay with you," I said.

Abby looked at me carefully, assessing. "Okay."

When my mother and Nana had gone in, Abby turned to Steve. "We haven't made any arrangements yet. We're going to call around to funeral homes tomorrow morning. We'll have one of them pick him up as soon as possible."

"Okay," he said, and, to me, "I'm sorry."

"Thanks."

Abby and I stood outside the door. I could hear my mother and Nana inside, talking. I couldn't hear what they were saying.

"Are you sure you don't want to go in?" Abby asked. "You could wait until your mother and grandmother came out and go in by yourself."

"No. I don't want to see him like this."

"Okay."

266

"He'd be pissed that we were at the Kanki."

"From what you've told me, I think he probably would."

"He'd have wanted a death bed vigil. He'd want the world to stop turning."

"It stops turning one person at a time," she said.

"As soon as we've dropped Mama and Nana back at the house, I want to go for a walk. Is that all right with you?"

"Sure. Where would you like to go?"

"Shelley Lake."

She frowned. "It's dark," she said.

"We always walk there in the dark, Abby. It's a tradition."

She sighed resignedly. "Why don't we ask your grandmother if we can borrow a flashlight? I've reached the age now where I'd like to make our traditions a little safer."

Abby had never been enthusiastic about any of my girlfriends. She liked Susan "well enough," as she put it, and one or two others also fell into this category. Most she merely tolerated, and the rest she actively despised. Not that she was ever rude to any of them; she was just rude on the subject of them. She mocked their charms and berated my tastes. She shook her head or rolled her eyes and, invariably, we both agreed that the relationship wasn't serious and that I needed to figure out just what it was that I wanted.

I depended on Abby's disapproval. It ensured that I'd never commit to anyone else. No more Susans, just safe Susan look-alikes. Abby would be the great constant in my life, and I'd be content with that. The only thing that could have come between us was Rosalyn. It never occurred to me that I might come between them, not until my grandfather had to be involuntarily committed to Dorothea Dix Hospital.

Two years after Jean died, he was still living in the trailer they'd shared. Fred had moved into the trailer directly across the road, a rundown silver Airstream that looked like a relic from the Apollo space program. Fred wasn't old enough to retire, but he'd been unable to hang onto his job at Bloom's after Hunter left. He took a series of low-paying jobs—attendant at a car wash, janitor for a company that sold restaurant supplies—and was fired in turn from each and every one. He carried on in this fashion until Miss Agnes died. The family farm was sold and the proceeds were divided more or less evenly among all of her children. Fred took his thirty thousand dollars and disappeared on the bender of a lifetime. By the time Hunter located him two months later, he was down to exactly nine thousand five hundred. Under pressure from my grandfather, he used it to buy the Airstream, and he became the trailer park's maintenance man. He mowed grass, trimmed hedges, and reported park violations to the management, stuff like abandoned cars or residents allowing their dogs to run loose.

It was Fred who called my mother the night Hunter slipped off the deep end. By that time, my grandfather's drinking had gone unchecked for seven years. He and Jean were rarely sober, and once she was gone, the occasions when he was unimpaired disappeared altogether. I stopped checking on him or answering his phone calls. So did my mother. There was no living with what he'd become.

Fred intervened only because my grandfather tried to kill him. The position of trailer park maintenance man didn't pay especially well, so Fred supplemented his income by noticing when residents were absent or inattentive and helping himself to a few of their belongings. He stole the occasional lawnmower or television set and sold it down at the pawn shop. One night, my grandfather caught him out in the shed stealing his lawnmower. Hunter went back inside, loaded up his shotgun, and blew half a dozen holes in Fred's Airstream. He missed Fred, but only just.

The police were called, and they found Hunter sitting in the middle of his living room. He'd drunk two bottles of Aqua Velva aftershave and taken apart a plastic razor, using the blade to slash his wrists. The police called an ambulance, Fred called my mother, and she called me.

I called Abby. She and Rosalyn were moving to Cleveland, Ohio the next day, and I was due to move to Columbus exactly one week after that. When I told her what had happened, she said she'd be right over. We went together to the emergency room. She waited in the lobby while my mother and I consulted with the ER physician. The commitment wasn't an easy process, and Abby decided that she'd stay the extra week and drive up to Ohio with me. She said Rosalyn didn't need her—Case Western was paying for her relocation, and they'd hired professional movers to transport their stuff—and Vivian was planning to drive up with them to see them settled into their new apartment. Rosalyn and Vivian could go, and Abby would stay.

It all made perfect sense. Abby went back to Chapel Hill the next morning to pack a suitcase, and she met me at my apartment that afternoon. As soon as she stepped in the door, I could see she'd been crying.

"What is it?" I said.

"It's nothing. Are you ready? You said you'd meet your mother there at three."

"We've got time. What's the matter?"

I took her suitcase and made her sit down on the couch. She wouldn't tell me what it was for a long time. I had to guess.

"Rosalyn?" I said finally. I'd exhausted all of the obvious choices— death, illness, and catastrophe.

"She has a problem with you," Abby said. "She has a problem with us. She always has. I know, she hides it well, and she likes you, she really does. But . . ." she sighed and looked away. "Rosalyn's not perfect. Sometimes she's jealous."

"Abby . . . why? You love her. She knows that. We've been friends for a long time, but I don't flatter myself. If she gave you an ultimatum, I know who you'd pick. That's how it should be."

"Maybe that's how it should be," she said. "But that's not how it's going to be." She looked up then and her eyes were bright. "She'll never make me choose because I won't stand for it. I won't be controlled, not by anyone. Not because they love me or because I love them. I was my own woman before I met Rosalyn Bodie, and I'm my own woman now."

"I can't do this," I said. "Abby, go back. I can take care of this problem on my own. I shouldn't have called you in the first place. I panicked. A suicide attempt . . ."

"Listen to me." She took my face between her hands and held it

269

firmly. "You should always call me because I always want to be able to call you. I rely on you. You've never let me down. I'm not going to let you down now. Rosalyn has got to understand that this is who I am. If she can't accept that, then she doesn't want me, not the real me. Lovers change. Sometimes, they walk out on you."

"You learned that from me," I observed dryly.

She let go of me and sat back. "I learned that from my aunt Pearl, and Kim DiMarco, and Rosalyn herself. Do you know how many women she's loved and lost? Until I came along, she was worse than you."

"Rosalyn?"

"Rosalyn. It's not that I don't trust her; I do. And I love her. But I need you, too. We'll work it out. It was just an argument, and we've had plenty of those before. Don't look like that—they weren't all about you."

"Thanks. I feel so much better."

"That's nice. You're supposed to be making *me* feel better."

I stood up and held out my hand. "Come on," I said, pulling her up. "We've got half an hour to spare before we have to put my grandfather in the booby hatch. Let's go to the Char-grill. I'll buy you a Hamburger Steak and a strawberry shake."

"Excellent idea, but first, I want to do this." She wrapped her arms around my neck and pulled me close. I held her tightly for a moment, and then we both pulled away.

"What was that for?" I asked.

"It's been about eight years since the last time I hugged you. I thought you were due."

"If you're this stingy with Rosalyn, no wonder she's pissed."

"Asshole," she laughed. "The shit I go through for a damn crazy white girl."

270

Chapter Twenty-Seven

The flashlight Nana loaned us was a tiny penlight she kept in her pocketbook. Every other flashlight in the house—and there were six of them—had dead batteries. It took us half an hour to establish that none of them worked and another fifteen minutes to convince her that I wasn't going to lose her penlight.

She said, "I keep that in my purse in case we get home after dark and someone has unscrewed the porch light."

"Why would anyone unscrew the porch light?"

"Because," she said knowingly. "You don't know what all is out there."

"That is so paranoid."

"You think you know everything, but you don't live here. There are gangs roaming the streets at all hours of the night. Robbers, rapists. A woman just over on Glascock Street had her house broken into not three weeks ago. She was there all by herself and . . ."

I interrupted. "I won't lose your penlight. If I break it, I'll buy you a new one. In fact, as soon as the Wal-Mart opens tomorrow morning, I'll buy you six brand new flashlights. I'll buy you a lifetime's supply of batteries. I'll buy you a burglar alarm and a stun gun. Just let me borrow that damn penlight for tonight."

"I don't know why in the world you want to go to Shelley Lake," she said. "Not in the dark. You don't know who you're going to run up on out there, a killer, maybe—what will you do if you run up on someone like that?"

"I'll throw the penlight at him."

"I don't think that's funny. It's not funny, is it, Barbara? Why don't you talk some sense into these girls? They don't know how dangerous it's gotten here. They live way out there in Oregon . . ."

"We have crime in Portland," I said. "It's a city, not a logging camp."

"Then you ought to know better. Barbara . . ."

"They're grown women," my mother replied. "You've warned them. They're going to do what they want to do. Be careful," she said to me, "and call us when you get back to the hotel. It doesn't matter how late it is. We'll be up."

"You have until exactly one a.m.," my grandmother said. "One minute after that and I'm calling the police."

I kissed her on the cheek. "You do that," I said. I kissed my mother as well. "I'll see you both tomorrow, just as soon as we've made the arrangements. Don't worry about a thing. We'll take care of it."

"Thank you," my mother said. "And thank you, Abby. You don't know how much I appreciate this."

My mother looked tired. So did Nana. Neither of them had cried at the hospital, and I wondered if they'd cry now. My mother perhaps, but only late at night, long after my grandmother had gone to sleep. Nana, probably not. I'd never seen her cry, not when pets died or sad movies came on television. She was a complainer, not a weeper.

I wasn't even sure that this was an occasion for crying. In life, my grandfather had been an emotional black hole. He sucked up anger, and fear, and sadness and channeled them into a swirling vortex, a hurricane wall surrounding a calmer but constant eye of self-pity. And yet I didn't just miss the good man he could sometimes be—a part of me that I didn't like to acknowledge also missed the turmoil and the excitement.

Abby and I said goodnight. Nana yawned. Perhaps she was sorry that the man she'd married twice, the man she'd had a child with, was dead. Maybe she felt old or worried about her own mortality. There was no telling. She might just as well have been thinking about bunions and duct tape.

Ⅎ Ⅎ Ⅎ

We listened to the radio as we drove to the lake. I found an eighties flashback program featuring greatest hits from our college days. I'd never given Abby an answer about rooming with her at N. C. State. At the end of that week, on the day I'd promised to tell her, we left for the beach. Hunter and Jean took off the following Tuesday. Mike called, Susan left, and Jack reported for duty at Camp Lejeune. He went on to fight in the Persian Gulf War. Kim missed her period. I received my financial aid packet from UNC. They offered me full funding. I turned them down.

Abby and I roomed together for the next two years. I met my first post-Susan girlfriend in the fall, a woman who played on the N. C. State volleyball team. Her name was Jimmie. She was six-foot one, the only woman I ever dated who was taller than me. Abby didn't like her, so we met in her room rather than mine. She lived in the international dorm with a roommate from Cyprus, a raucous Greek with wild brown hair. The roommate had very orthodox ideas about what was and was not appropriate behavior, and we shocked her terribly on more than one occasion.

When Abby moved with Rosalyn to Chapel Hill, I was involved with a sorority sister. Leesa with two e's. Leesa had been hammered by God, her mother, and the state of Virginia from the original template of true Southern womanhood. She was a debutante, an equestrian, and she called her father "Daddy." She'd been the N. C. State homecoming queen. Her closet was so wide and deep I didn't think she'd ever find the way out. She did, though—she left me for one of her sorority sisters. They graduated, moved to Atlanta, and had a baby via donor insemination. Leesa sent me Christmas cards every year, always including a copy of the latest family portrait.

Natalie Merchant and 10,000 Maniacs were singing *What's the matter here?* It was a song I'd nearly forgotten, though I'd been a big fan when the album came out. I'd played it over and over, driving Leesa to distraction. She liked country music.

"You remember this album, Abby?"

"Of course. You gave me a tape of it."

"That's right. I suppose if I did that now, I'd be sued for piracy. You know, Napster and all that."

"I don't know," she said. "You forget, I work with human bodies, not computers. The digital age has passed me by. I can surf the web, but that's about it."

She pulled into the gravel parking lot on Millbrook Road. There was a larger, paved parking lot farther along, which constituted the official entrance to Shelley Lake. It led to a dock and a boathouse, where, during the day, you could rent rowboats and paddleboats by the hour. We'd rented a rowboat on many a summer day gone by. Sometimes we came alone, but more often Kim was with us. She always wanted to row until we were just out of sight of the boathouse, and then she'd dive head first into the water. Swimming in Shelley Lake was strictly forbidden. It was actually a small reservoir, home to a few ducks and a copious assortment of water weeds. The risk of drowning seemed slight, though I suppose if she'd gotten tangled up in the weeds, we'd have had the devil's own time pulling her out. Abby didn't learn to swim until college, and I was no Esther Williams.

Abby switched the engine off. "Do you have your penlight ready?"

"No."

"Do you just want to sit here?"

"For a minute."

"Do you want me to turn the radio back on?"

"No. Stop asking questions. I want to talk."

"How can we talk if I can't ask questions?"

"Abby," I warned.

"Sorry. I'm listening."

I found then that I didn't want to talk. I wanted to convey what I thought and felt without saying a word. The sky was clear and the moon, just as bright as two nights before, was hanging heavy and full just above the trees. It seemed to me that it should have been raining. Huge drops should have been beating down on the car's roof and hood, with claps of thunder echoing off in the distance. Abby was afraid of thunderstorms. All I needed was a dramatic flash of lightning, a crack of electricity, and Abby would be out of her seat and into my arms.

Instead, I turned the penlight on and off. I shone it onto the floor, the dashboard, and out the window.

I held it beneath my chin and said, "Boo."

"Boo," Abby replied.

I switched the penlight off. "At home, I have dozens of photographs of myself with Hunter. Especially when I was little, maybe three or four. In all of the pictures, I'm either sitting on his lap or right up next to him. He's always got his arm around me, and we're looking at one another, smiling and laughing."

"You were close."

"In a strange way, I guess we were. For a time. I only have one picture of myself with Lucky Eddie. You've probably seen it. I'm seven or eight, and we're sitting on opposite sides of my grandparents' sofa. I'm staring glumly into the camera and Eddie's looking off in the opposite direction. He's smoking a cigarette, one of those thin, brown things he always smoked. I think they were called More cigarettes. If I ever decide to go in for psychoanalysis, I'm going to take those pictures with me. Pictures don't lie. Not about family dynamics, anyway."

"I only have one picture of me with Edna," Abby said. "The one Vince DiMarco took at high school graduation. He had it blown up into an eight by ten and sent it to her."

"That was nice."

"It was. I think Kim might have arranged it. She was always good about things like that. She organizes all of her photos into scrapbooks. I keep mine in a junk drawer."

"Why do you think Edna never remarried?"

"I don't know. I guess she never met anyone who could compare to my father. She loved him. He was fifteen years older than she was, a real radical. He was a member of the Black Panther Party."

"I didn't know that."

"I don't suppose I ever told you. I don't think about him very often, probably because I never knew him. He wrote poetry, Amiri Baraka sort of stuff. They'd only been married for a year when he died. Six months later my mother had me. It was a good thing I was a girl— the only name they'd discussed was Abia. No boy's names."

"Poor Edna."

"I know. How many men have heart attacks at thirty-four? He died of an aortic rupture. He was really tall and really skinny—I think he might have had Marfan's Syndrome."

"Isn't that genetic?"

"Don't worry," she said. "I don't have it. Look at me. I'm not tall, and I'm certainly not skinny. I probably ought to diet. I've put on twenty pounds in the last five years."

"You don't need to diet. You're just right." I started to run my hands through my hair and then I stopped. That was what Hunter used to do—run his hands through his hair and despair over circumstances that he could have changed if he'd tried.

"You've always been just right," I said. "And I like your hair. It suits you. If it would be okay—if you wouldn't mind—I'd like to go with you sometime when you're having it braided. I want to watch."

She laughed. "You want to sit in a beauty parlor for six hours reading old copies of *Ebony* and *Essence*?"

"Yes."

"Then you definitely need to get out of this car and walk."

She opened her door. Her face was illuminated by the soft yellow glow of the overhead light. She was beautiful, from the arch of her eyebrows to her small round chin. When she smiled, deep dimples appeared in her cheeks.

"Are you coming?" she asked.

I put the penlight in the glove box to stop myself fiddling with it. The moon cast enough light that we didn't need it anyway. I followed Abby up the embankment to the top of the reservoir. There were a few other cars in the parking lot, but there was no one in sight.

"Should have parked around front," Abby said, breathing heavily. "Not so steep."

"A little exercise won't hurt either of us."

"Speak for yourself. It's hurting me plenty. Which way now, left or right?"

To the left was the boathouse, to the right, empty grass fields and then the trees.

"Neither," I said. "This is as good a place as any."

"As good a place as any for what?"

"My speech. You made a speech here to me once. Now I want to make one to you. Do you remember the night we came here and you asked me what I'd decided about N. C. State?"

She turned her head to one side and gazed at me warily. The beads in her hair made a quiet clacking sound. "I remember."

I took a deep breath and launched myself into the void. "I want to live with you, Abby—no, that's not quite right. I want you to live with me. I think my place would be better for Belvedere. I have a bigger back yard."

"You want to be roommates?" she asked, frowning.

"No. Yes. I want to be more than roommates. I want to be more than friends." She opened her mouth to speak. "Wait," I said. "Don't say anything yet. I don't want you to answer until I'm finished."

I took a deep breath. "Abby, if we never have anything more than what we have right now—if all we ever have is this friendship— then that's still better than anything I could ever have with anyone else. I love you. I've loved you for a long, long time. If I'd had any brains at all, I'd have told you that in ninth grade biology class. Maybe we'd be in Atlanta now sending out baby pictures in our Christmas cards."

During the long pause that followed, I gave up and ran my hands through my hair. I was surprised to find that it made me feel a little better, and I wondered for a split second if it had worked that way for Hunter, too. I sat down on a bench and stared out over the lake. After a moment or two, Abby sat down next to me.

She said, "I don't get the Atlanta part."

"Do you get the rest?"

"Yes."

I continued to look at the lake. A path of light from the moon bisected it neatly. It looked as if you ought to be able to walk right across it. I was tempted to try.

"I think you're the biggest thumb-twiddler in the world," she said.

I looked up then. "The biggest what?"

"Thumb-twiddler. Procrastinator. Time waster. You know why you didn't tell me this twenty years ago? Because you prefer to be a victim of circumstances. You think you want certain things to happen, but you're not sure, so you just let the chips fall where they may. Susan happened to you. Leesa happened to you, and the other Lisa, and Tracy, and that damn vegan from Yellow Springs, and . . . God, I can't remember all the rest."

"It's an illustrious list. I gather you don't want to add your name to it."

She shook her head. "Not if this is another one of your idle offers. You're always making idle offers. That's how you've managed to rack up five thousand ex-girlfriends. You ask, just out of curiosity, if they'd like to, you know," she lifted one eyebrow suggestively. "And you're always surprised when they say yes. You're surprised, and then you're stuck. I don't want to be your latest . . . sticky situation."

"Fine, don't be. I don't know why I thought . . ." I stopped. "What if I want to be stuck? Have you ever considered that?"

"No. Do you?"

"Yes."

"Okay, why? Why me? Why now?"

Her tone was belligerent. I was familiar with angry, irritated, and downright snappish, but this was new to me. I found it aggravating, provoking. I stood up, the better to glare down at her. "Why do I want to be stuck? Because, goddamn it, I am stuck. I'm in love with you. Can't you see that? And as for why now, I can only tell you that this didn't happen all of a sudden. I didn't wake up this morning and think, 'I'll brush my teeth and then I'll fall in love with Abby.' I've been getting more and more stuck as each year has passed. This feeling—it's always been there, constant, reliable, and comfortable. That's why I didn't notice it. You don't notice the things you depend on. Your heart, your lungs, your . . . your . . ."

"Your uterus?" she suggested.

"Your uterus. Who the hell ever thinks about her uterus? But without it, no children. No monthly reminder that you could, if you wanted to, have a baby. You don't think about anything important until it all gets shaken up."

"And what about Susan? Three days ago . . ."

"Three days ago I thought I might find it painful to see her again. And guess what? It was. But I've learned something. I won't love Susan Sava until the day I die. I don't want to—she's not worth it. You are."

She didn't miss a beat. "Your speech was better than mine," she said, "all those years ago. Although mine was a lot shorter."

The belligerent tone was gone, and in its place was calm assurance. I liked this even less. I wanted to shake her, shake her and then throw her into the lake. I sat back down, defeated.

I said, "How can you just sit there like you're attending a second grade piano recital? You're polite, but you're bored. You're waiting for it all to be over."

"Is it over?"

"Yes."

"I think," she said, moving close enough to put her arm around me, "that that was a very brave speech. Especially for you. I admire your courage."

"Gee, thanks. I feel like an idiot. I've been yelling for the past five minutes." I leaned forward. Her hand, which had been squeezing my shoulder, dropped to the small of my back. "I want to throw you into the lake."

"Don't. You'll only have to fish me back out."

"I hate it when you're like this."

"Like what?"

"Calm. Cool. Collected."

"I can afford to be calm," she replied. "I know something that you don't."

"Oh, yeah. What's that?"

"I love you, too." She tugged on my shirt. "Come on, sit up. I can't talk to your back."

I sat up. I didn't want to look at her, and I didn't want to cry, so I closed my eyes.

"No," she said, "that won't do. You have to look at me. Can you do that? Good. Do you know what funeral sex is?"

"What?"

"Sometimes, when someone close to you dies, you feel the need to reaffirm the fact that you're still alive. You have sex with someone."

"Oh, for God's sake. I don't want to have funeral sex."

"I did," she said. "After Rosalyn died. I met a woman in a bar, and I went home with her. I'd never done anything like that in my entire life. When it was over, I wished I were dead."

"Abby." I reached out to touch her shoulder, but she leaned away.

"No," she said. "Not yet. Please. I'm telling you this so that you'll understand. I still feel guilty. I feel, right now, like I'm cheating on Rosalyn. I don't know if I'll ever get over that. As much as I love you, I still love her, too. I always will. She wasn't perfect, God knows, but she was a part of me."

"I understand."

"No, you don't. Honey, I want to cheat on Rosalyn. With you. Tonight."

"With me," I repeated slowly. "Tonight. You mean you want to have sex?"

"Yes, if we can figure out who kisses who first."

"What about feeling guilty?"

"I can live with it if you can," she replied. "I just wanted you to know that it's there, and that it might always be there. Rosalyn looms pretty large, Poppy. Just like she did in life."

I took her by the hands and helped her to her feet. "Thanks for the warning, but I've made my decision. It's you, me, and Rosalyn. I just hope she doesn't hog the covers."

"What about our other problem?"

"The who kisses who first thing? It's not a problem."

Before she had time to panic or object, I kissed her. I caught her off balance and held her there, with my arms wrapped tightly around her waist. When she reached up and put her arms around my neck, it felt like a triumph. I had no illusions about making her forget Rosalyn. I was content to live with Abby's memories just the same as I lived with my own, but I'd be damned if I'd let them occupy the space between us. In that intense moment of physical connection, as Abby tangled her fingers in my hair and kissed me back with a rare passion, I knew that we could push Rosalyn and Susan and everyone else into some far corner, and even if we couldn't keep them there forever, it would be enough for us to go on.

Several minutes later, giddy and breathless, I asked if she was ready to drive us back to the hotel.

"Yes," she said.

"Can you drive quickly?"

"I can get a speeding ticket."

I glanced at the illuminated dial of my watch. "I don't care about the speeding ticket. Put your foot down."

She laughed. "You'd think we'd never done this before."

"*We* haven't, but that's not what I'm worried about. We've got exactly fifteen minutes before my grandmother calls the police. Unless you'd care to be interrupted by Raleigh's finest, we'd better get back to the Velvet Cloak."

Chapter Twenty-Eight

There are disadvantages to making love with your best friend, especially if she's a nurse and you're recovering from surgery. Once you've overcome the fear of experiencing the familiar in a new context, and the potential embarrassment should you get it all horribly wrong, she still might stop right in the middle of things and examine your hysterectomy scar.

Abby traced her index finger over the skin just beneath my incision. "It looks better," she said. "The swelling's gone down."

I raised myself up on my elbows and glared down at her. "Just for your future reference, that's a real mood breaker."

"Sorry. Want me to start over?"

"No. Now I feel like you're reading from a manual. Begin with the breasts and then work your way down past the navel, being sure to stop . . ."

"At the five-inch long incision in your lover's abdomen." She laughed. "Okay, I apologize for the clinical interruption, but listen— you need to relax. You're so tense I could bounce a quarter off of your stomach."

"And how do you propose I relax? That damned surgeon . . ."

"That damned surgeon what?"

"She cut out something I might actually need."

"Go on."

I laid back down and covered my eyes with my hands. "My cervix. She took my cervix. It was attached to my uterus."

"I know what the cervix is," she replied. "Why would you need it?"

"Because. She explained to me at great length that it was . . . that it might be . . . goddamn it, for some women, the cervix is part of the sexual response. At a certain pivotal moment, it clamps down. It's . . . it might be important. I don't know."

"Okay," Abby prompted, "and now you're afraid that you . . ."

I stared up at the ceiling. She resumed her tracing of the skin beneath my incision, slowly sweeping the tips of her fingers from one side of my abdomen to the other. The sensation this generated was on the verge of being ticklish.

"I'm afraid that nothing will work as well as it used to. I'm afraid that I won't be able to, you know, and that . . . oh, hell, I'm afraid that it's like Frankenstein's monster in there. A jagged seam, and pieces missing, and God knows what all."

She smoothed the skin beneath my navel and then kissed it. "Can you feel that?"

"Of course."

She moved lower and kissed me again. "How about that?"

"Uh huh." I shifted on the bed, allowing her to slip a hand beneath my hips.

"And that?"

My tongue was suddenly stuck to the roof of my mouth. "I . . . wow."

"I don't think we have a problem," she said.

A flashing light in the dark room woke me. Abby was sitting up with her back propped against the pillows, watching television with the sound off.

"What time is it?"

"I'm sorry," she said. "I didn't mean to wake you. It's a quarter to four."

I sat up. "Insomnia?"

"Sort of."

"Freaked out?"

"A little."

I yawned and squinted at the TV. "Anything on worth watching?"

"No."

The sheet was tucked up under her arms, covering her chest. I reached between her breasts and tugged on the fabric, untucking it. She let the sheet fall to her lap.

"Want to do it again?"

"Definitely."

Hunter had finally passed out. He was lying on his back in the middle of the living room floor, snoring loudly. It was long past midnight, and Nana and I were both too tired to sleep. We were watching a western on television, something featuring a very young John Wayne.

"He was kind of handsome, wasn't he?"

"I suppose so," Nana said. "I always preferred William Holden."

"They're both drunks."

"They might be," she agreed.

"They both look like drunks, anyway. Do you think we ought to cover Hunter with a blanket? We don't want him to get cold and wake up."

"He's going to have a terrible backache," she said, "sleeping on that hard floor."

"Serves him right," I replied. "Look at him—mouth hanging open, snoring like a buzz saw. Why'd you ever marry him?"

"I don't know. Crazy, I guess."

"And not once but twice." I shook my head. "I know he was good-looking once upon a time. I've seen the pictures."

"Pretty is as pretty does," she said.

John Wayne walked into a bar. "Want a drink?" one of the patrons asked.

Hunter sat bolt upright. "What's that?"

"For goodness sake," my grandmother said. "That was someone talking on the television. Lie back down and go to sleep."

As soon as he was settled again, I took the afghan off the sofa and covered him up. I had to resist the urge to kick him. As I sat back down, I caught Nana's eye. She put her hand over her mouth and began laughing. Soon, we were both rocking back and forth, the tears rolling down our faces, laughing until it hurt.

While Abby took a shower, I found a funeral home in the telephone book. My mother would have shopped around. I just wanted to get it over with. I called, made the arrangements for my grandfather to be cremated, and paid for the whole thing on my credit card. Apart from the cost, which was astronomical, it was all very easy. We just needed to stop by to sign the paperwork, and they'd send an ambulance to pick up the body. The funeral would take place in two days' time. I said I'd drop off the obituary just as soon as I'd written it and that I'd let them know what we wanted by way of a service. We might have to call upon Nana's preacher after all.

"Would you like to purchase a cemetery plot?" the director asked. He had a pleasant voice, light and casual and not at all sepulchral. I don't know what I'd been expecting. Boris Karloff, maybe.

"Why would I need a cemetery plot?"

"Some people bury the ashes," he said.

"Why?"

"To have a place to visit on the deceased's birthday or Memorial Day."

"If you're going to do that, why bother to cremate? No, I think we'll keep the ashes. We can put them in an urn or something. Keep them up on the mantelpiece. To tell you the truth, it'll be nice to have him at home for a change."

He discreetly ignored this last remark. "We have a very nice selection of urns here. When you come in to sign the paperwork, perhaps you'd like to look . . ."

"Perhaps so," I said. I looked at my watch. It was just past eight. "We'll stop by around eleven. Should I call the hospital and tell them you're coming?"

"No," he said. "We'll do that. We'll take care of everything."

"Thank you."

"You're very welcome."

I hung up the phone. "I'll just bet," I said, putting my credit card back into my wallet. Abby came out of the bathroom, a white towel wrapped around her body.

"Who was that?" she asked.

"The Tyson-Brewer Funeral Home. I've just arranged to have Hunter cremated. The funeral will take place day after tomorrow. We can go home after that."

She sat down on the edge of the bed. "Some women might have called room service. Ordered breakfast for two with a bottle of champagne and a dozen red roses on a silver tray."

"If you're hungry, we're only two blocks from the IHOP."

"The International House of Pancakes. You are romance incarnate."

"I know." I sat down next to her. "The funeral director asked if I wanted to bury the ashes. I suppose then he could gouge out the cost of a tombstone."

"What are you going to do with them?"

"If my mother doesn't want them, I don't know. Take them back to Portland, I guess."

"You realize," she said, leaning back and resting on her hands, "that we'll be flying home with two dead bodies?"

"I hadn't thought of that." I looked at her closely. She'd headed off for the shower as soon as she'd woken up, so I hadn't had a chance yet to examine her for signs of dismay or regret. "How are you this morning?"

"Pretty damn good," she said. "How about you?"

"Excellent. Never been better, in fact."

"Really? I'll take that as a compliment."

"I meant it as one."

"You have a lot of technique," she said. "A lot of . . . skill."

"Honed through years of experience. I see where this is heading. Yes, I have gone out with a lot of women. I have not been chaste. I'm sorry, but . . ."

She put her hand under my chin and closed my mouth. "I don't care about any of that except insofar as it affects us. If we can't make this work, Poppy, I don't think either of us will ever get over it. I know I won't."

"Me either. I don't know if that's a comfort to you or not." I laid back on the bed and pulled Abby back with me. "If you're wondering what will happen should my wandering eye start wandering again, I can only tell you that it won't. I don't leave women; they leave me. Well, some of them stalk me, but you know what I mean. I will never cheat on you. Never."

"I know you won't, but if you get bored or restless . . ."

"Honey, if I was going to get bored or restless with you, I'd have done it a long time ago. I've never lost interest in you."

"You had a lot of outside entertainment," she remarked wryly.

I sang, *"But I'm always true to you, darling, in my fashion; yes I'm always true to you, darling, in my way."*

"That's not Shakespeare."

I rolled over onto my side, facing her. "No, it's Cole Porter. *Kiss Me Kate.* Do you really need that towel?"

"Listen, just because I said you were good at sex—really good—that doesn't mean that you can derail the conversation by propositioning me whenever the going gets tough. Now why did you take my towel? It's cold in here."

"So I see. *Kiss Me Kate* is based on a Shakespeare play. *The Taming of the Shrew.*"

"I'm insulted."

"Don't be." I kissed her. "I love you. I can't promise it'll always be smooth sailing. We might argue."

"I expect we will. Would you . . .?"

"Of course. If you'll lift up for just a moment, I'll toss this wet towel onto the floor. There, much better. What will we argue about?"

"Your family," she said. "My mother. This part is turning out to be less awkward than I thought it would be."

"I'm glad to hear it," I said. She moved beneath me, pressing herself against my knee. I pulled my T-shirt off and tossed it onto the floor next to the towel. "I think it's working out very well."

"I won't want to go back to work."

"Don't. You can stay at home. Be a kept woman."

"Um," she said, burying her face in the space between my neck and shoulder. "A kept woman. Edna's going to kill you."

We picked up my mother and Nana before going to the funeral home. Nana had already been on the phone to her minister, the Reverend Dale Dwighty, and he'd agreed to deliver a few remarks suitable to the occasion.

"Brief remarks," my mother said. "Or so we hope."

"We should pick out a Psalm for him to read," Nana said. "I was thinking we might use the twenty-third."

"How does that one go?"

I said, *"The Lord is my shepherd; I shall not want. He maketh me to lie down in green pastures; he leadeth me beside the still waters. He restoreth my soul; he leadeth me in the paths of righteousness for his name's sake."*

Everyone stared at me.

"How in the world do you know that?" said my grandmother. "You don't go to church."

"No, but I did go to graduate school. Just when was Hunter ever led down the path of righteousness for anyone's sake? I think a better bet would be Psalm 102. *Hear my prayer, O Lord, and let my cry come unto thee. Hide not thy face from me in the day when I am in trouble; incline thine ear unto me. In the day when I call answer me speedily.'* That seems more suitable. He was fond of calling and crying and getting in trouble."

"Sounds good to me," said my mother. "Let's go with it."

The funeral home was on New Bern Avenue, halfway between downtown and the beltline and less than a mile from the hospital. It was a single-story brick building that looked as if at some time it might have been a private home. The interior was quiet and dim, and the director, William Tyson the Third—the Turd, I thought—looked exactly like his voice. He was a small blonde man in a lightweight wool suit, gray rather than black, and he spoke softly but audibly. My mother signed the paperwork, I signed the credit card receipt, and Mr. Tyson assured us that we were in good hands. Soon, we were stepping back out into the afternoon sunshine.

"I'll pay you back just as soon as I sort out his insurance," my mother said.

"There's no rush. I don't mind racking up a little finance charge."

"What about the ashes?" my grandmother asked. "Where will you sprinkle him?"

"I was thinking either Miss Agnes' pond or the parking lot of the Jones Street Tavern."

She punched me on the arm. Abby laughed.

"It's good of you to take them," my mother said. "I wouldn't know what to do with them."

"I'll find someplace nice," I assured her. I glanced at Abby. "I expect we'll be visiting some suitable locations in the next few months. Maybe we'll take a drive down the Pacific Coast Highway."

"Oh, he'd love that," Nana said. "He loved the ocean. Are y'all hungry? There's a new seafood place out at the Tower Shopping Center. It's not very expensive, and they give you a pure platter."

Vivian Bodie owned a café and gourmet grocery store in Durham. It was in the oldest part of downtown in a restored tobacco warehouse, a rustic brick building with uneven wide-board floors and tall arched windows. The café, which was in the front of the store, spilled out onto a covered porch, and on warm sunny days, diners crowded around the wrought iron tables and ate North Carolina haute cuisine. Fresh butterbeans, fried okra, field peas with snaps, and a wide variety of dishes featuring, seasoned with, and celebrating pork fat. Vivian had published a cookbook with a Durham press and acquired a devoted following among the local gourmands and gastronomes.

I'd met her several times before, first when I was living with Rosalyn and Abby, and later, in Ohio, when Rosalyn was dying. Vivian was younger than her sister, only a year or two older than Abby and me, and the family resemblance was slight. Vivian was slender where Rosalyn had been stout. Her features were more delicate, and she lacked Rosalyn's ability to glower impressively. She was, however, just as imposing a presence as her late sister. Neither of them knew how to whisper. When they tried, their voices just carried further.

Vivian sat down with us now at one of the outdoor tables. She was wearing a pair of blue-and-white checked trousers and a white chef's jacket with her name embroidered in blue over the left breast. I liked Vivian, just as I'd liked Rosalyn, but I regarded this visit as the first official test of my relationship with Abby.

I sipped a cup of coffee with chicory. "You know, as long as I've been in Portland now drinking Starbuck's, I still prefer my coffee this way."

"You want something to go with that?" Vivian asked. "How about a sandwich, a black forest ham on focaccia with roasted red peppers and fresh mozzarella? I serve that with a spicy mayonnaise that will knock you out."

"No, thank you."

"Brunswick stew with cornbread?"

"I don't need a thing, Vivian. This coffee is perfect."

She shook her head and said to Abby, "She's just as damn skinny as you said. Is she anorexic? When did she stop eating?"

"I've done nothing but eat since we got to Raleigh, and I am far from anorexic. My clothes are loose because I recently had some surgery."

"Hmm," she said skeptically. "You can at least eat some banana pudding. I bake my own vanilla wafers, and the custard is made with organic cream and bourbon vanilla. It's delicious. I know Abby won't say no."

"It's no use saying no," Abby replied. "Not that I want to. And you could use a few helpings," she said to me. "I like a woman with a little more meat on her."

I waited for a reaction from Vivian. She smiled and raised her hand, and two seconds later, a waiter came bustling out. "Two banana puddings and some more coffee. And tell Ernesto to step out of the kitchen and come visit with us for a minute. Sarah can take over."

"Who's Ernesto?" I asked.

Vivian laughed. "Abby didn't tell you? Ernesto is my delight and my mama's shame. Isn't that right, honey?"

She turned to address a short fat man with shiny pink cheeks and curly black hair, who looked for all the world like a fully grown Kewpie doll. He wiped his hands on a towel tucked into the front of his apron and sat down heavily in the chair next to Vivian.

He shrugged. "Vivian's mama. She don't like Italians." He had an accent as thick as Bronislawa's and Wojcek's. "What can I do?"

"Not a thing in the world," Vivian said. "Honey, this is Poppy Koslowski, Abby's friend."

"Hello. Ernesto Moretti." He held out a pudgy hand for me to shake. "Poppy—it's a funny name."

"It's short for Popeye, I'm afraid." I pointed to my eye. "For obvious reasons."

"Oh, a nickname. I get it." He smiled broadly, an expression that utterly transformed his face. It was the happiest expression I'd ever seen on another human being. His teeth were so straight and white that they looked almost unreal against the red of his lips and the black of his mustache. I smiled back at him.

"Not just a friend," Abby said quietly. "Not anymore."

Ernesto turned his beaming countenance upon her. "What do you say?"

"Yes," echoed Vivian. "What do you say?"

"We are not just friends."

"Hmm," said Vivian. "I hate to say I told you so, but I told you so."

"Told you what?" I asked Abby.

"Nothing."

Vivian laughed. "What's your favorite color, Poppy?"

"Blue," I said, puzzled. "Why do you ask?"

"Uh-huh. And what color are the beads in this sister's hair?"

"Shut up, Vivian."

"And what color was that silk blouse? We shopped all over the city of Durham for that thing. Teal would not do. Neither would sky blue. It had to be that particular shade of bright, primary blue. Someone," she paused significantly, "was trying to send you a psychic message because she couldn't bring herself to be direct."

"It worked," Abby said shortly. "Let's leave it at that."

"I hadn't known Ernesto six months when he moved in with me," Vivian went on. "Life is short. I told her, there's no point in wasting time. You can't sit around waiting on other people. You've got to take the tiger by the tail."

I turned to Abby. "And I'm a thumb-twiddler? What a nerve. You've got . . ."

"Banana pudding," Abby interrupted. "And look, you've got some, too."

The waiter set plates down in front of me, Abby, and Vivian. He glanced at Ernesto, who shook his head.

"I have to cook," Ernesto said, standing up. He shook my hand again and blew a kiss at Abby. Vivian he kissed on the mouth. "You ladies must go on with your argue alone. Arrivederci."

Vivian kissed two fingers and waved them at him. "Ciao, honey. I need to take these girls by the house, but I won't be gone more than half an hour."

"Take the time," he said. "And enjoy the pudding."

"Isn't he adorable?" Vivian's whisper was loud enough to carry past Ernesto's retreating back and on into the café's kitchen. "I could eat him up with a spoon. Mama's beginning to warm to him, although it'll be a long time before she lets on that she likes him." She fixed Abby with a significant stare. "Have you told Edna?"

"More or less."

"That's news to me," I said. "When?"

"Oh, for God's sake." Abby rolled her eyes. "What do you think Edna and I were fighting about the other day? I told you I said something she didn't like."

"Yeah, and as I recall, I asked you what it was. You wouldn't tell me. You just gave me some vague answer."

"I said I told her the truth, and so I did. Now eat your banana pudding. You're going to need some ballast for that swollen ego. Thank you," she said to Vivian. "You had to talk."

"Never mind that," Vivian said. She pointed at us with her dessert spoon. "I'm happy for you, and I'll tell you something—Rosalyn would be happy, too. She loved you, Abby. She would never have wanted you to spend the rest of your life alone."

"I know that," Abby said quietly.

292

"Good. Now is that or is that not the most delicious banana pudding you have ever eaten in your life? Ernesto says it's better than sex. If I had any sense, I'd slap him for that."

On the way back to Raleigh, I asked Abby why Vivian's mother didn't like Ernesto. "Is it because he's white?"

"No," she said. "It really is because he's Italian. Mrs. Bodie's older brother was killed in Naples at the end of World War II. The fighting was over. He was just there visiting, killed by a gang of Italian boys who robbed the corpse."

"A little rough on poor Ernesto. Are you going to tell me what you said to your mother?"

"Why should I? Just how many more declarations of my devotion do you want?"

"Prior to this past couple of days, the last time you said you loved me was 1984. Sixteen years ago. You've got to make up for a lot of lost time."

"I love you," she said. "Now don't expect me to say it again until the year 2016."

"And if anything changes?"

"You'll be the first to know."

Chapter Twenty-Nine

My grandfather's attempt at suicide didn't amount to much. He made a few experimental cuts on his wrists with the razor blade, all very shallow and superficial. At the hospital they dressed them with antibiotic cream and Band-aids. It was enough, however, to have him involuntarily committed. I thought of that day as the beginning of the end. He was admitted to Dorothea Dix Hospital for a week's observation and then spent another two weeks there while we looked for a nursing home.

The doctors put him on Thorazine and an anti-psychotic, and he stayed on a combination of mood-altering drugs for the rest of his life. He lost the ability to carry on a coherent conversation. He shuffled. He threw away his glasses and his false teeth, and then he threw away their replacements.

Drinking the Aqua Velva was a little more problematic than Hunter's efforts with the razor blade. He was obliged to eat a charcoal compound to absorb the alcohol. The emergency room doctor informed us that it would be expelled in a few days time in the form of a very painful bowel movement.

"Think of the worst constipation you've ever had," he said. "This'll be a little worse than that."

"Damn him," my mother replied. "I hope he shits a brick."

"As for man, his days are as grass. As a flower of the field, so he flourisheth. For the wind passeth over it, and it is gone; and the place thereof shall know it no more."

We were deep into the 103rd Psalm. Nana's preacher, it turned out, had a mind of his own. Though we had requested no sermon, he'd given us one anyway. He'd begun with a passage from the first book of Samuel. *The Lord maketh poor, and maketh rich: he bringeth low, and lifteth up.* When he got to the part where the Lord lifteth up the beggar from the dunghill, I let my gaze wander over the flowers on the dais at the front of the room. There were half a dozen wreaths resting on stands around a framed photograph of my grandfather, sprays of roses, white lilies, and a few mixed bouquets.

The photo itself was a prize I intended to take with me back to Oregon. It was an eight by ten of Hunter in his Masonic fez. A black tassel hung down from the crown next to his face, and the name of his temple, the Sudan, was stitched across the front in colored glass beads. The picture had been made just before my mother and I had moved from Michigan. There was a companion portrait of my grandparents together, Hunter grinning so as to show off all of his teeth, and Nana smiling with her mouth shut. My mother kept that one in a brown photo folder in the top drawer of her dresser.

There were about twenty-five people in attendance. My grandfather's sisters, Lucy and Dot, were there, as was Lucy's daughter, Linda, and Linda's daughter, Nancy. Nancy looked rough, not surprising since, according to my Aunt Dot, she lived on Slim-fast and methamphetamines. Dot had brought Uncle Fred from the nursing home in Selma. He was in a wheel chair, and, though he was just as awful an old gnome as ever, he was sober and his shoes were on the right feet.

Just before the Reverend Dwighty had begun to speak, I'd seen Susan slip into the back of the room. She sat in the last pew, elegant in her dark green suit. I glanced down at my own attire, blue shirt and khaki pants, and wondered if I'd be seen as deliberately disrespectful or just ignorantly under-dressed. "Can't do a thing with her," the Southern women would say. "I don't believe she even owns a dress."

I laughed, prompting Abby to squeeze my hand. She'd been holding it throughout the service, a fact that had not escaped my mother's notice, nor my grandmother's. I supposed I should have told them about us, but when would have been a good time? Surely not while we were eating a pile of greasy seafood at the Tower Shopping Center. Abby and I spent the rest of that night coping with heartburn, and the next day, we were with Vivian.

We talked for a long time after we got back to the Velvet Cloak about our expectations and our denials and our mutual desire to get things right. Edna had not been pleased, but she didn't in fact want to kill me. She'd suspected we were a couple ever since we'd moved to Oregon together, and, as Abby said, she'd had years to get used to the idea. Apart from suggesting that I was in it for the free health care, Edna had been fairly tame by Edna's standards. She'd once accused Rosalyn of being a predatory bulldagger, out to seduce vulnerable virgins. I was spared that sort of opprobrium.

The Reverend Dwighty finished his sermon. He was as round and fat as a butterball, and as he'd walked up to the lectern, my mother had leaned over and said, "I'll bet he's never preached a sermon on gluttony." I noticed that his feet were spilling up and over the sides of his black loafers.

He stopped in front of my grandfather's picture. His hands were clasped together at his waist, holding his red leather bible.

"Go in peace and serve the Lord," the preacher said.

"Thanks be to God," the congregation replied.

"Goodness gracious me," said Nana.

"You got that right," my mother said. "Your preacher is one hell of a windbag. Does he always go on like that?"

"It was nice of him to come," Nana said, "and on such short notice."

"How much notice do you usually get for a funeral?" I asked. "Not everyone dies on a schedule."

"These flowers are beautiful," Abby said. "Did your grandfather like roses?"

"Loved them. He sent them to Nana on her birthday, their anniversary, and whenever he'd been especially drunk and obnoxious. She got a lot of flowers."

"And you see how much they meant," Nana said. "I tell you, pretty is as pretty does."

After the funeral, the Bloom's men came up and hugged us all, mumbling their condolences. A few of the old boys milled around next to my grandfather's portrait and talked to one another. Fletcher Bloom spoke with my grandmother. He told her what an excellent mechanic Hunter had been and how much they'd missed him when he retired. Although it was horseshit, it was the right thing to say.

Dot invited all of us back to her place for dinner. She said she'd baked a ham and some biscuits, which I knew meant she'd prepared a full meal. Lucy and Linda begged off, saying they had something else they had to do. Nancy had disappeared immediately after the service to shoot up or score some crack or whatever it was she did that kept her twitching like she was wired to 220 volts. I was sorry not to speak to her, as I was glad that she had come. My grandfather would have wanted as many people as possible in attendance, especially at an event where he was the undisputed center of attention. My mother, Nana, and I thanked Dot and said we'd come right out. Dot had charge of Fred, so his presence was a given. I also let it be known that I was bringing Abby.

"Is there something you want to tell me?" my mother whispered. Nana and Abby were engrossed in a conversation about plantars warts, my grandmother maintaining that she'd heard they could be cured by a generous application of chlorine bleach.

"We're together," I said. "And we're very happy."

"How long?"

"Only recently. But much longer than that, really. It just all worked out."

"Good for you," she said. "She's a sweet girl. I've always liked her."

"And to think you went to segregated schools. When should I tell Nana?"

"Let me do that. I'll give it to her between the eyes when you get on the airplane. She won't be surprised. She knows a lot more than she lets on."

"If she says, 'It's the children I feel sorry for,' don't tell me."

"Whatever she says, I won't pass it on. But deep down, you know, she'll be happy that you're happy."

"Let's hope so."

Someone put a hand on my shoulder. I turned around to find Susan standing next to me. I hugged her.

"I'm glad you came."

"Of course," she said. She hugged my mother.

"Thank you for coming," my mother said.

"Of course," Susan replied. She and my mother made polite conversation for a few minutes, and then my mother joined Nana and Abby over by the wreaths.

"I guess you'll be heading back to Portland soon?"

"Tomorrow," I said.

"I'm sorry. I'd hoped we could see more of one another."

"It would have been nice," I agreed.

"Well, I'm not settled down yet. Perhaps when I've figured out what I'm going to do, when I've gotten an apartment and moved out of my father's house, I'll come out to Portland and see you."

"You'd be very welcome. We've got plenty of room."

"We," she said quietly.

"We," I repeated. It felt good, and I was only mildly sorry that it unnerved Susan. "You have my phone number. Just give us a couple of days' advance notice so we can hide the dirty clothes in the closet and throw some clean sheets on the bed."

"I'll do that," she said. She kissed me lightly on the lips. "You take care of yourself, Poppy."

"I'll do that."

"I will call you."

"Okay." I watched her walk away. I felt a small, lingering desire to run after her. It didn't worry me. I wouldn't have traded a pleasant afternoon with Susan for a month of arguments with Abby. As if on cue, I heard her voice behind me.

"She'll stay in our house over my dead body."

"Jealous?"

"Yes."

"Good. Now you won't take me for granted. Are you ready to make your debut as my bride at my grandfather's wake?"

"Yeah," she said. "I'm going to ask Uncle Fred for your hand in marriage."

"He won't give me away," I replied. "But I'm sure he'd be more than happy to sell me."

"How much?" she asked skeptically.

"Two six packs of beer and a carton of cigarettes."

"Cheap at the price," she said. "It's a deal."

Epilogue

I upgraded us to first class for the flight home, and it was worth every penny to be able to stretch out in a wide seat that actually reclined. Rosalyn's ashes were packed in Abby's carry-on. I'd put Hunter's into my checked luggage. We didn't talk about what we were going to do with them until we were standing in my living room, now our living room, waiting for Louise to bring Belvedere home.

I took Hunter's box out of my suitcase. It was wrapped in plain white paper, like a box of See's Candies. "What should I do with this?"

"I'm going to put Rosalyn on the mantle," Abby said. "You could put Hunter there, too."

"I don't think Rosalyn would like that very much. Hunter was the kind of old white man she had to fight to get a decent education."

"Then it's perfect that they should be on the mantle together— triumph for her and punishment for him."

I put the box next to Rosalyn's urn. "*In death they were not divided,*" I said.

"What are you quoting from now?"

"The Bible, for goodness sake. Well, actually *Mapp and Lucia.* E. F. Benson. This is only a short-term solution, you know. I'm not going to keep Hunter's ashes in this house forever."

"I won't keep Rosalyn's either," she said. I looked at her in surprise. "Mortal remains don't mean a thing to me. The body's just a container for the spirit. When the spirit's gone, it might as well be an empty milk carton."

"Nurse," I accused.

"Poet," she shot back.

She'd just come over to kiss me when the doorbell rang.

"Damn that Louise," I said. "What timing."

"Belvedere," Abby cried happily.

Belvedere did seem to be doing better on the Rimadyl. The stiffness was gone, and he pranced around Abby, jumping up and licking her face. He also treated me to a lick or two. Louise stayed for over an hour, talking non-stop about the things Belvedere liked to eat, including a special concoction she'd learned about on the Internet, featuring a mixture of liver and boiled tripe.

"He's put on two pounds," she said. "The vet was worried that he'd lost a little weight. Older dogs do that sometimes. They get fussy about their food. I've been wrapping his pills in a slice of bologna, and he eats them like a champ. You can get tripe at the Fred Meyer. Just ask the butcher for it. It smells a bit when it's cooking, but the vet says that if he likes it, he should eat it."

We both thanked Louise for her exquisite care and, as soon as we could politely manage it, ushered her out the door. With the least encouragement, she'd have offered to stay and demonstrate the fine art of tripe cooking.

As soon as she'd closed it behind Louise, Abby leaned against the door. "Lovely woman," she said, "and a godsend of a dog sitter, but she's as nutty as a fruit cake. Tripe." She reached down to rub Belvedere's ears. "It's back to Science Diet for you, my friend."

"He looks good, you know."

"I know. He's getting old, Poppy."

"Maybe we should get a puppy. Someone for him to play with. We could name it Beauregarde."

"Do you want to train a puppy?"

"Sure. Why not?"

"Oh, I don't know. Whining all night for two or three weeks. Peeing and pooping on the floor. And then, of course, the inevitable getting old and dying. A puppy is not going to save me from the coming disaster."

"I know." I put my arms around her and held her close. "We could have a baby."

"It wouldn't look anything like you." She pulled back and looked at me. "Tell me—are you just after me for my uterus?"

"Kind of. I'm more interested in the general vicinity."

"I'm going to ignore that vulgar remark." She considered me seriously for a moment. "I'm thirty-four, you know. I'd be what they call an elderly primap. That's a woman who's pregnant for the first time."

"Yes, I know what a primap is. I'm not completely ignorant. So, you might actually be interested in a baby?"

"Maybe. But if you're just looking for a picture to send out with your Christmas cards, we'll get a puppy."

"You, me, Belvedere, and Beauregarde?"

"That sounds good," she said. "For now, anyway."

"And if we do that other thing?"

"You're breaking the news to Edna."

Joan Opyr is a Southern expatriate living in exile in Moscow, Idaho. By day, she's a pre-nursing student at Lewis-Clark State College; by night, she's a CNA on an Alzheimer's and Dementia Care Unit. When does she write, you might ask? Typically when she's procrastinating on a school assignment or doesn't want to study for a test. And in the summer—she always writes in the summer.

Joan is a graduate of North Carolina State University with a BA and MA in English and has been, for the past 18 years, ABD for her PhD at The Ohio State University. Her area of study is Old English with a sideline in feminist theory and Foucauldian analysis. Will she ever finish her dissertation? Never say never. It could happen. But it probably won't, as every time she sits down to write about *Beowulf,* she gets an idea for another novel.

Joan has a wife, two kids, two dogs, and a guinea pig named Tim.

Bywater Books

I CAME OUT FOR THIS?

Lisa Gitlin

"outstanding, hilarious debut novel"

—Akron Beacon Journal

"Debut novelist Gitlin's breezy story is told through freelance writer-character Joanna Kane's sometimes manic, sometimes maudlin, and sometimes simply wonderful journal entries, a narrative point of view that propels the tale with enchanting wit."

—Richard Lebonte, *Book Marks*

"This book is a bona fide page-turner; there's no suspense—it's not that kind of page-turner—but it is compelling from the first sentence to the last.... Gitlin has a razor-sharp insight into the foibles of love and human nature and Joanna's first-person narrative reads like the rantings of a real live woman who is alternately in love, angry, sad, embarrassed, verklempt and ultimately incredibly strong and vibrant.

"It's difficult to imagine who wouldn't love this book."—Victoria Brownworth, *Lambda Literary*

Paperback Original ♦ ISBN 978-1-932859-73-7 ♦ $14.95

Available at your local bookstore
or call 734-662-8815
or order online at www.bywaterbooks.com

Bywater Books

MISS McGHEE

Bett Norris

"Any reader will love this intelligent, richly detailed, altogether satisfying portrayal of a resourceful woman's struggle for love and self-determination in 20th century small-town America. *Miss McGhee* signals the arrival of an impressive, gifted storyteller."

—Katherine V. Forrest

World War II is over, and like millions of others, Mary McGhee is looking for a future. A new start, a new job, a new place. But in the small Alabama town she's chosen, she soon finds it's not so easy to leave the past behind.

Set in the shadow of the civil rights movement, *Miss McGhee* is a sweeping tale of forbidden love in a turbulent time. First-time author Bett Norris portrays one of the darkest and most troubling times in American history with exceptional skill and sensitivity, giving us a unique insight into our own recent history.

Miss McGhee is a runner-up for the
first annual Bywater Prize for Fiction.

Paperback Original ◆ ISBN 978-1-932859-33-1 ◆ $13.95

Available at your local bookstore
or call 734-662-8815
or order online at www.bywaterbooks.com

Bywater Books represents the coming of age of lesbian fiction. We're committed to bringing the best of contemporary lesbian writing to a discerning readership. Our editorial team is dedicated to finding and developing outstanding voices who deliver stories you won't want to put down. That's why we sponsor the annual Bywater Prize. We love good books, just like you do.

For more information about Bywater Books and the annual Bywater Prize for Fiction, please visit our website.

www.bywaterbooks.com